Sep 2018

DRAGON'S CODE

DRAGON'S CODE

Anne McCaffrey's
DRAGONRIDERS OF PERN

GIGI McCAFFREY

DEL REY / NEW YORK

Copyright © 2018 by Georgeanne Kennedy

All rights reserved.

Published in the United States by Del Rey, an imprint of Random House, a division of Penguin Random House LLC, New York.

DEL REY and the HOUSE colophon are registered trademarks of Penguin Random House LLC.

DRAGONRIDERS OF PERN is a trademark of Anne McCaffrey Literary Trust.

LIBRARY OF CONGRESS CATALOGING-IN-PUBLICATION DATA
Names: McCaffrey, Gigi, author.
Title: Dragon's code: Anne McCaffrey's Dragonriders of Pern / Gigi McCaffrey.
Description: New York: Del Rey, [2018]
Identifiers: LCCN 2018018896 | ISBN 9781101964743 (hardback) |
ISBN 9781101964750 (ebook)
Subjects: | BISAC: FICTION / Science Fiction / Adventure. | FICTION / Action & Adventure. | GSAFD: Science fiction.
Classification: LCC PR6113.C356 D73 2018 | DDC 823/.92—dc23
LC record available at https://lccn.loc.gov/2018018896

Map by Bob Porter

Printed in the United States of America on acid-free paper

randomhousebooks.com

2 4 6 8 9 7 5 3 1

FIRST EDITION

Book design by Susan Turner

This book is dedicated to the present and to the past:
With love to my brothers, Alec and Todd,
to my husband, Geoff, and to our son, Owen.
Thank you all, gentlemen,
for your enduring love and support.
And for your near-perfect understanding of
the delicate dichotomies and abundant
absurdities of "the Geej."
And to the memory of my loving parents:
H. Wright Johnson and Anne Inez McCaffrey.
I know you're both out there,
somewhere, in the cosmos.

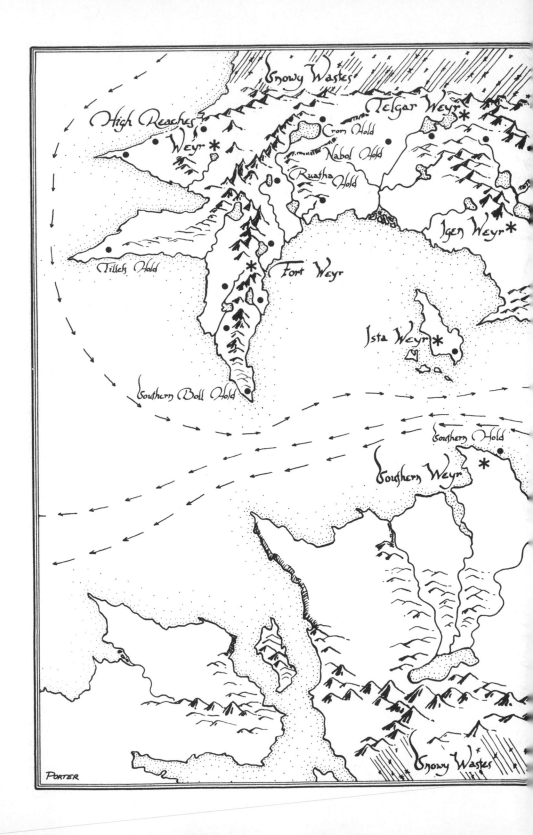

PROLOGUE

AFTER THE DEVASTATING HORRORS OF THE NATHI WAR, HUMAN-kind spread farther out into the stars, seeking solace and a new beginning. Among the worlds colonized by such refugees was the third planet of the star Rukbat, in the Sagittarian sector. Pern, as this world was named, was beautiful, habitable, and far enough from the standard trade routes that the colonists felt secure in turning their backs on the past to build a new future. They took little notice of the planetoid they called the Red Star . . . until the path of its wildly erratic elliptical orbit brought it close to Pern.

Suddenly, strange spores that looked like silver threads began to rain down on Pern, devouring any organic material in their path and, once on the ground, proliferating with terrifying speed. Only metal or stone could stop them; only fire and water could destroy them. The initial losses the colonists suffered were staggering, and during the subsequent struggle to combat the Thread—as they called the aerial menace—Pern's tenuous contact with the mother planet was broken.

The survivors, having cannibalized their transport ships and everything within to create weapons that might destroy the Thread, turned to genetic engineering as a longer-term solution. Fire-lizards—indigenous winged life-forms that displayed some telepathic abilities and could emit a flaming gas after chewing a phosphine-bearing rock—were bred into enormous creatures that the humans called dragons, after the mythical Terran beasts they resembled. Bonded from birth with their empathic human riders, these dragons could travel from one place to another instantaneously and, soaring on their huge wings, could flame Thread in midair, before it could reach the ground and ravage the land. Additionally, in the more temperate lands of the Southern Continent where the colonists had settled, grubs were altered to burrow after and consume any Thread that did make it to the planet's surface.

But the Southern Continent proved unstable. After a series of catastrophic earthquakes and volcanic eruptions, the entire colony was forced to flee to the Northern Continent, where the land was more stable and mountain caves provided refuge from the Fall of Thread. When the first new settlement, named Fort Hold, proved too small to hold the growing population, other Holds were carved from the western cliffs and the mountains to the east. At the same time, the fire-breathing dragons had evolved to a size too large for a comfortable life in the cliffside Holds. And so the dragons and their riders moved into the ancient cones of extinct volcanoes high in the mountains, where huge caves and calderas provided space for the settlements that came to be known as Weyrs.

The dragons and their riders in their high Weyrs, and the people in their cave Holds, went about their separate tasks, and each developed habits that became custom, which solidified into traditions as incontrovertible as law.

Then came an interval of two hundred Turns of the planet Pern around Rukbat, during which time the Red Star was at the far end of its erratic orbit and no Thread fell on Pern. Freed from constant fear, the inhabitants grew crops, planted orchards from precious seed brought by the original colonists, and began to think of reforesting the slopes that had been denuded by Thread. They even managed to forget that they had once been in grave danger of extinction . . .

. . . until the wandering planet returned to perihelion, bringing fifty Turns of attack from the skies, and the Pernese once again knew deep gratitude for the dragons who, under the direction of their fearless riders, seared the Thread to char, midair, with their fiery breath.

Thus began the understanding of real life on Pern: cycles of decades-long, quiet Intervals punctuated by fifty-Turn Passes when the Red Star was near, bringing with it constant Threadfall and dread.

By the Third Pass of the Red Star, a complicated socio-political-economic structure had developed to deal with this recurrent evil. Six Weyrs of fighting dragons were pledged to guard Pern, each Weyr having a section of the Northern Continent literally under its wing. The rest of the population was divided into holders and craftspeople. Each Hold—under the leadership of a Lord Holder and with the support of the Crafthalls—tithed to support the Weyrs, where the volcanic landscape could not support agriculture and the dragonriders had to devote all their time to nurturing and training with their dragons, lest a Pass arrive and find the planet's primary fighting force unprepared.

On occasion, the conjunction of Rukbat's five natural planets would prevent the Red Star from passing close enough to Pern to drop its fearful spores. During one such Long Interval, the grateful people prospered and multiplied, spreading out across the land and becoming so busy with their daily pursuits that most began to believe the Red Star had finally passed beyond any danger to them.

Within five generations, only one Weyr—Benden Weyr—was left inhabited. These last descendants of the heroic dragonriders fell into disfavor, as the tales of their brave exploits faded into legend; without Thread to fight, the dragons and their riders seemed to have no more part to play in the world—and no reason to be supported by the people of Pern. So when the Red Star at long last returned to perihelion and Thread attacked again, it fell to Benden Weyrleaders F'lar and Lessa to rally their almost defenseless planet against total annihilation.

But now, even as dragonriders and their dragons fight the valiant war against Thread, dissatisfaction and dissent have begun to simmer in parts of the world . . .

DRAGON'S CODE

ONE

CLOUDS OF WARM, DUST-LADEN AIR BILLOWED DOWN AROUND Piemur and whipped off his floppy hat as hundreds of dragons and their riders lifted off from the ground, steadily filling the sky overhead. Hastily he pulled his tunic over his head to protect his face from flying grit, clamping his mouth shut tight in the process. All the trees and vegetation around the Weyr bucked and buffeted under the huge downdraft generated by the wings of the bronze, brown, blue, and green dragons. Through the protective fabric, Piemur heard the comments the dragonriders called to one another as they took flight; heard, too, the muffled sound of dragons coughing as they rose higher off the ground. Listening, he wondered—not for the first time—what pernicious ailment still afflicted so many of the dragons of Southern Weyr, and why the Weyr Healer couldn't find a remedy to shift it from their lungs. Only when the sounds receded to almost nothing and he could feel the air settling did he risk uncovering his eyes to look skyward.

Piemur watched as the sun shimmered off their soft hides and made their jewel-like, faceted eyes sparkle. There was nothing like the sight of a sky full of dragons, he fancied—even dragons who were not in the full of their health. The fine membrane that made up the sails of the dragons' wings looked nearly transparent, and he wondered how wings that appeared so delicate could bear the weight of such massive creatures.

Today the Oldtimer dragonriders were traveling to harvest a fresh crop of numbweed, which they would later pound and boil into the noxious unction that, once set, would be used as a hallowed salve. Only twoscore riders and their dragons remained behind in the Weyr with the queens, the most senior of whom had just returned from a lone sojourn. A brown dragon was curled up in a wallow, coughing desultorily as if to dislodge a tiny irritant nestled deep inside his vast lungs. His rider rested with him, in the curve of his forelegs.

A few other dragons basked in their wallows or relaxed under the ministrations of their riders, while the rest simply slept, their old bones soaking up the plentiful sunshine. Numerous weyrfolk—men and women who lived at the Weyr but were not dragonriders—went about the compound, washing or tending to clothing, preparing food, or assisting the older dragonriders with the task of bathing and oiling their dragons' soft hides. Nothing was more important than caring for the dragons. With their abilities to fly, teleport, and breathe fire, the dragons were the best and most effective weapon the world had against its mindless enemy, Thread—an insatiable organism that, when the orbit of its host planet was close enough to Pern, would shower down in a fifty-Turn cycle, devouring anything organic in its path. And if the dragons couldn't char every last Thread from the skies before they touched ground, the deadly strands would burrow underground to continue their terrible course of destruction. The dragons were truly the most precious things on the planet, and supporting them and their riders was the job—either directly or indirectly—of every person in or outside of the Weyrs.

But Southern Weyr no longer had that kind of support. The Oldtimer dragonriders had cut ties with Benden, the premier Weyr in the northern hemisphere, effectively alienating themselves from their peers and, ultimately, everyone else. Never in living memory had any group broken free, seeking to go it alone in the hostile environment of Pern without the support of the other elements of their social structure.

Piemur was here at the behest of his mentor, Masterharper Robinton. He hadn't started out as a spy. Three Turns earlier, Piemur had been virtually wrenched from his comfortable position in the Harper Hall and sent to the Southern Hold to teach the resident harper the new drum measures, vital for maintaining communications with neighboring smallholdings. But it hadn't taken long for Saneter to memorize the new measures . . . and for the Masterharper to task Piemur with a seemingly endless stream of structureless chores, almost all of which were completely outside his training as a singer. If not for his deep-rooted sense of loyalty to his craft and his mentor, Piemur would have gladly forgone the exhausting and never-ending job of mapping Southern, a vast continent far larger than anyone had ever imagined and, in many areas, actually impassable.

He didn't mind standing in to teach the local children when Saneter was away or indisposed. In fact, he quite enjoyed passing on the information contained in the teaching ballads, imperative for every child to know in order to survive. And the mapping, while often monotonous, hot, and uncomfortable, sometimes had its moments of discovery and adventure. Piemur's most unsatisfying task by far, and the one he found so disturbing to perform, was as a spy: observing and assessing the demeanor and welfare of the dragonriders of Southern Weyr. He gleaned no joy in snooping around the noble dragons and their riders, pretending to be someone he was not, visiting the Weyr on one pretense or another while trying to catch every snippet of conversation or grievance he could. It felt grossly wrong to Piemur to behave so duplicitously toward a group of dragons and riders who had spent a lifetime defending the planet. But the Masterharper, in his role as Pern's custodian of culture and heritage, and the discreet harmonizer of her interconnected social relationships, was anxious to know how the outcasts were faring. He regularly stressed how important it was for Piemur to take note of any little details in the Weyr's daily life that might be the slightest bit out of the ordinary, and report these. The most trivial snippet could be what helped to reunite Southern Weyr with the rest of dragonkind—and as a harper, Piemur was trained to observe details.

So he noticed when T'reb landed his green dragon and, instead of flying out again to harvest numbweed with the other members of the Weyr, headed for B'naj's dwelling. To Piemur's sharp eye, the subtle signs of agitation in the green rider's posture were unmistakable. Straightening his tunic over the top of his loose leggings, then scooping up his hat and setting it firmly back on his head, Piemur moved from the shade of the trees to cross the compound in the direction T'reb had taken.

Trying to look nonchalant, Piemur circled around B'naj's wooden cabin so he could eavesdrop from the quiet side of the building where leafy trees offered him a hiding place from which to remain unobserved. Once behind the building he dropped down onto his hands and knees, crawling quickly toward a pair of open windows. He sat on the ground, his back pressed hard to the wall of the cabin, head cocked to one side as he tried to make out what was going on inside. He could clearly hear the sound of feet pacing.

T'reb was talking hurriedly, his voice several octaves higher than was comfortable for Piemur's trained ear. No doubt: T'reb was very upset.

"My mind is made up now, B'naj. No more dithering over what's right or wrong. I've arranged to meet him and set everything in motion."

"Calm down, T'reb." That was B'naj's voice, speaking in a placating tone.

"But don't you see, B'naj? We have to *do* something."

"Maybe you're overreacting," B'naj said.

"But you didn't see her, B'naj. It was unbearable!"

"What exactly did you see, my friend?"

"Mardra! Trying to coax Loranth from the Hatching Grounds. She was moaning."

"Mardra or Loranth?" B'naj asked.

"Loranth, you dolt!"

There was silence for a few moments, and Piemur could only surmise that B'naj was glaring at T'reb in response to the ill-mannered remark.

"It was like no other dragon sound I've heard before," T'reb continued finally. "It put my nerves on edge."

Not a hard thing to do, Piemur mused, knowing how volatile T'reb could be—even at the best of times.

"It wasn't the usual keening, nor the sound dragons make while feeding; no, it was a slow, heart-wrenching rumbling that came from deep inside. And the sound kept increasing, B'naj, to a cry so pitiful I thought she was in mortal agony."

Piemur heard B'naj murmur something indistinguishable, and then T'reb continued.

"Mardra was pleading with Loranth: 'Come away, my love,' she said, 'we cannot keep revisiting this loss.'"

Loss? What loss? Piemur wondered. What was T'reb talking about? And why was Mardra at the Hatching Grounds when the Weyr didn't even have a new clutch of eggs to harden? Perhaps the old queen and her rider were simply visiting the Grounds, a hallowed place for all dragonkind, to ensure that they were still, as was the custom, in perfect order?

"Such a note of despair was in her voice, B'naj. I saw her weeping, and I thought I might weep with her, too. I can't get the image out of my head!"

No wonder T'reb appeared so edgy, Piemur mused. What could possibly be causing the Weyr's senior queen dragon so much distress?

"But what were they doing there?" B'naj asked.

"Loranth dug up those old egg shards and was poking around at them," T'reb replied.

Egg shards? Piemur felt a moment of confusion. Why had the queen dug up old eggshells? Hatching Grounds were revered among dragonmen and -women! Everyone knew that the Grounds were where the future riders first met the young dragons they would partner; the place where, for the very first time in their lives, the specially chosen men and women would form their unique mental bonds with the giant, fearless, and noble creatures. To make that bond, to Impress a dragon, was to make a telepathic connection so strong that it could never be broken. Piemur had often wondered what it must be like to be a dragonrider, to have the unconditional friendship, love, and support of one of those magnificent beasts, a bond so strong that it lasted for life. From what he understood, the wondrous relationship he shared with his own Farli, his little golden fire-lizard, was only a tiny fraction of the deep connection between dragon and rider.

Piemur gave himself a mental shake; he couldn't let his thoughts distract him, or he might miss a crucial exchange between T'reb and B'naj.

"The Hatching Grounds should've been thoroughly cleared ages ago. It's not proper for the queen to do that, nor to leave the place in such a state."

"Yes, but Mardra wouldn't have it, would she?" The pitch of T'reb's voice was rising again.

"And no amount of weeping or moaning will change the fact that Loranth won't produce any new clutches of eggs. She's just too old." Piemur thought he heard a note of sadness in B'naj's voice.

"It's more than that, B'naj."

"You're right. Loranth has been off color ever since that shaft collapsed when the Weyr was mining firestone. I'm glad I didn't go with you and the others."

"We should *never* have gone on that cursed venture—over half the Weyr was exposed to those noxious fumes."

"Yes, yes, we've spoken about this already. And we *still* cannot change what is done, T'reb!" B'naj was growing impatient.

"But we can't just sit by as the Weyr falls apart. That's why we have to *do* something now!"

"That's a matter for our Weyrleader, T'reb, not us."

"Ha! You still think T'ron will do something? He's no more use to us now than a spent glow in a basket!"

"Shh, keep your voice down!" B'naj hissed.

"I'm not going to stand by anymore, B'naj. We have a duty to our queen and our Weyr!"

"What are you up to?" B'naj asked.

"There's this plan—half-cocked at that—but perhaps we can use it to our advantage."

"What plan, T'reb? You can't go behind our Weyrleader's back, my friend." B'naj sounded alarmed.

"During my sojourns north, I traded with a group of men from Nabol. One of them pointed out similarities between us."

"Similarities? What are you talking about, T'reb? They aren't dragonfolk!"

"No, they aren't, but just like us they've fallen afoul of Benden!"

"I don't understand," B'naj said.

"When they sought help over a family feud, Benden said they couldn't interfere in Hold matters. Benden—F'lar and Lessa so high and mighty, as if their Weyr rules all the rest! Some leaders, yeah? Left those Nabolese out in the cold just like those other meddlers, the harpers. Honestly, B'naj, I hardly listened to all the details of their silly feud. The nub of it is that they want us to help secure a holding promised to their father by Lord Meron."

"Meron," B'naj said, enunciating the two syllables slowly and with so much distaste in his voice that Piemur had little difficulty imagining the dragonrider's facial expression. And no surprise there: The late Lord Meron had been cruel and uncaring; even Piemur had fallen afoul of the Lord Holder. "He always was a sneaky lick of a man. We never should've traded with him."

"But we did, and strange as it now seems, his kin may actually have thought of an idea that will benefit our Weyr. We just have to assist them in securing lands to hold."

"They can have plenty of land down here—as much as they like."

"They won't travel south."

"Why not?"

"They say they can't stomach the sea crossing. And anyway, they want lands in the north—just as was promised to them."

"And what would *we* get in return?"

"Exactly what we need, B'naj. New blood."

"How in the name of the First Egg—" B'naj's response increased in volume until T'reb cut him short.

"Shh!" T'reb said.

A long silence followed.

"What?" B'naj asked at last, and Piemur guessed that T'reb must have whispered something. He tried to press his ear even closer to the cabin wall. There was the sound of movement inside and a low murmuring, but Piemur couldn't make out what was said. He held his breath, straining harder to hear the two dragonriders. Suddenly a chair scraped against the floor and Piemur heard what sounded like a hand slapping bare flesh.

"You cannot stop me, B'naj!" T'reb said heatedly. "It's obvious to me now, the less you know the better."

What had T'reb said? Shards and fire blast! Piemur wished he'd been able to hear. It felt like all the hair on his body was standing on end, warning him of some ominous event in the offing, as sure as the dreaded Thread fell from the sky.

Footsteps marched purposefully inside the cabin, and then there was the sound of the door opening. Piemur crouch-crawled quickly to the end of the cabin and then ducked around the corner. From his new hiding place, he could see T'reb marching across the compound toward his dragon, Beth.

Without a backward glance, T'reb approached Beth and grabbed her flying harness. The green dragon turned toward her rider, and Piemur saw the color of her many-faceted eyes change from a soft green to a darker hue that was flecked with amber. *Beth's not a happy dragon*, he observed in silence.

From the cover of the building Piemur tilted his face up, closed his eyes briefly in concentration, and then let out a sharply pitched, three-toned whistle that sounded just like a birdcall. Then he sat back on his heels, looked up into the sky, and waited.

He felt the barest change in the air pressure above his head, and for the briefest moment it felt as if his ears were about to pop. Then the sensation ceased and Farli appeared, hovering in front of him, her golden wings easily maintaining her position at the same level as his eyes. Piemur smiled and with a single shrug offered his right shoulder as a landing pad. Farli was a queen fire-lizard, one of the small winged creatures that were distant cousins to the dragons. Fire-lizards shared almost all the attributes of their huge relatives, including telekinesis and telepathy—though due to their frivolous nature, the latter ability tended to be weaker and often inconsistent. The Southern Continent, with its warm climate, was the fire-lizards' natural home, but more and more were being adopted by people in the north. Farli had seemed happy to join Piemur when he came south, and here, where he was so often alone, he appreciated her companionship more than ever.

Without saying a word, Piemur looked intently at Farli, one hand stroking the soft hide on her back as he sought her complete attention. He thought hard, mentally showing the little queen what he wanted her to do, repeating his command several times to ensure she understood. Farli's faceted eyes whirred as she looked intently at him; then she leapt off his shoulder and, from one wingbeat to the next, vanished *between,* to that other place, the empty void that dragons and fire-lizards alike used to teleport from one space to another.

Piemur crept back toward the edge of the building and peered around the corner, hoping that on this occasion his capricious fire-lizard would do as he asked. He watched T'reb checking the tautness of one of the flying straps as Beth minced from one foot to the other, a sound not dissimilar to a hiss issuing from her mouth.

T'reb quickly mounted his dragon and urged her to take flight. With several strides, the green dragon gained enough speed to leap into the air. She rose slowly skyward as Piemur watched, nervously searching for Farli. *Quickly!* he thought. *Quickly, Farli, before they blink out of sight and go* between!

As T'reb and Beth climbed higher, Piemur saw a little speck of gold dart into the sky below them, keeping time with the dragon and rider. Once they'd reached sufficient height above the ground, T'reb and Beth disappeared, flying *between,* and Farli went with them.

Confident that Farli was successfully tailing the green dragon and her rider, Piemur stood up, wiping his hands across the sides of his thighs as he began to walk around the side of the building.

"Hey! What're you doing there?" B'naj called from the doorway, from which he'd been watching T'reb's departure.

Piemur, caught off guard, quickly ducked his head between his shoulders and kept walking as if he hadn't heard the dragonrider calling to him.

"Hey!" B'naj yelled again, louder. "You, there!" Several of the other dragonriders around the compound looked up.

Piemur twisted toward B'naj, one hand raised above his head in a jaunty wave, but he kept walking, his hat pulled down over his face.

There was nothing for it, he thought—he had to get out of there, and fast. He cupped his hands around his mouth and called, "That's grand then! I'll have those supplies ready for you in the next sevenday!" His gaze was fixed at a point beyond B'naj and slightly to the side; he hoped B'naj would think he was addressing someone else, while onlookers would assume he was speaking to B'naj.

He waved one more time, then turned his back to B'naj and walked purposefully across the clearing toward the tropical forest, hoping that any dragonriders whose attention had been caught by the interchange would lose interest and resume whatever they'd been doing. Piemur knew he'd be safe once he'd made his way into the cover of the forest surrounding the Weyr. Hoping that B'naj was no longer watching he slipped into the woods and set out at a quick jog, ducking and bending to avoid low tree branches and tenacious vines. With any luck Farli would come back to him quickly, with a clear and accurate mental picture to share exactly where T'reb had gone in such a hurry.

At last reaching his little camp near the Weyr, he could see the distinctive shape of Stupid, the runnerbeast he'd rescued as an or-phaned foal. The hobbled beast, now fully mature and standing level with the top of Piemur's head, was dozing in the shade of a fellis tree, his long neck extended to the ground and his lower lip protruding beyond the upper lip as if in a pout.

Stupid had grown accustomed to being left alone, happy to for-age and graze unchecked, though he seemed the most content when Farli was nearby. Piemur had ensured that the runner was within reach of a source of fresh water, and as he always did, he tied a raw-hide fringe to the halter to keep flies and other pesky insects from Stupid's eyes.

Seeing Piemur, Stupid made a noise in his throat, a sound that always reminded Piemur of a mix between a hum and a hiccup. Responding with a soothing hum-buzz noise of his own, Piemur made short work of readying the runnerbeast, smoothing the hair on Stupid's back and quickly checking for any insects that might have burrowed under the skin.

Finally, he slipped the bridle over Stupid's head and gently eased the left ear into the loop of the single ear strap. Then, still hum-buzzing, he placed the saddle pad on Stupid's back, behind the last neck bone. The runner blew through his muzzle gently, a sure sign he was relaxed, and shifted his weight from one forefoot to the other. Piemur tightened up the saddle pad cinch, which was positioned behind the two pairs of front legs, doing so slowly to ensure that Stupid wouldn't be pinched by the saddle girth, a seemingly minor injury that could result in the dreaded, hard-to-cure girth galls. Stupid stomped his rear feet but didn't seem upset.

Piemur passed a critical eye over his handiwork, still pleased, after all this time, with the way he had modified the design of the saddles he'd grown up with in Crom. His customized saddle suited the specific needs of the Southern Continent's warmer climate, where a hide-made, wood-framed saddle would be far too hot, heavy, and cumbersome for both rider and mount. Piemur had not been in Southern long before he'd realized that a soft saddle pad would work much better: It was easier to make and maintain, it dried more quickly, and it was far less likely to harbor any pesky bugs or biters that could riddle the back of a runner with poxy ooze-sores and painful lumps.

Piemur unfastened the hobble, then, pursing his lips as if he were spitting a small seed from his mouth, he made the distinctive *brrup-phut* noise that seemed to enchant all runnerbeasts, sounding like wind passing from the guts of a well-sated ruminant.

Stupid lifted his head at the sound and walked forward, unguided, on a path only he seemed to know. Keeping pace on the left side of his mount, Piemur deftly grabbed the reins of the head harness in one hand, along with a hank of the beast's long mane, and sprang from the ground in one lithe movement, swinging his right leg high and wide, to land gently on the pad without causing the beast to flinch or break stride.

He reached out silently to Farli again, but his summons remained unanswered. He hoped she'd been able to trail T'reb. Where could the dragonrider have been going? He'd said he was going to help Mardra, the most senior queen rider in Southern, and that some men from Nabol had a plan that would help the dragonriders of Southern Weyr. What could that possibly be? Even Piemur, who wasn't weyrbred, could see that the members of the Southern Weyr were experiencing a steady, inexorable decline. All the dragons in Southern were of an older generation, and with no young blood among them to invigorate the Weyr, and none of the queens rising to mate in recent times, that left only the few smaller females, the green dragons, as an inadequate source of release for the virile males.

Piemur thought of how much change the Oldtimer dragon-riders had had to endure—and now this. They came from a different time—the last time in the past when Thread had fallen—and they had fought valiantly, keeping their own generation safe. But the end of that Pass and the start of a new two-hundred-Turn Interval, free of Thread, left them unmoored, bereft of purpose. So when Lessa, the Weyrwoman of Benden Weyr, had crossed four centuries to implore them to help fight Thread in the current Pass—Piemur's time—they must have felt they had only one option: to agree to her request to accompany her four hundred Turns into the future.

Until the arrival of the Oldtimer dragons, the modern-day dragonriders had been too few in number and insufficiently trained in aerial combat. Alone, they would have been ill equipped to survive the ravages of Thread, much less protect their planet. Piemur knew that *all* the inhabitants of Pern owed a huge debt to the time-traveling older generation of dragonmen who had sacrificed so much. But they also faced a different kind of challenge. In the four centuries that had elapsed between their time and the current Pass, attitudes, customs, and even aspects of the language had changed, and while most of the Oldtimers had managed to adapt to their new lives, some of them had collided disastrously with the newer generation of weyrfolk, craftspeople, and holders.

Piemur knew all about the numerous clashes and claims of foul play that had occurred while all the Oldtimers resided in the Weyrs of the north, clashes that had grown so frequent that they culminated in a group of more than two hundred Oldtimers moving to the Southern Continent where they could live by their old ways, unchallenged. But in a cruel twist of fate, while their northern peers embraced a new life as heroes, the Southerners' inability to accept change not only made them exiles but also tarnished their reputations, turning them from heroes to castoffs.

Piemur felt a stab of empathy for the Oldtimers of Southern—he felt like a discard, too. No longer of any use as an apprentice at the Harper Hall, where his young singing voice had been extraordinary until the dreadful day when it broke, Piemur was now, at the age of just seventeen Turns, a castoff, stuck doing odd-jobber tasks until his Master found an alternative role for him. He clenched his jaw and shook his head slightly, determined not to let his feelings of misfortune engulf him yet again. He'd been working hard to get past the loss of his voice and had no wish to wallow in self-pity anymore. *What's done is done,* he reflected.

There was no point in waiting idly for Farli to return, and besides, she could usually locate him no matter where he was, so Piemur decided to scout out the Hatching Grounds and see firsthand what had disturbed T'reb so much. And so he guided Stupid through the denser parts of the forest to clear ground and the place where he knew the Southern Weyr Hatching Grounds were located. He'd never been here before; no one outside the Weyrs ever visited the Grounds except by express invitation.

Hatching Grounds, hallowed by dragons and their riders alike, were always kept immaculately clean, the sand raked regularly to keep it free from debris or potentially sharp objects. After every Hatching ceremony, those fortunate enough to Impress a dragon often kept a small shard of their dragon's eggshell as a treasured keepsake, while the rest of the spent dragon shells were buried with great care and solemnity.

Here, however, withered seaweed and tumbleweed mixed together in a gnarled mess among the sands. Other debris was strewn all around the sand; sharp rocks and flotsam, washed up from the beach, littered the site. Clumps of what looked like old feces dotted the ground, and one clump appeared to be made up of bone, hide, and sinew. Piemur's lips pursed in distaste as he wondered if any of the other members of Southern Weyr, apart from Mardra, T'reb, and now B'naj, knew how sullied their Hatching Grounds were. As he passed a critical eye over the rest of the area, looking for some kind of evidence that might explain this dereliction, his gaze fell on a few egg shards, smashed and scattered around the sand. Though hold-born, not weyrbred, even Piemur knew it was unthinkable for dragonfolk to allow their most treasured space to fall into such disorder.

He walked slowly through the Hatching Grounds and then returned to the indeterminate clump of bone and hide to examine it more closely. He felt uneasy, fearful of what might greet him when he looked closer. But with a compulsion bordering on morbid curiosity, Piemur knew he *had* to determine what was in the mangled clump of tissue. He sidled up close, dropped down to the ground to squat on his heels, and peered at the mass. He sniffed the air tentatively but detected no noxious odor. No form or definitive skeletal structure was obvious, and from all appearances the clump was so old it was in the last stages of decay. Searching among some of the nearby detritus that littered the Grounds, he picked up a stick and used it to poke at the clump. His heart lifted when he nudged it further and recognized a little matted wad as a rib of feathers amid the remains.

Sweet shards, what a relief! Dragons, even in their shells, didn't have feathers. *It's probably only the remains of a wherry,* he speculated. The clump looked like something that had been eaten and then regurgitated. *Do dragons vomit?* he wondered.

Deeply thankful that the clump was not the remains of a dragon embryo, Piemur looked around at the other shell shards. The fragments had been broken up and scattered about, but as he picked up a piece of shell to examine it, he thought it seemed curiously insubstantial, brittle even, in his hand, and far more fragile than he thought a dragon's shell should be. While he was carefully replacing the fragment where he'd found it, he saw a partially intact egg hidden behind a small boulder. Nervously, Piemur moved closer to examine it.

The crown of the egg had been broken through to the size of a grown man's head, but the rest of the egg was intact. Piemur leaned in close, and a faint rotten odor assaulted his nose. Peering inside, he could see what looked like the dried remains of a malformed yolk and some fluid at the bottom of the shell that had almost completely congealed. He'd seen enough. It was time to leave these desolate Grounds.

Trying desperately to clear his mind of the disturbing scene, he focused on calling to Farli. Where was she? Unable to shake off the dreadful feeling of malaise that had settled over him, he started walking back along the beach to where he had tethered Stupid. Suddenly Farli burst into the air overhead, chirruping to Piemur in a trill of notes and flashing a blur of images at him while she flew in erratic circles around his head.

"Hold on, there, Farli! Slow down, little sweet. You're showing me too much too fast," Piemur said, smiling at the gold fire-lizard.

He stretched out his arm and Farli settled on his hand, careful not to cling too hard with her sharp talons. Piemur brought her down and held her close to his chest, gently stroking her with his free hand. Unbidden, a little sigh of satisfaction traveled up from his chest, and he could feel Farli relaxing in his hand. When he stroked the skin on the ridges above her eyes, she crooned at him with delight.

"Wonderful Farli," he murmured. "Where did the green dragon fly?"

An image of a sunny beach flashed in Piemur's mind, and he mentally nudged Farli to show him more of the scenery and any specific landmarks she might have noticed. Farli fluttered her wings impatiently, but he persisted, easing the subtle pressure on his fire-lizard's mind until she was calm enough to reveal what he needed to know.

"You've done a good job," he said as he continued to stroke her. The little queen preened, furling her wings along her back. Piemur could tell she was delighted with her achievement, because the color of her eyes had changed from a deep purple to blue.

"There you go," he said, raising his hand up to his shoulder. Farli delicately extracted her talons from his hand and hopped to his shoulder, where she stretched along the back of his neck in her favorite position, her head and forelegs resting along one side of his face, with her back legs and tail along the other.

"You rest, sweet thing, while I mount up. Then I have to ride fast to where T'reb was headed. You'll guide me, won't you?" Piemur reached his hand up to scratch the skin above Farli's left eye ridge, and the little queen crooned at him again.

"I have to find out more about what T'reb is planning, Farli, because it sounds like trouble!"

TWO

PIEMUR HELD HIS BREATH, NERVOUS THAT THE MEN MIGHT SEE him. With a lot of backtracking, traipsing around in dense jungle, and more than a little cursing, he had finally reached the site Farli showed him, nearly falling off Stupid with fright when he heard the sound of voices coming from the direction of the beach. He must be more careful: He had nearly blundered onto the beach and risked exposing himself! He slowly retraced his steps a safe distance to where he could tether Stupid, deciding to leave Farli there, too, since she had a knack for keeping the runnerbeast calm and quiet.

Crouching lower than he felt was physically possible, he approached slowly, all the while keeping his eyes glued on the two men.

Piemur tried to recall every detail of what he had overheard back at the Oldtimer Weyr, hopeful that the thick grasses and giant ferns would conceal him as he knelt down and peered through the screen of lush plants. One of these two must be the man T'reb had spoken about when he was arguing with B'naj. Had he mentioned a name? And in what way was he going to help T'reb realize his so-called plan?

Letting his senses heighten, he listened intently to the men who, a mere dozen paces distant, seemed blithely unaware of their eavesdropper. By the look of them Piemur pegged them as hold-bred, though he was only hazarding a guess. One of them, a lanky, mop-headed man, suddenly turned in Piemur's direction as he made expansive gestures with his arms, pointing up and all around at the dense forest. For a moment it seemed as if the man was looking directly at him. Piemur froze. He could feel a pulse beating in his neck, and his heart sounded like a quickening roll of drums in his chest.

Don't forget to breathe, he reminded himself, and drew in a measured breath before exhaling quietly. Sweat rolled down from the crown of his head, skidded over his brow, and tracked down the side of his face. He felt exposed here on the ground. Quickly he scanned the surrounding trees and bushes for a safer vantage point.

The second man was not as tall as the first, and had copper-colored, wavy hair and a scar on his upper lip. The taller man mumbled something Piemur couldn't hear. The copper-haired man looked at his companion, and because he was facing Piemur, his next words were easily discernible.

"It just seems unusual to me, Toolan. 'Sall I'm sayin'." Piemur watched the man as he lifted his hands up high in the air, fingers spread wide.

The other man—Toolan—scowled. "And the dragonrider told *me* that this is the place he wants drawn! Anyhow, what do *you* know about what he wants? You just met him. I'm the one he's dealing with, not you, Cramb!"

The note of contempt in Toolan's voice was clear to Piemur. He wondered why the man named Cramb didn't seem to react to the snide remark. Glancing away, he caught sight of a tree with branches that might make a perfect hiding place. *It's now or never,* he thought.

Careful not to make any noise, Piemur crept to the tree and eyed the stout branch above him. It was only about two meters from the ground. Piemur wasn't very tall, but he was compactly built, and all his time scouting and mapping in Southern had given him strong leg muscles. Lowering himself into a semi-squat, he stretched his arms out by his sides, fists clenched. He took a deep breath and then in one powerful thrust shot up into the air, grabbed the branch, and clasped it tightly with both hands. A large bird flew off its perch somewhere above him, causing branches to shake and leaves to rustle. Piemur wanted to gasp but held his breath instead, hanging perfectly still.

"What was that?" Toolan asked, staring intently in Piemur's direction.

"It was just a bird, Toolan," Cramb said. "This place is alive with birds and wild animals."

Toolan turned away from the tree and Piemur exhaled, thanking the First Egg for the man's lack of curiosity. Slowly he hauled himself up and onto the branch, where he settled himself with his back resting against the tree trunk and his legs stretched out in front of him. He felt well covered by the dense leaves all around him, while he could clearly see the men below.

Cramb was running his tongue over his scarred upper lip as he stared at Toolan. Piemur craned forward, intent on seeing what transfixed Cramb. Slowly, careful to make no sound, he extracted the single-lens distance viewer from under his tunic, in the small pack he carried around his waist. He had been given the viewer for mapping the skies in Southern with N'ton, and had found it a useful tool while scouting, as well. Now he focused the lens on Toolan's face.

Was that a giant gob of spit bouncing about on the man's lips? Piemur grimaced when he realized that it was, but he couldn't stop himself from staring at it as Toolan spoke, the glob moving up and down, occasionally stretching in a thin thread between the two lips before snapping back into position.

Please lick your lips, Toolan, or I might just heave, Piemur silently pleaded.

"I think it's an odd choice. That's all," Cramb said. He licked his lips again, and Piemur suddenly caught himself licking his own lips, too.

"Well, don't bother . . . to think, that is!" Toolan said loudly, and then paused before adding, "I know what's wanted. You're just here to make a sketch of it, so get to work," he barked. "Shards, but this place is hot!" He wiped sweat off his face with his arm as he looked around the clearing. "I hate when it's this hot!"

What a foul character this Toolan fellow is, Piemur decided. By contrast, Cramb seemed a rather pleasant man, and Piemur wondered why he was mixed up with an obnoxious crud like Toolan.

Piemur watched as Cramb pulled at two leather straps that crisscrossed his chest, lifting them over his head to reveal the rawhide satchel he'd been carrying on his back. He opened it and pulled out a little fold-up stool. Then he rooted around in the satchel for a moment before taking out a piece of chalk and a midsize slate.

"Take your time, Cramb. I need a rest," Piemur heard Toolan call imperiously from where he'd settled at the base of a stout, fronded tree. He watched the lanky man fold his arms behind his head and then slide his legs out in front of him, crossing one ankle over the other as he closed his eyes.

"You'll get plenny a' that, Toolan. This is just a rough sketch I'm laying down on the slate. I'll have to copy my work onto fine vellum and then add more detail before I make the final rendering in color. After that's done, I'll make another sketch when the sky's dark. You said that's what T'reb wanted."

"Hmm," Toolan acknowledged, not bothering to look at his companion.

Cramb bent his head and got busy paring his stylus with a sharp knife; Piemur noticed the man's smile of pleasure as he briefly glanced at the somnolent Toolan.

The landscape along this part of the Southern Continent's coast was really quite outstanding, Piemur reflected, as he looked up and down the shoreline as far as he could see. Might even be the prettiest spot on all of Pern, he thought, and worried that it might be marred by whatever scheme these two men were realizing for T'reb.

Once Cramb arranged his equipment ready to hand, he completed the sketch quickly and set about redrawing the scene on the fine vellum that he carefully removed from his satchel and rested on a thin piece of bark that he laid across his thighs.

Nestled in the tree, Piemur wondered why in the world T'reb wanted a drawing of this place. With a slow sigh he forced himself to relax a little. Toolan was snoring quietly in the shade, one hand, palm upward, resting over his eyes as if in mock horror. *I'd better stay alert,* Piemur thought, *and not fall asleep like this Toolan fella.* He'd been sent by Master Robinton to scout out any unusual incidents involving the Oldtimers, and to fall asleep on the job wouldn't put him in very good favor with his Master. That was a certainty!

The thought of the Masterharper reminded Piemur of his life at Fort. Just the thought of it elicited a sharp pang of regret, which Piemur felt as a physical stab in his chest. He shook his head. Why, even though his life as a first-line singer was over, he was lucky to still be apprenticed to the Masterharper! A memory flashed into his head from three Turns past, before his voice broke, and he closed his eyes, unconsciously savoring every detail.

He was in the main music hall, on the day the choir was practicing an incredibly difficult piece of a cappella music Master Domick had composed. Not that Master Domick ever composed anything *but* complex music. Piemur had the lead, as usual, but the choir members were struggling to perfect the discords and counter-melodies that made the madrigal so unique—and difficult to master.

"No, no, *no!*" Domick had shouted, his voice rising on the last word as he simultaneously smacked his baton off the music stand. "You sound like a herd of shrieking runnerbeasts being devoured by Thread. Read the music score, for pity's sake! Do *not* sing the last phrase like that!" The Mastercomposer's face was turning a disturbing shade of red as he shouted, and the boys and girls of the choir started to squirm in their places, which only added further to their teacher's obvious ire.

"Piemur. Please," Domick had said as he drew in a deep breath, tapping his baton once again while gesturing with the other hand for Piemur to step from his place in the line of apprentices and stand facing the assembled group. As Piemur made his way to stand next to Master Domick, he saw the door to the practice hall open and the

Masterharper of Pern enter, followed by Journeyman Masterharper Sebell.

"Sing the base phrase, Piemur," Domick ordered, looking all the while at the choir members to see that they were paying attention. Piemur opened his mouth, drew breath, and then, as always, time seemed to slow down for him as he exhaled the first note and the sweet sound flowed around the big hall. As Piemur's voice filled the room it was like a window had been opened, flooding the space with delicious sound.

"Excellent. Now, Dilis, you sing just as Piemur is singing, please," Domick said, and Dilis did as instructed. Piemur adjusted his voice, easily singing in harmony with Dilis as he let the other boy take control of the base phrase. Domick nodded with approval.

"Now, Shern, I want you to join in and take over the harmony from Piemur. Don't err on the notes," Domick commanded. Shern began singing, and Piemur immediately changed his refrain and sang in counter-harmony with the two other lads. The effect was spine tingling.

"Now all of you: Trebles, sing your parts; sopranos, too. Follow Piemur's lead," Domick said, raising his arms and indicating on the downbeat when the singers should join in. As all the voices of the choir joined in, they filled the room with a multilayered, complex melody. The Mastercomposer closed his eyes, his head bouncing up and down in tempo with the singers. Without any further direction from Master Domick, and perfectly on cue, Piemur took a breath and sang his solo part, filling the air with his sure, high treble voice. The song was beautiful, captivating everyone in those few moments of perfection.

Then Domick's composition neared its coda and all the voices of the choir sang in tight bursts, sounding like gusts of wind, and Piemur's voice, singing higher than the others, sounded like a small, frightened creature being tossed about on the ebb and flow of air.

When the final note of the song was sung and all the voices ceased, everyone in the room remained silent momentarily, hushed by the fading echo of the beautiful sound they had created together. Then the singers turned from one to another, delighted smiles spreading over their faces, and in a rush they all started talking at the same time, thoroughly pleased because they knew they had finally sung the difficult song as it was meant to be heard.

Piemur remembered standing in front of his peers and quietly beaming along with them. Then, without any fanfare, he had resumed his position in the front row of the group, spreading his arms over the shoulders of the two on either side of him while turning to nod at the others.

Piemur would never forget that moment! He had barely noticed the looks of approval on the faces of the Masterharper and journeyman masterharper, though he was aware that they were pleased. No, Piemur knew his singing voice was perfect, not because of any vanity but because it had been meticulously trained to be just so, and nothing less. He knew, too, that for a little while during the rehearsal he had been the focus of everyone's attention, but that wasn't what had been most important to him as a singer. All he'd ever cared about was the satisfaction and inexpressible joy he experienced when singing with a group, joining in with other voices to create one single, superb orchestra of sound. That was what was most important to Piemur. When he sang with a group he felt as if the sound were actually amplifying from inside his body, tingling every cell, and filling him with pure delight.

But now, perched in the tree watching Cramb, he knew singing with a choir would never be the same for him. He wasn't sure if anything could ever make him feel so passionate again. How time changed everything!

Piemur shook his head. He'd better keep his attention on the job, he mused, and redoubled his efforts to stay fully alert. The day was wearing on, and the light in the sky was changing with it. Night would fall soon, and quickly.

The location Cramb was drawing had an excellent expanse of pure white, undisturbed sand set back from the shoreline by two full dragonlengths. As Cramb tilted his head, Piemur followed his gaze and saw that the artist was scrutinizing a cluster of boulders set to one side. He started drawing again, and Piemur reckoned that he might be adding in the boulders.

Cramb stopped drawing and tilted his head again, looking pleased with himself as he viewed his work with a critical eye. Piemur watched him, captivated; he had never seen a landscape artist at work before.

Cramb carefully secured the sketch onto a flat piece of bark. Then he placed five small dollops of colored powder on a smaller piece of bark and mixed water into each pile to form a smooth, loose paste. Piemur couldn't help but smile when he saw Cramb's tongue poking out of the corner of his mouth, his lips curling upward unconsciously. *The artist must like this part,* Piemur supposed.

Piemur watched, fascinated, as Cramb used the five basic pigments to create a varied range of colors, all of which could be found in the local scenery. Starting at the top of the vellum Cramb quickly and meticulously filled in the colors of the scene. Piemur wished he could see Cramb's work, even though the scene was right in front of his eyes.

Sighing, Cramb carefully set the finished drawing aside to dry. Then he took a smaller rectangle of vellum from his satchel and quickly started sketching again, glancing over at the sleeping form of Toolan once or twice as he worked. Finally, Cramb retrieved his color palette and added paint to the second drawing. *Perhaps he doesn't want to waste the leftover pigment on his palette,* Piemur speculated.

From his place under the shady tree, Toolan woke with a snort, making a disgusting noise as he cleared his throat. He sat up and peered in Cramb's direction.

"Best get a fire started and fresh water hauled in," he said, directing his comment not to Cramb but rather to the general area of the little campsite.

"The dragonrider won't mind waiting another day for my finished sketches then, d'you think? I'll have my work cut out drawing the nightscape when darkness falls," Cramb said, his tone moderate. Piemur couldn't be certain, but he thought he saw a little smile pushing up one corner of Cramb's mouth.

"Right, yes! You'd better stay put then, Cramb, and get that work done. We need those sketches ready first thing tomorrow. On you go, now!" Toolan said, flapping one hand at the artist.

Toolan stomped off in search of dry kindling and made a great deal of noise on his return as he set about making a fire, finally placing unlit, moss-covered torches to either side of Cramb's stool for later use. Piemur noted with a grin that Cramb remained intent on his work as Toolan crashed and harrumphed around the campsite. Either Cramb was so absorbed that he was completely oblivious to his colleague's efforts, or—more likely, Piemur mused—he was a master at ignoring him.

Finally, when darkness began to fall, Toolan lit the torches next to Cramb, illuminating the artist's face as he worked. Of course, Piemur couldn't see the drawings, but he watched in fascination as Cramb made deft brushstrokes on the vellum, adding one or two final touches to his work.

The delicious smell of brewing *klah* wafted through the campsite, tantalizing Piemur as he sat on his perch, reduced to sipping the warm water from his flask to help wash down the hunk of dried meat he had to chew on. As night fell, the daytime birds and animals slowly ceased their calls and chitters, and nocturnal creatures began to fill the air with their cries. Cramb had finished his drawings and set them in a safe place to dry, and he ate the meal Toolan had prepared in silence, as Toolan sulked, seemingly put out, in Piemur's view, that his companion didn't appear more grateful.

When the meal was finished, they both stretched out in front of the fire and after some time settled down for the night. Piemur waited until he thought Toolan and Cramb were soundly asleep before he dropped quietly from his perch to stretch and relieve himself. He'd decided to move out of the tree for the night, and hide among some dense sedges several paces away, so he could be more comfortable and remain undetected. If luck was with him, when T'reb returned in the morning he might learn more of what the dragonrider was planning.

Piemur wished he could call Farli to keep him company, but he didn't want to risk being discovered, and anyway she was better off with Stupid, keeping him quiet.

Too bad, he brooded, because he could've coaxed her to bring him one of the juice-filled red fruits that grew in abundance along the coast; it would've been a welcome addition to the warm water and dried meat. *Ah well,* he thought ruefully as he settled himself under the tree, *I've had harder nights before and it hasn't hurt me yet.*

The morning calls of birds roused Piemur before Toolan and Cramb. He watched, from his position back on his branch, as Cramb woke first and then stood up, stretching his arms skyward, tilting his head to his left shoulder and then to his right. Then, with an expression that looked like a malicious grin, he walked over to Toolan's sleeping form and poked him sharply in the butt with his boot.

Without warning a small flock of birds flew out of Piemur's tree, crying raucously. He tensed up, willing himself to become invisible as Cramb turned to look in his direction.

"What's all the commotion?" Toolan called to Cramb as he walked toward him.

The birds' shrill cries clanged in Piemur's ears as he felt the change in air pressure that signaled a dragon emerging from *between*. Cramb and Toolan also obviously noted the change: Both looked skyward. Piemur watched as T'reb and his dragon appeared out of nowhere, flying on a path that would pass directly over Piemur's tree. Fearful the dragon might spot him, he eased as quickly and quietly as he could from his position against the tree trunk, slithering and stretching until he clung along the underside of the branch. Dismayed, he heard the sound of the leaves rustling with his movement. And then, both Toolan and Cramb peered in Piemur's direction as he hung, clinging like a lizard to the tree.

"Is something in that tree, Cramb?" Toolan asked, but Cramb had no time to reply as the green dragon made her descent toward the sandy beach, her wings beating powerfully as she drew closer to the ground, her forelegs and haunches stretching downward in preparation for landing. Toolan and Cramb stood stock-still, seemingly unable to move, the huge draft of air created by the green's descent swirling sand up and whipping it all around them.

They mustn't be used to dragons, Piemur reckoned, *or they'd surely have moved far enough away so they wouldn't get hit by all that sand.* He frowned as he watched them. He'd gingerly dropped from the tree while the two men were distracted by Beth's arrival. He looked on as the dragon landed, all four feet finally touching the ground. *Shards, but she looks in poor condition,* Piemur noted critically, observing from close quarters the lack of luster in the color of her soft hide and the slight hollow just above her rib cage. Her eyes looked dull, too, if he wasn't mistaken.

Beth furled her wings and then daintily extended her right foreleg so her rider could dismount. As soon as T'reb's feet hit the ground, Beth turned and, making a deep rumbling noise as she coughed, walked across the hot sands toward the clear waters of the ocean.

T'reb was no taller than Piemur and he had a hard, lined face. He removed his flying helmet, revealing a heavy peppering of gray hairs on his head that mingled with the brown and made his hair appear as if it were metallic in color. The fringe was cut blunt and straight across his brow, and his eyes, set too close in his face, appeared to look smaller because of the dark circles that ringed them. *He looks worn out,* Piemur reflected, *even for an Oldtimer.*

The dragonrider turned to watch his green as she walked to the water's edge, and then, swiveling around, he lifted his chin, assessed Cramb and Toolan briefly, and pointed a gloved index finger in their direction, peering down his nose at them. The two men were still knuckling sand out of their eyes and spitting it from their mouths, so they didn't see the summons.

"You there, Tortle!" T'reb called imperiously, flapping one hand before he removed his gloves and opened his flying jacket. The dragonrider's voice, Piemur noticed again, was high-pitched, shrill, and unpleasantly nasal. Piemur puckered up his mouth at the sound.

"Ah, pardon, Dragonrider T'reb," Toolan said, offering a rather clumsily executed bow. "My name is *Toolan.* This is Cramb."

"Yes, yes," T'reb said dismissively as he walked toward the two men. "Do you have what I want?" *Straight to the point,* Piemur mused: *There's no messin' around with this one, nor time wasted on good manners.*

"Yes, the sketches are complete," Toolan said, bowing again, deeply. Cramb regarded his colleague with one raised brow and then dipped his body slightly in an elegant, though less obsequious, show of respect. He handed the two drawings to T'reb, who took them with a sniff.

"Hm," the dragonrider said reluctantly, scanning the paintings, "this isn't bad work." His tone suggested that he hadn't been expecting anything of such quality.

"Thank you, Dragonrider," Cramb said. "It's a beautiful place. I wish you great pleasure from my works."

T'reb looked at Cramb sharply for a moment, as if he didn't know what he was talking about, and Cramb tilted his head to one side, frowning, his unspoken question in the gesture.

"Yes, well, they look accurate and will serve our purposes well," T'reb said with an insincere smile. "The night sky has been copied with absolute accuracy, Toober, as I instructed?"

Toolan made to protest again at T'reb's failure to recall his name properly but desisted at the last moment with a little sigh. Cramb nodded in affirmation at T'reb's question.

T'reb looked edgy, Piemur noticed, watching as the dragonrider glanced quickly at Toolan, who shook his head in a tight, quick movement.

Then, without any regard for creases or folds, T'reb roughly stuffed the two drawings into his flying jacket, ignoring the shocked intake of breath from Cramb. The dragonrider chucked a small cloth pouch at Toolan, nearly hitting him in the face, and, without a farewell or final word, turned and walked toward his dragon as she waddled from the water's edge to the shore.

Piemur looked from Cramb to Toolan and then to the dragonrider, wondering what he'd missed.

As T'reb and his dragon took to the air, climbing high into the sky, Cramb closed the distance to Toolan and grabbed him by the arm. A second later, as T'reb and Beth blinked *between* out of the sky, Cramb roughly turned Toolan to face him.

"What the shards was that really about?" he demanded. Toolan pulled his arm from Cramb's grasp and walked away from the campsite toward the open beach.

No, no! Piemur thought in desperation, as he watched the two men. *Don't go that way—I won't be able to hear what you're saying!*

Cramb pulled at Toolan's shoulder, making him stop dead in his tracks.

"You told me the dragonrider wanted a painting of this place because it held great sentimental memories for him. You said he wanted to put it someplace prominent in his weyr. Then you told me he wanted a nightscape of the same scene as well! Just what the shells have you gotten me mixed up in, Toolan?" Cramb's voice was tight, and although he kept his anger under control it was obvious he was furious at the deception.

Toolan's expression turned devious, and Cramb crossed his arms in front of his chest, glaring at his companion.

"He plans to use this place as a secure hide—from what I can guess," Toolan said finally, with a smirk on his lips. "Probably more of the goods he and that sorry group of Oldtimers have been trading. It's why he chose this particular little cove, I reckon. It's hard to reach, and nestled among so many other coves that look exactly the same, it'd be easy to bypass or overlook." Then he turned and flounced away from Cramb, who hastily followed. They continued talking, though Piemur caught only snippets of what they said, and not enough at that to make his long day and night of surveillance truly worth the while.

As the two men walked away from him, deep in heated conversation, Piemur debated whether to follow them. He could cut his losses now and relate what he'd seen to Master Robinton, or stay on in the hope that the men would reveal more of T'reb's scheme. He hastily decided against leaving with such scanty information and carefully crawled through the undergrowth, drawing level with the two men.

Cramb had stopped Toolan midstride, one hand on his shoulder.

"You don't need to know any more than that, Cramb!"

"Oh, yes, I do, Toolan! You don't honestly expect me to believe that the dragonrider is going to put valuable goods out here? In the middle of nowhere?" Cramb lifted one hand, gesturing around him at their remote location. "Unless, of course, what he wants to hide would be safe here, in this heat, where any curious animals could find it."

Toolan shrugged his shoulder out from under Cramb's hand, his face contorting in anger.

"I can't tell you any more, Cramb! My cousin sent me down here because I've done a few trades with T'reb before. Serra thinks the Oldtimers should honor the connection they once had with our great-uncle. We all want land of our own, and Serra's convinced the dragonriders can help us take what we want."

"So you and your kin are going to hold land of your own?" Cramb asked, shaking his head. Piemur gasped and then quickly clapped a hand over his mouth. Cramb knew, Piemur thought, just as everyone did, that lands fit for holding were not easy to come by. They were handed down from kin to kin or, in the rare case of Lord Toric of Southern Hold, earned from many Turns of brutally hard work. He could only hazard a guess about Cramb, but he was full certain now that Toolan was from Nabol.

"And what are you giving the dragonriders in return?"

"That's all I can tell you, Cramb, because it's all I know," Toolan said, a stubborn note creeping into his voice.

"I bet you know more, Toolan," Cramb said slowly, his voice taking on a threatening edge as he stepped closer to Toolan. "Spit it out!"

"Serra thinks they can get land across the border from Nabol. That's all they told me!" Toolan's tone was final, his right hand cutting through the air like a flat blade.

Piemur's mouth fell open. Crom, where he was born, where all his kin lived, was across the border and not far from Nabol. Were they planning on ousting some unsuspecting smallholders in Crom? He sat up in alarm, banging his head against an arching branch of the bush he was crouching under.

Toolan and Cramb heard the thunking noise as Piemur's head connected with the branch and looked in his direction as the bush shook violently.

"Hey!" Toolan yelled. "Who's in there?"

Piemur crouched lower, trying to disappear into the ground as Toolan and Cramb marched toward him.

"You! You in there! I can see you!" Cramb called.

Swallowing hard, Piemur clamped his jaws together and scuttled out from under the bush on all fours, then stood up, quickly scanning around for the best escape route. Hoping he could outrun them, Piemur darted through an opening in the forest, threw his head back, and ran for all he was worth, allowing all the tension he'd stifled while spying to propel him away from Toolan and Cramb. He ran fast, covering the ground easily, dodging around trees and swaths of dense bushes and ferns. As he ran he could hear the sounds of the two men as they pursued him. *Faster!* Piemur urged himself on, checking over his shoulder to see if they were close. Toolan, with his lanky legs, was ahead of Cramb and looked to be about ten meters behind Piemur. *Too close!*

Piemur pressed on, propelling himself forward as the adrenaline he'd been dampening was finally let loose into his bloodstream. His arms pumped at breakneck speed and he ran on and on, darting and ducking through the forest until his lungs felt like they were on fire. He took a quick look over his shoulder, checking to see how close Toolan was, but the path behind him was empty. Slowing his pace, he checked in all directions, but there was no sign of Toolan anywhere.

Piemur stopped behind a huge hardwood tree, panting heavily.

The muscles in his legs quivered from his prolonged dash and he forced himself to concentrate on his breathing.

All those Turns of voice training were coming in useful now, he thought wryly, as he took in a huge lungful of air. He could feel his diaphragm fall and rise with each deep inhalation and exhalation, and his breathing steadied quickly. He straightened up, scanning the sky above for the sun.

"Pooly shoots," he muttered, realizing he had a long hike ahead of him to reach the clearing where he'd tethered Stupid. He reached up to pull his hat down firmly on his head, but it was no longer there. It must have flown off during the chase. There was nothing he could do about that: He would just have to go bareheaded all the way back to the hold. He clipped his thumbs around his belt loop, checked the sun's position once more, and then turned forty degrees eastward. Piemur sighed, looking all around at the dense tropical forest. He had a long trek ahead of him.

THREE

PIEMUR ARRIVED AT SOUTHERN HOLD HOURS LATER, EXHAUSTED, thirsty, and sunburnt. He brought Stupid directly to the runner-beast corrals where there was shade and a huge trough of fresh water. Toric, the accepted though unconfirmed Lord of Southern Hold, crossed the compound to greet him.

"'Day, Piemur. You look scorched, lad. Lose your hat?"

Piemur nodded briefly, then scooped up a handful of water from the trough and splashed it over his head and along the base of his neck before he stooped to drink. He felt like he'd spent the morning on a fry griddle.

Toric wasted little time with pleasantries, getting right down to what had clearly been foremost on his mind. "The Oldtimers sent word yesterday: They're no longer permitting anyone from outside to enter their Weyr."

Piemur jerked upright, sending droplets of water flying from his hair. He stared at Toric, his thirst forgotten, a frown creasing his burnt brow as he wondered if this latest development had anything to do with T'reb and the two men he'd been spying on.

"Can you believe it? Mardra and T'kul say that we've brought illness to their Weyr," Toric spat, and Piemur had no trouble hearing the disgust in the Lord Holder's tone. "Not a word from T'ron, though. His opinion on this matter is *anyone's* guess!" T'ron was

Southern's Weyrleader; T'kul, though he had been the Weyrleader of High Reaches before going into exile with the other Oldtimers, now acted as T'ron's wingsecond. More and more, though, Piemur reflected, T'ron seemed to be leaving the talking to T'kul.

Toric paced as he spoke, swinging his heavily muscled arms and huge hands as he moved. Those impressive arms, Piemur guessed, must have been the result of his younger days as a fisherman at Ista, before he agreed to take hold of lands on the Southern Continent. Berry brown from his Turns in the hot climate, the skin around his light-green eyes was marked with a fine web of lines, and like most folk who lived on the Southern Continent, Toric wore his hair cropped close to his head.

Piemur shook his head, feeling slightly dizzy. It was a dreadful shame, he thought, that the Oldtimers were isolating themselves further. Even though the Southern Weyrfolk were no longer in favor with Benden Weyr, Piemur didn't think they were *all* such a bad bunch. He reckoned only a small group of the Southern Oldtimers were actually troublemakers, and that the other members of the Weyr had stayed on with them out of loyalty.

"I'll have to send a message to the Masterharper," Piemur said absently as he searched the rooftops for Farli. "I wonder where Farli's gone."

"It's nigh-on impossible to keep track of all the fire-lizards around here, Piemur," Toric said, gesturing with a flick of one large hand. "She could be with the fair nesting at the back of the Hold, for all I know. But there's no need to send a message to the Masterharper—I sent word to him myself. N'ton should arrive with him soon enough."

"Good, and thank you, Lord Toric," Piemur replied, not voicing the thought that he also had interesting news to relate to the Masterharper.

In fact, it was several hours more before N'ton arrived with Masterharper Robinton and Journeyman Masterharper Sebell. The two harpers were seated behind the Fort Weyrleader on his dragon's huge back.

Wearing wide-brimmed hats to protect their heads from the heat of the sun, Piemur and Toric were watching as a stock hand familiarized a young draft beast with harness and tackle when Lioth's bronze form appeared high above the Hold complex. As the on-lookers watched his careful descent, the dragon appeared to change color in the sunlight. Minute flecks of gold, brown, green, and blue caught the reflection of the sun, making the soft bronze hide glow with iridescence.

Lioth was a superb example of a bronze dragon, measuring slightly more than thirty-seven meters from tip to tail; his head was finely sculpted, and his features distinctly defined by taut muscle and sinew. His eyes, like those of all dragons and fire-lizards, were many-faceted and reflected the mood of the creature through the color spectrum, whirling blue with contentment through to red for anger or alarm. Lioth's eyes were a shade of deep green and shim-mered brightly, Piemur noted. It was obvious that Lioth was fighting fit. The majestic bronze backwinged several times as he made his descent, N'ton sitting astride, his back straight and body motion-less, stuck by invisible glue to the base of his dragon's neck while Robinton and Sebell, seated behind him, clung on tightly to the har-ness straps.

N'ton raised one arm casually in greeting to those below, ap-pearing to all intents as if he were waving from the comfort of a stationary herdbeast cart rather than from the back of an immense dragon going through the motions of a rigorous descent. With one final wingbeat Lioth extended his hindquarters, dropping all four legs to the ground, his long tail resting gently on the dirt as the sails of his huge wings pinioned back and inward toward his body, folding neatly into place along his back and flanks. Suddenly the air all around Piemur and Toric was laden with the wonderful, aro-matic smell of dragon. There was no other animal smell as beguil-ing, Piemur thought; he could breathe that scent in from daylight to dusk and never tire of it.

"'Day to you, So'holders," N'ton called to Piemur and Toric as he unclipped himself from the flying harness. N'ton turned toward the Masterharper, who had already freed himself from the harness straps, and offered the older man his hand so he could dismount. Lioth obligingly extended a foreleg to aid the harper. With practiced

ease, Robinton climbed down from the huge dragon, Sebell quickly
following suit as Piemur and Toric closed the distance to the new ar-
rivals, waving the settling dust away from their faces with their hats.
Tris, N'ton's brown fire-lizard, flew in a lazy circle around Lioth and
then darted off to join a group of other fire-lizards sunning on the
Hold roof.

From his perch on Lioth's neck, N'ton bent forward from the
waist and, in one agile, seemingly breakneck action, fell, headfirst,
toward the ground. At the very last moment, he flick-pivoted his
legs together in a snapping movement, using them like a fulcrum to
force his body upright, and landed straight and steady at the side of
his mount.

"Shards!" Piemur whispered under his breath. N'ton's acrobatic
dismount filled him with awe even though he'd seen it dozens of
times in the past. Dragonriders, Piemur reminded himself, being the
guardians of their world, were truly a breed apart.

"Well there, N'ton, welcome. Welcome, Master Robinton, Journeyman Master Sebell," Toric said, inclining his body in the customary show of respect. He clasped hands with the two harpers and
finally with N'ton, looking up at the tall dragonrider.

Standing almost two meters in height, N'ton, like most dragonriders, was supremely physically fit and carried his long, strong
frame with a casualness that matched his easy manner and pleasant nature. All dragonriders had an indefinable presence, a strength
akin to an electric force that radiated around them. Some folk at-
tributed the dragonriders' unique energy to the lifelong connection
they shared with their dragons, or to their higher-than-average lev-
els of empathy. Whatever its source, when dragonriders entered a
room, they often charged the atmosphere with a buzz that could
also infect those around them. N'ton, though still relatively young,
carried himself with an air of maturity as if he were much older
than his Turns. His light-blue eyes had one or two creases at the corners; his symmetric, handsome face bore a straight nose and strong
chin, and he seemed to be utterly unaware of how striking a figure
he cut. Piemur had heard women gasp when they saw the Fort Weyrleader for the first time.

"My thanks, Toric, you're ever gracious, though I've visited here so much of late, Lioth has fairly beaten a permanent path to your door," N'ton replied, gesturing toward his dragon with an affectionate smile, who had moved off to sunbathe a short distance away.

"Good day, Master Robinton," Piemur said excitedly, wishing he could simply blurt out everything he had seen and heard in the last two days instead of observing the customary niceties. He approached his Master, and then suddenly remembered his manners. "And Journeyman Sebell, Weyrleader N'ton, good day to you both."

"Ah, Piemur," Robinton said, a smile on his face. "Well now, my lad, you look as eager as ever, though somewhat singed. Let's get ourselves settled out of this heat, shall we?"

The Masterharper raised one brow a fraction and exchanged glances with Toric before moving hastily toward the shade of the Hold porch. Like N'ton, he and Sebell wore heavy flying gear, and the trio were intent, first and foremost, on divesting themselves of their outer clothing. Life on the Southern Continent was all about winning the unrelenting battle against the heat.

"Make yourselves more comfortable," Toric said, "while I call for some refreshments." Turning from the group he walked through a set of wide, open doors and into the Hold proper, calling, "Meria. Where is everyone? Meria!"

Southern Hold, like all other holds on Pern, was built as the central structure of the compound, designed to house, facilitate, and above all protect the immediate community from Thread. Built off the ground, on short plinths, thus allowing the maximum amount of air to circulate under the dwelling, a communal space dominated the center of the hold leading from the huge, bi-folding front doors. On either side of the large room, double doors on both side walls led to a corridor off which the hold's sleeping quarters were situated. Each sleeping area had large, floor-to-ceiling windows leading out to a deep veranda—and though spartan in design, one room could house a small family if the bedding was arranged accordingly.

Piemur took a seat on one of the benches shaded by the roof of the deep porch, only realizing as he sat down that his head was pounding fiercely and his stomach roiled with queasiness. He rubbed a hand over his forehead and then yanked it away, his badly burnt brow stinging from his touch. All he wanted was to make his report to Master Robinton so he could withdraw to somewhere cool and quiet to lie down.

With a heavy sigh, Robinton took a seat and Piemur glanced at him. *He looks fatigued,* Piemur thought. Probably traveling around too much doing more than any other man his age would consider prudent. The Masterharper had a great many demands on his attention, and although he still carried his tall frame with easy grace and an amiable demeanor, Piemur could readily see new lines creasing the corners of his Master's mouth. His hair seemed grayer, too.

"Meria, Meria!" Toric called again. Then, "Ah, there you are!"

Piemur had met Meria on the day she first arrived at Southern Hold. She had left Southern Weyr and, needing shelter—no one on Pern, even on the Southern Continent, would choose to live in the open, under the threat of Threadfall—had sought succor from Toric. As far as Piemur knew, Meria had never offered an explanation as to why she'd left the Weyr, which was something Piemur often speculated about.

Toric returned to the porch, harrumphing gently under his breath as he assured his guests that refreshments were on the way. Moments later Meria arrived with a tray, followed by a drudge who carried an even larger tray laden with refreshments.

"Good day," Meria said, smiling as she placed her tray on a side table. "My apologies for keeping you waiting, but it's best to serve refreshments at the very last moment before the heat spoils them."

With quick movements she poured fresh juice into cups, which she then offered to the guests. Meria winked at Piemur as she handed him his drink, but with his aching head he was only able to manage a weak smile in return. When they all had a glass in hand, she gestured to a plate of bread, hard cheese, and soft yellow berries, then withdrew.

Toric cleared his throat and looked at the Masterharper.

"I wish to thank you for making the detour here from your planned journey," the Lord Holder began, and when the Masterharper nodded, Toric quickly continued. "We have unsettling news from the

Weyr, Masterharper. As my message stated, the Oldtimers—my pardon, I mean the Southern Weyrleaders—formally closed their Weyr to us yesterday. This means we are unable to offer our tithes in exchange for their protection from Thread." He paused here, his brows meeting in a frown as he mulled something over in his head. Then he went on.

"Since the lands in Southern are well seeded with grubs we tend to manage quite well on our own, without the help of dragonmen. But regardless of our own efficiencies, it still sits poorly that they have chosen to isolate themselves so. I wonder, too, if we'll no longer have dragons protecting our skies." Toric crossed his arms in front of his chest and looked from Robinton to N'ton and then Sebell and Piemur.

"This is, indeed, a most disturbing development, Lord Toric," Robinton said. "Have you told Benden of this news?"

Toric shook his head. "Not that it would do any good, I fear, since those in Southern no longer have anything to do with F'lar and his Weyr." Toric cast a quick look at N'ton: Everyone knew that the Fort Weyrleader—as, indeed, all the Weyrleaders in the north— looked to Benden as the premier Weyr.

Piemur fidgeted in his seat, overcome with the heat and his exhaustion. *Why can't I focus?* He just wanted to tell Master Robinton what he'd seen. He was so tired. He shook his shoulders.

"This is awful," N'ton offered.

Robinton nodded and turned to Sebell, his second. "Do I take it, then, Sebell, we don't have anyone keeping tabs on Southern Weyr other than Piemur?"

All eyes turned to Piemur. Suddenly he felt light-headed, and the cup of juice he held in his hand began to slip out of his grasp. He put it down on a nearby table and wiped his burning brow with the back of his hand, trying to gather his thoughts into a semblance of coherency. Everyone was staring at him.

"That's so, Master Robinton," Sebell answered. "A month ago I moved a scout from Southern up north to Nabol, as matters there dictated. Since then, Piemur has been our only pair of eyes and ears in the south."

"Report, please, Piemur," Robinton said, smiling.

Piemur cleared his throat. His eyes felt odd, and he wanted nothing more than to lie down and close them.

"Well," he began hesitantly, "I saw two men in a cove on the eastern shores?" His words came out like a question rather than a definitive statement. "They met with—" Piemur could feel the Master's eyes on him, but try as he might, he seemed unable to articulate his news. "—with T'reb." He frowned and then wiped his brow again, wincing slightly at the sting. "He'd exchanged terse words with B'naj the day before I saw him with the men in the cove."

"Two men on the eastern shores? We're discussing Southern Weyr, Piemur. What news do you have from there?" Robinton sounded puzzled and, Piemur thought, uncharacteristically curt.

"But I haven't been in the Weyr for several days, Master. Or is it just one day?"

Oh, dear, Piemur brooded, *why am I blathering?* His brows furrowed again as he tried to recall the order of events, then he shook his head. He could feel Robinton staring at him, so he continued.

"I was following two men from Nabol. Or at least I'm quite certain they're from Nabol. Well, one of them, at least, is probably Nabolese. They met with the Oldtimer T'reb. I think he's up to no good, Master . . . and those Nabolese are looking for holds! T'reb spoke about Mardra, too! She was on the Hatching Grounds," he exclaimed all in a rush, his thoughts racing. "Loranth was coughing and upset, because she's sick or something." He could sense himself beginning to falter.

Now Piemur could see the doubtful expression on his Master's face and the nervous movements of N'ton and Toric as they watched him floundering to make his report. Only Sebell remained completely still, watching Piemur closely.

"But this report is of no consequence, Piemur. What about the Weyr?" Robinton asked.

Piemur's head started to spin and he swayed a little in his seat. How could the Masterharper think his news was of no consequence when it obviously was? Piemur felt aggrieved that he wasn't being taken seriously when he believed, most strongly, that what he'd seen was of the utmost seriousness.

When Piemur didn't respond immediately, the Masterharper frowned and turned his attention to Toric, asking a question that Piemur barely heard. Piemur felt his stomach sink. T'reb had mentioned a plan and how he wanted to help Mardra. Had he said that to the Master? He wasn't sure. On an impulse Piemur decided to push his point.

"But don't you see, Master?" Piemur said, interrupting the Lord Holder in midsentence. "What happened at the Hatching Grounds will create further ripples."

The Master was fond of talking about people's actions as if they were pebbles cast into a pool of water, and how their actions created ripples even after the pebbles had sunk out of sight. "T'reb said that Mardra sounded desperate, and she promised to make everything right again!"

"Piemur," Master Robinton said sharply. He turned to Toric. "My apologies, Lord Toric, Piemur's allowed his enthusiasm, and possibly too much time in the hot sun, to override his sense of courtesy." Robinton raised a brow at Piemur in subtle warning.

"But I know more will come of this!" Piemur blurted. "Some of the Oldtimers aren't happy at all, Master. I think they're planning on doing something drastic."

Too late, Piemur saw the color in Robinton's cheeks heighten and realized that he'd pushed his point too far. Quick to ease the tension, Sebell placed a hand on Piemur's shoulder and then stood up, urging his friend to do likewise, as he led him from the porch and gestured with an outstretched arm toward a long table set in the shade of some fellis trees.

"I see you've been kept busy, my friend," Sebell said quietly, his tone reassuring, indicating with one hand that Piemur should take a seat next to him at the table. "I'm sure you see that the Master is focused on other matters today."

"But, Sebell, you should've heard what I heard! T'reb saw Mardra and Loranth on the Hatching Grounds. He said it was terrible, and they were both upset! And then T'reb met with Cramb and Toolan in that cove. They gave him two drawings, paintings, really, I suppose." It was all rushing out of Piemur now and he was hard-put not to stumble over his words.

"What were the drawings of?" Sebell asked, one eyebrow arching upward.

"Well . . ." Piemur frowned. "I never really saw them, Sebell, but I watched him—Cramb, the painter, that's who—he was facing me as he worked, so he *must've* been sketching that cove. I heard them talk about it, too!" He could feel that he was growing overly animated again and saw that Sebell had a curious expression on his face. *Sebell thinks I've been chasing down shadows, too!*

Piemur suddenly felt uncomfortable and quickly looked over his shoulder, noting that Master Robinton was absorbed in discussion with Lord Toric and N'ton.

"Piemur, before N'ton fetched us this morning, the Master and I discussed your role as a scout. This new position the Southern Weyrleaders have taken has changed everything. The Master thinks it might be best if you concentrate on mapping again. You've done more than your fair share of scouting for now."

"But, Sebell, I *know* something bad is going to happen. Those two men said T'reb might use the cove to hide something!"

"Did T'reb speak to them about what he wanted to do?"

"No, but . . ." Piemur stopped, pinching his face in worry. Was he remembering correctly? He *had* been hunkered in that tree for an inordinate amount of time with hardly any sleep.

"Toolan told Cramb that T'reb wanted the drawings so he could hide something there. More of the goods they've been trading illegally, he guessed. But Cramb thought that was nonsense. They spoke about taking a holding near Nabol, too, Sebell. I was worried they might try and oust my family from their holding in Crom. Then Cramb got cross with Toolan!" Piemur said. His head was really pounding now and he wanted nothing more than to have his report accepted so he could go lie down.

"Hold on, Piemur, go back a bit. Did T'reb *say* he was going to hide something in the cove?"

"No . . ." Piemur's shoulders sagged; he felt thoroughly deflated.

Sebell shook his head slightly and then his expression brightened. "You've done good work, Piemur, but I think you may have been out in the hot sun for longer than is healthy. It's obvious to me that you're not behaving like yourself. Why don't you get out of the heat and rest? When you're ready, the Master thinks you should map the terrain near that steep bluff to the west of here. You know where I mean, don't you?" Piemur nodded. "You always talk about how much you like climbing, so this should be a welcome task."

Piemur looked at Sebell's steadfast brown face and the journeyman master gazed back, his brown eyes kind and unwavering. Sebell had become somewhat of a mentor to Piemur since he'd left the Harper Hall, often liaising with him instead of Master Robinton, who had to attend to so many other matters. In Piemur's opinion Sebell was the finest of harpers, second only to Robinton, and a master of all a harper was supposed to be: educator, mediator, and most important custodian of the heritage and culture of Pern's unique society.

Perhaps Sebell and the Master were right; maybe there really was nothing to take from what he'd seen and heard. Perhaps what T'reb had been up to wasn't truly sinister at all. Nonetheless, he couldn't forget what he'd seen with his own eyes on those desolate Hatching Grounds. Spurred on by that thought, and what his gut instincts were telling him, suddenly he felt inclined to forget what the Master wanted and find out for himself just exactly what plans were brewing among the Oldtimers in Southern Weyr. Just as soon as his head stopped pounding!

Piemur mopped the sweat off his head and face and checked the knot in the tunic he'd tied around his waist. He'd need the tunic later when he reached the top of the cliff face, but for now it was too hot and awkward to climb in, especially in the unrelenting heat. Satisfied the tunic was secured, he tested the first handhold he'd use to haul himself up the rock face and then began the arduous task of climbing.

It had been a sevenday since he'd left Southern Hold. He'd left Stupid behind, because the terrain he'd be mapping wasn't suitable for the six-legged ruminant. N'ton and Lioth had obligingly flown Piemur close to the cliff face to shorten his trekking time, but even so Piemur had started his journey in an unnaturally foul humor, unable to shake the feeling that Master Robinton no longer valued him, and that he'd made a fool of himself in front of Sebell, N'ton, and Toric. Ever since that afternoon it had been hard to keep his spirits buoyed and on an even keel. He felt as if he didn't fit in anywhere anymore. Throughout the last fourteen days he'd mentally argued with himself about returning to Southern Weyr to discover more of what the Oldtimers were planning with the men from Nabol, and every time his better sense won out and he convinced himself *not* to act contrary to Master Robinton's orders, he felt like a coward, willing to do anything in order to fit in. Where had his gumption gone? Had he lost so much of his strength of character along with his singing voice that he was no longer able to act on his own?

His foster mother, Ama, had always reminded him—as she did all her fosterlings—to heed their instincts. And before Piemur left Crom to be an apprentice at the Harper Hall, Ama reminded him that if he ever felt uncertain of the direction his life was taking, all he had to do was let his instincts guide him toward a decision.

"Don't fret, my lad, or overthink things," Ama had said, beaming at him. "Let your guts guide you and then just go with it. Let it rip, my Pie." At the time he hadn't understood what she was saying, but he reckoned now she may have been telling him that he didn't have to be an apprentice harper if he felt that wasn't his destiny.

As he climbed the cliff now, all alone save for Farli's sporadic company, he found himself lapsing into dark reveries and had to consciously shake himself out of his funk. Right now, he reminded himself, it was important that he focus all his concentration on his ascent. Slowly, as he got into the pattern—climb, haul, find a foothold, then climb again—Piemur stopped thinking and unconsciously began to hum a song he'd learned as a young boy. It was a gentle tune that lilted from one note to the next in a steady rhythm and always made him smile when he heard it.

He'd just navigated to one side of a large gouge in the rock face, a recess that looked like one of the very shallow caves that pockmarked the cliff and slowed down his climb. He placed both feet on the far-right side of the cave mouth and reached for the next handhold, still humming, when his voice suddenly failed to rise easily, croaking unattractively instead. Abruptly he stopped humming. Holding on with both arms, his feet still on the ledge, he cleared his throat and then tried the note again. Another ragged croak filled the air. He frowned and turned his head to one side of the cliff face, spitting saliva from his mouth.

Ha! he thought bitterly, leaning into the cliff face as he spat over his shoulder again. So much for all the advice he'd been given: "You have to give your voice time, Piemur, let it settle naturally," or, "You'll see, Piemur, it'll be no time before you find your mature range." But no one said what everyone knew—that there wasn't any guarantee a young man's voice would settle into a good tenor or baritone once he'd matured.

Leaning heavily against the cliff face, Piemur closed his eyes at the memory of his old voice as the hairs on the back of his neck stood on end—it was as if the songs he'd sung three Turns ago still filled the air, and he tried in vain to stop the familiar feeling of loss from piercing his heart. This is what he did now: map the Southern Continent; or spy on the Oldtimer dragonmen; or teach the children of Southern Hold; or do whatever the Masterharper of Pern asked of him. Piemur did what he was told, and without any grousing, but he felt as if he'd been discarded, as if all his Turns of vocal training never existed. The thought cut through him.

"Ha!" he exclaimed out loud this time. He couldn't help himself.

A group of tiny birds, nesting in a crevice in the cliff face, were startled by the harsh sound Piemur made and flew out of their nest in a panicked frenzy.

If anyone had told Piemur three Turns ago that he'd no longer be a first-line singer or even a full-time drum messenger in the Harper

Hall, but, rather, become an odd-jobber on the Southern Continent, he would've told them in no uncertain terms to char off! Had he really been such a disappointment to his Master and Crafthall?

He thought of the Masterharper, and how dismissive he'd been of Piemur's opinion about the Oldtimers. Now, as Piemur clung to the cliff face, he shook his head and a spray of sweat flew off him.

He continued to climb, hauling himself higher and higher, while his mood seemed to go lower and lower. His thoughts were on the verge of turning decidedly dark when he felt a sudden, gentle whoosh of air over his head and Farli appeared above him. Her delicate wings maintaining a hover, she chirped at him, her eyes whirling brightly while she broadcast a series of mental images that were too jumbled for Piemur to comprehend.

"Ah, here, hold up there a minute," Piemur said gently, smiling in spite of himself. "Completely out of the blue you decide to come chattering back to me. You've grown tired of your friends, is that it? Well, you may well be able to fly and chat at the same time, Farli, but *I'm* not able to climb a rock face and stop midway to casually decipher your ramblings. *I* have to pay attention to what I'm doing, you know. Just give me a moment."

A chap couldn't stay broody for very long when he had a fire-lizard, Piemur mused. He smiled at the sight of his little queen, and knew how lucky he was to have her, even if she did wander off on her own from time to time. Even though Piemur felt he didn't fit in anywhere else on Pern, he knew that Farli was a perfect fit for him. Attuned to his thoughts as always, Farli flitted close to Piemur's shoulder as he climbed, thrumming gently, moving to keep her delicately sculpted head close to his.

Then, without warning, Farli's thrumming changed to a shrill chittering, and she broadcast an image of Piemur climbing very fast up the rock face.

"Yes, Farli, that's a good, clear image. Well done, you're getting much better at that," Piemur said encouragingly. It was hard work training a fire-lizard, but he reckoned his gold had really improved.

Unexpectedly Farli screeched loudly in Piemur's ear again and then abruptly vanished *between*. Piemur chuckled to himself and shook his head, amused at the small queen's antics. Something on the periphery of his vision caught Piemur's attention and he whirled his head around, craning to see behind him.

Thread! It wasn't supposed to fall for another day! He could see a wide bank of the mindless, voracious strands moving toward the cliff like a giant curtain of gray.

Move! Fast! Piemur thought frantically, searching above him for another one of the cavelike blemishes in the face of the cliff. He didn't dare climb down, because it was too hard to see foot- and handholds to move quickly in that direction. He had to go up!

One more frantic look over his shoulder at the approaching thick band told him that the Thread was barely three meters away. He called on all the dragons of Pern, present and past, to guide him to the nearest opening as he hauled himself upward. If even one strand of the deadly filaments touched his body he wouldn't stand a chance: The searing burn would surely cause him to lose his grip on the rock face, and it was a long fall down.

His left hand pawed around above his head as he hauled himself upward with his right. There, an opening—he could feel it! He pulled his body up with all his strength, scrambling to get into the little fault in the cliff face before the Thread reached him. At last his head and shoulders were in the cave; all he had to do was drag the rest of his body into the small, irregularly shaped opening.

I hope I fit in here!

With one last mighty effort, Piemur pulled his legs into the little cave. His head banged against the hard, unforgiving rock. He forced himself to ignore the pain. As the leading edge of Thread hit the cliff face, Piemur squeezed himself as tightly as he could into the back of the cave. If a wind started to blow, Piemur thought in horror, even a little gust of it, Thread could blow in and he'd be done for. He watched in terrified awe, pressed tightly against the back of the crevice, as the silver strands made contact with the cliff face and then, unable to penetrate the rock, slithered and fell toward the ground. He had never been this close to Thread before in his life! He closed his eyes.

What was that sound? He could hear something like gushing

liquid or rushing air—or maybe a combination of the two. It grew louder. Through his tightly closed eyelids Piemur could sense an orange glow. His eyes snapped open just as flame spewed in front of the rock face, and Piemur wondered if he was dreaming. Then another burst of fire flared in front of his eyes and, hissing, Farli flew into the cave.

She must have flown off to find firestone when she first caught sight of the Threadfall, Piemur thought in amazement. He knew that fire-lizards, like dragons, could chew firestone in order to breathe flame, but he'd never seen it before.

Now his gold fire-lizard stood firm, all four feet planted squarely on the rock and her head thrust forward while she flamed the Thread, answering an instinctive urge to extinguish her ancient foe.

"Farli, you amazing girl!" Piemur cried. "Keep flaming!" Then fear washed over him as he realized there was only a limited amount of flame his little queen could produce before the gases from the firestone she had chewed would be spent.

"Farli, you're going to have to get help for me. Save your flame, Farli, you're going to need it!"

Farli cheeped once to Piemur in reply, then closed her mouth, a tiny wisp of smoke floating up and over her head.

"We need help, Farli. Can you go get help?"

As Piemur spoke, Farli looked intently at his face. Then she pushed an image of a brown fire-lizard at him as her eyes flashed from red to brown and then red again. She let out a quick set of trills, spewed a burst of flame from her mouth, then hopped off the ledge and was gone *between*.

Piemur sat, alone and very frightened, his eyes huge as he watched the falling curtain of Thread and waited for help.

A roaring noise, faint at first and then growing louder, filled Piemur's ears. He wondered, having never heard about it before, if this was the sound Thread made as it fell where it could find no fuel to feed on. He had never before been out in the open when Thread was falling!

The roaring noise grew even louder, and Piemur could see an orange glow in the light around his cave.

"Piemur! Piemur!" N'ton's voice called.

"Yes, I'm here, N'ton!" Piemur hollered, hands cupped around his mouth to broadcast the sound of his voice. He didn't dare put his head outside the cave.

"Hang on!" N'ton called, and Piemur could see the orange light growing brighter.

"You'll have to jump, but wait for my command," N'ton told him.

Jump? Piemur could feel fear creeping up the back of his neck again and he swallowed hard, trying to muster the courage to fling his body out of the cave into the midst of Thread. Well, if Thread didn't kill him, the fall most likely would, he thought. He didn't appreciate the irony.

The noise of Lioth flaming grew louder, and now Piemur could feel the fiery heat. He saw a wing tip, and then the dragon wheeled in the air and sank out of sight.

"Piemur, I'm right below you. Jump now!" N'ton shouted, and with barely a second thought Piemur sucked in a big breath and pushed with all his strength, flinging himself out of the cave.

He fell with arms wide and legs splayed, amazed that he wasn't screaming. Lioth was below him, his mouth wide open, spewing flame to keep the space all around them clear of Thread.

With a thud, Piemur hit the bronze dragon's back, landing hard, and all the air whooshed out of his lungs. Then slowly, to his horror, he began to slide—down, down, and away from Lioth's body, unable in that brief moment to do anything to stop his progress, unable even to draw breath. *There's N'ton's foot,* Piemur thought calmly. *I'm falling away from Lioth through Thread.*

And then Piemur felt something clawing at his back, and with a mighty yank that seemed as if it might cut him in half, N'ton had caught hold of his tunic.

"I've got you!" the dragonrider shouted, one hand grasping Piemur's tunic while he held on tight to the straps of his flying harness with the other.

Lioth swerved violently to avoid a thick clump of Thread, and Piemur could feel the force of the movement pulling against his body.

Lioth! Quickly, my friend! My grip on him is loosening! Take us between! N'ton said to his dragon on a tight mental note.

We will not let the man-boy fall, Lioth replied, as his wings thrust air downward with powerful force and he flamed a path clear above them.

Lioth, he feels like a deadweight. I don't think I can hold him, N'ton said. *Take us to water!* He flashed a mental image of the nearby shoreline to his dragon.

In an instant Lioth transported them *between,* a cold, frighteningly dark place where the absolute silence was a noisy pressure in human ears, and where the freezing temperature was a striking blow to all but dragon hide. Piemur felt a massive shock as the cold assaulted him, and he closed his mouth on an overriding urge to scream. He couldn't feel Lioth's hide against his body, or N'ton's grip on his tunic, or any air in his lungs!

Then they burst into daylight, and as Piemur was finally able to drag air into his starved lungs again, he felt his fear slip away. They were flying over the sea, Lioth adjusting his altitude quickly to draw close to the water's surface.

I cannot land with him. He must go in alone, Lioth told N'ton.

"Hold your breath, Pie!" N'ton shouted, leaning over toward Piemur. Then he let go.

Piemur hit the water feetfirst, his arms spread out wide, plunging into the warm seas of the Southern Continent with a flamboyant splash, plumes of water flaring up around him in a rainbow of spray that settled into groups of ripples as he submerged.

Surfacing quickly, he spread out his arms and legs and lay on his back while he worked to steady his breathing. Lioth landed half a dragonlength away, furling his wings along his back as he bobbed gently in the water. N'ton looked over at Piemur, an expression of awe on his face, his blue eyes wide.

"Piemur?" the dragonrider called, a line of concern evident in his creased brow.

"Just . . . give . . . me . . . one . . . moment." Piemur spoke each word slowly, as the rippling water lapped around his mouth and he floated on the waves.

A slow smile started to spread across N'ton's face as he looked across the water at his young friend. "I guess you might need a moment to gather yourself after that," he said, the relief evident in his voice.

"Ah, here," Piemur said slowly as he lifted his head to regard N'ton and Lioth. He managed a weak smile. "I don't think I will *ever* want to do that again."

FOUR

IN THE NORTH, THE WEYRS AND MAJOR HOLDS TENDED TO BE carved out of rock in the mountains that were so plentiful on that continent. Southern Weyr, like Southern Hold, did not have access to all that stone, but here in the south it wasn't as important, because the land was rife with the grubs that had been seeded in the soil hundreds of Turns in the past, and which the present generation of Pern's people had only recently rediscovered. The grubs devoured Thread, eliminating the deadly parasites before they could burrow into the ground and wreak havoc.

As well as protecting the verdant lands of the Southern Continent, the sightless little grubs seemed to have enhanced the soil to such a degree that trees and other vegetation, through some unknown exchange, had a remarkable ability to self-heal any score marks left by the Thread that did land. Certainly the southern vegetation was more robust than that which grew in the north.

Southern Weyr was positioned on a grassy promontory near a small freshwater lake. Cavelike rooms—weyrs—had been dug into the steep sides of the bluff, below a plateau with natural barriers where the Weyr's herdbeasts could be safely corralled. Since an actual cavern could not have been excavated there, a central hall was situated on the plateau above, built from hardwood trees and topped with black reef-rock tiles. The wooden buildings suited the

heat of Southern, built as they were above ground on stilts, with
reef-rock foundations, wide windows, and deep porches to keep the
baking-hot sun at bay. The Weyr was far more spacious than any
of its northern counterparts, and though unconventional, it lacked
none of the amenities to which weyrfolk were accustomed. During
the day the dragons rested on the plateau in wallows they'd made
in the bare black soil, baking in the sun's heat. Groves of giant,
arching spongewood and fellis trees offered shade for the structures
the humans used, and scattered beyond the central hall were other,
ancillary buildings.

Under the brilliant blue, clear skies of late morning, the dragonriders in Southern were going about their usual duties. To any casual
observer, the dragons and riders of Southern Weyr should have been
content with their lot, living in a tropical paradise away from what
they viewed as meddling by Benden Weyr and the other northern
Weyrs, but that was not the case. A small group of men were deeply
dissatisfied with their lives in the Weyr, ill at ease and increasingly
dogged in their wish for change. Their disquiet could be felt as a
palpable energy by the other members of the Weyr and was beginning to fester and spread, like a disease. It didn't help that so many
of the dragonriders and their dragons were actually ill, poisoned
by their ill-fated attempt at mining firestone. Now a heated debate
spilled out of the open windows of the Weyrwoman's quarters, easily audible for any weyrfolk to hear.

"We are too *far* from our *time,* T'kul!" T'ron, the Southern
Weyrleader, shouted. He raised his head to glare at his wingsecond
and at the same moment crashed his closed fist down on the table,
punctuating his point with the violent gesture. An echoing rumble of discontent could be heard outside, coming from his bronze
dragon, Fidranth. But as soon as the words had left T'ron's mouth,
his shoulders drooped and he unconsciously placed one hand on his
abdomen, over the site of an old wound. He looked around at his
surroundings, scowling deeply. His face was hard and deeply lined
from a lifetime spent fighting Thread.

"We've been over this topic so many times before—" T'kul said,
trying to keep the tension out of his voice.

"—And there's naught to be done about it. I know, I know!" T'ron stared hard into T'kul's eyes. "I should *never* have let you talk me into flying our five Weyrs into this Pass—on the conviction of that wretched Benden Weyrwoman, Lessa. Bah!" His scowl was more dour than usual as he glanced over at Mardra, the woman who had once shared his bed. Mardra held his gaze briefly and then turned her stony expression to T'kul.

"When our generation's Pass of Thread came to an end, T'ron, we all began to notice that emptiness—the lack of purpose. Well you remember it, I know you do!" T'kul said, trying to mask the weariness he felt as he reiterated his argument for the umpteenth time. He coughed hard, his face suffusing red.

There had been a time, back when he'd been a Weyrleader with hundreds of dragons and their riders under his command, that T'kul had radiated vitality. Now he stood in front of T'ron, one shoulder slumped lower than the other, as if a small chunk had been gouged out of it.

"And if we'd stayed in that time," he went on, "we would've lived out the remainder of our long lives trying to fill each day, nay, hour, with some act of worth or some sense of meaning. Our dragons were growing frustrated by their redundancy and we were helpless to counter it." He paused before continuing, "And though I *detest* this admission, Lessa's insight was faultless: We *were* meant to come forward in time to fight Thread in this Pass. Every dragon, rider, man, and woman from the five Weyrs was destined to make that leap forward with her."

"But it has cost us dearly, T'kul," T'ron retorted. "The evidence is all too obvious—we're not the same anymore. Why did *we* have to pay so huge a price for what was an honorable act? Our dragons are off kilter, they've lost their vitality, their health suffers, too—as does ours. This imbalance has infected us all!"

"If our situation was entirely due to traveling forward four hundred Turns, then every dragon and rider in the north would be affected just like us," T'kul said, rubbing his chin. "No, something else is the cause."

"It's this blasted heat!" T'ron burst out. "No one should have to suffer in such a stew of sweltering heat!"

T'kul frowned at T'ron. "Are you blind? The dragons love this heat!"

"It's not one thing or the other," Mardra said. "We should've broached these concerns with Benden long ago. I've told you this already!" She glared first at one man and then the other, a thinly veiled look of contempt in her expression. "Your perverse desire to protect the autonomy of the Weyr has pushed us all too far!" An uneasy silence followed before she spoke again.

"Relations between our Weyr and Benden are now at an irrevocable low, and *they*, most likely, would not aid us now even if we possessed the gumption to swallow our pride and ask for help!" Mardra's tone was reproachful. She began to pace the length of the table with slow, deliberate steps, her arms crossed in front of her body, hands holding opposite elbows, a bitter expression on her face.

"But what should we do?" T'ron asked, looking first at T'kul and then to Mardra, an air of desperation in his tone.

"Must I hear that question again and again, until I fear my ears might bleed?" Mardra snapped, staring skyward, a note of disgust in her voice.

T'ron rubbed the middle of his abdomen distractedly. "We should never have come forward, my friends. I'm sorry. Isn't hindsight a curse?" He shook his head, his shoulders bent forward, as if he carried a massive burden.

"I'm sorry," he repeated, not looking at the others as he quickly left the room.

T'kul and Mardra watched as the figure of their once vibrant Weyrleader crossed the compound to where his bronze dragon slept beside a giant fellis tree.

"No one wants to say this, but our Weyr *will* fail soon if we don't take adequate measures." Mardra spoke in a low, measured voice. "Loranth will not make another mating flight, this is a certainty. She was too disturbed, nay, obsessed with the abnormal egg born from that false cluster." She paused, a fleeting look of grief in her eyes. "In truth, Loranth was too old to take even *that* last regrettable flight. It's a wonder that there was any outcome to it at all, given that she hadn't flown to mate in such a long time."

"And Merika's queen won't rise to mate, either," T'kul replied grimly, referring to his old partner. "But a solution to our failing Weyr might be closer than we think."

"What do you mean?" Mardra asked sharply, both hands resting on the table as she gave T'kul a hard look.

Without replying, T'kul walked to the threshold of the door and called T'reb in to join them.

"What do you mean, T'kul?" Mardra repeated.

"T'reb will explain," he replied. T'kul opened the door of Mardra's cabin and the green rider, quick to answer the summons, entered the room, quietly closing the door behind him. He offered a perfunctory salute to the Weyrwoman.

"Tell her," T'kul ordered.

"Weyrwoman." T'reb looked at Mardra for approval. She nodded for him to explain.

"During the time we've been south I've continued to trade with a group of men in Nabol even though the rest of the Weyr has fallen out of touch with them—" After the briefest pause, T'reb continued. "—since Lord Meron died. These kinsmen of Lord Meron's were deeply aggrieved when he failed to honor his promise to provide holdings for them. They sought redress with the new Lord of Nabol, but their claims failed. They hoped to earn lands of their own here in the south, but too many of them couldn't face the hard sea crossing. One of them, though, had been at sea before and didn't mind it, so he was sent south to meet with me. He said they recall the strong trading ties we had with Lord Meron when we were first exiled, and he and his kinsmen wish us to honor that old connection."

"They do, do they?" Mardra asked, her tone full of contempt.

"Let him go on," T'kul said intently.

"They want us to help them take land of their own. Up in the north, near Nabol. They know the young lord of Ruatha has not yet been confirmed, so his lands would be in contention if he were to suffer a misadventure."

"Jaxom?" Mardra asked. "Wasn't his sire that upstart Fax? The man who took whatever he wanted?" T'kul and T'reb both nodded. "Jaxom's that hold-bred youngling who cracked the unhatched egg on Benden's sands several Turns ago."

"That's correct, Weyrwoman. The egg bore a white dragon," T'reb replied.

"An aberration if ever there was one," Mardra exclaimed, her lips curling back from her teeth in distaste. "The egg should've been left unhatched!"

"No one has ever heard of a Lord Holder being a dragonrider, Weyrwoman. The men from Nabol think it vastly unfair that the young Ruathan lord has been allowed to keep his lands *and* have a dragon. Of course, Benden has sanctioned this—with Lessa's familial connection to the lad."

One of Mardra's brows rose up. "And what do they expect us to do?"

"They want help disposing of Jaxom so they can take his lands in a coup. If he's dead, his runt of a dragon will fly *between* and suicide. No loss to any of the Weyrs, to my reckoning."

"Have you agreed to help them?" Mardra asked.

"Not yet. They wanted to know what we need in return, Weyrwoman." Encouraged by Mardra's look of interest now, T'reb continued. "I told them new blood—that we need new blood. They suggested we should simply take a queen egg. Benden has one hardening on its sands as we speak."

"You mean *steal* an egg?" Mardra whispered in awe.

"Yes. We deserve it," T'reb said emphatically.

"After all we've done for the other Weyrs, it could hardly be considered stealing," T'kul interjected, speaking intensely, though his voice was low. He looked from T'reb to Mardra and slowly smiled, his lips stretching across his mouth as a look of cunning spread across his face. Mardra straightened suddenly, rubbing both her hands across her cheeks.

"Well, I don't know. I think . . ." she said and then paused. "I think it would be too much," she finished in a rush and looked at the others, anxiety clouding her eyes.

"But they owe this to us! Don't you see? Without our help they would've perished before the end of the first Turn of this Pass!" T'kul stepped closer to Mardra, as if trying by sheer proximity to bend her viewpoint to his.

"And all their precious upstart crafters and holders would have perished, too," T'reb added sourly.

"It sounds like madness," Mardra said. "How would it even be done?"

"Taking the egg wouldn't be the problem, Weyrwoman. Many of our riders know the layout of Benden's Hatching Grounds intimately. The problem would be in keeping the egg safe and its whereabouts secret until the new queen hatched," T'kul said.

"But what if we had a plan?" T'reb offered, his eyes lighting up. "If we knew of a place to hide the egg where no one could find it?" He looked at Mardra, searching her face.

Several heartbeats passed as the Weyrwoman paused in thought, and then an almost imperceptible shift in emotions flashed across her face.

"Do you have any idea what would happen if we got caught?" Mardra asked, clasping her hands together, her fear supplanted by the burgeoning possibility of hope. She knew then, as she uttered those words, that she had given her full approval and commitment to an unheard-of and deeply deplorable act.

When N'ton had brought a dripping-wet and unusually quiet Piemur back to Southern Hold, he admonished his young friend to stay under cover until it was confirmed that Thread had ceased to fall over Southern. Piemur could see from the look on N'ton's face that the irregular Threadfall patterns were a serious concern for the Fort Weyrleader, so he promised to remain at Toric's hold until an all-clear message arrived at Southern Hold.

Later, after he had washed and changed into fresh clothes, Piemur sat on the back porch of the Hold with Farli, who was draped across his shoulders, fast asleep and deeply contented. Piemur had spent a long time praising her for having the wit to send N'ton to his rescue. N'ton had explained afterward, during the damp flight back to Southern, that Farli had almost attacked his own brown fire-lizard, Tris, in her urgency to get help. Once Farli had gotten Tris's full attention, her message was relayed to N'ton, with Tris's help. Farli had done exactly the right thing, Piemur mused, stroking his queen's head.

It was well past time *he* did the right thing, he brooded. But what *was* that? He rubbed the side of his head. He'd been feeling so lost for so long now. He sighed heavily and closed his eyes, tired of his own feelings. How would he ever feel like he truly belonged anywhere if he always felt like an outsider? He wished there was someone he could talk to, but whom? He couldn't think of a single person who would understand how it felt to be a failed singer with no discernible harper skills.

But for the first time, he felt impatience with his despair. It was as if a new resolve had begun to creep up on him after his terrifying escape from the cliff. *Perhaps it's time I'm as brave as Farli*, Piemur mused, *instead of always waiting to be told what to do. Perhaps it's time for me, Piemur of Crom, to make my own decisions and strike out on my path through life.*

Despite his scouting report being disregarded, he had been unable to quiet those niggling thoughts he had about T'reb and the men from Nabol. No matter what Master Robinton said, Piemur *knew* that T'reb was up to no good with those men. Was T'reb's resolve to help Mardra also something to worry about? No, he reckoned T'reb was just being his usual edgy, irrational self.

He recalled Toolan and Cramb's conversation after T'reb left their campsite. Toolan had mentioned kinsmen who felt the Old-timers could in some way assist them in securing lands of their own. T'reb had taken Cramb's drawings and thrown a pouch of money at Toolan in payment. That *must* mean there was more to their deal than Piemur knew about. The Oldtimers probably wanted to secure better trading arrangements in the north in exchange for helping the Nabol men secure land in Crom. Piemur couldn't sit back and let a bunch of Lord Meron's unscrupulous relatives undermine what his own family had worked so hard for. If only he knew *when* they were going to strike, he could warn someone!

Piemur slapped his hand against his thigh. He had to do what he thought was right! He knew he would be going against the Masterharper's decision, but someone had to do something before a disaster occurred. As soon as he had the all-clear for Threadfall, he'd sneak over to the Oldtimers' Weyr to find out more about their plans with the Nabolese.

He only hoped he hadn't left it too late.

Sebell strode purposefully, heading for the main hall of Fort Hold. He'd told his queen fire-lizard, Kimi, never known to stray too far from him unless she was delivering messages, to wait instead on the fire heights with a group of fire-lizards preening in the sun. N'ton's message had indicated that he and Piemur would be at the Harper Hall within the hour, and Sebell felt it was important to speak with the Masterharper prior to Piemur's arrival.

Two young apprentices walking in the opposite direction passed Sebell, nodding at him politely though they were hard-pressed to hide their curious glances. Sebell wasn't wearing the normal harper-blue attire, or the shoulder knots that would've indicated his rank. Instead he wore a broad-brimmed hat and nondescript clothing that bore not one single shoulder knot or patch of distinctive color. In the Harper Hall, or any Crafthall, seeing someone without markings or colors on their clothing was as unusual as seeing a two-legged tunnel snake.

A journeyman clattered up the corridor, approaching rapidly, all full of purpose. He cast a cursory glance at Sebell in his nondescript clothing and was about to forge on past him without a word, but just as they drew abreast he recognized the unmistakable features of the Masterharper-in-the-making and his mien changed.

"Good morning, Journeyman Master Sebell," he called out brightly, smiling in greeting though he hardly broke stride. As Se-bell nodded in reply, he heard gasps of shock coming from the two apprentices who'd just passed him. He smiled to himself. It was difficult to remain anonymous on one's own turf, he mused, regardless of attire.

He arrived at the end of the corridor and stopped, marveling, not for the first time, at the sight of the splendid Great Hall of Fort Hold. Fort was the very first Hold to have been founded when people first settled in the north. Very little was changed about the natural stone face of the mountain that formed the exterior aspect of Fort. A rugged cliff with a hanging curtain of rock, two meters thick, hid the immense natural cavern that lay within. More than fifty meters deep, the cavern tapered slightly at either end. At the back a further eighteen openings led into deeper tunnel complexes, but it was in here, inside the huge cavern, that the settlers had made their mark. It was obvious that they'd used great skill and care to create the ornate and elegant living space. Some folk thought the fancies and follies that formed the detail work in the Great Hall were outright wasteful, but there was no denying that they were beautiful.

The interior design of Fort reminded Sebell of frozen music. All the doorways and arches in the Hall were embellished with exquisite carvings of floral vines and leaves. The great doors that led into the Hall, closed during Threadfall but otherwise, as now, left wide open, were fabricated from a unique metal that was nigh-on indestructible and burnished a deep bronze color that glowed with a centuries-old patina. High above, Fort's first settlers had fashioned hanging sconces for glowbaskets, which could be lowered for replenishing by intricate pulley systems.

Smiling, as he always did when he entered the beautiful Hall, Sebell nodded at colleagues and other craftsmen and craftswomen as he walked, and waved a special greeting when he saw Silvina, the headwoman of Fort. He crossed to the opposite side of the Hall and climbed a set of stone steps, two at a time, to the workrooms assigned to more senior craftsmen and -women as well as the Masterharper.

The door to Master Robinton's rooms was rarely closed, and this day was no different. Two windows had been cut into the outside wall, and though they were recessed and could be shuttered, they let in welcoming shafts of light. One of the windows, the one nearest to the Masterharper's desk, was flung open wide. The other window was closed, and sunlight streamed through the glass. Nestled on its sill, curled up on top of a wad of soft fabric, lay a sleeping bronze fire-lizard, the Master's Zair.

Robinton was on his feet, his tall, lean frame bent over a workbench, intently studying a large piece of fine-grade animal skin that was covered in a series of star charts.

"Ah, there you are. Well, I hope, Sebell?" Master Robinton said without looking up. "Do come in, please."

Sebell smiled slightly at Robinton's acute awareness as he entered the room and closed the door behind him. At the sound of the door latch clicking home, Robinton looked up and Sebell offered a bow of respect. Slowly, Robinton straightened, rubbing a knot out of his lower back as he peered at his second, fatigue evident in his eyes.

"As bad as that, is it?" the Masterharper asked, giving the closed door a quick glance as he lowered himself into a chair.

"Matters in Nabol have moved on apace." Sebell's tone was bleak, and Robinton looked closely at him, searching the younger man's brown eyes.

"Go on," Robinton said.

"Any hopes we may have had of tensions easing among Lord Meron's kin have been dashed," Sebell said.

Robinton rubbed a hand over his eyes and then sighed, gesturing for Sebell to continue, though his manner showed that he'd really prefer not to hear any more.

"It's remarkable, really: All these Turns after his demise, Lord Meron's plans to sow conflict within his family have, quite unbelievably, taken seed. Though Lord Deckter has a firm hand and has vastly improved the Hold since he inherited, it seems he's been powerless to undo the damage created by Meron when he was alive."

"Shells, but the man's reached out from beyond to disoblige us yet again! He behaved vilely to all beholden to him, playing one branch of his family off the other for the sheer pleasure it gave him. And with the tenacity of a tunnel snake, he fell ill and stubbornly took an age to die! His legacy, it seems, is set to thwart us once more." Robinton spoke heatedly and then held up a hand in a beg-pardon gesture at his uncharacteristic outburst.

"He was a deviant, indeed," Sebell said, a fleeting look of dis-taste on his face before his features settled back into their usual benevolent demeanor. "The latest news from Candler in Nabol," he continued, "is that a group of his kin, and a few holdless rogues from farther afield, are bucking to take matters into their own hands."

"But it's been *Turns* since Meron died! Why would his kin cause a stir now?"

"We heard they tried to branch out on their own, and worked odd jobs to earn the marks for passage to the Southern Continent. That took a long time, but it seems they believed they could get holdings of their own there. I don't know exactly what happened between then and now, but they're back in Nabol and stirring up old grievances."

"Trust Lord Meron to have the last laugh—he deliberately cre-ated discord when he was alive because his every little whim wasn't appeased, as he thought was his due," Robinton said with disgust. "I never did like that hard-flung crud of a man," he added under his breath.

"It's a pity those few men never found a way to fit in with Lord Deckter," Sebell said, shrugging.

Robinton's expression turned grave. "Do you think Lord Deck-ter's position is in peril, Sebell?"

"No, I believe his position is secure. He's kept his head down and gotten on with improvements that have satisfied his holders, and he has a strong body of loyal men around him," Sebell said, adding, "But there are those few, disgruntled by the treatment they received from Lord Meron and unwilling to recognize Deckter as their lord."

"And they're tolerated by Lord Deckter?"

"Oh, yes. He hopes they'll come around in the end. We know that a small group of them left the safety of Nabol recently. They didn't venture far, toward Ruatha's border, though Candler wasn't able to confirm their exact destination. He thinks he followed too close, because one of Meron's kin, Jerrol, has grown suspicious. That's why we can't use Candler anymore to watch them."

"So what could that gang of rabble be up to, I wonder?" Robinton asked.

"Piemur mentioned something, Masterharper, after he reported to you in Southern Hold," Sebell said carefully, watching the Masterharper to gauge his reaction. Robinton raised one brow briefly and then nodded for Sebell to continue.

"Piemur said he overheard the Nabolese talking about getting a holding. I think what he heard may have more merit than we gave him credit for."

Robinton's expression changed to one of alarm and he leaned closer toward his second. "What did Piemur hear?"

"He was worried they're going to oust his family from their holding in Crom. But now that I think of it, Piemur said the men spoke about getting a holding *near* Nabol. That doesn't actually mean they're focusing on Crom, does it? Both Crom and Ruatha are Holds *near* to Nabol." Sebell began to pace the length of Robinton's workroom, his hands clasped behind his back. "Sun-addled though he was, Piemur was distressed by what he saw and heard in Southern, and he believes something is going to happen. At least one of the men he spied on was from Nabol. He and the other man met with an Oldtimer named T'reb. Piemur said Mardra was mentioned, too."

"Yes, he did, though none of what he said made much sense, Sebell. The lad's been traipsing about all alone for too long. It's my fault, I fear," Robinton said.

"He mentioned T'reb hiding something in one of those isolated coves," Sebell continued.

"More of their illegal trades, most likely," Robinton offered.

"Probably," Sebell said. He'd halted his pacing and gave a little shake of his head, as if something was niggling at the back of his thoughts, then he continued. "I guess the Oldtimers are the least of our concerns compared with these men from Nabol."

There was the clattering of footsteps on stone outside Robinton's room, and both Sebell and the Masterharper fell silent before a knock sounded on the closed door. Robinton called out: "Come!"

Piemur entered Robinton's room, slightly out of breath and exuding an air of urgency; his eyes were bright with excitement. N'ton followed Piemur into the room, quietly closing the door behind him.

"Piemur, this is unexpected. What's brought you to Fort?" Robinton asked.

"I have a report, Masterharper." Piemur walked over to Robinton's desk and stood in front of it, his shoulders squared and his eyes shining in his deeply tanned face.

Robinton shot a quick look at N'ton and gestured for Piemur to proceed.

"After I mapped the steep bluff to the west of Southern as you instructed, Masterharper, and was forced back to the Hold because of Threadfall, I decided to go back to the Weyr," Piemur explained. When he saw a puzzled expression flit across Robinton's face he swallowed hard, focusing his attention so he could report what he had heard clearly and concisely. "Southern Weyr, Masterharper." Piemur could see the open expression on the Master's face slowly changing to a frown, so he continued quickly.

"What I overheard led me to believe that a small group of men from Nabol plan to oust settled holders and take their lands from them. I thought they were going after land in Crom, but now I know differently."

Sebell, who had come to stand beside Master Robinton's chair, placed his hands on the table and leaned forward intently. "Tell us exactly what happened, Piemur," he said.

"I decided to follow T'reb. Been following him for the last two days. He seems to be behind what's going on. I wasn't able to get past the watch dragon at the entrance to the Weyr, but by creeping around the margins of the compound I was able to overhear enough. T'reb spoke with some other riders. I couldn't see who, but I know Mardra and T'kul were there." Piemur drew in a deep breath, silently telling himself to get to the point and stop adding unnecessary details. "I heard them mention Lord Jaxom."

"Jaxom?" Robinton exclaimed, but then he flapped a hand at Piemur to disregard his interruption and continue.

"I only arrived at the tail end of their conversation, but T'reb told Mardra they had to ensure Lord Jaxom was out of the way or the men from Nabol wouldn't keep silent."

Against all the odds, Jaxom, the young Lord-to-be of Ruatha, had Impressed a dragon five Turns past and now straddled two disparate social spheres: He was a dragonrider but did not live in a Weyr or fight Thread, and he was a Lord Holder, though his Hold was managed on his behalf to allow him to tend to his dragon. Jaxom's tenuous position would remain so until he was formally confirmed by the other Lord Holders.

"Sweet shards, I *knew* we should've pushed the point and had Jaxom confirmed with the Lord Holders at the last Council meeting." Robinton shook his head with regret, his lips clamped together in a taut line.

"Wouldn't keep silent? About what?" N'ton asked very quietly. Piemur looked at Sebell quickly; he had noticed how N'ton had come to rigid attention when Jaxom's name was mentioned. Everyone knew that N'ton helped Jaxom with his dragon, Ruth, and that he had become protective of the young lord.

"I'm not certain, N'ton, but something else has been bothering me—T'reb meeting with those two men in the secluded cove—it doesn't make sense." Piemur frowned and shook his head. "Perhaps he meant they wouldn't keep silent about the Oldtimers' involvement in ousting Jaxom."

"What else did you hear, Piemur?" N'ton asked tersely. Piemur thought the atmosphere in the Master's rooms couldn't get any more intense.

"T'reb asked the other riders if they were certain they knew exactly where they were going. They said they did, and then T'kul asked when it would happen. T'reb said within the week, but they'd have to wait for the message telling them when the time was right. T'reb sounded quite certain that a message *would* arrive. That's all I heard," Piemur finished, letting his arms fall to his sides.

"Very good, Journeyman Piemur, you've done well," Robinton said, standing up behind his desk.

Sebell reached across the worktable and clapped a hand on Piemur's shoulder, squeezing it briefly. Piemur felt deeply relieved that he had avoided a reprimand for his surreptitious foray back into Southern Weyr.

"Do you think they could pull it off?" he asked, searching first Sebell's face and then Robinton's.

"It's a good-sized holding, and with no real means of protection—not since Fax's day. They could easily split Ruatha into several smaller holdings," Robinton said, slicing his hand through the air several times to punctuate his next words, "and carve up that noble Hold to suit their needs."

Piemur felt queasy at the thought of the repercussions such an act would provoke. Pern in turmoil once again—and just when the Masterharper thought they were making progress. Memories from the not-so-distant past, when the tyrannous, self-styled Lord Fax invaded Ruatha to further expand his acquired, rather than inherited, holdings, were still fresh in the collective consciousness. It had been a dark period indeed, nearly culminating in senseless, province-wide bloodshed.

N'ton's expression darkened, and Robinton cleared his throat.

"This is a serious concern. If these men are successful in taking Ruatha, then others, elsewhere, could also try to buck the system and take whatever they want. The order we live by is far too fragile to endure such a fracture." Robinton's tone was solemn.

"I agree," Sebell said, "but nothing has happened *yet*."

"I wonder why someone is always trying to run the rightful Lords out of Ruatha?" Piemur muttered under his breath.

"They must not see Ruth as much of a threat if they think Ruatha could so easily be plucked," N'ton said.

"Hm . . . yes. That's where I need to clarify some other news Candler reported hearing," Sebell said, looking at the Masterharper.

"What was that?" Robinton asked.

"Exactly how hard it would be to get rid of a dragon like Ruth."

Piemur felt a wave of unease ripple around the room. All four men fell still, as if all holding their breath.

How could anyone in their right mind think to harm one of the noble creatures who unconditionally risked their lives for their world and everyone on it? Piemur was shocked. The very idea beggared belief!

Sebell drew a deep breath and continued. "They were debating whether Ruth was fierce like other dragons—they know he hasn't learned to flame yet. Candler heard one of them say they'd have no real difficulty in dealing with a runt like Ruth."

"He's not a runt!" N'ton exclaimed, trying to keep his voice under control. "He's a sport!"

"Yes, of course, but these men are not well educated in the ways of dragons and the Weyr. They only know about land."

"All they need do to put Ruth out of the picture is get rid of Jaxom." Piemur realized too late that his uncensored thoughts had just tumbled out of his mouth.

"Oh, no! My pardon, please, N'ton. I meant no disrespect at all. I *like* Jaxom! And what little I know of Ruth, too." Piemur's face started to color under his deep tan.

"Piemur has a point, blunt though it may be," Sebell said, raising one brow as he shot a look at Piemur.

"The lad has a dragon to protect him, for shards' sake! It's no matter that he's different," Robinton said, referring to Ruth's unusual color. As a white dragon, he was the only one of his kind.

"But he hasn't yet flamed," N'ton cut in quickly.

"Yes, and being smaller, Ruth might be an easier target, especially as he's living in Ruatha Hold, outside the protection of the Weyr," Sebell said.

"Only a dim-glow would try and meddle with him. As small as he is, Ruth is still a dragon," Piemur said.

"But your point is correct, Piemur: If someone interfered with Jaxom," N'ton offered, "and killed him for his holdings, Ruth *would* suicide."

"No, no, we cannot have that," Robinton said, shaking his head. "We must watch out for the young lord of Ruatha until I can convince the Lord Holders to confirm him. And the sooner the better," he added, planting a fist on the worktable to punctuate his point.

"More than just watch over him, Master Robinton, we have to ensure that Jaxom is protected—and discreetly." N'ton sounded deadly serious. "Just as a coup of Ruatha would upset the balance of the holders' lives, so would the death of the little white dragon affect our Weyrs. Difficulties with the Oldtimers have caused disquiet among dragonmen, and the needless death of one of our dragons would make matters far worse."

Piemur listened to N'ton, realizing that Robinton had wisely allowed the Weyrleader to speak on behalf of the Weyrs even though the Masterharper was well aware of how delicately the balance of life on Pern swayed in tune with the sum of its parts.

"Can you help us, N'ton, and spare another man, too? We'll need more than one pair of wings if we're to keep up with Jaxom," Sebell asked.

The Fort Weyrleader nodded his immediate assent. "I'll ask J'hon to help. He's a good man," he said, referring to his wing-second.

"I'll get Menolly in on this, too," Robinton offered. "She's friendly with Jaxom. If she works with Finder, our harper in Ruatha, and you and J'hon, N'ton, we should avoid raising Jaxom's suspicions. Or anyone else's, for that matter."

"Perhaps it would be better if as few people as possible knew the exact details of what we've heard regarding Lord Jaxom and his Ruth. Would you agree, Masterharper?" Sebell said, looking to his mentor for the definitive word.

"Indeed, Sebell."

"I dread to think how the Weyrs would respond if they learned what that lot had in mind for Ruth," N'ton added.

"Those men from Nabol," Robinton said, gesturing vaguely with one hand, a look of distaste on his face. "The sooner we can expose their plans and halt them, the sooner they'll be dealt with by their own. Piemur," the Master added, looking at his protégé with a smile, "I have a very special task I want you to undertake."

"Yes?" Piemur said expectantly, reassured that he was now firmly back in favor with the Masterharper.

"I want you in Nabol. First thing tomorrow."

Piemur felt his heart sink; he hated that rotten, landlocked, dreary old place. Why him? Didn't the Masterharper realize that sending him to Nabol would be like a punishment? Piemur had never been secretive about his complete distaste for that northern Hold.

"We could do with a good set of eyes up there, Piemur, and a clever head, too." Sebell smiled at Piemur.

"But Nabol? I never thought I'd have to go back there, Master," Piemur said, unable to hide his disbelief.

"My apologies, Master Robinton," N'ton said, interrupting, "but I'm overdue at the Weyr."

"Yes, of course, N'ton, and thank you." Robinton smiled at the dragonrider. "We'll work out the finer details now and let you know precisely how we plan to keep Lord Jaxom out of harm's way. Piemur, you can go now, too. Well done, lad."

With a weak smile and a single nod, Piemur followed N'ton out of the Masterharper's rooms. N'ton swiftly descended the stairs to the outer courtyard where Lioth waited. Piemur watched as the big bronze dragon uncurled his long tail and pushed himself upright, ready to fly the short distance from Fort's Harper Hall to the adjacent Weyr.

"Don't look so glum, Piemur. You're clever enough to insert yourself quickly in Nabol and find out what we need to know. I bet you'll be out of there in three winks of a dragon's eyelids," N'ton said as he grabbed Piemur's forearm in a firm grasp. Then he turned on his heels and, in a few short strides, closed the distance to his lifemate. Leaping effortlessly onto Lioth's proffered foreleg, N'ton pulled himself up onto the dragon's shoulder and was settled astride the base of the dragon's neck before Piemur had time to insert his thumbs into the loops of his belt.

N'ton waved his left hand over his head with a clenched fist—the dragonriders' salute and signal to take flight—and smiled down at Piemur in farewell. As Lioth lifted into the air, he turned his head

and looked down, rather than skyward, and Piemur felt surprised
when he realized that N'ton's dragon was looking at *him*. Staring
back at the huge bronze's eyes, Piemur waved in awe, wondering
if he were seeing things. He could've sworn the big bronze dragon
winked at him.

The courtyard was growing increasingly busy and Piemur realized that a regular break in the Harper Hall's daily routine must
have occurred as he stood watching N'ton and Lioth depart. *That's
funny,* Piemur thought; *I didn't even hear the change-chime.*

Several groups of apprentices clattered across the courtyard,
talking loudly to one another in friendly banter. Other students,
clumped together in groups while they walked, crisscrossed the
courtyard, bound for wherever their timetables decreed, and six
young apprentices, lumbering under the weight of a large, gleaming
kettledrum, made their way intently toward the other side of the
compound, heading for the drumheights.

Piemur felt a little regret as he watched them, and then the sharp
pang of remorse that his days as a singer were done crowded against
his ribs. The camaraderie of singing, and being surrounded by music from daybreak to dusk, had made up some of the most memo-
rable moments of his life. How he did miss that. Perhaps it was for
the best that he was so rarely in the Harper Hall. How could he
remain so close to the thing he loved most—music—when he was
no longer able to sing? It felt a tad too much like torture. Piemur
shook his shoulders and walked purposefully toward the main hall,
suddenly aghast that he should be so self-absorbed when far more
important things were happening all around him.

FIVE

"I SEE SOME THINGS NEVER CHANGE," THE FAMILIAR VOICE CALLED
from behind Piemur. "You're still nothing more than a walking
stomach, Piemur of Crom! I'll have to tell Cook to bring in another barrow-sized load of provisions lest we run out while *you're*
back in the hall."

Piemur sat at a table in the food hall at Fort, a heaped plate of
food in front of him. A few nearby diners fell silent to assess what
the commotion was about and just as quickly resumed their conversations when their curiosity had been fed.

"Ah, here, Silvina, it's only a little bite to eat," Piemur said
through a mouthful of wherry meat as he looked over his shoulder
at Fort's headwoman.

"That's what I'm worried about, lad: If the whopping great
mound of food I see on your plate is only a 'bite,' I'd hate to see
what you call a meal these days!"

"But it tastes so good, Silvina. I never cease to wonder how
Cook always makes such scrumptious food," Piemur said, wiping
his mouth with the back of his hand.

Seemingly from out of nowhere, Silvina produced a small square
of cloth and deftly draped it across Piemur's lap as she sat down
next to him on the long bench. He took the hint and raised the cloth
in his hand, making a big show of daintily dabbing at the corners of

his mouth to prove to Silvina that all her Turns of trying to knock manners into him had actually paid off.

"It's good to see you, Piemur," Silvina said with real warmth in her voice, briefly resting a hand on Piemur's shoulder. "It's been alarmingly quiet around here without you."

"And it will be once again when I head off tomorrow, Silvina. The Master has plans for me," he replied and then filled his mouth with a huge forkful of wherry stew and mashed tubers.

"I'm surprised you didn't bring your fire-lizard with you," Silvina said with a note of mild dismay in her voice. She watched with maternal satisfaction as Piemur chewed intently.

"She hasn't half gone bossy, Silvina! I think she's growing too fast for her own good—and mine and Stupid's!" He put down his eating utensils and was on the verge of wiping the back of his hand across his mouth when he snatched up the cloth again and pointedly lifted it to pat at his mouth.

"She came north with me, but then I guess she flitted back to Lord Toric's again after we arrived. She might have gone back to check on Stupid. They've been together all their lives, you see, ever since I rescued Stupid from beneath his dead mother's carcass."

"I see," Silvina said, looking at the young journeyman harper with a sharp eye. "And you don't half smell of them, Piemur. You decided to fill your stomach first before attending to the finer things in life, I see, treating us all to your own brand of personal perfume." A light note of disapproval colored her voice as she looked fondly at the young man who'd once been the source of so much mischief at the Harper Hall and Fort Hold.

"First things first, Silvina. First things first," Piemur offered by way of excuse, and grinned at the headwoman as he lifted his utensils for her to see before plowing another forkful of food into his mouth.

"Well, I'm pleased to see that some things never change, and even though my young folk go away and grow up, they always come back to me—with their hearty appetites intact." Silvina smiled affectionately at Piemur as she swung a leg over the bench and stood up.

"I'll have one of the drudges make up a cot for you in the sleeping quarters, Piemur, and leave out a fresh tunic and trews for you, too. Just make sure you have a thorough wash, young man, before climbing into, or on top of, anything in *my* Hold." But her tone was teasing as she gently patted Piemur's shoulder again and turned to go.

Suddenly Silvina turned back toward him. "Have you seen Menolly yet?"

Piemur shook his head.

"She's been marking exam papers for Master Domick all week. I bet she'd appreciate a little diversion from you," Silvina suggested and Piemur nodded, eyes wide, to let her know that he'd follow her advice. Silvina smiled and started to walk away, only to stop again a few paces later.

"You're still partial to a bubbleberry pie or two, aren't you?"

His mouth still full, Piemur nodded vigorously.

"I'd best warn Cook to put on an extra dozen for the evening meal, then," Silvina replied, and finally left to attend to other duties.

Piemur scraped his plate clean and quaffed down a large beaker of water, wiping his mouth thoroughly with the cloth Silvina had given him when he was done. Feeling replete, he took his used dish and cutlery to the serving hatch and placed them on the tray provided. A drudge winked at him, whistling a little tune, and swiftly lifted the dirty tableware from the tray and splashed it into a huge sink of steaming, sudsy water.

Grabbing up the flying gear he'd deposited on the seat next to where he'd been eating, Piemur made his way through the hall and down the familiar corridors that led to the bathing chambers and beyond to the sleeping quarters.

True to her word, Silvina had instructed someone to leave fresh clothing and even a thick, fluffy towel on one of the cots at the far end of the sleeping quarters, in an overflow area that was always reserved for visitors. Dropping his flying gear on a stool beside the cot, he loosened the clasps on his boots, slipped his feet out with a sigh, draped the towel over his shoulder, and made his way to the bathing room.

The baths at Fort were formed from a series of interconnecting pools that were continually fed and refreshed with hot water from a source buried deep beneath the cavelike series of rooms. Turns past, as a young apprentice, Piemur had loved to stand directly in front of the stream of fresh water; too often he had lingered past the point of being clean, long enough to make him late for his apprentice duties, which got him into trouble.

Now he doused himself with a bucket of water, then grabbed two handfuls of sweetsand and scrubbed himself all over. He took his time scrubbing his feet, knowing full well that his soles were a dirtier shade of brown. When he was satisfied that the heaviest of the dirt had been washed clean, he hopped from the ledge into the warm waters of the bathing pool, where he rubbed the sweetsand off his skin. At last with a mighty sigh he relaxed and simply floated in the warm bath, ripples of water flaring away from him as he lay motionless in the pool and soaked the last of the dirt and the exhaustion from his skin.

Once he'd dried himself off and returned to the sleeping quarters to change into the fresh clothing Silvina had supplied, Piemur felt energized, and quickly made his way to the room Menolly occupied.

He knocked on her door in a series of *rah-ta-ta-ta-ta-tah*s that could only come from the hand of someone who understood rhythm and drumming.

"Come in," Menolly's voice called from within.

Piemur opened the door and peered into the room.

"Silvina said you might need a break from scoring exam slates. Want some company?" he asked tentatively.

"Do I ever!" Menolly replied with fervor, smiling warmly at Piemur. "Have a seat, Pie. It's good to see you. What've you been up to?" She pushed away from her worktable, stretching her arms above her head to ease taut shoulder muscles.

"Oh, I haven't been doing anything new—only mapping and snooping," Piemur said with a frown. He pulled a stool close to Menolly's desk and sat down, hooking his feet around the top stretcher as he had done a hundred times in the past. "I see you've graduated to marking Master Domick's tests. What's the new batch of apprentices like?" he asked, peering at a stack of slates piled up against the leg of the desk and another pile in front of Menolly, waiting to be graded.

"A few bright ones know their stuff backward, and then there's the rest, who'll be good musicians but never truly outstanding," she said as she peered at Piemur. "Your face has grown," she added, a smile slowly spreading across her face.

"Don't be wherry-brained, Menolly," Piemur said, chuckling. "My face is the same as it's ever been."

"No, I mean your face looks longer. And have you gotten taller, Piemur?" Menolly asked. She stood up from her chair, gesturing for her friend to do likewise. They stood facing each other, and Menolly suddenly gasped.

"You're taller than me!" she exclaimed, with a look of mock horror.

"Had to happen sometime, Loll," Piemur replied, grinning from ear to ear as he sat back down.

Menolly's appearance had changed, too, Piemur reckoned. She was no longer the shy, gangly, all-arms-and-legs girl he'd befriended when she'd first arrived at the Harper Hall. Her curly dark-brown hair and sea-green eyes were still the same, but there was something different about her, something he couldn't identify. And then it dawned on him: Menolly looked completely at ease. She had once been the new girl who was treated as an outcast: maybe because she came from a seafaring hold, maybe because she had an unusually large number of fire-lizards answering to her. Now as Piemur looked at his friend he saw that she was truly content, comfortable with her life. *She's found the place where she belongs,* he mused.

A gifted musician, Menolly had flourished under the tutelage of Robinton and the other music masters, Master Domick and Master Shonagar, but at the core of her skill was a talent for composing. There had been a time, Piemur thought, when it seemed that Menolly had written all the new music circulating around Hall and Hold. She had a fine singing voice, too, and she was also the first person Piemur knew who had Impressed a fire-lizard. In fact, Menolly had arrived at the Harper Hall with a group of *nine* young fire-lizards all answering to her, and somehow over the last few Turns she'd inadvertently Impressed a tenth. It was through Menolly that Piemur had learned so much about the little winged creatures. He'd helped Menolly feed her brood until they were old enough to hunt for themselves.

Glancing around, he saw that nearly all her brood seemed to be absent. As was often the case with mature fire-lizards, they answered their instincts first, often disappearing for days at a time; no doubt they were currently nesting on the roofs of the Hall with the other fire-lizards, or had flown farther afield, hunting for food. Her queen, however, named Beauty, was Menolly's constant companion. At the moment, Beauty lay on Menolly's bed, dozing in a sun puddle next to the last addition to Menolly's fair of fire-lizards, bronze Poll.

"How's your voice, Piemur?" Menolly asked, cutting to the chase as she peered tentatively at him from under her lashes.

"Ah, here, let's not talk about my voice, Menolly. It's gone, and I may never develop a mature voice worth bothering about, either," he said, trying to sound matter-of-fact, though saying out loud what might be the truth stung sharply.

"Have you *tried* singing?"

He wished he could explain to Menolly how much it hurt to be reminded about his voice, but he didn't want to burden her with his problems. He didn't think she'd understand, anyway. How could she? Her voice was still perfect.

"A few times—Farli keeps nagging me—but my voice always breaks into a warble or a croak, Loll."

Menolly nodded as she absently stroked Beauty. In response, the little queen started to hum, and then Beauty and Poll trilled in unison, as if they were tuning instruments.

"Poll's got a bit of catching up to do in order to follow the other fire-lizards musically. We've been working on impromptu vocalizations," Menolly explained. "It's great fun. Why don't you join in, Pie? You'll know what to do." She tapped the index finger of one hand on the desktop in four-four time, then hummed a series of

notes. Beauty followed suit, and after a few beats the young male
sang with his queen, his voice adding a deeper timbre to the sound.

I can't do this! Piemur thought, trying not to let his sudden sense
of panic become obvious to his friend. He clasped his hands between his knees as he sat on the stool and smiled briefly at Menolly,
then he looked down into his lap, forcing himself to remain seated
as he listened to the music. Menolly allowed the fire-lizards to har-
monize freely with each other, adding her own voice to their trills
or occasionally leading them away from the base refrain to explore
new chord groupings. All the while, their music seemed to build in
momentum, though the tempo remained true. Piemur slowly began
to relax. It was hard to remain tense when he was being treated to
such a lovely performance.

Beauty took the lead again and brought the chorus to a conclusion with an incredibly high note. The young bronze fire-lizard
shook out his wings and promptly flew away as if dismissed.

"She always shows off when she's had enough," Menolly said,
chuckling. Then she turned to Piemur. "Tell me what've you seen in
the south," she said, and Piemur was grateful that she had changed
the subject. "Anything interesting?"

"Disturbing more than interesting. We've heard a *rumor* about
some men from Nabol who think they can take some of Jaxom's
holding," Piemur told her.

"Jaxom?" Menolly looked incredulous.

"I know," Piemur replied. "You'll hear all about it from Sebell
and the Masterharper. For now, they're planning a roster to keep
Jaxom safe, just in case. The Master wants you, N'ton, J'hon, and
Finder to make sure he's otherwise occupied while we get to the bottom of this rumor."

"Are you serious?"

"Never more so, Loll. But Jaxom's land isn't the only part to my
news. When I was in Southern, I followed two Nabolese men who
were scouting out a site for one of the Oldtimers, T'reb."

"More men from Nabol?" Menolly interrupted. "Is that a coin-
cidence, Pie?"

"I'm not sure, Loll, but I'd bet a Gather worth of marks they're up to no good." Piemur's tone was grave.

"And what does the Masterharper think about it?"

"That's just it, Menolly. He's distracted about this business with Jaxom, so he didn't think my hunch amounted to much." Piemur shrugged. "And now he's sending me to Nabol in the morning." He sighed heavily.

"Hmm." Menolly looked at him carefully. "And it's not your favorite place, either, is it?"

Piemur's head shot up, his eyes shimmering with distaste as he held up a hand, touching off his fingers one at a time as he spoke fervently. "It's cold! The people are half-wits! The food is dire, and the water smells like wherry poo!"

Menolly lifted a finely arched brow at Piemur, a little grin tugging at one corner of her mouth. Piemur could see the smile slowly creeping across her face, so he continued.

"The skies there are never anything other than gray, so it looks as if Thread is always about to fall. And the Hold is in a shambles!" He spluttered as he spat out the last word and Menolly tried hard not to laugh.

"And it's rotten with damp!" he added.

Menolly's brows lifted slightly higher, and Piemur guessed that she might be pondering how an entire region could be damp.

"And not just the Hold," he exclaimed, knowing perfectly well that he was being melodramatic, but he was enjoying himself. "The whole region is awash with damp. Place reeks of the stuff!" A little smile tugged at one corner of his mouth.

Menolly's smile slowly stretched and then burst wide open as she chuckled heartily.

"And did I mention that it smells?" Piemur concluded, beaming back at her.

The usual traffic of early-morning drum messages was, for some reason unknown to Piemur, quite clearly audible from where he lay on the guest sleeping cot. It must be something to do with the acoustics in this part of the cave complex, he reckoned, turning on his side and bending an elbow to prop his head on his hand. The messages arrived in the steady stream he had grown accustomed to when he still lived at the Harper Hall, rolling out their transmissions in a rhythm that seemed to reverberate through his bones in a deeply comforting thrum.

During the period right after his voice broke and before he began working for the Masterharper outside of the Harper Hall, Piemur had become a proficient drum messenger, so he had no difficulty deciphering the various requests that rolled in and out again as the messages were passed on to their intended destinations. Tillek Hold requesting a healer from Ruatha to assist their own who'd broken her leg; a herdbeast master requesting advice on how best to deliver a ruminant of what might be triplet calves; and a group of holders from Keroon offering to barter, to anyone and everyone, sackloads of tubers from their bumper crop, for literally anything else that was on offer. Piemur smiled: *Trust that lot from Keroon to always want what they don't have!*

Yawning so deeply that his ears popped, Piemur nearly missed the next drum message that rolled in from Igen Weyr, warning that Thread hadn't fallen as was expected. He threw off the quilted blanket and swung his legs over the edge of the cot, mentally reaching out to find Farli. His little gold had flitted off hours before, unaccustomed to sleeping in the depths of a mountain. A faint answer came back to him and he sensed, rather than knew, that she was outside, roosting with the other fire-lizards resident at Fort Hold and the Harper Hall. Jumping to his feet, he hastily shook out the blanket and smoothed it in place—lest he get an earful from Silvina. He'd slept deeply, and for the first time in a very long while, his dreams of music hadn't disturbed his sleep.

He was mulling over his dream, trying to recapture the ethereal images that had played out in his head, when a sound, once familiar, floated toward him. The change-chime was sounding. Cripes, it was later than he thought! He jammed his feet into his boots, shoved his flying gear into his bag, which he threw over his shoulder, and then ran at full pelt from the sleeping quarters to the main hall. He was supposed to meet J'hon in the Bowl of Fort Weyr and he was late! Sebell had arranged for an envoy from Nabol to meet Piemur when he landed, so he'd have a safe base from which to learn more about the plot to oust Jaxom. If he was late meeting J'hon, he'd be late meeting Sebell's escort!

Dashing through the main hall, Piemur had just enough time to scoop up a handful of bread rolls and a hunk of cheese before he dashed on toward the tunnel that led to the Weyr. Giving Farli a mental shout to join him, he hoped that the usual morning stream of folk traversing the tunnel had eased off; otherwise, it would take him an age to reach the Weyr.

Jogging into the tunnel, he was grateful to see that it was almost empty of foot traffic. Without breaking stride, he crammed his clothing farther into the bag, tossed the food on top, and quickly secured the buckles. Slinging the bag over his back, he pumped his legs hard until he was in a flat-out run. He easily dodged two holders deep in conversation and a harper clasping half a dozen flat drums, though he nearly collided with a woman who was walking down the middle of the tunnel carrying two bulky baskets. When she saw Piemur pelting down the tunnel, she did a little dither-dance, bobbing from left to right repeatedly, her eyes wide as she tried to guess which side he would run toward. In the end, he only had to veer from side to side twice before the woman, hands held protectively over her head, gave a little cry and crouched down on the spot, allowing Piemur to leap to one side of her, laughing a little at their silliness as he did. He looked back over his shoulder, checking to make sure she was all right. Then, all of a sudden, he'd reached the end of the tunnel and, hard-pressed to slow down in time, all but charged into the Bowl of Fort Weyr.

There wasn't anything, Piemur mused, his head cranked back on his neck as he looked skyward, that could make a fellow slam on the brakes faster than seeing a Weyr at full fighting strength in the final moments of preparation before they flew to meet a Threadfall.

From his position in the Bowl of the caldera that Fort Weyr occupied, Piemur heard a clamor as the weyrfolk assisting the dragonriders called to one another. While the noise ebbed and flowed all around him, Piemur stood openmouthed as he watched scores and scores of dragons, bronze, brown, blue, and green, flying overhead at varying heights and in no apparent order. They whizzed through the air, this way and that, creating a surge of energy that Piemur believed he could actually feel through the downdrafts of air their wings created. How they didn't collide with one another, midflight, was a mystery he'd never understand. What an altogether uplifting and magnificent sight!

Most of the dragons were ready, perched on the upper rim of the Weyr Bowl, their fighting harnesses drawn tight and bulging sacks full of firestone slung from them on either side of their necks. They were waiting for the formal command from their Weyrleader signaling them to take to the skies and meet their old foe once again. Some dragons were launching from the mouths of their weyrs to swoop down and land in the Bowl, attending to last-minute necessities, while others waited patiently as sacks of firestone were hauled and pushed to their backs by their riders and attendant weyrfolk. *What organized disorder!* Piemur marveled.

"Piemur!"

He looked toward the sound, trying to locate the source, but there was too much dragon flesh in his way.

"Over here, Piemur, to your left!" It sounded like N'ton's voice.

Piemur followed the voice, careful not to get in the way of running weyrfolk, or a dragon tail, or furling wings, as the members of the Weyr single-mindedly prepared to fight. The Fort Weyrleader called out again, and Piemur located N'ton just as sacks of firestone were being lifted into place on Lioth's back. The big bronze dragon stamped one huge foot as he stood, impatient to be airborne.

N'ton was dressed in full fighting gear, his helmet already strapped tight and goggles at the ready as he leaned down the side of Lioth's neck so Piemur could hear him.

"A drum message came in from Igen Weyr, Piemur. Thread hasn't fallen when or where it should, so we're taking flight earlier than planned, lest we get caught out, too. I'm sorry, but you'll have to wait for a lift to Nabol. I'll send word to you later." The tall dragonrider reached his hand down to clasp Piemur's, a smile on his face.

Piemur smiled back. "Safe skies, N'ton!"

There was nothing for it, he ruminated, hoping the escort would wait for him in Nabol, or he'd simply have to make do on his own when he eventually arrived there.

As Piemur watched, Lioth moved into a clear space in the center of the Bowl and, bunching his limbs underneath him, made a huge leap upward, launching into the air to fly the short distance to where the other dragons were waiting along the edge of the rim.

Moments later all the dragons and riders had completed their preparations and were assembled along the rim of the Bowl. Looking to their Weyrleader, the riders waited mere seconds before N'ton lifted one arm over his head and pumped the air with his closed fist, signaling for the wings of dragons to take flight.

They lifted in a steady stream, one wing at a time, flying upward in their hundreds, up above the huge Star Stones of Fort, said to be the largest on Pern, and when they had gained enough height to hover on the thermals, then, without a further gesture or a single command Piemur could hear, they answered the unspoken call of Lioth and N'ton and blinked out of sight, *between,* into that frighteningly dark place where silence was a noisy pressure and the cold unforgiving and absolute.

A mere two hours later, while Piemur sipped a cup of hot *klah* in Fort's main hall, with Farli perched along the back of his neck, a young lad from the Weyr brought a message to him from J'hon. The dragonrider was ready to take Piemur to Nabol. It seemed odd to Piemur to hear from J'hon so soon. Threadfalls usually lasted for at least three or four hours, after which more time was spent on the final checks that ensured no Thread had been allowed to reach the ground undetected.

Piemur quickly scooped up his bag from the bench and jogged back through the tunnel to the Weyr, Farli zooming on ahead of him. More than three-quarters of the Weyr had returned from their flight and now stood in the Bowl, waiting for helpers to divest them of their firestone sacks, or hauling them off their dragons themselves. The air was charged with misspent energy. Piemur could hear several dragonriders calling to one another in desultory tones, and another group arguing among themselves about landmarks and wind patterns, their frustrations all too evident. They must have had a bad flight, Piemur surmised.

He searched for the bronze wingsecond and finally located him at the far end of the Bowl, standing near his dragon, Mirth. As he approached, Piemur heard J'hon talking to a much older dragonrider who, he realized, must be one of the many Oldtimers who'd remained in the north, adapting to life in their own world's future.

"I'd think it's best if your dragon remains tacked up with the sacks in place, J'hon," the Oldtimer was saying, "or you'll likely kick yourself when the call comes that the forward scouts have sighted the leading edge of Thread." He smiled at J'hon and clapped a hand on his shoulder as he turned toward his brown dragon to run a critical eye over the straps that held his own sacks of firestone in place.

"Sound advice, D'rah. My thanks," J'hon said, nodding to the more experienced dragonrider. Then, when he saw Piemur approaching, he called, "Hey, Piemur, you got my message!"

At a scant twenty-one Turns, J'hon was the youngest dragonrider at Fort to hold the position of wingsecond. Not as tall as his wingleader, J'hon nevertheless had a commanding presence and carried his frame with a lithe grace. His hair was dark and thick, his face pleasant, and his eyes were a remarkable gold-flecked hazel. He was well known in the Weyr for his rapid-fire wit and pithy jokes, and Piemur felt at ease in his company.

"My thanks, J'hon, though I've no wish to go to Nabol." Piemur clasped hands with the dragonrider who, he noted with a jolt of pride, was only slightly taller than he. The unmistakable smell of firestone smoke clung to the wingsecond's clothing, and Piemur realized that his dragon must've already tested his flame even though no Thread had yet fallen to char.

"No thanks are needed, Piemur—it'll be a welcome break from waiting for the call to fight Thread. If we can actually determine when and where it's going to fall." J'hon's smile was rueful. "Igen reported earlier that Thread fell out of sequence there, too."

"How will the Weyr adjust to this kind of unpredictability?" Piemur asked.

"That's a good question, Piemur. We checked and double-checked our charts last night, in preparation for today, but something has changed the pattern of the Fall. F'lar sent a wing to sweep the skies over the southeastern border of Ruatha, hoping to properly pinpoint where the Fall will begin. There wasn't any point in the whole Weyr remaining in flight, so N'ton sent most of us back to wait it out. It was a shrewd decision—otherwise we'd all get too edgy. If you're ready, Mirth and I can take you to Nabol now."

"I'd best get it over with," Piemur said, a forced grin flashing across his face as he quickly stepped into his heavy leggings and then toggled the fastenings closed on his jacket before finally pulling his fur-lined helmet onto his head. Pulling the strap of his bag over his shoulder, he scanned around him, trying to spot Farli, but he couldn't see her anywhere. She must've gotten spooked by all the commotion from the dragons and riders, he guessed. No doubt she'd find him later.

Already settled between the last two ridges at the base of his bronze's neck, J'hon leaned down and offered Piemur a hand to help him climb up the tall shoulder and around the bulky firestone sacks. Mirth, on some signal from his rider, turned his head toward Piemur, gently nudging him with his nose. Glad for the boost up from behind, Piemur landed on Mirth's back with a chuckle, and made short work of clipping the straps of the flying harness around his waist. The addition of the firestone sacks and the harnessing that secured them gave Piemur the comforting feeling that he was wedged in place like a pip between two teeth.

"All set?" J'hon asked over his shoulder. Piemur nodded.

Mirth walked clear of the other dragons and then, extending his wings, ran several paces on all four legs before leaping into the air. He beat down powerfully with his wings and, in a few strokes, rose up and up, high into the air until he was level with the rim of the Bowl. With a few mighty strokes he climbed higher until the change in the air all around them signaled to Piemur that they were gaining lift with the help of the thermals.

J'hon turned his head toward Piemur, cupping one hand to his mouth so the sound wouldn't be blown away on the wind. "I'm going to fly just beyond the Star Stones and then we'll go *between*. We'll arrive a good distance out from Nabol Hold. I want to find the best approach to the settlement so as few people as possible see us."

Piemur nodded in agreement, quickly pulling his flying gloves from his jacket pockets. He put them on and then secured the side flaps of his leather helmet over his ears in preparation for the icy cold of *between*. After every flight he'd made into that huge, cold void he was certain that the *next* time he'd be ready for the experience. Yet there wasn't anything that could prepare Piemur adequately for the silent nothingness, or the panic that rose up in him as all sensations fell away, sparing him nothing, not even the comfort of touch. They seemed to hang there, and time, too, played out strangely *between*. Although Piemur knew they would emerge into daylight in the same amount of time it took him to count to three, those few moments always felt like hours. Just when he thought he couldn't bear it any longer, they burst out into the skies southwest of Nabol Hold.

Nabol is grayer than I remembered, Piemur thought with irony, snorting gently under his breath as he scanned the skies around them. Suddenly J'hon's body froze and Mirth tensed, too, as dragonrider and bronze dragon looked up in unison. Piemur followed J'hon's gaze, and then he saw it: a silver mist of descending Thread raining down across the sky.

Panic washed over him. How could they have arrived in the middle of Threadfall?

"Thread!" J'hon roared at Piemur. "Hold on tight!"

Mirth reacted immediately, beating his wings faster and stretching his neck out in front of him, his body elongating like an arrow as he climbed up and away from the path of the approaching mass of streaming silver strands.

The bronze dragon wheeled midair, wrenching Piemur's head about on his shoulders, and Piemur wondered how dragonriders remained hale and hearty when they endured such aggressive airborne maneuvers. A belch of flame burst from Mirth's open mouth and seared a large clump of the silver threads to mere char. Mirth turned his head back toward his rider, and Piemur could see the huge eyes whirling a deep shade of red as J'hon fed him lumps of firestone from the sacks slung across his neck. While Mirth quickly crunched the stone, J'hon craned his neck around.

"I've called for support from the Weyr, Piemur, but we can't leave now! My wing will be here soon." Then he turned back toward Mirth to feed him another lump of firestone.

Piemur grimly nodded as he clung onto the fighting straps for dear life, realizing that J'hon couldn't possibly see his feeble movement unless he had eyes in the back of his head. Mirth flew on, ahead of the silver rain, dodging clumps that fell around them and flaming those that were directly in his path. The bronze dragon climbed and dove, pivoted and wheeled through the air, his attention completely focused on fighting his ancient foe.

They were moving so fast and changing direction at such high speed that Piemur thought his arms might be ripped from their sockets. Later, when he recollected that terrifying flight, he wasn't quite certain how he'd heard it, but the sound of a hiss coming from behind his left ear caught his attention, and he turned just in time to see a single strand of Thread land on top of his bag.

The horror of being so close to Thread galvanized Piemur into action. In a flash he pulled the strap from his back and shrugged the bag off as the Thread writhed grotesquely. He mustn't let the Thread touch him! In a rush of fright, Piemur flung the bag away from him, and for a moment it seemed to hang in the air before it began the inexorable plunge downward, the strand of Thread seeming to swell and grow as it mindlessly consumed the bag and its contents.

"Nooo!" Piemur roared, unconsciously grabbing J'hon's shoulder as he watched in horror while the bag fell through the sky. What had he done? The bag would hit the ground and Thread would begin burrowing, its energy bolstered by the organic matter of his bag and its contents!

Without missing a beat Mirth wheeled midair and plummeted down to follow the hurtling bag. As he drew near, the bronze began to backwing and rolled his body skyward again. Then, just as Piemur thought Mirth was going to let the bag fall unchecked, the dragon turned his head and belched out a long, funnel-like stream of red-hot flame. Piemur's bag—what was left of it—and the writhing strand of Thread were engulfed in a fireball, exploding in flurries of sparks and smoldering ash.

Piemur gulped in a lungful of air, released his death-grip on J'hon's shoulder, and slumped against his harness. J'hon reached back one gloved hand and slapped Piemur's knee reassuringly.

Mirth began to ascend again, and between one wingbeat and the next the sky was crowded with dragons. A full fighting wing—thirty strong—filled the air, bursting into the empty spaces all around Piemur. He'd never seen anything so spectacular and heartening before in his life. Bronzes, browns, blues, and greens—all flew together in tight formation, their eyes whirling deep amber and red. Little plumes of flame escaped from several of the dragons' mouths, followed immediately by full jets of fire streaming out to sear the Thread from the sky. Piemur stared, incredulous at how agile the smaller green and blue dragons were as they darted in and out around the larger browns and bronzes, catching any errant Thread that might have escaped their larger wingmates.

The wing pressed onward and Piemur realized that the dragonriders must have established the exact measure of the leading edge of Thread as it stretched across the sky like a swath of silver rain, because J'hon pumped his arm several times and half a dozen dragons responded by peeling off in either direction. Working as a finely drilled team, the thirty dragons and riders blazed through the sky, systematically wiping out the deadly spores before they could make landfall.

When the skies finally looked clear and their frenzied flight slowed, Piemur's arm muscles were burning; he'd been holding on to the fighting straps so tightly that he was certain he'd never be able to unclench his hands again.

All around them, the other members of the wing were slowing the pace of their flight, dragons and riders turning their heads slowly from side to side as they scanned the skies. When it was clear that no more Thread was falling, the riders called out to one another, exchanging comments of praise, or mild teases, the urgency and tension of their hasty combat immediately forgotten in their easy badinage.

"We've got it under control now," J'hon said, lifting his goggles from his eyes as he turned to face Piemur. The bronze rider's face was covered in a dark layer of sooty ash, save for where his goggles had rested. He flashed Piemur a toothy grin, his golden eyes sparkling with elation. "Are you still in one piece?" he asked, and Piemur nodded, feeling as if his eyes might pop out of his head.

"It wasn't a heavy Fall. Must've been a break-off clump," J'hon continued with a shrug. "I can take you to Nabol now, Piemur."

Piemur nodded, all too aware of the irony of his situation: Never, in a thousand Turns, would he have thought he'd be relieved to be going to Nabol.

They touched down at the edge of a large field, far from the outermost cotholds of Nabol, and farther still from the main Hold, where Lord Deckter resided.

Piemur removed his flying jacket and heavy leggings and handed them to J'hon to keep safe—it would be too difficult to explain to anyone inquisitive enough why he had such distinctive dragonrider garb when he was trying to fob himself off as a holder.

There was no sign of the promised escort, and while he and J'hon stood together on the ground debating the best alternatives, Mirth suddenly trumpeted in anger, stamping his forefeet on the ground and darting his wedge-shaped head from side to side in agitation, his mouth wide open and his huge teeth bared in a snarl. J'hon turned toward his dragon, the flying gear forgotten where it lay draped over his arm. He was frozen to the spot as he silently communicated with Mirth.

Piemur wondered if more Thread was falling where it wasn't expected. But then the bronze dragonrider turned and looked at Piemur, his dirty face a mask of panic.

"What is it, J'hon?"

"Ramoth has gone berserk!" J'hon said, and his eyes glazed over again as he listened to Mirth. Piemur looked at J'hon in confusion, his brows furrowing.

"She has a clutch of eggs on the Hatching Grounds," J'hon explained quickly, his features hardening as he continued, "and the queen egg has been stolen!"

"Stolen! There must be a mistake. Who would take it?" Piemur asked, a dozen other questions colliding in his head as he stared, aghast, at the Fort wingsecond.

"Mirth says three dragons flew into the Hatching Grounds and took the queen egg. Ramoth doesn't know what Weyr they came from. N'ton's been called to Benden—the Weyr's in chaos!"

Piemur was about to ask another question when J'hon spoke again with Mirth, whose eyes were whirling a disturbing shade of red.

"Lessa wants revenge!" J'hon reeled in shock.

"Revenge?" Piemur shook his head, grabbing J'hon's arm to steady him.

"Against whoever did this!" J'hon responded.

"But I don't understand, J'hon, there must be some mistake. Who would steal the queen egg?" Piemur asked, still holding on to the dragonrider's arm. Mirth bugled again loudly.

"It could only be the Oldtimers—the exiled ones down in the south. Their queens no longer rise to mate, and their bronzes are dying off."

Piemur shook his head as he stared, disbelieving, at the shocked dragonrider.

"With the illegal trading they've been doing—and all those covert raids and routing parties, plus the endless flaunting of our ways and customs—the Oldtimers have been doing everything they can to get the attention of the Weyrs in the north. It's as if they actually *want* to incite discord among us all."

"But I can't believe it, J'hon. There must be some mistake. Some way to settle this—you're all guardians, after all."

"And they've betrayed us, Piemur. Betrayed our code!" J'hon shouted, giving full voice to his anger and outrage.

Piemur stared at the young wingsecond, slowly shaking his head in denial.

"Don't you see? It's as if they've stolen a newborn child from his parents, Piemur! Stolen the most precious, the most revered among us. They've been fighting every little improvement we've brought about, always flouting the changes we've made. And even though all of us look to Benden as the premier Weyr, they refuse to do so. Now this, Piemur! It's absolutely the final straw!"

Piemur stared at J'hon, an expression of horror on his face. Was J'hon really saying what he *thought* he was saying? He couldn't believe it.

Mirth stamped his feet again, his head darting in a tight motion from side to side.

"What do you mean, J'hon?" Piemur had to ask.

"They're trying to force our hand, Piemur! They want to go back to their old ways—the way they lived four hundred Turns ago! And they're trying to force Benden's hand to step down, to yield to them." Mirth turned his head toward J'hon, who locked eyes with him.

"What is it? What's he saying now?" Piemur asked.

"They're talking about dragon fighting dragon!"

"No!" Piemur cried. "Dragons don't fight *one another*!"

"I have to go, Piemur, N'ton is calling us back!" J'hon shouted, having lost all composure. He looked frantic, Piemur thought, seeing the strange expression in J'hon's eyes as the bronze rider submitted to a summons too strong to ignore.

It was a distressing sight to see—a dignified and noble dragonrider caught in such a tumult of wild emotions. If only this was a horrid mistake, Piemur thought. Or, if not, at the very least if the egg was found and safely returned to its rightful place . . . soon!

J'hon dumped Piemur's flying gear on the ground and without a word vaulted onto Mirth's shoulder, quickly pulling himself onto the bronze's back.

Mirth looked as if he were ready to hop out of his skin, mincing from one foot to the other, a deep rumble rising up through his gullet and culminating in an anguished bugle as he waited for J'hon to settle himself in place. In powerful, frenzied wingbeats they rose up into the air over Piemur's head, Mirth bellowing his distress, and then his cries were cut short, swallowed up, as they flew *between*.

SIX

THE RISING SUN FELT WARM AS THE LONE, MUD-CAKED DRAGON and his rider arrowed in over the backs of the drowsing bronze dragons and their napping riders. It was crucial the pair from the north succeeded in recovering the egg from the Oldtimers, returning it from this place and time, back to its rightful home in Benden Weyr. Too much would be lost if they failed.

They flew in fast and, in one deft swoop, before the startled bronzes could rise to their feet, the mud-covered dragon grabbed the egg in his sturdy forearms and lunged upward. They'd done it! They'd snatched back the queen egg!

The rider looked over his shoulder as they were gaining height and, to his horror, he clearly saw a blue dragon with his rider and a passenger flying in low over the backs of the three startled bronzes.

Shards! Have they seen us? the rider asked, but his dragon didn't reply as he beat his wings down hard through the air, quickly achieving enough height so they could go *between*.

The looting dragon and rider went unseen by Meria and B'naj as Seventh flew them into the cove, toward the sunrise. Their attention was wholly focused on the ground, not the air, so they failed to see the dragon clutching the queen egg.

Meria was afraid B'naj hadn't timed their flight correctly. She knew exactly when and where T'kul, B'zon, and the other rider had taken Benden's queen egg, but from her position on Seventh, behind B'naj, she couldn't see any sign of it in the sands below. It was imperative that they be quick and remain unseen as they snatched back the egg! But where was it?

Meria fervently wished her eyes would adjust quicker to the change in light from where they'd just been, *between,* to the light they were flying into now. If the rising sun were only a little higher in the sky she could see more clearly. She could make out the shadow-like figures of two dragonriders as they ran out from under the shade of a grove of frond trees. They were waving their arms and shouting something. They ran toward their dragons, and then she could hear them shouting again.

Meria squeezed B'naj's shoulder to get his attention. "Can we get any closer, B'naj? I can't see the egg."

"If we fly any lower they *will* see us, Meria. One moment," and he fell silent as he conferred with his dragon.

"Seventh says the egg is gone!" B'naj sounded alarmed.

"Gone! Gone where?" Meria exclaimed.

"Seventh says the bronzes don't know. They only saw a dark shadow."

"Take us down quickly, B'naj! We have to find out more!"

Meria swallowed hard, trying to stop the panic that was rising up in her chest from overwhelming her. The egg *had* to be returned to its rightful Weyr! The consequences of not doing so were too huge to imagine.

At B'naj's command his dragon arrowed down toward the ground. Displaying remarkable agility for such a mature dragon, Seventh drew dangerously close to ground level, but just as it looked as if he was going to crash, he swooped upward out of his dive, backwinging dynamically to slow his forward momentum. He hit the ground with a resounding thud, landing squarely in front of the two bronze dragons, his wings billowing air in mighty sweeps. The force of his maneuver hurled Meria forward and she bumped heavily against B'naj's back, but hastily she righted herself, jumped off Seventh's back, and ran to the two bronze riders.

T'kul saw her first. "What are *you* doing here?" he shouted. "Was it you, healer? Did you take the egg? You traitor!" He was furious. "It was almost ready to hatch—just another day, maybe two. We could've had new blood for our Weyr!" His tone was full of venom, and Salth, his dragon, growled, halting Meria in her tracks as she shook her head in denial.

"Wait T'kul! B'zon, please, you have to listen to us," B'naj pleaded, running up to stand beside Meria, arms straight and fisted hands taut on either side of his big, barrel chest. He was a tall man and well known for his strength, but T'kul, swelling with outrage, seemed to tower over him.

"It's a brave man who lands a mere brown in the path of two bronzes, B'naj. Or a foolish one. Get out of our way!" B'zon, the other bronze rider, hollered. Both bronze dragons hissed and bared their teeth at Seventh, spurred on by the anger and sense of urgency they felt from their riders. The smaller blue dragon, however, stood his ground unflinchingly. The bronzes bristled, stamping their feet.

"Please!" Meria said fervently, as she stood in front of Seventh, one arm raised in entreaty. "Please, T'kul, B'zon, listen to us. B'naj and I only want what is best for all of us. Stand down, I implore you." She pointedly looked at the two bronze dragons, whose eyes were whirling a dangerous shade of burgundy, willing them to listen as she mentally begged for calm.

Salth, T'kul's bronze, rumbled low and slow, his eyes sparkling as they were lit by the rising sun.

"I know what you tried to do, T'kul, and I respect you! You did what you thought had to be done to save the Weyr. *Our* Weyr." Meria's voice resonated with pride. "But this was not the way to do it," she added, trying to sound calmer, gentler.

"Leave off with your healer platitudes, Meria," B'zon called snidely. "You left our Weyr of your own free will." He pointed his index finger at her and then stabbed his chest repeatedly to punctuate his next words. "You mean nothing to us now!" His cruel tone cut through the morning air like a scythe. Meria caught her breath in a single gasp and then looked away. This had been her greatest fear: that she would not be able to get through to them—now, when they needed help the most.

"But what can you possibly do now?" B'naj cried, indicating with one sweep of his hand the hollow indentation in the sand where the egg had lain. "The egg is gone. Who knows to where or when, but it's no longer in your possession, Weyrleader."

T'kul's furrowed brows softened briefly when he heard B'naj call him by that title. T'kul had been the leader in High Reaches Weyr for most of his life, in the old times, and for all too short a time in this Present Pass. But then F'lar exiled them to the Southern Continent and another dragonrider took his place. It had been Turns since anyone had called him Weyrleader. Still, fury overrode his pleasure at being addressed with appropriate respect.

"Shards!" he shouted vehemently. "Somehow Benden must've followed us to this place, this time"—he slapped his hand against his thigh—"and waited for the perfect moment to catch us off guard."

Meria had to stifle a smile: If T'kul was, indeed, correct, then at the very least the egg was back where it belonged. But she knew that it would've been far better if the egg had been returned by members of the Southern Weyr. That small act would have clearly shown to Benden that the majority of dragonriders in Southern were aware of and would not condone the grave offense a small handful of them had committed.

"How many dragons were there?" she asked. "What did you see?"

B'zon rubbed his forehead with one hand, but it was T'kul who replied, though he didn't look at her.

"We didn't see anything, but Salth says it was just one dragon, a dark one. Probably a blue. Strange, though, Salth said he was too small to be a blue." T'kul shook his head wearily. "He took the egg so quickly we had no time to react."

"We should go look for him and take back the egg!" B'zon said.

"Look for him where? When?" Meria asked, keeping her voice gentle. She didn't want to rub salt into their already raw wounds.

"There won't be another chance to take back Benden's egg, B'zon. Or any other eggs, for that matter," B'naj said. "The Weyrs will guard against such an occurrence. You may be sure of that. *All* the Weyrs will be wary of other dragons henceforth." He shook his head, the true import of his words not lost on any of them. He suddenly had a startling thought and could feel dread dropping like a heavy stone into the pit of his stomach. "Just how long did you have the egg in this *when*?"

"Ten days," B'zon replied, his tone leaden.

Meria couldn't stop herself from gasping; the situation was worse than she had imagined. If the egg had been returned almost immediately after the theft, then the affront to Benden Weyr wouldn't have been so grave, so unthinkable. But to have kept the egg for a full ten days, hardening outside its rightful Hatching Grounds, showed the thieves' utter commitment to their plan: to keep the egg for one of their own Candidates to Impress. If Benden chose to wage all-out retribution on the members of Southern Weyr, they would be well within their rights. A profound and deeply uncomfortable silence fell over the group as they stood facing one another in the pretty little cove.

B'zon broke the silence with the thought that was uppermost in all their minds. "What are we going to do now?" he asked, his tone bleak. "Our dragons are all off color, more than half of them. And none of the greens in our Weyr fly to mate anymore—they're too old."

"I think I know why the dragons are off color," Meria declared, trying to sound encouraging. "And it has naught to do with the lack of an active queen."

"No!" T'kul shouted, his face purple with rage. "You don't get to do anything now, when it's too late. I won't allow you to ease your guilt for abandoning the Weyr!" He stood staring fiercely at Meria for what seemed like an age, and then he turned and mounted Salth without a backward glance. B'zon quickly followed suit and the pair took to the air, climbing into the bright, early-morning sky before finally disappearing into the lightless void of *between*.

. . .

The lone pair timed it so they flew *between* one Turn in time ahead of their sunrise theft. They were back in the pretty little cove, exactly where they had been mere moments earlier, but now they were completely alone. The dragon landed carefully and, with the last bit of strength remaining in his forearms, gently lowered the egg to the warm sands; his rider hopped from his back and checked the egg for any signs of cracks with gloved hands. It seemed hard enough, and still warm, and quite possibly no worse for wear, even though it had traveled through the cold nothingness of *between*.

The rider quickly scooped armfuls of sand over the egg, banking it as high as possible to maintain the heat. A dragon egg was a delicate thing, and this one was more precious than any the rider had ever handled—apart, of course, from his own dragon's egg. When he was satisfied the queen egg was well covered, he collapsed on the hot sand, panting to catch his breath.

"We can't stay long," he said between gasps. "They might try to find us by jumping forward in time day by day. They'd know we can't take the egg far at once or we'd risk damaging it in the cold of *between*." The dragon signaled accord, his sides still heaving from his exertions. Then he froze, taut with alarm. Startled, his rider turned, too, and saw two fire-lizards, a gold one and a bronze, watching them from the edge of the beach. But as soon as he clapped eyes on them the pair took to the air and disappeared from sight.

"Do we know them?" the rider asked his dragon.

No.

"Where'd those two queens go?"

They showed me when *the egg was taken to. That's all you wanted.* The dragon lowered his head, bereft, like his rider, that he hadn't insisted the queen fire-lizards who'd guided them here should be made to remain. He noticed a pile of firestone and his eyes, whirling in alarm, caught sight of flame scar on the ground nearby, faded somewhat and overgrown with weeds, but discernible nonetheless.

The rider didn't feel safe and knew he wouldn't feel at ease until the egg was back in Benden where it belonged. His dragon began crunching some of the firestone.

What are you doing? You're not going to flame dragons! the rider said, aghast.

No, of course not, but will they dare approach me if I am flaming?

The dragonrider was unsettled enough not to protest. After a brief pause, he set to loosening the rope he had tied around his waist to make a sling with the fur rug he'd brought to protect the egg. When his makeshift sling was assembled, the rider fitted it comfortably around his dragon's shoulders and placed the egg carefully inside. He started to check the knots one last time, but then some inner caution urged him to leave immediately, so he ceased his actions and quickly mounted the waiting dragon.

As the dragon made the series of jumps *between,* into and out of that place where the piercing cold ate at human bones, his rider had time to worry if he was making the jumps too long to keep the egg warm. What if he wasn't correctly judging the forward jumps through time? Had he killed the little queen trying to save her? His mind reeled with thoughts of *between* and paradoxes until he latched onto the one idea that made the most sense: At least the most important act, returning the stolen egg, was in process. And dragon had not fought dragon—not yet!

The shimmering midmorning heat of the Keroon desert, a safe haven they'd visited before, warmed their bodies as well as their spirits when they landed in the soft sand, out of imminent danger. Under the caked, black mud, the dragon looked a ghastly color, which added further to his rider's worries.

Resolute, they released the egg from its sling and lowered it to the sand, covering it to keep it warm after the flight *between* times. It was not far from the hour when the egg had to be back in the Hatching Grounds, and they still had some time-distance to cover, too. They were both very tired and rested awhile in the hot desert before they made the last, the trickiest, jump. It was imperative that when they jumped *between* they came out in a position just inside the Hatching Grounds, where the arch of the entrance sloped abruptly downward, obscuring the view of anyone who might be looking from the Bowl into the Grounds.

Without warning, the rider and dragon were roused from their respite by a sudden, utter stillness and a minute change in air pressure. Instinctively they glanced upward, expecting a wing of flaming dragons to bear down on them to reclaim their prize, but the sky above was still and clear and hot. Then they saw it: the silver mist of descending Thread sheeting down across the desert.

They scrambled to the egg, dragon and rider both frantically digging it free of the sand, and then the rider pushed it into the sling, mounted, and glanced up at the sky. Why were there no fighting dragons filling the skies?

They had worked quickly to secure their precious burden in its sling, but their efforts had not been quick enough. Just at the moment the rider urged his dragon upward, the leading edge of Thread fell in a hissing, writhing mass to the sand around them. The dragon gave a belch of flame, trying to clear a path far enough above ground so he could go *between,* but a ribbon of fire sliced across the rider's cheek, down his right shoulder, through his wherhide tunic, and down into his forearm and thigh. The pain was excruciating! Somehow, they made the jump *between,* away from the thick sheet of falling Thread, but not before the dragon's foot and leg were also seared.

The cold of *between* immediately halted the Thread's progress through their flesh, killing it and cooling their wounds momentarily, and then they were back in light again, finally in the Hatching Grounds at Benden Weyr, where they could hear a distraught Ramoth bellowing. They'd been here before and witnessed the moment the theft had been discovered. The rider started to worry again about the consequences of time paradoxes but quickly shook his head to cast aside those fears. Despite all their traveling between times and places, they had managed to return the egg to Benden Weyr, and only a very short while after it had been taken.

As they landed, the hot sand bit into their wounds, and both dragon and rider were hard-put not to cry out from the cruel pain as they lowered the egg. They were almost home free!

But as the egg slid out of the sling, it began to roll down the slight incline of the Hatching Grounds, away from them.

Oh, no, we'll be seen! the rider silently cried as he clambered onto his dragon's back. *Hurry!*

In one final, powerful jump, the mud-caked dragon and his weary rider leapt toward the vaulted ceiling above the Hatching Grounds and then vanished.

T'ron shouted vehemently, pounding his closed fist on the table.

"By the First Shell, what have you *done*? Your actions have put us all in an indefensible position!"

When Mardra had haltingly told T'ron about the foiled attempt to get a queen egg, his initial response was one of shock, but those feelings were quickly supplanted by outrage. How had matters grown so distorted that the members of his *own* Weyr had forgotten their purpose? Had he failed them—and himself—so badly? In the past, he might have wallowed in his own ineffectiveness, his sense of inadequacy as a leader, but now a steely resolve ignited in T'ron's gut and exploded outward. *He* had to force them to see their error and then lead them out of this disastrous mess. He felt as if he had shrugged a heavy, ill-fitting cloak from his shoulders, and divested himself of an unwanted weight.

"You should be flogged in turn by each and every member of this Weyr! What have you done?" he demanded again, his voice rising as he spat out the last word, glaring darkly at Mardra and T'reb, and then at the ashen faces of T'kul and B'zon.

"But, T'ron, it would've given the Weyr a fighting chance—" B'zon started to explain, but T'ron didn't allow him to continue.

"A fighting chance for what?" he hollered, glaring first at B'zon and then at the silent faces of T'kul, Mardra, and T'reb. "Pitting dragon against dragon? Have you lost your minds?"

"But I couldn't bear it any longer, T'ron," Mardra said beseechingly, clasping her hands together. "Loranth's been off color for so long—and then she was so distraught after that last clutch. I had to do something to ease her grief—our grief!"

"We had to help our queen!" T'reb cried.

"And you thought stealing *another* queen's egg was the answer? I see time has not only deprived you of youth, but also taken your sanity with it!" T'ron roared, and his audience stared at him in silence. He felt as if he was growing stronger, as if this new feeling of purpose was coursing through his veins like an extra life-blood, injecting him with authority and vitality.

T'reb looked as if he was going to be sick to his stomach, T'ron noted, and T'kul, possibly for the first time in his life, had a look of worry stamped across his countenance rather than his usual mien of arrogance. Granted, the jump *between* times twenty-five Turns had turned his wingsecond's face a sickly shade of gray, but he could tell that there was more than timing fatigue at work in T'kul.

As the other dragonriders stood around him in silence, T'ron racked his brains, wondering what he could possibly do to salvage his Weyr and repair the damage these riders had done. It was a pity that B'naj and Meria hadn't been successful in regaining control of the egg and returning it to Benden. That would have been the best outcome. T'ron had been astounded when T'kul and B'zon had flown into the compound, roaring wildly at all the other riders, demanding to know who had snatched the egg from them. But no one in Southern Weyr admitted responsibility, and T'ron could tell, from the looks of shock on their faces, that no other members of his Weyr had taken the egg, much less known about the foiled plan.

He sighed heavily, knowing that they had only one option left to them.

"We must leave. Right now," he declared decisively. Outside, his bronze, Fidranth, bellowed and was answered by many of the other dragons. A low murmur of voices could be heard coming from the dragonriders who waited tensely outside.

"Leave the Weyr?" Mardra looked about her frantically.

"Yes! We must leave here, right now, every last one of us. Leave this time, this Pass, so no other dreadful event can occur to compound the situation. If we go to some other *when,* then at least we'll be able to think clearly and carefully. Think of a way out of this mess. Time, at least, will favor us in this instance. It's not the best solution, but for now it will have to do."

"But what good will that serve? They have the egg back," T'kul said.

"It will keep us alive, you fool," T'ron spat, but T'kul frowned at him.

"You don't understand, do you?" T'ron glared at his wing-second fiercely and then straightened his shoulders, feeling as if he was standing taller than he had in Turns. He cast his gaze on the other dragonriders, noting that they were unable to look him in the eye. How odd, he thought, that he should feel so invigorated in the face of such disaster.

"You foolish people have breached an inviolable code. Your desperate actions have contravened every fiber of what we are—and debased the valor of all our dragons. This act has undermined the very foundations of our purpose—and our future—violating the code of trust our dragons placed in us from the moment their minds graced ours."

"But the egg would have saved the Weyr!" B'zon cried.

"And what would have happened when the egg hatched? The Weyrs in the north would have retaliated. Think about it! Our fragile order would've fallen asunder with tit-for-tat squabbling that would escalate among the riders into outright fighting, pushing the dragons to the point of combat! Then our focus would get skewed from our true purpose and, quite possibly, Threadfall would go unchecked. Imagine the devastation. Can you?

"If Thread were to gain the upper hand and be allowed to fall unchecked, it could ruin a Holder's entire crop, leave us short of food supplies, burrow underground, and spread. That would lead to more arguing, blame laying, fighting, until the very fabric of the Weyrs, the Holds, and the Crafts would be irreparably rent."

"But *they* have the egg! They took it back!" Mardra cried, her features contorting in anguish.

"And still you cannot see what you have done?" T'ron shouted, shaking his head. The dragonriders looked at their Weyrleader, varying degrees of defiance mingling with confusion on their faces.

"You may have defeated our defenders!" T'ron roared, glaring from T'kul to Mardra and then to B'zon and T'reb.

Shouts rose from the dragonriders outside, and scores more dragons joined in. Mardra suddenly seemed to understand the import of T'ron's words, for her shoulders drooped and she covered her face with her hands. T'kul stood immobile next to her, slowly shaking his head as if the true outcome of their actions was finally resolving into a clear picture in his mind.

Once a proud and respected member of her Weyr, Mardra reacted as if wounded, the cries from the riders outside seeming to cripple her, and as if all the stuffing had been knocked out of her with one invisible blow, she crumpled to the floor. Her hands slid from her face as she wept, and Loranth, feeling her rider's dreadful despair, keened loudly in response. All the dragons, nearly twelve-score of them, added their voices to Loranth's lament, filling the air with the shocking, heartrending sound of their anguish.

T'ron stood motionless, appalled to see the woman who'd once helped him lead Pern's oldest Weyr through Turns of fighting Thread so thoroughly undone. T'kul knelt beside her, his face suffused with shock.

A chill ran down T'ron's back as the dragons keened together, and he felt their grief like a physical blow. Crossing the room to the open doorway, he looked across the compound to where his dragon, Fidranth, stood.

My friend . . . he said as he looked into the eyes of his noble lifelong partner. Connecting with his dragon's distraught consciousness, T'ron found that he was utterly unable to articulate any coherent thought.

Fidranth's huge eyes, dull with dread, grew a deeper shade of amethyst as he stared at his lifemate.

What has been done?

. . .

Piemur stood in shock for a long time, scanning the skies at the empty space where J'hon and Mirth had been. Could he actually be dreaming all this? Had Ramoth's queen egg *really* been taken from the Hatching Grounds at Benden? The whole world felt as if it were tottering on a very precarious and dangerous edge.

As if trying to prove that his reality was, indeed, a dream he suddenly remembered his bag and reached one hand behind him, patting his back—but of course the bag was no longer there. Had he really been a witness—practically a participant—in a battle against Threadfall? He'd nearly gotten himself scored by Thread—quite possibly devoured by it!

But his near miss during a Threadfall was nothing compared with what might happen if the dragonriders exercised their anger rather than restraint. Dragons fighting dragons? It was unthinkable!

Piemur couldn't bring himself to imagine what the outcome of such an event would be. How would they be able to fend off Thread if the dragons were fighting one another? His thoughts reeled. Why take the egg? It was difficult to understand why anyone would jeopardize the safety of their world: It just didn't make sense. Piemur knew that if any Weyr fell short of its necessary complement of dragons, the deficiency was made up whenever possible by the other Weyrs. Weyrleaders only had to make the request, and the required dragons were moved accordingly, even queens.

Piemur recalled the Masterharper and Sebell discussing how F'lar had instigated the revision of antiquated practices. Despite the resistance from some of the Oldtimers, F'lar's foresight had improved how the Weyrs functioned, and especially how they interacted with one another and with the other societal groups. From what Piemur knew, all the Weyrs except Southern were up to fighting strength, and although none of them, apart from Benden, had a clutch of eggs currently hardening on their Hatching Grounds, the queens in the other Weyrs were all in good health.

Could J'hon really be correct? Could the Oldtimers in Southern Weyr have taken Ramoth's egg? And then it hit him, with the force of a physical blow, and he opened his mouth in astonishment.

Of course, it all made sense now: T'reb talking to B'naj about Mardra's "idea" and his own, *better* "plan"; old Loranth moaning over empty eggs; the Oldtimers isolated and too hidebound to break with centuries-old customs and *ask* for help! And those two chumps T'reb had paid to draw the pretty little cove. The Oldtimers really *had* stolen the egg! That cove must be where they'd hidden the egg after taking it. He had to get a message to the Masterharper—but how?

Farli! He'd get her to take a message to Robinton!

He tried to quiet the frenetic thoughts bouncing around in his head and took a deep breath. He'd never get Farli to respond to him if he wasn't thinking clearly. Had she followed behind J'hon and Mirth when they left Fort, arriving in the middle of a Threadfall? What if his little friend had been caught in the Fall and gotten threadscored? It didn't bear thinking! He took another breath. Farli was too clever to get threadscored; she would've blinked *between* the instant she saw what they'd flown into. He had to believe that.

Farli! Farli, to me. Farli, come to me, he called, pushing the thought out to where he hoped his little queen might sense his summons.

He waited, straining for any whisper of Farli's reply. Nothing. He could feel no thought or nudge, not even a twitch from the firelizard's mind.

"Think, think!" he told himself, frantically looking all around as he racked his brains. J'hon had set them down in a clearing near the base of a rocky hill; a scattering of trees and other forest vegetation grew on the periphery of the clearing. He focused his thoughts and broadcast an image of the clearing, and then realized that what he was looking at could be in any number of places on Pern. He had to show Farli a more precise picture of where he was, with clear landmarks.

Piemur quickly made his way up the side of the hill, grabbing a long stick from the detritus littering the forest floor and using it to beat down the more robust plants that impeded his progress. When he reached the top of the hill and ran out past the trees, the landscape stretched out before him in a huge patchwork of fields and meadows bounded by hedgerows, dotted here and there with small copses and larger groves of trees.

The sky overhead was still dark and heavy with cloud. One mass to his right was full of rain. He could see the curtain of water as it fell, looking at first glance like a descending gray fringe. Guessing that the rain was heading his way, Piemur hunkered down under the shelter of a large, leafy tree and concentrated. He called again to Farli, this time showing her a precise image of the landscape and what he could see from his place at the base of the tree. He pushed his thoughts out hard, hoping Farli could hear them.

There! Down the slope, in the distance! Was that Farli? Two gold bodies flitted through the air toward him, seemingly twinning their wings together in flight, then separating again into two distinct bodies.

"Farli!" Piemur called, standing up from the base of the tree and waving his arms to attract her attention.

At the sound of Piemur's voice, Farli flew ahead of the other gold fire-lizard and immediately landed on Piemur's proffered arm, chittering constantly as she broadcast terrified images of angry dragons. He could see a small piece of cloth tied to Farli's left hind leg. A message!

The other gold fire-lizard, who cautiously followed Farli, looked at first glance to be Sebell's Kimi, but when she settled on the branch of a tree, her eyes whirling amber in alarm, Piemur realized that he was mistaken: He'd never seen this fire-lizard before.

"Shh, shh, Farli," Piemur said softly. "You don't need to be afraid," he said, placing a gentle hand on her to calm the frenzied images she kept showing him. Farli flexed her wings, chittering again and showing him the same image of angry dragons. She was mincing from foot to foot on Piemur's arm, and her talons, usually sheathed so as not to hurt him, were digging painfully into his flesh.

"Here, now, Farli, settle yourself. Settle," he crooned to her, tenderly rubbing her eye ridges. The soothing gesture had the desired effect, and Farli submitted just long enough for Piemur to remove the message from her leg. As he was unfurling it, she flew off to join the other queen on her branch, where she huddled, her eyes whirling an alarming shade of amber mixed with red.

The message read: *The egg is safe! Stay put. I'm coming, S.*

The egg was safe! Piemur looked at the little scrap of cloth again, worried that he might have misread it, but no, the message was clear. The egg was safe! The Oldtimers must have realized the huge mistake that had been made and returned the egg. Perhaps T'ron, as Weyrleader, had stood up to the troublemakers and forced them to take the egg back. Who returned the egg wasn't important now, Piemur thought, relieved that a disaster had been averted.

"Woo-hoo!" he shouted, slapping one hand against his thigh. He tucked his thumbs into his belt loops and grinned from ear to ear as he rocked back and forth on the soles of his feet. This was great news!

However, it was hours later when J'hon, not Sebell, arrived, and his news wasn't as good as Piemur had hoped. As soon as Mirth landed, Farli and the other queen darted off in a frenzy of wings and terrified screeches.

"Benden has mounted a full guard on the Weyr since the egg was taken and returned," J'hon said, his tone grim as he handed Piemur a message from Sebell wrapped around a small pouch of marks, along with a satchel containing basic provisions and items of clothing better suited to the cooler, damper climes of Nabol.

A question had been nagging at the edge of Piemur's thoughts throughout his long wait until J'hon returned: Which of the Oldtimers had actually been daring enough to return the egg? He asked J'hon.

"We don't know," J'hon said, frowning. "N'ton told me that after the theft there was a lot of confusion. Benden's dragons were incensed, and the egg was returned during that frantic time."

"But didn't anybody see, for shells' sake?" Piemur was astounded. "How could no one have seen an egg being put back on the Hatching Grounds?"

"So much was going on, and no one was looking at the spot where the egg had *been*! Ramoth was storming around the Bowl, bellowing, making all the dragons crazy for revenge, and then F'lar and Mnementh flew out of the Weyr with a group of dragons in search of the egg. He'd already called the other Weyrleaders to Benden when the egg was taken, so the extra dragons only added to the confusion." J'hon wiped a shaky hand across his brow, and it suddenly dawned on Piemur how much of an impact the theft had had on the dragonriders—as well as their dragons.

"J'hon, I'm fairly sure the Oldtimers in Southern took the egg, but why is everyone in Benden also certain it was them?" Piemur asked.

"That was the first question on everyone's lips, but Ramoth would know, of course. You see that, right? After all, she can speak with every dragon, in every Weyr. She would know! She tried to reach the dragons in Southern, but they aren't there anymore."

"They aren't there? Where are they?"

"We don't know. Southern Weyr's empty. It's like they just got on their dragons and . . . vanished."

Piemur rubbed the back of his head, deep in thought. Why right a wrong—return the egg—and then go into hiding? With the theft of the egg, the Southern Oldtimers had put themselves in an impossible position, but disappearing into thin air only made them appear guilty of something more. What had they been thinking? Piemur knew exactly what it felt like to be on the fringes, part of something yet not, included and discarded, all at the same time. Shards! Didn't the Oldtimers know they could never fit in if they stayed in hiding?

Piemur searched J'hon's face and saw that the wingsecond was wrangling with his own ragged thoughts.

"Well, at least the egg is back," he offered, trying to reassure J'hon.

"Tensions are still high at Benden, though. They've put additional dragons on guard with the watch dragon." Watch dragons were always on guard at every Weyr, alert to the external threat of Thread, not internal threats—or threats from other Weyrs.

"Every dragon approaching any Weyr must immediately announce their arrival or suffer the consequences," J'hon continued. "And Lessa is furious because the egg has noticeably aged since the theft—by about ten days! She fears the thieves may have exposed the egg to their own Candidates and it might not Impress any of the girls brought to Benden on Search." Concern creased the skin around his eyes.

"I see," Piemur said, unable to think of anything else useful to say.

"Lessa's even put an all-out ban on fire-lizards," J'hon added wearily.

"Why ban fire-lizards?" Piemur asked, thinking, in that silly part of his brain, how impossible it would've been for little fire-lizards to steal a queen egg.

"Because only fire-lizards could've alerted the thieves when Ramoth left the Hatching Grounds—it was when she went to feed that the egg was taken," J'hon explained. Piemur looked at J'hon, his brows still furrowed in confusion.

"Shards, Piemur, you know how the Weyrs work: We all know one another, we live together, as a team, and if anyone else comes into the Weyr we know about it. The only explanation for how they grabbed the egg from under Ramoth's nose is that fire-lizards were used to spy on the Hatching Grounds, waiting for the perfect time when the egg would be left unguarded."

"Oh," Piemur said, the one syllable word wavering on a downward note as J'hon's meaning hit home. "That might explain why Farli is so scared—and why she has a crazy image in her head."

"What of?"

"Darkness, a single egg, and flaming, angry dragons," Piemur explained, shaking his head at his fire-lizard's confused ravings.

"She's right, harper. The dragons *are* angry."

SEVEN

WHEN J'HON MADE HIS DEPARTURE A LITTLE LATER WITH A single, grim nod and a firm handshake, Piemur remained in the clearing, taking stock. Farli flitted back to his shoulder briefly, flashing her disturbing images to Piemur one more time before she and the other queen flew *between*. Piemur was concerned about Farli but, used to her occasional bouts of whimsy, he figured that the theft of Ramoth's queen egg was probably the reason for her disturbing images and erratic behavior. It was probably just as well, he mused, that she had gone off on one of her jaunts: It would be easier to complete his mission in Nabol without her flitting around distractingly.

Piemur was thankful that J'hon had thought to stuff a parcel of food into the bag of supplies, and ravenously devoured the cold cooked tubers and slices of meat before consciously slowing down to drink from the small flask of water. He saved the hunk of bread and cheese for later; longingly, he eyed the smaller parcel that looked, from the sticky spots that had oozed out between the seal, as if it contained cooked pastry filled with soft, sweet fruits, but decided to save that, as well.

After he'd eaten, he changed into the nondescript clothing that would disguise him as a holder in Nabol, pulled the cloth cap firmly onto his head, and finally took his ease under a tree, unrolling the message from Sebell.

It read: *Go west. Follow river. Cross footbridge, Marek 5th cot. All haste—J STILL AT RISK. S.*

Piemur had no difficulty finding the cothold belonging to Marek, where he was offered the use of loft space in an outbuilding with clean, dry bedding. Once he'd thanked Marek for his hospitality and settled his small bag in the loft, Piemur left the outbuilding and set to work finding out as much as he could about the men who planned to oust Jaxom.

Deciding it was easier to stick to a story that was close to the truth, he passed himself off as a herdbeast handler from Crom, hopeful of setting up a holding of his own. Knowing that the men he was seeking wouldn't be in Nabol Hold proper, but rather on its outskirts, he concentrated his energies on the smaller cotholds in the populated areas outside the main Hold. With an ease that surprised him, Piemur drew on his harper training and worked quickly to talk with as many people as possible. He found that in Nabol *everyone* had time for chatter and gossip, so he made a point of lingering long over his evening meal in the main hostelry outside Nabol Hold, and by spending a few marks extra to stand a round of cider for the more tight-lipped denizens, he was able to loosen their tongues enough to glean even more information.

On the second night, Piemur struck up a conversation with a bandy-legged cotholder named Hedamon, who was happy to answer any of the casually posed questions he asked him, though he seemed intent on getting more than at least one free drink out of Piemur's pocket. After they'd been talking for a while, Hedamon lifted his empty glass for Piemur to see, tilting it from side to side as he looked him up and down, before exclaiming with one squinty eye, "Yer a nosy liddle git, aren't ye?"

Hedamon winked conspiratorially at Piemur and, even though he was already well in his cups, accepted the fresh glass of ale. After making short work of downing it, the holder insisted that Piemur accompany him to another location that specialized in making its own unique brews and was, in Hedamon's opinion, where *every*one in Nabol went to socialize.

Piemur was utterly unable to resist Hedamon's urgings as the boozed-up man draped an arm over his shoulder, grabbed a handful of his tunic for better purchase, and clung to him as if he were a lifeline, jovially hauling him out of the hostelry and into the cool night where, a short walk away, Skal's renowned brewhouse was located. As he got his bearings, Piemur realized that they weren't far from Marek's cothold.

An old woman, who was standing in her doorway as they approached the brewhouse, tut-tutted and made a shushing sound when the raucous Hedamon tottered past her, leaning heavily on Piemur, her disapproval settling on her shoulders like a shawl.

"Ah, shush yourself, Fronna," Hedamon called loudly, adding, "ye frigid old cow," and then belched to punctuate the insult.

Piemur strained against Hedamon's immobilizing hold on the front of his tunic, casting a quick, apologetic look over his shoulder at the woman in the hope that she hadn't heard Hedamon, but it was obvious from the resounding sound of her front door slamming shut that she had.

Hedamon stopped abruptly in front of the last house in the group of cotholds, tilting his head back to give it his full scrutiny. The effort of leaning back while he looked up had the effect of making Hedamon lose his balance, and he tottered backward a few paces, dragging Piemur with him. With a huge effort, Piemur, slightly tipsy himself—though nowhere near drunk—managed to halt Hedamon's backward progress and they stood for a moment, taking in the nondescript, unmarked façade of Skal's brewhouse.

"This, young lad," Hedamon slurred, holding up one finger to stress his point, "is the finest brewhouse outside Nabol proper. Ye won't get any bedder beer near here." He guffawed at his choice of words. Then, with a huge lunge forward on one bandy leg, Hedamon marched onward purposefully, dragging Piemur with him. He pushed open the front door of Skal's brewhouse and crammed them both through together as if the doorframe could in no way pose an impediment to their progress.

As his shoulder was bashed painfully against the stone, Piemur finally broke free of Hedamon's grasp and pulled back a little, allowing the older man to precede him over the threshold and through to a narrow hallway with an open door on either side and another at the end. As they passed, Piemur could see that the room beyond the left door was empty of people, though it contained some chairs and tables, a padded seat under the deep window embrasure, and a fire burning invitingly in the hearth. The other doorway opened into a room where a group of older women were seated around a table, playing cards and holding glasses of amber liquid in their free hands as they laughed unreservedly at some comment one of them had made.

Hedamon ignored the women and continued down the hall to the far door, which he pushed through. Suddenly they were outside again, in the night air, surrounded by throngs of people.

Piemur quickly realized that Skal's brewhouse was, in actual fact, his home. He used his rooms as demand dictated; one of them, the empty room they had passed by, could serve for smaller, more private parties, but when a large group of drinkers descended on Skal's house, he opened up the courtyard area at the back to accommodate the extra guests.

At the far end of the courtyard a long counter had been set up under a lean-to shale roof. It was from here that Skal served his brews of ciders and ales to his guests. Two helpers, a man and a woman, were stationed alongside Skal, busily pouring drinks for the thirsty traders and other assembled folk.

Hedamon, obviously a frequent visitor to Skal's house, called out to some of the men around the serving counter and was answered in turn with varying degrees of greeting, ranging from lukewarm hellos to icy-cold stares. A few men noticeably turned their backs when they saw Hedamon. It was at that point that Piemur thought it prudent to step away from the older man so he didn't limit his options for gathering information. It wasn't hard to distance himself from Hedamon: Piemur wasn't even sure if the man was still coherent after their walk through the fresh evening air; his speech had degenerated noticeably, and he swayed continually from foot to foot as if he stood on an oceangoing vessel. When Hedamon bellowed out an order for drinks above the noise of the crowd, one of the servers behind the counter gestured with a nod of his chin toward Piemur who, sensing the perfect opportunity, made a shrugging motion with his shoulders, shook his head, stretched his lips wide over his closed mouth, and raised his brows in a sheepish expression; at the same time, he darted a glance in Hedamon's direction as if to suggest that he hadn't a clue about the identity of the man standing next to him.

His ploy worked and the server promptly placed a single glass of ale on the counter and then quickly moved away to take the next order. As Hedamon bellowed again, trying to attract the server's attention for a second glass, Piemur ducked in behind a group of large traders dressed in heavy furs and slipped into an empty, snug little booth positioned out of Hedamon's line of sight.

He sat in the enclosed space soaking in the sounds and trying to pick up on snippets of conversation that floated across the courtyard in his direction. The fur traders, talking in their deep, resonating voices about their next port of call, drowned out the chatter of the other patrons. Thankfully, they were frugal men and only stayed for the one drink before vacating the premises and freeing up the space for a new batch of drinkers. A server interrupted Piemur's solitude to clear away several empty glasses and offered to bring Piemur a drink if he wished. But Piemur only ordered a small glass of cider, not wanting to risk getting drunk and missing out on any potentially noteworthy snippets of information.

Apart from the occasional curious patron who popped a head into the booth to see who its occupants were, it turned out to be the perfect hiding place from which to eavesdrop on nearby conversations.

His ears pricked up and he grew very still when he could've sworn he heard a voice say "Lord Meron." Trying to quiet his breathing so he could hear better, Piemur leaned back against the booth's partition, closed his eyes, and concentrated on listening. There it was again: the long-dead Lord Meron's name!

"Meron said he'd behest *me* that parcel of land near the high ground bordering Ruatha! But then the old bollox recanted."

"I'll bet he promised that same piece of ground to every single one of us," another voice proclaimed bitterly.

"For certain he was no good at keeping his word, and far better at stringing us all along for his own use."

"He's wuined us all, is what he's done," a third voice piped up. "Why, I had the chance to take hold of land my mothuh's bwother offered. But Lawd Mewon kept danglin' his promises in fwont of me in that way of his, the malice-widden old git, telling me not to settle for less than I deserved. So I wefused my uncle's offuh, and he gave the land to someone else!" The third speaker clearly struggled to pronounce *R*'s.

"Listen," a deeper voice commanded. "We know too well what Lord Meron did to us all. We can talk it to death but it won't change anything. We have to *do* something about it or give over the belly-aching once and for all. I don't know about you lot, but me and Serra have had enough talk."

Piemur nearly gasped. He had heard that name before! Toolan had spoken about his cousin Serra. Piemur quickly silenced his own thoughts, determined not to miss a single word the men uttered.

The deep voice continued: "If you're in with us, say so now or stop wasting our time. We all worked hard to prove our worth, and little thanks we got for it. Nothing but empty promises, and then when that old fart finally died, we were cast aside and forgotten. No one's going to give us land—as is our right—so we'll just have to take matters into our own hands."

There were a few low murmurs in response, and then the speech-impeded voice said something too low for Piemur to hear. Another man excused himself from the group, claiming he wanted to wait and see how matters panned out.

Piemur wished he could leave the safety of his little booth to see what the men looked like, but the need to hear more of what they had to say was far greater, so he remained where he was. With any luck, when they were leaving Skal's he'd get the chance to follow them out of the brewhouse and match the faces to the voices.

The group of men moved away from Piemur, their numbers re-duced, possibly by half, he reckoned, and he could no longer hear what they were saying. Were they still in the brewhouse yard, he worried, or had they all left? Piemur didn't want to miss any of their talk, but he couldn't be too obvious and brazenly follow them around. There was nothing for it: He'd have to play the drunkard in the hope the men would see no threat in his behavior and carry on with their conversation.

Piemur pulled the soft cap down firmly on his head, slopped a little cider onto his tunic and boots, and then pulled the collar of his jacket up around his ears. In his best imitation of a legless drunk, he tottered out of the booth, cup in hand, and made the drunk's equivalent of a straight line for the service counter, zigging and zagging a little as he walked. He completely ignored the men, now numbering only three, he noted from the corner of his eye, and continued toward the counter with what he hoped looked like great determination.

He ordered another glass of cider, a large one this time, so as to appear fully committed to furthering his state of inebriation, and then made an impressive show of looking for someone around the courtyard before finally taking a seat at a table beside a brazier that was near to where the three men were now seated. Pretending to take a long pull from his glass, he then leaned back in his seat, resting the glass on his chest. He nodded slightly from time to time as he peered around the courtyard, an asinine grin on his face. Moments later, he allowed his chin to settle on his chest and let his glass list slightly in his hand as he feigned sleep.

"Are you certain we should go for Ruatha?" Piemur heard one of the men ask in a hushed tone. "Crom's closer."

"Have you seen those men Lord Nessel has holding with him? Some of 'em are as big as herdbeast bulls! Nah, I'd put my chances on Ruatha—the Hold is barely guarded, if at all," the deep-voiced man said.

"That young dragon-lord spends his time flittin' here an' there, doing nothin' for his Hold. What a waste! Who'd miss him?" another voice said.

"Aye, but his connections make him that extra bit special for our purposes."

Piemur nearly sucked in his breath and was hard-pressed to keep up his pretense of slumber.

"Might make 'em sit up and take—" the deep-voiced man continued, but his words were suddenly drowned out as Hedamon shouted from several paces away: "There you are! Thought I'd lost ye! It's your round for the drink."

Piemur felt like groaning. Thinking fast, he guessed that now Hedamon had drawn attention to him it was probably best if he didn't give the three men an opportunity to scrutinize him too closely. He reacted quickly, harrumphing and clearing his throat as he stood up, turning away from the three men as he left his seat and swaying slightly when Hedamon laid a possessive arm across his shoulders. Piemur didn't resist, allowing the older man to lead him back toward the bar.

What can I do now? Piemur thought frantically. He was too far away to hear what the other men were saying, and even if he could manage to lead Hedamon back to his table, the older man would drown out all other conversation or, worse, drive the three men from the courtyard altogether. *Think, think!* Piemur ordered himself.

Piemur pushed his half-full glass at Hedamon's chest, gesturing for him to take it before he staggered away from the older man, claiming, "I'm gonna be sick."

Keeping up his drunken pretense, he half staggered, half tottered across the courtyard and into Skal's house. Once over the threshold, he quickly made his way through the hallway and out into the night. He would find somewhere to hide in wait for the three men, then follow in the hope that they would talk more about their plans for Lord Jaxom. It was a weak plan, but it was the only thing he could think of.

In the end, the three men came out of Skal's house and split up, two of them walking together in one direction and the other walking on his own the opposite way. Piemur felt he had failed: He hadn't found out anything truly useful. But then, after the men made their farewells for the night, the lone man stopped and called out to the other two.

"Jerrol!"

The deep-voiced man stopped and turned, his sullen-looking companion stopping, too.

"I've changed my mind," the lone man said. "You can count me in. Meet at your place in two nights' time?"

"Yes, Jentis," Jerrol replied with a nod, and then he lifted one hand briefly and continued on his journey.

Making a snap decision, Piemur followed Jerrol and his companion. Even if he didn't hear more about their plan, at least he now knew the names of the men and that they planned to meet again in two nights. And soon he'd know exactly where that meeting was going to take place.

Jerrol and his companion walked for almost an hour, leading Piemur up to the edge of the settlement of dwellings close to the ramparts of Nabol Hold. When Piemur finally saw them enter a small cothold, he retraced his steps to Skal's and didn't have much farther to go before he was back at Marek's cot. It was very late at night when Piemur wearily climbed up the ladder into the loft and flopped onto the straw. He was physically worn out but had, fortunately, walked off the effects of the cider, and now his head was ringing with thoughts.

He wanted to tell Sebell what he'd found out, but where was Farli? She was never around when he needed her. He steadied his breathing to slow his thoughts and then pushed out hard for his little queen, calling her to him with quiet urgency. But as his breathing steadied and Farli failed to show up, fatigue overtook him, and Piemur couldn't fight against his body's need for sleep.

A single, solitary shape—an egg, bathed in darkness—edged into his mind. He felt cold. Suddenly the face of a dragon flashed before him, eyes spinning bright red with anger and a gush of fiery breath spraying from his mouth. Then the dragon faded away, and Piemur saw the lone egg once more before it, too, faded away and he drifted into darkness again.

A muffled chirp and then a twitter filtered through his hearing, gently pulling Piemur up from his sleep. Something warm pushed against his shoulder. He pushed back. As he grew more alert, he realized that whatever was pushing against his shoulder extended over the crown of his head in a curve, touching either ear. He opened his eyes and lay still for a moment, trying to get his bearings. Had he really seen an egg, or was it a dream? And what was all this about a flaming dragon? As he rolled onto his side, the faint, sweet-musky scent of fire-lizard filled his nostrils, and without looking he knew Farli had found him and curled up around his head during the night.

"Hey, Farli," he whispered. The little queen sat up and stretched slowly, her back arching languorously, the motion extending through her front and back legs as she opened her eyes and peered at Piemur. She chirped once and then her eyes quickly changed from a calm cobalt color to anxious amber.

"What is it, Farli? Why are you so upset?" He reached a hand tenderly toward his fire-lizard and rubbed just above her eye ridges, trying to calm her, but the same image of an egg in darkness and angry dragons flashed through his head again.

"You've been sharing your dreams with me, I see. Well, Farli, I can't explain it, but if the egg you're seeing is what I think it is, you needn't worry any longer. The egg is safe. D'you hear me, girl? The egg is safe." Piemur reached for his bag, quickly writing a message on a piece of cloth with his scriber.

"I need you to take a message to Sebell. It's important," he said, looking fixedly at Farli as he showed her an image of Sebell. "Take this to Sebell, Farli, and then come back to me." He pushed the image of Sebell at her and then, pushing his thoughts harder, he showed Farli an image of her flying back to him. The little fire-lizard squawked once, as if he'd pushed a little too hard, but she hopped onto his arm. As soon as Piemur had secured the message to Farli's leg, the little queen flew out of the building and was gone.

Piemur didn't have to walk far from Marek's cothold to their meeting point, on the edge of a heavy copse of trees, and was there when Sebell arrived, riding behind the Fort dragonrider, T'ledon, on his blue dragon, Serith. Piemur offered a respectful bow to the blue dragon and his rider and then nodded to Sebell, who was attired in a tunic made from the distinctive blue cloth of the Harper

Hall. It had been a very long time since Piemur had seen his mentor in clothing other than nondescript holder or trader garb.

"Piemur," Sebell called when Serith touched down. "Tell Farli to meet us back at Fort. The Masterharper wants a full report from you, in person." Sebell offered Piemur a hand onto Serith's back.

Once Piemur had settled on the blue's back, Sebell tapped T'ledon on the shoulder, and the dragonrider signaled to his dragon. Serith, in no way burdened by the extra weight, loped several paces away from the trees and then made his leap up into the air, unfurling his wings before beating them down to gain lift. It was a brief flight *between* from Nabol to Fort Hold; nevertheless Piemur felt the cold clamping into his bones as he counted to three, waiting for the moment they'd leave the dark nothingness and arrive back in the light again.

Piemur was surprised, when they'd made their way through the Great Hall and into the Masterharper's workroom, to find not only Master Robinton but also N'ton, Menolly, J'hon, Candler, and Finder. The group exchanged greetings and, at the Masterharper's urgings, helped themselves to steaming cups of *klah* and warm bread rolls.

They conversed amicably as they sipped their *klah*. Piemur hungrily ate two bread rolls and gulped down his *klah* between mouthfuls. Once replete, Piemur asked Menolly and Candler if they'd found out who had returned Ramoth's egg, but no one knew.

Piemur was relieved when he heard that Menolly and the other members of the group had experienced exactly the same frantic behavior from their fire-lizards, and that they had also been shown identical images of an egg in darkness along with flaming dragons. Clearly, Farli wasn't the only one to have been deeply affected by the theft of Ramoth's egg. At least the fire-lizards could settle down now that the danger was over.

"Very good," Robinton said, beckoning to the group for silence, "everyone's here so we may as well begin. N'ton informs me that Lord Jaxom is suitably occupied in the company of Lytol and Brand, so we need not worry about his safety while we convene this meeting." He paused for a moment and then looked at Piemur intently. "What have you discovered in Nabol, Journeyman Piemur?"

Piemur dove right in: "About half a dozen men met in Skal's brewhouse last night to discuss their lack of holdings and how Lord Meron had deprived them of their right to hold land. It's safe to say that they all still feel hard done by. But when talk turned more serious, such as how they could—" He hesitated, trying to find the appropriate word. "—*acquire* lands of their own, three of the men had no stomach for it and left the group soon after." Piemur glanced at the Masterharper, realizing as he paused to gather his thoughts that the room had gone completely silent. He looked over at Menolly, who winked at him encouragingly from her seat next to Sebell. Then he looked to N'ton and J'hon, who stood side by side, both nodding at him to continue; and then he glanced at Candler and Finder and saw something in their expressions he'd never noticed before: respect for his harper skills, not merely his singing.

"When the three remaining men resumed their conversation, I only had a short amount of time to hear what they were talking about before I was interrupted. But the gist was this." He held up his hands, touching one finger at a time as he listed off the key points of the Nabolese men's discussion: "Although Crom Hold is closer, they still think it's best to take their chances with Ruatha because they reckon the Hold isn't guarded well enough." Piemur saw Robinton and Sebell exchange glances before returning their attention back to him.

He went on, "They know that Lord Jaxom has been distracted. In their opinion, he does a scant amount of work for his Hold. One of the men said something very curious—that Lord Jaxom has 'connections which make him that extra bit special' for their purposes. He probably meant his blood connection to Weyrwoman Lessa. Unfortunately, I was interrupted at that point and couldn't eavesdrop safely any longer."

Piemur could see the disappointment in Master Robinton's eyes when he looked at him, so he continued quickly. "I followed the men when they left the brewhouse and heard the names of two of them:

Jerrol and Jentis. They made a plan to meet again in two nights in Jerrol's hold." He dropped his hands at his sides, his report complete.

"Very good, Piemur," Robinton said. "We can use this!"

The room, which moments before had been silent and still, erupted into excited chatter, and Piemur realized with a dawning sense of awe that he could now command the attention of those whom he once thought he would never be equal to. The realization made him glow with a burgeoning sense of pride.

Robinton cleared his throat, subtly calling everyone back to order.

"Piemur, I want you to go back to Nabol and try and get more information when those men meet again. And I think Sebell should go with you. Two men can do twice as much as one." The Masterharper didn't have to say what everyone was thinking: that there was safety in numbers, and that the youthful form of Piemur, by all accounts, was no match for three deeply disgruntled men should the situation turn sour.

"Menolly, I want you to continue to guard Jaxom with the roster we already have in place. Finder and Candler can relieve you when necessary—or when the young lord grows tired of you tagging around after him," Robinton added, a note of mirth in his voice. Menolly chuckled.

"N'ton and J'hon," the Masterharper said, looking at the two dragonriders, "can we count on you to help Menolly and Finder keep Lord Jaxom protected?" They nodded again, and Robinton was on the point of continuing when N'ton held up a hand. The expression on his face changed suddenly, and Piemur knew that the Fort Weyrleader was speaking with Lioth. J'hon's face, too, had that distracted, almost dazed look that meant his dragon was speaking to him.

"Ramoth calls us," N'ton said, and Piemur instinctively held his breath, fearful that more bad news had come from Benden. Everyone else in the room stood perfectly still, obviously thinking the same. Then both N'ton and J'hon smiled.

"We're called to Benden for the Impression. The queen egg is ready to hatch."

Once again Robinton's work room erupted into a melody of talking voices.

"Master Robinton?" N'ton asked, a smile spreading across his handsome face as he gestured to the harper. "It would be our great pleasure if you'd accompany Lioth and me to Benden. As usual," he added.

"I'd like Sebell, Menolly, and Piemur to come along, N'ton. Additional pairs of harper eyes and ears will be useful in judging the prevailing mood in Benden. Things have been too fraught there of late. Candler and Finder, you two will have to keep an eye on Jaxom for now," Robinton instructed.

The group quickly disbanded, filing out of the Masterharper's rooms to retrieve their flying gear before reassembling in the courtyard of the Harper Hall. Robinton and Menolly would fly on Lioth with N'ton, and Sebell and Piemur would go with J'hon on Mirth.

Piemur could hardly believe his luck! Earlier in the day, he'd thought he'd be stuck in Nabol with no respite in sight. Now he was going to a Hatching! Maybe there *were* some advantages to doing all this legwork for the Master.

Farli chirped in the air above Piemur, and Menolly, who was walking ahead with the Masterharper, turned. "You'd best tell your little queen to stay behind, Piemur. We haven't the time to band her now, and she'd receive a harsh welcome if she arrived in Benden as is. I'm leaving mine behind, even though they *are* banded." Four of Menolly's fire-lizards were flitting around overhead, and Piemur noticed they all wore bands with harper blue on top of Fort's background of lattice yellow. "Best not to upset the Weyrwoman," Menolly explained.

"Menolly's right, Piemur," Robinton added. "It's the least we can do to show our respect to Benden in light of what's happened. I know I shall feel naked without my Zair as company, but it must be so." He looked up at N'ton, who had already mounted Lioth and was clipping extra flying straps onto the dragon's harness to accommodate the additional passengers. "Are we going to arrive there in good time, N'ton? I don't want to be late for *this* Hatching."

Piemur and Sebell were standing behind the Masterharper and heard him murmur quietly, "I'd do anything to ease matters with Benden Weyr right now."

"Your concern is appreciated, Masterharper. Lioth is certain we'll arrive in good time," N'ton replied.

Piemur thought he saw one of N'ton's brows lift briefly, and he wondered if the dragonrider had also heard the Master's heartfelt wish. Sebell subtly nudged Piemur's arm. So Sebell had seen that momentary acknowledgment from the dragonrider as well!

"This will blow over soon," N'ton assured Robinton, reaching down a hand to the older man while Lioth dipped his shoulder and proffered a foreleg to help him mount.

Ha! Piemur mused. So he was right: N'ton *had* heard what the Master had said.

"I cannot imagine, N'ton, what will ensue if this queen does not hatch whole and hearty, or if she fails to make a fast and firm Impression."

"Never fear," N'ton said, and Piemur watched with pride as the dragonrider bowed, a gesture of high regard for the foremost custodian of Pern's heritage, the man who held the welfare of every person, not merely those of his own craft, close to his heart.

EIGHT

THE GROUP FROM FORT WEYR AND THE HARPER HALL WERE NOT among the first guests to arrive at Benden Weyr, so the lower tiers of the viewing stands were nearly full when they made their way across the Bowl to the Hatching Grounds. Master Robinton took the seat reserved for him, and N'ton and Menolly flanked him on either side. Piemur and Sebell happily took seats farther up the viewing stands. Any seat at a Hatching, no matter how far from the floor of the sands, was a treasured one, Piemur mused as he rubbed his hands together in eager anticipation and looked around at all the open, expectant faces, nodding or smiling in greeting to his immediate neighbors.

Within the hour, dragons from every Weyr across the northern hemisphere of Pern had delivered all the guests invited to Benden with an alacrity that even the efficiency-obsessed Mastersmith, Fandarel, would've deemed remarkable.

Ramoth, the senior queen dragon in Benden Weyr, stood protectively on the hot sands of the Hatching Grounds, close to the queen egg. It had been pushed away from all the other eggs in the clutch, which were still many days away from hatching. Piemur had heard that Ramoth was the largest dragon on all of Pern, and as she stood over her egg she made an awe-inspiring sight, her golden hide gleaming with good health and the muscles of her huge body rippling with vigor and strength. Piemur couldn't help but make a mental comparison between the queen he saw in front of him now, vibrant and powerful, and the lackluster, unhealthy state of Mardra's queen, Loranth.

Up on the ledge of the Weyr, where all the other dragons perched, he could see F'lar's dragon, Mnementh, who was Ramoth's mate, watching her, his eyes an intense shade of green.

Ramoth lifted her huge, wedge-shaped head and looked around intently at her clutch, her whirling green eyes tinged with a faint shade of mauve. She was still uneasy, Piemur guessed, and no wonder: It had been a tense wait, these past few days, to see whether her most precious egg had suffered any lasting damage from its travels.

An imperceptible vibration traveled along the hot sands, and Piemur could feel the slightest of shudders coursing through the stands up to where he sat. The vibrations came from the mottled egg, which had begun to ripple with slight tremors. Without realizing it, Piemur reached out a hand and gripped Sebell's forearm; the older harper glanced at him quickly, then back at the egg, a smile of anticipation on his face.

Ramoth turned her head to where Lessa waited, and then the Weyrwoman of Benden strode to the edge of the Hatching Ground sands and stared at her queen. Lessa's long dark hair had been scraped back severely from her face—revealing her unusual, fine features—then plaited and twisted in a tortuously intricate weave that fell down her back in a heavy coil. The style expressed the stark frame of mind she'd been in since the theft of the egg. Her light-green robes hid her slight, wiry frame, and while there may not have been an extra pinch of flesh on Lessa's small figure, she stood tall, taut, and ready to spring into action at any moment.

As if prompted by some silent cue, several dragons filled the air with a few short bugling bursts. It was the noise the dragons always made to warn when a new queen was about to hatch.

The egg began to tremble and rock periodically, but no dragon emerged. A low thrumming noise, not as startling as the earlier trumpeted bugling, filled the Weyr as the dragons gave voice to the imminent arrival of a new queen and the further perpetuation of their species. The massive cavern, which had been an oppressive and unwelcoming place since the theft, and only an hour beforehand had felt dark and all a-hush with suspicion and fear, now buzzed with new energy as riders, weyrfolk, and all the assembled guests waited in silent anticipation. There was an indefinable energy buzzing all around him that Piemur knew was unique to dragonkind. He felt infected by it and awash with a greater sense of his own self-purpose.

Every Hatching was an important event for the dragons and their riders. No matter that this Hatching was unprecedented, like all Hatchings it afforded each rider and dragon the opportunity to renew their own bonds, as they vicariously relived the moment when they had made Impression with their own partners. Even the other attendees, from weyrfolk to lords, crafters to drudges, had the privilege of bearing witness to another wholly uplifting and uniquely special union.

Piemur saw a flurry of activity to one side of the Grounds and wrenched his gaze from Ramoth. The Weyrlingmaster and his crew hurried to the edge of the hot sands, offering last-minute tips to the female Candidates. Ramoth stood immobile next to the egg, hissing and rumbling loudly as her head whipped about, eyeing the increasing activity that dared threaten the safety of her progeny.

The dragons' thrumming increased in tempo and volume, adding to the sense of urgency. Only once before in the memory of any dragonrider living in the Present Pass, when Ramoth herself had hatched, did the safe Impression of a queen hold such importance to all the people of Pern. This Hatching would not culminate in the exultant celebrations enjoyed after a typical Hatching. In this situation it was best, Piemur ruminated with no little irony, not to count on anything until the egg had hatched.

The thrumming noise seemed to intensify the air of anticipation coursing around the cavern, and the sounds of excitement coming from the assembled guests rose and fell, as if on a wave.

Only ten female Candidates had been brought to Benden on Search, readied hastily when it was apparent the egg had been forced to harden, and thus hatch, before the others in the clutch. A few of the Candidates were slightly older than the others, having been added to the group at the eleventh hour when it was deemed that as much variance of choice as possible for the unique egg would be a sensible measure. It was imperative that the little dragonet, once safely hatched, made a decisive Impression.

The thrumming noise from the dragons suddenly increased in volume, all but drowning out the audience. It was the perfect cue, and an appropriate hush fell over the crowd.

Next to the egg, Ramoth hissed menacingly as the female Candidates were ushered from where they stood in the wings of the Hatching Grounds onto the hot sands. Even from his seat higher up in the tiers, Piemur could have sworn that Ramoth was scrutinizing each Candidate individually.

As tradition dictated, the Candidates were all dressed in identical plain, unbelted, white woolen robes; it was the mental energy and spirit of character that steered a dragonet toward her new lifemate, not the Candidate's physical appearance. Encouraged by shooing motions from the Weyrlingmaster, the Candidates nervously moved farther onto the sands. It wasn't that they didn't *want* the chance of Impressing a queen dragon, but the stories they'd heard about how enraged Ramoth had been since the egg's theft fueled their thoughts, and understandably the terrifying sight of the huge and menacing Ramoth standing in front of them now wasn't helping. It appeared, even after all the turmoil of the egg's theft and return, that Benden's senior queen dragon was intent on guarding her progeny up to the very last moment. The thrumming noise from all the other dragons grew more intense as the tempo increased.

Piemur watched as Lessa left her place in the seating area and walked to the edge of the Hatching Grounds to stand opposite the Candidates, her arms crossed in front of her body. It was clear to Piemur that, between Ramoth's hissing and darting head and Lessa's severe countenance, the Candidates were now too scared to move any closer.

Piemur saw F'lar as he slowly stood up from his seat, scrutinizing his mate's queen. Brushing a heavy lock of dark hair from his eyes, he hastily walked over to join his weyrmate on the hot sands.

When he gently touched her arm, Lessa turned her face to look at F'lar, a deep scowl clouding her features. What F'lar had to say to her Piemur could only guess, but it aptly served its purpose for, in a rare gesture of deference, Lessa slowly lowered her crossed arms, letting them fall limply by her sides. As F'lar walked back to his seat, Lessa's shoulders relaxed. Looking up at Ramoth, she raised one arm, then let it fall very slowly back to her side as she lowered her head, silently commanding her queen to retreat and let fate play out its plan.

Ramoth threw her huge head up toward the vaulted ceiling of the cavern as she roared loudly in defiance, pouring out all the pent-up frustration, anger, and insult she had borne over the last several days. The watching dragons abruptly ceased their instinctive thrumming. Ramoth's head shook violently as she bellowed, sending shivers down Piemur's back. He felt as if he understood what Ramoth was saying: that no queen dragon of Pern should ever have to fear for the safety of one of her own, not when the purpose of all dragons was so noble and selfless and true.

Her roar slowly died away and then Ramoth lowered her head, shaking it again vigorously before she blew heavily through her nostrils. She looked at Lessa, eyes whirling fiercely, and then made a single soft and forlorn cry and slowly backed out of the Hatching Grounds, relinquishing her precious egg. Piemur felt a lump forming in his throat but quickly gulped it down.

As if on cue, a loud crack rang out in the cavern and the egg rocked forcefully. The hushed crowd *ooh*ed audibly at the sound, in near-perfect unison, and then quickly fell silent.

Piemur heard muffled sounds coming from the edge of the hot sands as the Weyrlingmaster flapped his arms and cajoled the ten Candidates to move toward the queen egg. Two girls, far younger than the other Candidates, clung to each other as they wept in terror. Then one of them screamed and fell down in a puff of white wool, dragging her friend with her to huddle on the hot sands in a sobbing heap. Three other Candidates bravely stepped forward, ready to present themselves to the little queen when she finally cracked through the wall of her shell. Two of them, both blond and blue-eyed with plump, pink skin, looked so similar that Piemur was certain they must be sisters or, more likely, twins. They held hands, buoying each other to be brave through that simple contact. The third Candidate was older than the twin girls, for the soft and tender look of youth had all but left her face. Her expression remained somber as she tried to maintain some degree of calm in the midst of so much fear.

The egg rocked again, harder, and a crack appeared low down along its side. The last five Candidates stood immobile in a loose circle some distance back from the egg, reluctant to take any further steps forward. No doubt they were remembering the stories of dragonets who, as they lurched about in their first moments after hatching, had inflicted deep wounds on Candidates with their razor-sharp talons, mauling them unintentionally, some with everlasting or even fatal consequences.

One girl, who had been repeatedly pushed forward from the edge of the hot sands by the dragonrider who had found her on Search, cried out as the egg rocked again. Then she turned, screaming, and ran in blind terror from the Hatching Grounds, leaving behind her one chance of becoming the lifelong partner of a queen dragon. Piemur's heart went out to her: The loss was something she would live with for the rest of her life.

The egg cracked further and then rolled forward, leaving a large piece of shell behind on the sand. Piemur had returned his attention to the closest Candidates and saw the older one suddenly frown. She tilted her head to one side as if, Piemur reckoned, straining to hear something. She stared hard at the egg, and the twin girls moved closer, still holding hands. The older girl continued to peer intently at the egg and then, surprisingly, crouched down on her heels. Piemur saw a look of understanding wash across her face, and he moved to the edge of his seat as she dove forward toward the egg, frantically shoveling sand away from its base.

"Help me!" she cried. "She's lying upside down and can't move her head anymore to break free of the shell!" A rumbling of concern came from the crowd, added to the renewed thrumming of the dragons that ringed the Grounds. Piemur saw Lessa take several steps toward the Candidates and then stop, allowing the unfolding tableau to play out as it would, without any help from her.

Without hesitation, the blond girls answered the desperate plea of the older Candidate and flung themselves to their knees, helping to clear the hot sand back in a semicircular indentation at the base of the egg.

"We have to push it back!" the older girl cried. "Help me, please!"

Three pairs of hands pressed firmly against the top part of the egg and rocked it, trying to force it to roll backward. Seemingly of its own accord, the egg suddenly rocked to and fro and then settled into place, resting right-side up. But as Piemur looked on, to his horror he saw that the older Candidate had lost her footing when the egg righted itself, and fallen face-first onto the sands, her forearms trapped under the egg.

A great crack sundered the egg one last time, and the glistening, golden queen tumbled out, rolling over the fallen girl. Piemur couldn't believe it: Was the older girl really going to be injured after she'd helped the little queen? A profound silence filled the huge cavern, and Piemur later claimed he could hear the sound of his own heart beating as every man, woman, and dragon watched with bated breath.

The twins stood stock-still, frozen in crouched positions, expressions of shock on their faces and their arms spread out wide as they stared at the little golden dragon. The other Candidates, as if released from some torpor, moved forward to form a close ring around the dragonet as she walked toward them, her tail trailing over the fallen girl, who still lay prone and quite likely injured.

A piteous warbling rolled up out of the little queen's throat, terminating in a cry that sounded like a lament. She opened her mouth fully, her head thrown up, to reveal a fierce-looking set of teeth. She stumbled forward clumsily, moving her head from side to side, searching among the Candidates for the one she had to Impress. But where was she? Another soft cry, and then a deeply piteous moan rolled out of the queen's throat and she turned on her haunches, knocking down four Candidates as she swung about, desperately searching among them.

Noticing that the fallen Candidate was struggling to move, one of the twins bravely ran over to help her onto her side. There was a loud intake of gasped breath from the assembled crowd. Piemur watched, transfixed, as the little queen swiveled around and turned to face the two girls, her head held low.

Caught between the little queen and the fallen Candidate, the girl who had run to help fell backward in fright, landing bottom-first. The little queen lunged, and the girl scuttled farther backward and to one side, crablike, dragging herself through the sand in her haste to avoid being trampled. The other girl still lay on the sands, struggling to draw air into her lungs.

As the dragonet's momentum moved her directly toward the winded girl, Piemur held his breath, terrified that the poor girl would be seriously injured. But just at the last moment, the drag-onet stopped, head low, blowing air through her nostrils loudly, her eyes whirling a dazzling shade of turquoise blue. A little soblike croon escaped her throat. And then, in the profound silence that filled the cavernous Weyr, a single voice spoke in a wondrous tone.

"But you've *found* me, Nimath! I've been right here all the time, my beautiful queen."

The dragonet suddenly lurched forward, breaking the tender tableau, causing Piemur and everyone else to gasp again. But the queen carefully planted first one foot and then the other on either side of the girl, and then she lowered her head, gently blowing air through her nostrils. The girl raised her arms and laid her hands on either side of the little queen's head, caressing the glistening, golden hide as she rose to her knees and rested her forehead on the bridge of the queen's nose. The new partners remained motionless for several moments, content in silent communion.

The blond girl, who still sat sprawled on the sand a little dis-tance from the queen dragon and her new mate, suddenly burst into tears as the tension of the drama she'd been party to was finally de-fused. But slowly a watery smile spread across her face, and Piemur could see her exultation at bearing intimate witness to such a momentous Impression.

The viewing stands erupted with the sounds of happy people relieved of their worry. Piemur knew he was beaming from ear to ear as he reached for Sebell's arm once again, flushed with the joy he'd witnessed, and in which he'd shared. Sebell was smiling, too, his eyes shining and bright.

Released from the thrall of the Impression, the guests in the viewing stands lingered in their seats, chatting excitedly to one another, or they stood and stretched, turning to their neighbors to laugh or hug; some stamped their feet or clapped; others gently wept with joy, the dragonriders among them almost certainly reliving the moment that they, too, had first made Impression with their own beloved dragons.

Piemur, a smile still plastered across his face, watched as the Weyrlingmaster hurried forward to assist Nimath's mate, who proudly told him that her name was Mikay and that she was from a mountain hold in Crom. Carefully helping Mikay to her feet he was reassured, as was everyone else, when she calmly stated that she wasn't really hurt at all, just a little squashed and only slightly bruised.

The new queen and her rider stood together, Mikay never letting her hand leave her dragon's hide as Nimath crooned, ravenous. It was a piteous noise and Mikay immediately assuaged it with another gentle caress. They moved forward together as the Weyrlingmaster ushered the new queen and her rider toward their quarters, where Nimath would be given her first feed from Mikay's own hand.

As the tension that had mounted on the Hatching Grounds was dissipating, Piemur let go of Sebell's arm again as he looked around the great cavern. Lessa, he saw, had finally succumbed to the anxiety she had endured since the egg was stolen, allowing the taut fibers in her body to slowly uncoil. She stood alone, as she had throughout the Impression, several paces to the front of the viewing stands. He watched as the Weyrwoman of Benden lifted up one outstretched arm, palm open, to where her huge golden dragon waited on the edge of the Hatching Grounds, and slowly nodded. Their bond,

Piemur knew, was being reinforced, as it was every time they witnessed a new Impression.

Then Piemur saw Lessa slowly turn around, searching among the crowd. F'lar walked toward her, a tender smile on his face. Lessa stopped in front of him, leaning toward him in a rare moment of public intimacy as she tilted her head back to look up into his face. A lock of his hair fell forward, obscuring one eye, as F'lar looked down at her, and Lessa smiled as she pushed back the lock with one hand and stepped into his embrace. Then she gently touched his cheek, and he bent to kiss her on the mouth. Piemur watched Lessa relax in F'lar's arms as he kissed one eye and then the other, finally pulling her against his chest to hold her close.

Piemur wondered, somewhat embarrassed at witnessing this tender exchange, whether anyone on the Hatching Grounds other than F'lar and himself had seen the tears of relief that washed down Lessa's cheeks before she pressed her face against F'lar's chest.

When Nimath and Mikay had been ushered off to their weyr and the resident weyrfolk began to disperse from the Hatching Grounds, Piemur and Sebell slowly made their way from their seats higher up in the viewing stands to join the Masterharper, N'ton, and Menolly where they waited down below.

It was taken for granted that none of the usual post-Hatching celebrations would be observed after Nimath's Impression, but rather they would be delayed until the remaining eggs in the clutch hatched. No one could fault Benden's Weyrleaders in that decision, as none could have foretold whether the outcome of this Hatching would be a disaster or a success. But relief and exhilaration were both palpable in the air, and Piemur was pretty sure that plenty of weyrfolk would be celebrating anyway, if only in small ways.

He was surprised to find Menolly, N'ton, and the Masterharper talking among themselves with worried looks on their faces. As he and Sebell joined them, Menolly greeted them with, "Have you seen Jaxom?" Her voice was colored with anxiety. "He should be here—it's his duty. But we can't see him anywhere."

Piemur stiffened in surprise and dismay. Shading his eyes with one hand, he began frantically to scan the stands, but Sebell stopped him with a gentle pressure on his arm and a nod toward N'ton. The Fort Weyrleader's face had taken on the distracted expression that meant he was speaking with his dragon.

After what felt to Piemur like forever, N'ton's expression cleared and he looked directly at the others. "Lioth says Ruth is asleep in his weyr in Ruatha. Lioth cannot wake him, but Jaxom *must* be with him."

"We must assume nothing, Weyrleader," Robinton said forcefully. "We've witnessed the circumvention of a hideous tragedy today with the safe hatching and Impression of the new queen. We cannot let another disaster jeopardize the tenuous balance we have so carefully nurtured over the Turns." The Masterharper shook his head. "By the First Egg, Lord Jaxom *must* be all right, though what could have possessed him to miss such an important Hatching doesn't bear consideration. N'ton, quickly, take me to Ruatha! We must be certain that Jaxom is, indeed, safe and with his dragon."

He almost turned to leave, but then paused. "Menolly, my dear, come with me, please. Sebell, we cannot all descend on Ruatha, so you and Piemur should wait here until we let you know, *hopefully,* that everything is fine."

Not long after, Piemur and Sebell were back at Fort Hold, having flown there on Mirth after a very relieved J'hon informed them that Jaxom *had* been found in Ruatha. But the young lord's safety aside, it was still worrisome that he had missed an important event like a queen dragon's Hatching and Impression. If Masterharper Robinton hoped to convince the other Lord Holders to confirm Jaxom in his position, there could be no doubt in their minds about the young man's dedication and sense of responsibility. With no further information and deeply anxious to learn the whole story, Piemur and Sebell could do nothing but wait in the Great Hall, cups of *klah* in hand, and speculate about what might have happened.

By the time Menolly and N'ton arrived to fill them in, Piemur was buzzing with energy from one cup of *klah* too many. His leg bounced up and down and his fingers drummed the tabletop as Menolly told the tale.

"It was one of the most nerve-racking experiences I've ever had," she said. "When we arrived at Ruatha, all of us were hard-put to appear outwardly calm as we requested a meeting with Lord Jaxom and the Lord Warder, Lytol."

Piemur could see that Menolly was already assuming the harper role of storyteller as she recounted the events of their trip to Ruatha. She looked from one to the other of them, using that old harper trick of making each of her listeners feel as if she were talking to him alone. Her voice had a lilt to it; though not quite singsong, it flowed effortlessly and was wonderfully easy on the ear. Menolly chose her words well: They sounded practiced, as if she had scripted the story beforehand. Piemur found himself wishing that his own storytelling techniques were as well honed.

"After what seemed like an eternal wait, when a drudge, and then a steward came to speak to us, Lytol finally arrived. When he suggested that we wait in a small reception room nearby while he went to try to locate Jaxom, I was nearly fit to scream. None of us said it out loud, but I know we were all thinking the same thing: If even Lytol didn't know his ward's whereabouts, then where in the name of the First Egg *was* he?" Menolly's voice held all the strain she must have been feeling as she endured the suspense of waiting. She took in a long breath and then leaned forward.

"As we waited, even N'ton's nerves started to show. Why, he was twisting the fingers of his gloves so hard I thought he'd rip them clean off! And all Master Robinton could do was just sit immobile and ashen-faced in his chair." She looked to N'ton, who nodded in agreement.

"Then a drudge came into the room, startling us all half to death, and offered *klah*, which we refused. Who could drink *klah* at a time like that?"

"Was Lytol gone for very long, Menolly?" Piemur asked, feeling as if the tension they'd lived through was with them now.

"To be honest, Piemur, we probably didn't have very long to

wait at all. It just *seemed* like an eternity. I was the first to see Jaxom as he entered the room ahead of Lytol, and I think I must've said something out loud, because then N'ton swung around, saw Jaxom, and groaned."

"Why?" Sebell asked, looking to N'ton, not Menolly, for the answer.

"Because there was a fresh wound on Jaxom's face!" N'ton said. "At first glance I thought he'd been assaulted, but then I saw that it was actually threadscore."

"Threadscore!" Piemur and Sebell repeated in unison.

"Poor Master Robinton swiveled around in his chair so fast I thought he was going to be flung out of it!" Menolly added.

"The Masterharper did look surprised," N'ton agreed. "But Menolly sounded the most shocked of us all. Do you remember what you said? 'Jaxom, you're threadscored!' As if he wasn't already painfully aware of it!" Realizing that he'd embarrassed her, the Weyrleader smiled kindly at Menolly.

She rallied. "Well, I was shocked," she agreed. "I got so close to look at his wound, the poor man must've thought I was about to sit on him!" And then she laughed, shaking her head.

Piemur wasn't ready for levity. "But why would he take such a risk?" he asked earnestly.

"Believe me," Menolly said, nodding vigorously, "we all thought that very thing, and erupted into a barrage of questions about Ruth's health, and comments about Jaxom's recklessness."

"Where did he find Thread to fight?" Sebell asked, his voice very quiet. He looked to N'ton.

"I think he must've timed it. He *has* been pushing hard to take on more normal dragon duties with Ruth. In fairness to Jaxom and Lytol," N'ton said, glancing at Menolly to see if she agreed, "they answered or countered every one of our questions without batting an eyelid. Did you notice that, Menolly? How Lytol stood shoulder-to-shoulder with Jaxom? He was quite resolute and unapologetic. I've never seen their bond as strong before—like father and son."

"So, the young lord has taught his dragon to chew firestone and fight Thread. That's interesting," Sebell said, one brow arched.

Slowly, his lips curved up into a crooked smile. "Of course, his timing couldn't be any worse." Then he smiled broadly, and as Menolly and N'ton laughed at this play on words, Piemur finally broke out into a loud guffaw.

"It's moot, then," Sebell continued on a more somber note when their laughter had died down. "From what you've said, N'ton, there would be nothing to gain in alerting the Lord Warder to the threat that hangs over Jaxom from the men in Nabol."

"I honestly think this matter is best kept with as few of us as possible," N'ton said.

"But I feel the urgency to remove this threat against Jaxom has now increased," Sebell said. "Especially since the young lord's whereabouts couldn't be accounted for when we, ah, lost track of him. I'm sure the Masterharper has the same view." He placed a heavy hand on Piemur's shoulder. "I'm afraid you'll still have to go back to Nabol in time for tomorrow night's meeting, Piemur."

"Ah," Piemur said, frowning hugely.

"But I'll still be going with you. The sooner we take control of this trouble, the better. We'll use our fire-lizards to keep in touch."

"Speaking of fire-lizards, Sebell," Piemur said, looking around the Hall and then sucking in his breath slowly, "Farli might not be the best of help, I'm afraid. She's been really off color of late, and not at all reliable. I wonder if she's getting ready to—" But his words were cut off as Farli darted into the room and promptly landed on Piemur's shoulder, her eyes whirling a contented shade of blue as she rubbed her head against his cheek.

"She's made you eat your words, Piemur," Menolly said, and then laughed heartily. "That image of an egg and flaming dragons— was she showing that to you, too?"

When Piemur nodded, she flapped a hand at him as if his fire-lizard's behavior was nothing. "Everyone's fire-lizards were sharing the same images. It must've had something to do with the theft of the egg, or at least that's the best reason I can come up with. My lot settled down soon after Nimath made Impression. Master Robinton noticed it with his Zair, too."

"Well," Piemur said, rubbing the side of Farli's head gently, "it's good to have my old girl back again. You were behaving like a scatty wherry, my little friend." Farli cooed at him, her voice rising in a perfect trill to emphasize her point.

The Hall was steadily growing noisier as the residents of Fort Hold and the Harper Hall began to gather for their evening get-together. As usual, a large number of dragonriders from the Weyr were also arriving.

A young apprentice with bright eyes and a mop of short curly hair trotted up to Sebell with an ornately inlaid, twelve-string gitar and a flat drum in her hands, giggling nervously while she carefully handed over the instruments to the journeyman masterharper. Sebell placed the flat drum on the table and set himself to tuning the gitar while Menolly excused herself to retrieve her own instruments.

Piemur looked around the Hall, suddenly feeling ill at ease. Everyone was getting ready to make music. It had always been so easy for him in the past, when his voice was good. Back then he couldn't wait for the evenings, after the final meal of the day, when the harpers, holders, and dragonriders at Fort would congregate for the evening's entertainment. It was always a relaxed affair, and anyone who wanted to sing or play, relate a story, or tell an anecdote was welcomed wholeheartedly.

Piemur could feel his palms starting to sweat, and he wished he could disappear from the big Hall as easily as Farli flew *between*. He rose from his seat, on the verge of standing upright, and then he faltered, sitting back down again quickly. Everywhere he looked, harpers were pushing their chairs around to form loose circles, their musical instruments at the ready. Piemur saw N'ton and J'hon who, along with about a dozen other dragonriders, had found seats at a table with some of the younger singers. Scores of people were tuning instruments, and some of the younger apprentices were pummeling their tables with their hands, making rhythmic drumming sequences, eager to begin the music.

Sebell looked up from tuning his gitar and smiled distractedly at Piemur. Was it Piemur's imagination, or had the journeyman masterharper moved closer to him? He wasn't sure. Sebell cocked his head to one side, listening to his gitar while he tuned it. Then he looked across the table at one of the other harpers, who was holding a complex-looking set of wooden pipes.

"Give me a D, please, will you, Sousa?" Sebell said. "I can hardly hear myself with all this commotion, never mind tune my gitar."

Sousa promptly obliged, and Sebell made minute adjustments on two keys of his gitar and then looked up, satisfied. He strummed a major chord in D and then, while the notes were still reverberating, leaned a little closer to Piemur and spoke very quietly, so only he could hear.

"You shouldn't feel excluded tonight, Piemur, so I had one of my drums brought here if you wish to join in. You're a mighty fine percussionist, you know." Sebell smiled, seeming to understand that, possibly for the very first time in his life, Piemur was feeling uncomfortable among the harpers he'd known since he was nine Turns old.

Dumbfounded to hear that Sebell believed his musical talent wasn't limited solely to his obsolete singing voice, Piemur felt himself color. He picked up the flat drum from the table.

"I've got some sticks for you to choose from, too, because I couldn't remember which you preferred. There's a wooden tipper, and a bone one, too, as well as the beater."

"Thanks, Sebell," Piemur replied, pleased. "I always preferred the bone tipper over a wooden one. There's something about a bone tipper—I think it makes the drum-sound tighter, and each beat more distinct."

"Ha!" Sebell exclaimed, his brows arched as he absently strummed a series of chords. "I prefer a bone tipper, too, and for that very same reason."

All around the Hall harpers were strumming or blowing, tapping or humming as they got ready for the evening's music session. Lord Groghe, who had excused himself shortly after he'd finished his meal, reentered the Hall and took his seat at the top of the room. He was flanked by several of his sons on one side, and Masterharper Robinton and Voicemaster Shonagar on the other.

Piemur hadn't spoken to Shonagar in ages. He hadn't had the

heart to return to the Voicemaster's rooms, set in the depths of the Crafthall's caverns where the acoustics were so exceptional. He'd been afraid Shonagar would ask about his voice. Piemur couldn't bear to see the look of disappointment on his old tutor's face when he admitted that his singing voice was gone for good.

Shonagar was renowned for his droll sense of humor and florid speech, and although all the other apprentices in his group found the Voicemaster's archaic turns of phrase altogether boring, Piemur had always enjoyed Shonagar's witty company. The man certainly loved his words. It had been particularly hard for Piemur, after five Turns of being tutored almost exclusively by Shonagar, to be wrenched from the older man's company and cast out to learn other harper skills. On that horrible day, Shonagar had offered Piemur some advice, standing his young apprentice in front of him, hands on the boy's shoulders, expression earnest.

"I want you to remember something, Piemur: Just as there is more than one way to sing a note—as you very well know—there's also more than one way a harper's voice can be heard."

Shonagar had released his grip on Piemur's shoulders then and continued. "You're becoming a young man, Piemur, and will need to find young-manly tasks to fill your time. You are the most trouble-some, ingenious, lazy, audacious, and mendacious apprentice I've had to teach, but in spite of yourself, you've achieved some measure of success."

At the time, Piemur hadn't been quite certain if Shonagar was giving him a compliment or a rebuke, but later, indeed almost a full Turn after he was first posted to the Southern Continent and his duties returned him briefly to the Harper Hall, the Voicemaster had offered further advice.

It was in the evening, while everyone was relaxing and enjoying one another's company after the last meal of the day. A group of ap-prentice harpists had commandeered a corner of the Hall and were practicing a complex piece of new music. The more experienced harpers in the Hall left them to it, happy to continue conversing with one another while the mellifluous sounds of the harps played in the background.

Shonagar almost never stayed in the Hall for long after the evening meal; however, on this particular night he had remained at his table with the other music masters. Piemur only realized afterward that Shonagar must have been watching him throughout the evening, waiting for the right opportunity to speak with him.

"Ah, Piemur," the Voicemaster called as he approached the table where Piemur was seated with Menolly. Both apprentices stood to greet him when he arrived, exchanging pleasantries for a while until Menolly excused herself.

"You've turned as brown as a berry, I see," Shonagar said, smiling, though he was scrutinizing Piemur's face intently. "And much taller, too, my goodness! That means you're thriving. Tell me: Are you enjoying your pursuits in the south?" He raised his chin so that he seemed to be peering down his nose while he waited for Piemur's reply.

"It was difficult at first, and it took time before I grew accustomed to everything there. It's so very different from what I'm used . . ." To his own surprise, Piemur faltered as a rush of repressed emotions filled his chest and momentarily left him confused about who he was, where he belonged, and how he should phrase his next words.

He cleared his throat and then continued. "It's different from what I *was* used to—before." The last word sounded flat, as if it had simply fallen out of his mouth. He doubted that the astute voice teacher had failed to notice.

"Ah, but you've reached a juncture point in your life, Piemur, where you're bound to be assailed with many circumstances that are, as you say, most contrary to that to which you were once accustomed. You must bear in mind that you've left the young boy in you behind. Make room *now* for the young man you're becoming.

"Did you know, Piemur," Shonagar went on, a note of excitement lightening his tone, "that *this* is potentially the most remarkable time you'll ever experience in your life?" He raised both brows and smiled again as he placed one hand gently on Piemur's shoulder. Piemur hadn't a notion what Shonagar was talking about and his confusion must have been evident on his face, for the Voicemaster continued without waiting for a response.

"It is now, at this time, for a very brief while, that you will undergo more changes than at any other time in your life. Don't be daunted by the prospect, Piemur. Relish every new thing! Go find all the possibilities awaiting you and forget about what you knew—or what you could *do*—when you were that younger boy. It's not half as exciting as what's ahead of you, my man!"

Now, remembering that speech and the zest with which Shonagar had spoken it, Piemur looked across the room at his old Master and smiled. Shonagar had been a fine voice teacher and mentor for all those Turns, and now, Piemur mused, it seemed that Sebell had assumed that role. And honestly, he reckoned, he couldn't have asked for anyone better to fill Shonagar's shoes. He turned his smile to Sebell.

"It's been a long time since I've had a drum in my hands, Sebell. I bet I'm going to be as rusty as an old nail."

"Take it all in your stride, Piemur," Sebell offered, smiling.

With the flat drum in one hand and the sticks in the other, Piemur crossed the room to a group of drummers who'd assembled at a table positioned in an alcove. It was the perfect place for drummers to play so their measures wouldn't overwhelm the other harpers. He took a seat next to a young apprentice of about eleven, who was happily tapping out a rhythm on the table, instead of a drum, using two short wooden sticks. He kept hitting the table in the same series of taps, a look of deep concentration on his face, obviously having just mastered the new sequence. Piemur rested the edge of the round drum on one knee and looked around the room at the other harpers. Tonight he just felt like following their lead.

Sebell stood up from his seat and scanned the Hall for a moment before nodding at the young apprentice seated next to Piemur. That simple nod was Sebell's cue to everyone in the room that the young apprentice's rhythm was to be the starting point for the music to come.

Clever Sebell, Piemur mused: He was making use of the existing beat, and at the same time he was giving the young apprentice an enormous boost of confidence. As a few of the other, older drummers at his table joined in, adding the sound of their drums to the simple measure the young apprentice was playing, Piemur instinctively picked up his beater. Rather than tapping out the measure on the skin of the drum, he played the beat on its wooden edge, which made a very pleasing staccato sound that served as an accent to the other drums.

Maintaining the simple rhythm with unthinking ease, Piemur looked across the room toward Sebell, who had moved to sit on the tabletop so the other harpers could see him. The journeyman masterharper nodded once, never looking down at his gitar as he strummed out a line, and the other gitar players added their instruments to the refrain Sebell was playing.

All around the room, the different musical groups—harpists, flautists, fiddlers, drummers, pipers, percussionists, and singers—tentatively added their sounds to the basic rhythm the apprentice was playing, building on it subtly so the music grew in a complex layering of sounds. A chill ran up Piemur's spine as he heard the music grow, everyone adding their distinct part to fit neatly into the whole; from time to time an instrumentalist would break free from his or her group and play in counterpoint, before coming full circle again to play along with the others. This free-form music lasted a long time as the harpers toyed with the sound until, with yet another single nod of Sebell's head, the assembled players brought the music back to the original melody, which they maintained for several bars.

At the beginning of the next bar, an alto voice sounded out in the room, not with words but with simple scales of notes, la-las, da-das, and ululations. It was almost a primal sound, and when two other voices, a soprano and a mezzo-soprano, rang out, their song resonated through the room. Piemur looked around for the source and found it just behind Sebell's table. Menolly, seated with a group of pipers and harpists, had initiated the choral part of the composition. She sat comfortably at the table, a harp lying idly in her lap as she sang. She didn't have the highest, the finest, or even the purest voice Piemur had ever heard, but there was a timbre and a quality to Menolly's singing that was deeply pleasing to the ear. She seemed to have an innate knack for using all the right heart-notes to subtly tug at the listener's emotions.

Soon other singers added their voices, building up a harmony. Then the wind instruments joined the composition, and after a time Menolly stopped singing, allowing other voices to pick up where she had left off; everyone seemed to know exactly when to join the composition and when to exit.

Sebell stood up and played a counter-harmony in the higher register of his gitar, and then resumed the original piece of music, nodding twice, which was his signal to the room that they were to play two more bars and then finish. As the last bar was sounding, Sebell dropped one hand, and as it came up again, right on cue, all the harpers ceased making music.

It was a profound silence that followed, broken only by a spontaneous eruption of applause a moment later. Every last person in the room was smiling, laughing, or stamping their feet as they clapped. A wonderful buzz of energy filed the huge Hall as everyone felt united by what they had experienced together.

This, Piemur thought as he looked around the room at the other harpers, *this is one of the things I miss, this union of sound and the feeling of completeness it bestows on everyone, even on those who are simply listening.*

When the applause had died down and the room hummed with the gentle sounds of amicable chatter, one of the drummers at Piemur's table started drumming out the notes of a reel. Soon fiddle players at a nearby table joined in. Not everyone accompanied this impromptu piece; some chose, instead, to stand and stretch or talk among themselves.

Piemur looked over to the head table where Lord Groghe sat with the Masterharper. There was a smile on the Lord Holder's face, and although he was notoriously tone-deaf he clapped along in time to the reel. A yawn suddenly overcame Piemur and he realized that it had been a very long day, indeed. With one hand he rubbed tired eyes, the grittiness in them all too apparent as he blinked away fatigue. He'd best turn in before he fell over from exhaustion. With drum and sticks in hand, Piemur crossed the room to where Sebell was standing with his arm around Menolly, carefully placing the borrowed drum on a nearby table.

"Thanks, Sebell, that was fun," he said, smiling. "I'm going to call it a night and get some sleep."

"I'm pleased you joined in, Piemur. We haven't heard you play in an age."

"To be honest, Sebell, I wasn't sure if I could do it anymore. Or enjoy it," Piemur replied. "But I'd forgotten how much fun it is to make music." He smiled then and, with a wave of one hand, walked out of the Hall bound for sleep.

NINE

W HEN J'HON BROUGHT PIEMUR AND SEBELL TO A SECLUDED
spot about a kilometer from Nabol Hold, the morning
sky was a dull gray and rain fell on them in steady sheets.
Nabol seemed cursed with either wet and damp, or humid and hot
conditions; never somewhere moderately in between the two. It
wasn't a particularly cold day in Nabol, but the air was laden with
an insidious dampness, and as the rain easily seeped and soaked
through their clothing it quickly chilled them to the bone. Almost
as bad as the cold of *between,* Piemur mused.

Sebell's queen fire-lizard, Kimi, and Piemur's Farli flew with
them from Fort, broadcasting their excitement at this unusual expedition. But the two queens were less than happy when Mirth and
J'hon departed, both broadcasting to Piemur and Sebell their feelings about flying in the persistent rain. Piemur tried to mollify Farli,
who, he suspected, was ready to make a mating flight. Kimi, on the
other hand, seemed put out solely because of the rain and perched
on Sebell's shoulder, chittering irritably in his ear when he wasn't
rubbing her head. Suddenly Sebell stopped walking and brushed
Kimi off his shoulder with one hand. The little queen flew into the
air with a squawk and then pivoted on her tail and flew away.

"Go off, then," Sebell called after the retreating form of his queen, a scowl on his face as she flew on ahead toward Nabol. He looked at Farli, who was resisting all of Piemur's attempts to coax her to land on his arm. "And you can follow her, too, if you don't want to behave yourself. It's bad enough being soaked through with rain but having a pair of peevish fire-lizards grousing in our ears is just too much!" He flapped a hand at Farli, who squeaked once and then flew off after Kimi. Piemur could hear her chitter her disapproval as she flew away, broadcasting to him an image of his own face looking grumpy and cross.

"I am not grumpy," Piemur muttered under his breath.

"We're better off without them for the time, Piemur. I sent Kimi to roost near the eastern ramparts at Nabol. I suggested that she should wait there with all the other fire-lizards in Nabol as company until she's less put out—or more amenable."

Piemur shrugged, relieved not to have his high-strung fire-lizard distracting him from the task at hand when he and Sebell needed to have all their wits about them. Following a path he'd traversed before, he led Sebell to the cluster of five cotholds where Marek lived, trying his best to avoid puddles, steer clear of deep ridges in the path, and dodge the slippier parts of the route.

A young lad, no more than a dozen Turns in age, sullen and shabbily dressed, was banging a long stick on the ground when the two harpers approached the group of cotholds. Sebell knocked on Marek's door, and moments later it was opened by a tiny old woman with pewter-colored hair piled high on top of her head in a frothy corona. Piemur had never seen her before.

"Good day to you—" Sebell began, but the old woman flapped a hand at him and leaned her head out beyond the threshold. She was watching the sullen young lad as he banged his stick against the corner wall of her cothold. Flapping in his direction, she made an unpleasant guttural sound that sent the boy scurrying away. She muttered a few harsh words under her breath as she watched his retreating back, and when he was out of sight, she ushered Piemur and Sebell inside with a warm smile.

"Ah, cummin, cummin, Harper Sebell," she said when the door

was firmly closed, and beckoned Piemur and Sebell to follow her to
the hearth, where a glowing fire burned.

"I was visitin' my niece when your juryman was here to stay, so
I never got to meet ya." She reached for Piemur's hand and pumped
it vigorously, still smiling. "Cummin, cummin, youse are both well
come."

Piemur had actually never been inside Marek's home; during his
last visit to Nabol, he'd slept in the herdbeast shed and spent the
rest of his time snooping around the Hold for information. Now, as
he enjoyed the warmth of the fire, he looked around.

Although the room was small and in need of a fresh coat of
whitewash, it was warm and dry. A kettle of water sat on a trivet to
one side of the flames, steam piping in lazy wisps from its spout,
and hanging over the center of the fire on a hook and chain was a
large stewpot. On one side of the room, a small settle sat against
the wall, covered in lumpy seat pads that were stitched together
with odd pieces of material and stuffed with goodness knew what.
Hanging on another wall was a tapestry depicting the scene of a
harvest and obviously sewn by amateur hands, new to the craft of
textiles. The old woman took a seat on a stool next to the fire and
stirred the contents of the pot with a long-handled spoon.

"Marek'll be back soon. Youse just sit there now te wait on 'im.
We'll see ya roight. Feckin' rain has youse soaked roight through,"
she said, her voice quivery with age as she grinned at them through
her wrinkled face, tapping the side of her nose with one gnarled finger in a conspiratorial manner. She helped them take off their coats
and hung them up on hooks on the wall next to the fireplace.

As Piemur and Sebell took seats to one side of the fire, the
woman removed two cups from the shelf over the mantel and blew
into them loudly before setting them down, then tipped water from
the simmering kettle into each. Then she took a small nub of gray
root from her tunic pocket and wiped it clean with a quick scrape of
a knife. She laid it flat on a piece of board, which she rested on her
knees, and holding her knife so the blade was placed flat-side down
over the root, she gave it a quick bang with the heel of her hand.

When the knife was removed, Piemur could see that the root had been neatly squashed and moisture slowly oozed from its flattened sides. Then the old lady deftly cut the root in half lengthwise and plopped a piece into each of the cups.

"G'wan then," she said, gesturing for Piemur and Sebell to drink. "Tha'll take the chill off a' yer pins and make ye roight." She beamed broadly at the two harpers.

"Many thanks, Laida, this'll do the trick." Sebell smiled warmly as he blew on the contents of the cup before taking several tentative sips. Piemur, however, had never seen the root that Laida had used before and was more reticent in his approach than Sebell. He had bad memories of being forced to down noxious drafts by his foster mother, Ama, when he was a young lad. He blew on the cup several times, reluctant to commit to the first sip. The old woman peered at him from under frowning brows.

"Woan bite-cha, lad. 'Sgood for ya," she said, gesturing with one gnarled hand for Piemur to drink up.

Piemur closed his eyes and sniffed the brew; the earthy aroma was not at all unpleasant. Feeling only slightly assured, he took a little sip, allowing the liquid to settle on his tongue briefly, fearful it would release a foul taste as he swallowed it. But it was fragrant and sweet, spicy and aromatic—all in all, a satisfying surprise to the senses. Piemur blew on the cup a few more times, trying to get it to cool sufficiently so he could drink down the draft. When he'd swallowed every last drop, a contented "aah" escaped his lips, and it was with true regret that he allowed Laida to take the empty cup away. Laida chuckled and, without another word, tramped from the room through a small side door, leaving the harpers alone.

In the silence that followed, Piemur found his eye drawn to the mantel, on which were perched various odds and ends: a small paring knife next to a thimble, a square-shaped woven basket filled with dried summer flowers tied together with a strip of soft fabric, and in the very center a small picture, painted on a piece of wood, depicting a nightbird, wings furled and one bright, beady eye eternally watching the room.

Intrigued, he rose from his stool and reached for the little picture. He studied it briefly, admiring the skill of its creator, then showed it to Sebell before carefully replacing it and resuming his seat by the fire.

They waited in silence for a little longer, and at last Marek stomped into the cothold through the front door. Droplets of rain dripped from his thick, dark hair, and a strong animal odor surrounded him.

"How'sa goin' there, Sebell?" Marek asked warmly, and his voice seemed to boom around the little room as, hand outstretched, he closed the distance to Sebell. His heavily callused palms were black with ingrained dirt.

"Piemur," Marek said, offering a hand to him in greeting, as well. Piemur thought he would never get used to the way Marek's typical Nabolese accent stressed the second syllable of his name rather than the first: Pie-*mur*. He had to force himself to refrain from correcting him.

"I got your message 'bout those lads, Jerrol and Jentis. Cousins they are. Serra runs 'bout wit 'em. Surly git, he is." Marek nodded, poking the fire with a stick as he spoke. "What can I do fer ya, Sebell?"

"Piemur overheard them talking two nights ago," Sebell began, and Piemur suddenly felt surprised: It seemed much longer than two days since he'd been here in Nabol, what with everything that had happened in between then and now.

"Ah, they bin meetin' together a lot these past few months after they came back home. Can't help themselves but rock the boat till someone takes note and gives 'em what they want."

"After they came home, Marek, where were they?" Sebell asked.

"They mooched 'round fer a spell after the old Lord died, an' then they got the bright idea to make a go of it on their own down south. Didn't look like they made much of a go, from what I saw, ne'er mind that they were gone fer Turns. When they got home, they were in a woe-geous state, their tails well tucked twixt their legs. And they bin sulkin' ever since!"

"Hm," Sebell said, resting an index finger against his lips as he thought. "That would explain why they're stirring things up so long after Lord Meron's demise."

Piemur raised a brow at Sebell and then returned his attention to Marek. "They said they were going to meet at Jerrol's hold tonight, Marek, and we want to hear what they have to say. I don't know how we can do that, though—I've seen Jerrol's cothold," he said. "It's small so it's not as if we can hide inside it to eavesdrop on their plans."

"Lemme see what I can do 'bout it. Skal's bin makin' a new cider, an' if the lads hear there's drink goin' fer free, they'll be down at his brewhouse like hot snots off a shovel. Leave it wit' me, Sebell. I'll get word ta ye when I know they're headin' out. 'Sprobly better if ye wait near Skal's, then when ye see the three of 'em ye can follow 'em in behind." Marek's deep voice rumbled up through his chest like a slow, booming drum. Here was a man, Piemur thought, who would never be good at whispering.

"Thank you, Marek, you've been a great help," Sebell said. "We'll be off now."

"I'm happy to have helped ya, Sebell. I'll be leavin' early tomorrow, up north toward Crom. I've had m'eye on baggin' a wild boar for a long while, and my cousin says he knows where I can find one."

"Well, good hunting to you, Marek. And our thanks again to Laida, too—if you'd pass them on, please."

"Ah, Auntie Laida loves a bit o' intrigue," Marek said in a light tone. "It makes her feel useful and keeps her curious. And why shuddin she feel that way? 'Swat I say!" And he beamed at them, a huge, face-splitting grin that lit up his eyes and made both Piemur and Sebell smile along with him.

"There now, Harper Sebell, ye take good care," Marek said.

Piemur and Sebell left the cothold through the back door. They found shelter under a long, arching bank of bushes near a small field of ripening sourberries and waited for Marek to send word confirming that his "bait" had been taken. As they were waiting, Piemur noticed that he'd grown twitchy and edgy: he couldn't stop his knees from jiggling up and down as if they were playing out a rhythm on a set of foot drums. It was worse than when he drank too much *klah*.

"Shells, Sebell," Piemur said, "what was in the brew old Laida gave us? I have a fierce dose of the jitters."

"Here." Sebell took a cloth packet from his satchel and handed it to Piemur. "Eat this and the jumpiness should settle down. They call the root jango. It only grows here in Nabol. All the older folk up here take it, swear it gives them more pep. I think it's a bit of a cure-all, too, but it's best to eat something at the same time as taking it, as I've discovered. This"—he pointed at the packet in Piemur's hand—"should do the trick." Piemur unwrapped it and found a hard roll filled with cured meat and pickled root vegetables.

"Crafty Nabolese," Piemur muttered thoughtfully, taking a large bite of the roll. Sebell nodded and helped himself to a meat roll as well, and they settled down to eat in companionable silence.

Wiping crumbs from his mouth with the back of his hand, Piemur broke the silence. "Sebell," he said, "I keep wondering about the egg. Who do you think returned it?"

"That's a good question. It could have been *anyone* from Southern Weyr. But why would they return it and then vanish? Was it because the egg was ten days older? Somehow, I don't think that's the real answer, Piemur. The whole thing just doesn't make sense."

"I know. I can't figure it out. There must be something about this mess we're overlooking." Piemur sighed heavily and settled down to wait.

The sky above had lit up with stars, and sounds from night bugs and other nocturnal creatures filled the air when Piemur nudged Sebell. He could see Jerrol, Jentis, and the third man, who must be the one named Serra, walking toward Skal's house. The two harpers gathered themselves and quickly followed them.

Others, in couples and larger parties, were also heading toward Skal's. They were boisterous and jovial, walking past the two harpers quickly, obviously eager to get started with their night of socializing. A large group of traders came up behind Piemur and Sebell, overly loud with boastful talk of the deals they'd made in Nabol Hold.

"Right," Sebell said quietly as they entered the house, "we're on, Piemur."

Piemur pulled his cloth cap from his tunic pocket and placed it skew-ways on his head as Sebell pushed through the door and headed confidently down the hallway to the courtyard as if he'd done so a thousand times before.

Sebell walked up to the counter with a swaggering step, chin jutting out, giving off the aura of a man of some importance. One of the traders made room for him to lean against the counter where he could get the attention of a server.

"Two scoops of yer best cider, there, missus," he said, tapping a closed fist on the bar as he spoke. Then he let two full marks fall from his fist onto the counter. With those marks he could afford to buy plenty of drink not only for himself, but also for everyone else in the room.

"S'pose I'll have te give the lad a good sup for all the trade he's settled today. He made a deal with the steward over there in Ruatha for some a' their young runnabeasts. Steward even threw in a mare-in-foal. I guess we'll be shovelin' shite till the end a' this Pass!" Sebell said, and then burst into hearty guffaws of laughter, the delight at his good fortune obvious to everyone as he clapped Piemur soundly on the back and handed him a large beaker of frothy amber liquid.

"Drink up, lad, drink up. Ye'll not go thirsty ta-nite," Sebell exclaimed loudly.

The traders and other drinkers were a waggish lot, so while the drink flowed and tongues were loosened, they included Sebell and Piemur in their conversations as if they were all old pals. Skal was a canny man who knew how to make thirsty folk drink more, so when the noise in the courtyard had risen to a near-raucous level, he passed out free baskets of hot crackled meat strips and chunks of fried tubers, generously sprinkled with spices and salt. His customers fell on the food like a ravenous pack, polishing off every last morsel. But the salty food had the effect of drying their mouths, which made the drinkers quick to order more rounds of ale and cider to quench their renewed thirsts.

Just like everyone else at Skal's, Piemur tucked into the baskets of food with gusto, failing to notice the subtle warning look Sebell shot at him from across the counter. This was turning into one jolly and unexpectedly fine evening, Piemur fancied as he took a long draft from his third beaker of cider. Suddenly he remembered a joke his foster mother's son, Pergamol, was fond of telling.

"So, a man sat in a brewhouse all day gettin' full o' drink, see," he began, and someone shushed two noisy traders standing next to Piemur so he could continue uninterrupted, "and he'd been pesterin' the landlord for an age, trying to ask him a question, but the landlord was too busy, and couldn't understand the man's slurred speech anyhow, so he just ignored him."

Jerrol and his two companions had been standing at the end of the counter, not far from where Sebell and Piemur were holding court, and now Jerrol moved away from his companions to get a better place from which to hear Piemur. He seemed rapt by Piemur's story, a grin slowly spreading across his face in anticipation of the punch line.

"Finally, the drunk felt he couldn't be ignored any longer," Piemur continued, "so he bangs his cup on the counter and bellows at the landlord, trying to speak clearly. He finally masters his tongue, though his words are still a little slurred, and what he says becomes clear enough for the landlord to understand.

" 'I aksed you, mister brewman: Do yellow-sours have feathers?' the drunk said carefully, swaying in his seat.

" 'Of course they don't have feathers!' the annoyed brewer replied.

"And the drunkard held up one finger, hiccuping, and said, 'Then I've just squeezed yer tweety-bird into m'drink!' "

The group around Piemur erupted into laughter, the loudest of which came from Jerrol, who was now standing next to Piemur.

"You're a funny little lad," he said, clapping Piemur on the back roughly. "Have another draft of cider—at my pleasure. Perhaps you'll tell me a joke or two more."

Piemur laughed along with Jerrol and accepted the drink with a big show of gratitude.

As the evening wore on and the banter grew more intense,

Piemur remained in conversation with Jerrol, fabricating amusing stories about his life as a runnerbeast herdsman's apprentice and his home near Ruatha Hold. Sebell discreetly moved away from the group of men he'd been talking to and stood next to Piemur, holding his beaker of cider close to his chest and swaying slightly from time to time. He even contributed a few anecdotes to add to those Piemur was telling, endearing himself to Jerrol just as easily as Piemur had done.

Eventually Jentis and Serra joined Jerrol and the two harpers, appearing eager to share in their banter. As the evening wore on, the topics they discussed turned, as they always do when drinkers fill up and lose their inhibitions, to shared confidences. With a little help from Sebell, the subject swung back to Ruatha and its Lord-in-waiting, Jaxom. The three Nabolese men leaned in closer.

"D'you know Ruatha a-tall?" Piemur asked. The other men nodded in unison. "Well, I think tha's a funny ol' mess with the young Lord-to-be, don't ya think?" He'd been pretending to be drunk, but Piemur realized as he spoke that his words were actually slurring quite easily.

"Whadda ya mean?" Jerrol countered.

Suddenly Piemur could feel some bile rising up in his throat and he immediately covered his mouth, his cheeks puffing up involuntarily as excess air made its way out of his belly. He belched gently, his hand still pressed to his mouth, relieved that he hadn't humiliated himself in the brewhouse. Jerrol and his companions didn't seem to notice, eager as they were to hear more of what Piemur had to say. When Sebell saw Piemur's face, he quickly interposed himself and continued with the conversation.

"Well, it's just odd as a three-headed tunnel snake. The lad has a dragon, thassall."

"Yeah!" Piemur chimed in, having finally recovered himself. "How can he be lordly and a dragonrider as well? 'Snot right." He feigned a hiccup.

The remark met its mark, opening up a long and heated debate about how men should stick to what they know and not meddle in matters best left to weyrfolk. With a subtle push Sebell moved the conversation on to the difficulties of being holdless, and the three men threw themselves into it with gusto.

Piemur felt another belch traveling up his throat and was unable to stop it from erupting long and loudly, adding a rude punctuation mark to the conversation. He mumbled something and pushed himself away from the counter, making his excuses with a wave of his hand.

The room had shifted subtly, making it hard for him to walk without staggering a little. He tried to look over his shoulder to Sebell to wink at him that he was all right and would be back in a moment, but his vision was fuzzy and the room was too spinny. He had to get outside! *Wait a moment,* he mused, *I am* outside! And a little giggle bubbled out of his mouth.

Making his way through the crush of drinkers, he pushed through the door that led to the passageway and the front of the cothold. Bursting through the door a tad too forcefully, he all but fell outside onto the road, quickly recovering his balance as he assessed his surroundings.

I'll just wait out here, he thought, *where we sat before when we sat watching Skal's.* He giggled at his silly thoughts and then stumbled, lurching about in front of the cluster of dwellings until he finally found a place to sit down. He flopped to the ground, pushing himself up against the base of an arching bush, and tried to sit ramrod-straight so the world would stop tilting around him. A loud hiccup popped out, which made him want to laugh again. It would be a lot funnier, he reckoned, if his head would stop spinning. He leaned back, looking up to find something to focus on. The sky was clear and stars were beginning to appear, and he made a concerted effort to focus on just one star, hoping that would make everything stand still again.

Without warning Piemur's stomach purged itself. The process was over quickly, and with very little noise, but it was a messy and convulsive affair. Piemur felt decidedly wretched when the vomiting ceased, but he was hopeful he might now be in control of his actions. Careful not to crawl through the mess he'd made, he edged away to where the ground was dry underneath. He just needed to sit still for a while, he guessed, to stop everything from spinning. His eyelids drooped, and he fell into a stupor.

Piemur had no idea how much time passed while he lay under the bushes, trying to keep warm against the cool night air. Some of the time he was conscious, but for most of it he couldn't keep his eyes open, sleeping fitfully. When he woke, he was parched; he tried to roll his tongue around the inside of his mouth, but it was too woolly. Crawling out from under the bush, he could see that the night sky was brilliant with stars. He should go find Sebell. Skal's place, he thought, struggling to his feet, that's where he should go. Somehow, he managed to make it part of the way before he flopped down on the ground with a heavy sigh a few dozen paces from the brewhouse. He knew he had to pull himself together, but it was too difficult to keep his eyes from closing again.

Something plopped on the ground near Piemur and brushed against his hand. Seemingly from a long way away he heard a muffled groan and a shuffling gait and heavy footsteps, which vibrated through the ground.

"Youse don't fool us with yer harpy tricks. Herdsmen indeed!" Jentis's spiteful voice spoke from above Piemur. He felt a rough hand pulling at the back of his tunic, hauling him upward, then the hand released its hold and a heavy blow smashed against the side of his head, followed by a kick to his back from a large boot.

Jerrol's voice laughed close to his face, saying, "That'll soften yer cough." Excruciating pain radiated from above Piemur's ear and was echoed along his back. Then he fell unconscious.

When Piemur woke, the penetrating cold had crept into his bones and taken firm hold. He looked all around, hoping his eyes would become accustomed to the darkness. He had been dumped in a corner of a dark room, the only light coming from a crack in the door. He could just make out the shape of a person in the middle of the room, slumped on a chair or a bench, head bent forward and almost touching his chest. Was that Sebell? Piemur still felt queasy and his head began to spin if he moved it too quickly, so he crawled forward very slowly.

When he reached the middle of the room, Piemur's eyes had

adjusted somewhat to the darkness, and he could make out the face of the person on the bench. It was Sebell! His feet were tied to the lower part of the bench, at ground level, and his hands were tied higher, where the flat of the seat met the legs of the bench.

Very gingerly Piemur felt about for where Sebell's shoulders should be. The older harper didn't move at all.

"Sebell, is that you? Can you hear me, Sebell?" Piemur whispered. "Sebell, it's me, Piemur," he said again, this time gently shaking Sebell's shoulder. There was no reply.

"S-s-s-sebell," he said again, hissing in the harper's ear as he shook his shoulder more vigorously.

Suddenly Sebell's head jolted back on his shoulders and he cried out. "Aagh! Don't touch my shoulder!"

Piemur dropped his hand from Sebell's shoulder. "Sorry, Sebell, I'm sorry! What's happened to you?"

There was a long intake of breath from Sebell, and then, "I think my arm is broken, Piemur. Something's wrong with it. It feels dead at the shoulder and hurts unbearably if I move it even a fraction."

"All right," Piemur said, starting to feel around the ground for the taut ropes that bound Sebell's feet. "I'll try to free your feet first. Do you know where we are?"

"I think we're in the cellars of Nabol Hold," Sebell replied. "I can't get Kimi to come to me—I can't visualize where we are. I can feel her getting more and more distressed because she can't find me." Piemur detected the faintest note of despair in Sebell's voice and redoubled his efforts to untie the knots on the thick rope that bound him to the bench.

"Piemur, wait." Sebell said, his voice sounding steadier. "I want you to listen to me."

Piemur stopped what he was doing and sat back on his heels.

"When they come back I want you to try and get out of here. Pretend you're still unconscious, and if you see an opportunity, get out of here as quickly as you can. Will you do that?"

"I won't leave you, Sebell. Just let me get these ropes untied and then we'll get out of here together."

"No, we won't, Piemur. There are at least three of them to just us two, and I'm hardly fit to walk."

"I'll get your legs untied, Sebell, and then you'll be able to walk," Piemur said hurriedly.

"I can't walk, Piemur."

"What do you mean? Of course you can walk! I just need to get these ropes—" But Sebell cut him off.

"They beat me around the knees and shins, Piemur. I don't think I could walk more than two paces on my own without falling over. You're going to have to go without me. Get help and come back for me."

"I can't do that, Sebell!" Piemur cried but Sebell hissed in warning.

"Shh, I hear something!" Sebell whispered, and Piemur stilled his hands over the ropes, straining to listen. There it was: the sound of muffled footsteps approaching.

"Promise me, Piemur!" Sebell insisted, but Piemur shook his head, looking around the small room frantically for something, anything, he could use to overwhelm the men when they came into the room.

His head was pounding now and the footsteps were very close. What should he do? There was nothing he could use to hit them with, only the bench Sebell was tied to. *Think, Piemur, think!* He looked to where Sebell was tied on the bench one last time and heard him whisper, "Go, Pie," as the door was being unlocked from outside and voices were talking in the passageway.

Instinct took over and without realizing what he was going to do, Piemur made a lunge for the first man who entered the room, launching himself low as he aimed for the man's legs. As his arms wrapped around both legs Piemur opened his mouth wide and bit hard into the flesh of one thigh.

"Argh! My leg!" the man shouted, dropping the glowbasket he'd been holding and taking several steps backward. He crashed into his companions and that was all Piemur needed. He pushed hard with his legs and, head tucked low in a tackle, shoved with all his might, forcing the men back far enough to make a space in the doorway. He was out! He clambered and pushed, his feet making contact with one man's soft abdomen and his hands clawing at whatever else was in his way. Then he was pumping his legs, trying to run. Hands were grabbing at him and his jacket was pulling him backward. Quick as an eel, Piemur shrugged out of his jacket, and then he was free and running as fast as his legs could go. Sounds of heavy footsteps running behind him receded slowly as Piemur gained momentum down the long passageway, putting more and more distance between him and his pursuer.

He heard shouting from behind him and then a voice called out loudly. "Leave 'im! We have the other one, an' he'll be a better tool fer our purposes." Piemur looked back over his shoulder briefly, but there was nothing to see—the passageway was in complete darkness.

He had no idea where he was going, and twice he ran into a wall, almost crashing headfirst, but his arms saved him from the worst of the impact. Realizing he could very easily run in circles and haplessly end up back in front of his captors, Piemur slowed his pace. He had to find light, or fresh air—anything that would take him out of this darkness!

From what he remembered, the cellars of Nabol were vast and intertwining. He stopped and stood quite still, trying to remember how many times he'd met solid walls and in which direction he'd gone when he'd turned. He closed his eyes for a moment, drawing in several deep breaths as he stilled his thoughts. When he hit the first wall he ran left and then left again. So now he should turn right at the next junction in the passageway.

Jogging forward slowly, Piemur kept one hand on a wall to steady himself. He jogged on, meeting several junctions in the system of passageways. He had no idea if he was getting farther away from or closer to his goal. At some point he *had* to meet up with a part of the cellar system that was lit with glows, so he plodded on doggedly, his head pounding and his back aching with every step.

Piemur had no idea how much time had passed, but he felt he had been running through the cellars for far too long. What if he was lost here forever? The thought raced around in his head and panic started to grip him. His breathing grew faster and shallower until he was overcome with dizziness. He leaned against a wall, doubled over at the waist, and then slowly sank down to the dry ground. He was on the point of allowing himself to succumb to total despair and tried to rest his head in his hands, but when his hand touched his head he could feel a lump from where he'd been hit. A shot of pain ran along the side of his face and he sucked in his breath. Anger suddenly flared up, supplanting the fear that nearly paralyzed him.

How dare they hit him! How dare they beat and tie up Sebell, too. A journeyman masterharper! *We are not their enemies,* Piemur raged. No one was their enemy! His breathing grew heavy as his sense of outraged indignation mounted. But as he took control again and his breathing eventually slowed, Piemur began to realize just how desperate those three holdless, feckless men were. They were close kin of Meron, the late Lord of Nabol, so it was no wonder they acted so abominably.

There had never been any secrecy about Lord Meron, a thoroughly unpleasant man who did nothing to improve his holders' lot. He'd suffered from a long, wasting illness and had been slowly dying for several Turns, his next of kin fervently hoping all the while that he'd commit wholeheartedly to his condition sooner rather than later, but, alas, to his very last breath he failed to oblige. For Turns Meron kept his closest kin gathered around him, insisting they live cheek by jowl and at his pleasure—or lack of. He enjoyed goading them to bicker and fight with one another as he reveled in his handiwork.

Meron's kin had learned to expect that the holdings he promised to bequeath to one hopeful relative would be dramatically and whimsically wrenched out of their hands over some perceived slight, only to be given to yet another eager kinsman who would, in due course, suffer the same fate. Such was Meron's perverse predilection to bamboozle his kin and keep them all on tenterhooks that it was no surprise, Piemur reckoned, that they were all tainted with the same element of perversity and cruelty that had characterized every aspect of Meron's life.

Meron had been, quite simply, a wicked man who got no greater satisfaction from life than when he was brewing up malaise and discord among his nearest and not-so-dearest clansfolk. Such perverse depravity needed to be leached out of Meron's kin, Piemur knew, or it would never die, only spread and proliferate like Thread.

He sat there on the ground, and as he thought of the men who'd hurt him and Sebell, he absentmindedly grabbed handfuls of loose dirt from the ground. As he felt the dirt fall through his fingers he suddenly stopped. This dirt was dry! The ground in the cell where Jerrol had them locked up had been damp. What did that tell him? he asked himself. Think!

The damp parts of the cellars were probably no longer used, while the dry parts would be where all the provisions were stored. *So if I follow the dry sand until it becomes packed underfoot,* Piemur surmised, *I should be in parts of the cellars that are more regularly used.* He stood up and, with a greater sense of resolve, continued to walk along the passageway, periodically checking that the dirt beneath his feet was dry. If he erred in direction and the ground started to feel damp, he'd retrace his steps until he came to dry ground again.

He walked on, keeping one hand on the wall as he did until, with a jolt, his hand stubbed against something in the wall. Piemur felt it, a hard substance. Could this be a door? He ran his hand up and down the object, feeling what must be the frame, then he moved a few inches farther along and there it was—a door. He flattened his palm and rubbed it all over the door, but there was no handle. He pushed his weight against it, but the door wouldn't budge. *Never mind,* he thought excitedly, *if there's one door, there has to be more. It's a cellar, for shards' sake!* And he smiled to himself in the darkness.

Picking up the pace, Piemur walked farther along the passage, following it as it turned a corner. Another frame and door came up under his hand and he pressed his weight against it, but again it wouldn't budge. He started to jog, and within a few paces his hand met another frame and door. He was on to something! Suddenly there was nothing, no wall or doors, just empty space. He retraced his steps to the wall, trying to get his bearings again, but when he moved forward or to either side, the passageway was empty. *This must be an intersection, like a hallway.* He moved slowly across the passageway and walked forward until his hand touched a wall. On an instinct, he crouched down and felt the dirt. It was dry, but not as loose. He was on packed soil! He must be getting close to the parts of the cellar that were more frequently used. Then Piemur's foot banged into something hard, and with a shout of joy he reached down and felt the runs and riser of a stone step. Crouching down so he wouldn't trip, he quickly climbed a set of stairs. The walls were steep here, too, he thought, realizing that he could actually see where he was going. Light was slowly increasing the farther he climbed, and when he reached a small landing he looked up and saw daylight bathing the stairs and the walls of the passage. He ascended another set of stone steps two at a time and almost fell into a little vestibule, off which were two doors to the left and one to the right. He took a guess and pushed at the door on the right and, after a slight budge and then a shimmy, the door finally pushed open, and Piemur was standing in the open air. Rain drizzled down on his head and he beamed.

He ran his hand along the thick, outer wall of the Hold and jogged onward, quickly coming to a small door that, once opened, led outside of the Hold proper.

When he ran through the door, slamming it behind him with a dull thud, he stopped dead in his tracks: his surroundings were completely unfamiliar.

I must be on the other side of Nabol Hold, Piemur guessed. He ran down a narrow rampart, passing a group of holders pushing a cart out of a deep, muddy rut, and followed the walls of the Hold all the way around until he finally came to the other rampart he was familiar with. Now that he had his bearings, Piemur ran full-tilt in the direction of Marek's cothold, calling for Farli as he ran. His back was on fire and his lungs felt like they were going to burst. He wished he could stop for a drink of water, but he'd just have to wait.

Farli! Come to me, sweet thing. Farli!

Suddenly he remembered that Marek had gone hunting and wouldn't be at his cot. He ran on, past the lane that led to Marek's house, hoping that Skal might help him. As he ran, quickly closing the distance to Skal's, he passed a small grove of trees and felt the barest of mental nudges. Is that Farli? He turned his head to look back but couldn't see anything. There it was again, another nudge, but it wasn't familiar. He rubbed his eyes, still running fast, and then turned his head again to look behind him as he pelted along. Without any warning his forward momentum was abruptly stopped and a loud *thwack* rang out in his right ear as he plowed headfirst into the branch of a tree. He fell to the ground like a stone.

"Tsk, but look at the *state* of him."

Piemur heard the disdain in the voice and wondered whom the speaker could be referring to. His head felt like it was exploding in short pulsing bursts of pain. He couldn't bring himself to open his eyes; he knew it would hurt too much. Instead he lifted a hand to cautiously touch the side of his head and felt a lump the size of a fire-lizard egg just above his right ear. It was tender and sticky, too. Gingerly he felt above his left ear and, sure enough, the other lump was still there, though nowhere near as sore as the new one. *What's going on? Why am I all lumps and bumps?*

"Now, there's a lad who took too many scoops at Skal's last night. Didn't know when to stop, did he?" another voice commented in an equally critical tone. Piemur tried to sit up but failed at the first attempt, the ground seeming to slip right out from under his hand.

"Ah, but look at him, Fronna, he's got a nasty cut on his head!" the first voice said. "We have to help him."

"You've no idea where he's from or what he's been up to, Daisa. No, you'd best step away from him while I get Skal. He can sort this one out. *His* brew put him this way!" the grumpy voice said, and then Piemur heard the sound of feet stomping away.

His second attempt at pushing himself up succeeded, aided as it was with a gentle hand from Daisa, and he leaned back against a boulder just as Fronna returned with Skal. He opened his eyes, though his right one felt swollen and was hard to see out of. He decided it would be better if he simply closed that eye again, and the other one involuntarily closed in sympathy.

"I'll look after this one, Fronna. You've no need to bother yourself about him now."

"I certainly do, Skal! When you leave men littered around outside my cothold it becomes quite a bother, I can tell you! Shells, it's a wonder why he's fetched up here at all!" Fronna spluttered.

"Now, now, Fronna, it's not that bad. He probably fell and hit his head," Skal said as he gently leaned Piemur forward at the waist and eased in behind him so he could lift him up from under each arm.

"I can get up," Piemur said. His voice sounded croaky even to his own ears, so he cleared his throat, realizing that a faint taste of vomit still lingered in his mouth. When he tried to stand, a shooting pain in his back made him gasp.

"Here you go," Skal said, helping him to his feet. It was all Piemur could do not to wince, but he looked over at the two women who'd found him and dipped his head in acknowledgment, a weak smile of thanks on his lips.

"Ah, ye poor lad," Daisa said "Go sleep it off, and when you wake, have a big, greasy feed. Then you'll be all right."

Fronna said nothing, merely stamped her feet on the ground impatiently, and then she linked her arm into Daisa's and pulled her friend away.

"C'mon, lad," Skal said, "best get out of Fronna's sight till you're more yourself. How'd you hurt your head?"

"I—I think I ran into a tree. I'm not quite sure what happened before those women found me. What hour of the day is it?" Piemur asked but Skal made a soothing noise, shaking his head while he led him to his cothold.

Once inside, Skal maneuvered Piemur into the sitting room on the left of the passageway and told him to wait, returning shortly with a beaker of water and a cup of steaming hot *klah*.

"I should go and find my master," Piemur said. "He must be wondering where I am."

"Naw, naw, lad, you're goin' nowhere for now. Not until I've got you sorted. Sit here awhile and get some water into you. I find that always helps."

At first Piemur only sipped cautiously at the water, but once the liquid slid down his throat he responded to his body's urgent need and downed the remainder in one long draft. He hoped it wouldn't reappear again unbidden. As he set the beaker down, he noted that his hand was shaking slightly, and he quickly closed it into a fist to steady it.

"You must've gotten some bang on the head, lad. That lump's the size of my fist!" Skal said.

A sharp jolt of anxiety washed over Piemur. Sebell! He had no idea how long he'd been away from him. Had Jerrol and his men untied Sebell from the bench, or was the journeyman masterharper still confined in that contorted position? What if they had beaten him again? Piemur couldn't bear to think about it, but he couldn't help himself. Sebell was in trouble! And Piemur now knew that Jerrol, Jentis, and Serra were very serious about achieving their goal. What was it he had heard one of them shouting as he was running away? *He'll be a better tool for our purposes,* or something like that. *Enough,* Piemur told himself, *I have to find help and get Sebell out of those cellars!*

He took a last, big gulp of the *klah* and then thanked Skal for his help, cutting the older man off when he tried to insist that Piemur rest longer. He left the brewhouse, thankful for the small bonus of clear blue skies overhead, and set off at a jog, and when that pace didn't worsen the pain in his back he decided to ignore his throbbing head and accelerated to a full-blown sprint. He had to get help! Get a message to Menolly, or perhaps N'ton or J'hon. They'd know what to do. If only he could reach his little gold queen, she could find Kimi—who could find Sebell—or at least get a message to Menolly's fire-lizards! But every time he tried to focus his thoughts and push out hard to Farli, calling her to come to him, he felt as if he were reaching into empty space. It didn't help that his head pounded in a steady rhythm every time his feet hit the ground. But he ran on, closing his mind to the ache in his back and the pain in his head.

As Piemur got closer to Nabol Hold, the number of people using the path increased and he had to slow his pace to avoid crashing into anyone. Folk were going about their daily routines, exchanging greetings or waves of acknowledgment as they passed one another. Piemur got a few curious glances, no doubt, he guessed, because of his disheveled appearance.

When he finally rounded the corner to stand in front of the eastern ramparts of the Hold, Piemur came to an abrupt halt and his stomach sank.

There was Kimi, flying in frantic, erratic circles a meter above the ground, chirruping shrilly. Piemur pursed his lips and let out a sharp whistle. Kimi stopped in midflight, hovered momentarily, and then all but flung herself at Piemur in a frenzied flurry of wings and relieved cheeps and chirps. She flew too close to his head and her talons scraped against one of the bumps, causing fresh blood to flow down his face in a thin stream.

"Easy, Kimi!" Piemur said, holding one hand to his wounded head and the other one out for the agitated fire-lizard to land on but Kimi continued to fly around him, unwilling to settle down. A group of passersby glanced uneasily at Piemur before moving through the gates and into the Hold. Two little boys couldn't stop staring at the frenzied golden fire-lizard circling his head. Piemur smiled wanly at the boys and took a dozen paces backward, out of the flow of pedestrians; at the same time, he dropped his outstretched arm and tried to still his thoughts.

Easy, he thought, trying his best to broadcast to the queen, *easy, Kimi. We'll find Sebell. Be easy, Kimi, settle.* But Kimi continued her erratic flight, trilling loudly. *She must be calling for Sebell,* Piemur guessed, *and she can't get an answer from him. I knew I shouldn't have left him!* The thought ripped through him in a rush of panic and he felt as if he was going to be sick. His legs seemed to fold under him, leaving his body no choice but to follow, and he sat down hard on the ground, right where he stood. His thoughts raced around in his head and an unfamiliar feeling of panic spread outward from his gut. He had to calm down! And he had to calm Kimi, too, or they'd never be able to figure a way out of this.

In a very soft voice Piemur called Kimi's name over and over. She paid him no heed. So he hummed a gentle melody, one that was sung to every young child on Pern when they were scared or upset, hoping it would calm the frantic queen.

"Sh-sh, Kimi. I'm here," Piemur called quietly. "Come to me, Kimi, then we can find Sebell together."

The little queen's calls grew more raucous at mention of Sebell's name and Piemur could have kicked himself. He persisted, though, continuing to hum the gentle melody, pausing frequently to make shushing sounds and call Kimi to him. Finally, exhausted, Kimi slowed her frantic flight and with more encouragement from Piemur came to rest at last on his hand, her eyes whirling bright red. She gazed intently into his eyes and trilled at him. It was a piteous sound that articulated all her anxiety and fear, and tore at his heart.

"This isn't right," Piemur whispered. He stared intently at the fire-lizard. She must be unable to make a mental connection with Sebell, he brooded. And then he realized: *Shards, Kimi thinks Sebell is dead!*

He stared straight ahead, his eyes huge as panic gripped him. *No! There has to be some other reason why Kimi can't connect to Sebell right now. Sebell must be alive, he just needs help. If only I hadn't left him!* He called to Farli again but felt nothing, not even a murmur, from her. He shook his head; no point in wasting any more time in that quarter.

"Kimi. Kimi, look at me," Piemur said, forcing himself to remain calm. He had to get her to understand him and he didn't think sheer force of will would be enough. Shards, he wished he were as familiar with Kimi as he was with his own queen and Menolly's Beauty. He felt panic starting to rise again and took a few deep breaths. He made a clear picture of Menolly in his head and then called Kimi's name again.

"Kimi. Kimi, go to Menolly," Piemur said, staring into the little queen's eyes and hoping she could see the image he was broadcasting. Kimi's whirling eyes slowed slightly, and the color changed from bright, frightened red to a deep, alarmed amber. She tilted her head at Piemur and chirped once, as if asking him to repeat himself.

"Kimi, go to Menolly. I need help. Get Menolly, Kimi."

Sebell's fire-lizard looked at Piemur, her eyes still whirling amber, then she began to keen, a long and heart-wrenching sound that tore at him like the cry of a distraught child. Slowly Piemur reached out his hand to rub her head. Her keening was so painfully hard to bear that Piemur, close to tears, could only make gentle shushing sounds.

"Shh, Kimi, don't cry. We'll find him, I promise. But you have to help, Kimi. Get Menolly," he said and held his arm up high, trying to encourage Kimi to fly away and bring back help.

Kimi flew up into the air and circled slowly above Piemur's head. *Get help,* he thought, *get help, Kimi!*

With one final, sad trill, she flew straight up into the sky and was gone, flown *between*. The silence she left behind was oppressive.

Piemur hoped that the little queen had done what he'd asked, and not disappeared *between* forever, as all dragons and fire-lizards did when their human partners died. Sebell was not dead! Kimi had to believe that! Overwhelmed, Piemur lowered his head and wept.

TEN

ALONG TIME PASSED BEFORE HE FINALLY WIPED HIS TEAR-streaked face on his tunic and slowly stood up. What if Sebell really *was* dead? He had already been badly injured when Piemur left him hours earlier. What if Jerrol and his men had returned to beat Sebell again? Piemur's thoughts raced around his head at a frantic pace. It seemed ages since he'd sent Kimi to get help. What if she didn't come back? With a sinking heart, he began to believe that perhaps Kimi had indeed flown *between* forever, believing Sebell to be dead. Piemur had never before felt so helpless or hopeless.

His head was pounding again and he could feel an increase in the pressure in his ears, as if they were about to pop. He began gingerly to rub his temples; he was opening his jaws wide to unclog his ears when the space all around him exploded with fire-lizards.

First one, then two, then another pair . . . until a flurry of fire-lizards of all colors filled the air. They flew in tight circles around Piemur and chirped excitedly, calling to one another as if they'd found a prize. A gold quickly flashed in front of his eyes, too fast for him to see her clearly, and then flashed out of sight again, gone *between*. Was that Kimi? He didn't dare hope it was her. Piemur stood up, staring at the fire-lizards; there were nine in total. He rubbed his eyes to clear his vision. He saw that all the fire-lizards were banded with harper blue and light blue on a background of white, framed by a lattice in yellow. Their origins were as clear as day: These were Fort fire-lizards! And they answered to a harper—Menolly!

"Ha! Is that you, Auntie One and Auntie Two?" he called to a pair of green fire-lizards as they flashed past him. "Ha-ha! Rocky, I haven't seen you in ages, you handsome bronze, you!" The fire-lizards continued to fly around Piemur in lazy circles, comfortable in his presence. He'd helped Menolly feed her fair back when they were too young to hunt for themselves, but it had been a long time since he'd seen them.

"Diver, Lazybones, Mimic, and Brownie! It's so good to see you all," he said calling to another bronze and three brown fire-lizards. "Where's that old blue grump? Where's Uncle and the latecomer, Poll?" he called as the group flew around him.

A blue fire-lizard landed on Piemur's shoulder, and he held up his hand for it to climb onto.

"Ah, Uncle," he said, "it's been absolute ages! Look how handsome you are, my friend." Uncle chirruped at Piemur, as if his sentiments were identical, then he held out a foreleg where a message had been secured. "My flying friends, you cannot imagine how happy I am to see you all," Piemur said. Carefully he retrieved the message and read it: *Beauty brings help. Stay put. —M.*

Piemur laughed, slowly at first and then with more enthusiasm, letting the tension he'd been feeling ease from his body with his growing relief. Maybe everything would be all right, he thought. Maybe Kimi had been unnecessarily distraught and Sebell was alive after all.

Piemur didn't have long to wait before he felt a less subtle change in the air above him and looked up to see a dragon flying high overhead; he thought it was a bronze but he couldn't be certain because the sun was shining brightly behind him. The dragon circled down quickly and Piemur ran to meet him as they came in to land. It was J'hon and Mirth, and Beauty was darting around Menolly as she clambered off the dragon's back and ran toward Piemur. Without hesitation Piemur closed the gap between them and threw his arms around her in a tight embrace.

"I am so glad to see you, Menolly," he said, releasing her with a final squeeze. "And I've never been happier to see your fire-lizards, either—every single one of them!"

"Shells, Piemur, what's happened to you?" J'hon asked.

"Yes, what's happened?" Menolly said as she looked him up and down, taking in his disheveled appearance: the blackening eyes, the bloodstains on both sides of his head, and, when she sniffed, the rank odor of alcohol. "You need to have that wound dressed, Piemur. It looks nasty."

"I'll do it later," Piemur said. "Listen: Sebell and I were taken captive by Jerrol and two other men. I'm not completely sure what happened because I got hit on the head and passed out, but they brought us into the cellars of Nabol and while I was unconscious they gave Sebell a real hiding. His arm may be broken, and his legs aren't much better, either." Menolly's mouth opened in a silent O and she quickly covered it with her hand. Piemur clenched his jaw and then continued.

"They tied Sebell to a bench but left me unbound. I was trying to release him when they came back, so I knocked one of them over and ran for the door." The look on Menolly's face transformed to one of shock, and Piemur realized she thought he had abandoned the journeyman masterharper. He faltered before continuing. "While I was looking for help, I found Kimi. She was in an awful state. I don't think she can make a connection to Sebell."

"I know, Piemur."

"Shards, I should've stayed with Sebell! But he made me promise to run for help if I got the chance."

"What good would it have done if you were both kept captive?" J'hon asked.

"It's not your fault. We'll find Sebell," Menolly added in a determined voice as she gripped him by the shoulders.

"I shouldn't have left him, Menolly!"

"Don't think about that, Piemur, it won't do any good." Menolly shook his shoulders gently, then dropped her hands.

"Where did you get out of the Hold?" J'hon asked.

"On the other side."

"I'll send my fire-lizards to try and find Sebell," Menolly said. "And I'll have them ask the other fire-lizards here if they know anything. Goodness knows there're enough fire-lizards in Nabol to help."

"That's a good idea," J'hon said. He turned to Piemur. "Can you show us where you came out of the cellars?"

"I think so," Piemur replied, though even to his own ears he didn't sound very confident.

It took only a moment for J'hon and Menolly to strip off their flying gear and toss it in a small pile beside the huge bronze dragon. Then they set out at a run, Piemur leading as he sought to recollect exactly where he had exited the cellars. Periodically he stopped as he tried to find the small door he had come through, but each one he tried was shut tight and would not budge. How could he have failed to notice how many doors punctuated the perimeter of the Hold?

"Is this the one?" Menolly asked, but Piemur shook his head mutely and they ran on.

"How about this one?" J'hon suggested as they came to another door in the thick hold walls.

"That doesn't look like it," Piemur replied, and a growing sense of hopelessness began to cloud his thoughts. As they continued to run, Piemur's pace slowed substantially as he realized he had no clue how to find the right way back into the Hold.

"Should we retrace our steps?" Menolly asked, panic squeezing her throat and making her voice higher.

"I'm not sure . . . I don't know!" Piemur hated how much he sounded like a whining little boy. His head was pounding unbearably and the ache in his back had grown stronger with every step.

Piemur put his hands to his head, forgetting about the lumps above his ears. The careless act made him wince in pain. He fell silent then, fighting back the mounting despair, too embarrassed to look at his friends and ashamed because he had failed Sebell.

You can't hide from this, Piemur, he thought and forced himself to look up. As he slowly searched the faces of Menolly and J'hon he knew he had failed to hide his distress. Menolly started to fidget, and J'hon looked at the ground; both were clearly worried, and Piemur realized that nothing could be done to help find Sebell until he pulled himself together.

He took a few deep breaths and slowly rubbed his hands the length of his thighs, trying to remember how he had found his way out of the cellars.

"I came up out of the cellar through a wooden door. Then I saw the outer walls of the Hold and ran until I came to a very narrow door. I went through it and—" He faltered, trying to dredge the memory from his fuzzy head. "—and slammed the door closed. I remember that it made an odd sound—dull, like a thud, not a bang—but then I just kept running." Piemur was slowly regaining his composure, and as he did so, he began to feel—and, he thought, sound—more certain.

"I'm going to retrace our steps," Menolly said. "Piemur, you and J'hon keep looking in that direction." And she turned around and ran, stopping to push against the first door she came to before moving on to the next.

"C'mon, Piemur," J'hon said. "We'll find it, I know we will."

Piemur ran right past the correct door before he realized his error. He stopped, backed up, and stood in front of it, closely examining door and frame from top to bottom. Now he could see that this door wasn't mounted properly; warped by decades of use and disuse, it listed slightly on its metal hinges. That was probably why it hadn't sounded right when Piemur had slammed it shut behind him: It no longer met the frame squarely.

J'hon lifted the leg of his trousers, pulled out a sheathed dagger stashed in his boot, and began to scrape the blade along the bottom of the doorframe, loosening the dirt that filled the gaps around the edges of the door. Piemur jumped in to help, using the toe of his boot to pry at the dirt, and together they quickly cleared all around the door.

But even then, the door seemed to have no means by which it could be opened: no metal latch, handle, ring, or other device, only an empty hatch where a handle once had been. J'hon tried inserting the blade of his dagger into the hole, but it was too big. They both puzzled over it for several moments, stepping back a few paces to stare at it intently.

"Oy! Whadder you doin'?" a voice called.

Startled, Piemur and J'hon looked up but couldn't locate the source of the voice. They searched all along the huge expanse of wall, but no one was visible.

"Up here, you thick two-wits!" the voice called again. Piemur and J'hon took another step backward and looked up once more. High up in the wall of the Hold they saw a head protruding from a tiny opening.

"Whadder you doin'?" the head repeated.

"Ah," Piemur said, thinking quickly, "Lord Deckter wants us to check that all of these doors are working from the inside and the outside." He made a big show of scratching his head, trying not to wince when he touched the sore spots. "But we can't get in from this door, if you get what I mean." He scratched his head again.

"You'll never open that door from out there! Jaickers, there ain't any knob! Where did they find you two? I don't know why he wants you to check 'em all when the whole passway is going to be bricked up tight for good. But ne'er mind. Whadder *I* know?" the head yelled, shaking itself from side to side before continuing. "The Lord Holder knows best, I reckon. Listen here to me an' I'll tell you what to do. Go back to the rampart and in through the door; then go all the way down to the end of the passway. Take the second turn right, the third turn left, down two sets a' steps, and to the passway at the very end. That's where *that* door is!"

"Ah," Piemur said. Craning his neck back to look up was making him feel decidedly ill, and the fierce pounding in his head was making it hard for him to process the directions.

J'hon grabbed Piemur's shoulder and looked up, waving in understanding. "Ah! Er, yup!" he called. Then he muttered under his breath to Piemur, "I followed what he was saying, harper. Let's go—now!" J'hon propelled him back the way they had come. In moments they were met by Menolly, who'd heard their hollered exchanges with the head-in-the-wall and was running to join them, anxiety stamped all over her face.

"We know how to get into the cellars," Piemur told her quickly. "Let's get him out of there, Lolly." Menolly offered Piemur a weak smile and fell in beside him, following J'hon as he raced toward the Hold ramparts.

There was much more activity around this part of the Hold. A steady bustle of people and carts streamed in and out of the gates at the rampart. Piemur faltered at all the frenetic activity and stumbled several times. It was all starting to feel like too much to take: He just wanted to find Sebell so he could sit down somewhere quiet, lick his wounds, and forget about the awful events of the last day and night.

J'hon put a reassuring hand on Piemur's shoulder, applying enough pressure so that Piemur knew he wanted him to stop and look at him. Menolly stopped and turned, too, the three of them standing in an impromptu huddle.

J'hon's expression was intense, but when he spoke it was in his usual quiet manner. "We'll get into the Hold as quickly as possible and find him. Be certain of that, Menolly." J'hon nodded to punctuate his words, then continued. "Piemur, I can see you've been through the wringer, but just keep putting one foot in front of the other and if you need to, lean on me or Menolly." He paused. "Do you hear me?" And when Piemur gave him a weak smile in answer, they advanced into the heart of the throng.

Menolly and J'hon fell in step next to Piemur, walking close enough to act as virtual bolsters on either side of him. It was a simple gesture, but Piemur felt a rush of gratitude. *I must be more unsteady than I realize,* Piemur mused, and took several more steadying breaths.

When they reached the rampart walkway and found the door the bodiless head had mentioned, J'hon led the way through. Once inside, they moved quickly, snaking their way through the passageways and down into the bowels of Nabol Hold.

No one had followed them, Piemur was relieved to see. In fact, the cellars of Nabol were eerily empty, and he thought they could walk these passageways for days without attracting anyone's attention. The place seemed so abandoned that he was actually surprised to find a couple of glowbaskets on the wall of one intersection. Thinking fast, he grabbed them from their holders and handed one each to Menolly and J'hon.

"We have to search methodically," Piemur said, "or we might overlook a cellar room or dead end somewhere. Do you think we should split up?"

"I think we should stay together, Piemur," Menolly replied. "We can't risk any of us getting lost, and anyway, there's no telling whom we might come across down here."

"Safety in numbers, eh?" he asked, feeling hugely relieved. He didn't want to have to wander alone through these vast cellars . . . not again.

"Exactly," J'hon said, holding up his glowbasket and moving ahead.

Menolly followed with Piemur, sticking close in case he needed help. But the dimmer light level down here was soothing his headache, and since they had to slow their pace in order to check each door they passed, his back didn't hurt so much anymore, either. With his pain lessened, a wisp of optimism began to return to his spirit, even though he was ashamed to have barely enough strength to help Menolly and J'hon force open the most stubbornly stuck doors. As they made their way through the cellar maze, the light grew darker, the air dank, and Piemur began to see patches of moisture dripping down the thick stone walls.

"This must be the part they're going to brick up permanently. It looks like it hasn't been used in ages," he said, running his hand down a section of slick wet wall.

"And no wonder," J'hon said distastefully, ducking beneath the end of a broken, rotting beam that couldn't be doing much to hold up the ceiling anymore. He turned and held a protective hand on the splintered wood while Menolly and Piemur crept past.

The doors here proved nigh impossible to move, jammed as they were with Turns of dirt, water leaks, and neglect. Painstakingly, they forced each open and searched the room behind it, but each one they entered was empty, or contained only useless objects like broken baskets, discarded small furnishings, or moldering piles of rags. When they arrived, disheartened, at the last door, they automatically put their shoulders to it—but this door wasn't stuck closed. When the three of them pushed together, the door flew open with a whoosh, throwing them off balance.

Piemur, Menolly, and J'hon looked at one another, and Piemur could see that the others' expressions mirrored the hope he was feeling. Without a word, they entered the dank space.

But this room, too, was unoccupied, save for one rotten half barrel standing against the back wall. J'hon stood, stooping slightly in the middle of the low-ceilinged room, and looked all around at the empty space. Beside Piemur, Menolly dropped to a crouch, hunkered on her heels, and cradled her head in her hands. Piemur heard a stifled moan escape her.

How could Sebell not be here? There were no more cellars to search. Disbelief and despair warred in Piemur. He swung the glow around the room, high above his head, and kicked at the dirt floor in frustration.

"He has to be somewhere!" Piemur exclaimed. "We must've missed a room. Let's go back and search again."

"Huh?" J'hon was looking at the barrel pushed against the wall on the other side of the room. "Do that again, Piemur."

"Do what?"

Menolly slowly looked up.

"This," J'hon said, and stomped one booted foot on the dirt floor. As the dust flew up from his foot and then began to settle, all three could see that, rather than falling downward, the motes of dust seemed to be swirling toward them, as if being blown by a current of air. Coming to the same conclusion at the same time, dragonrider and harper all but threw themselves at the rotten half barrel and hauled it out of the way.

In the wall behind where the barrel had been, Piemur could see a small door set into a stone frame. If they hadn't moved the barrel they never would've known it was there! Menolly rose to her feet, eyes wide—and then she froze. She'd seen that there was no handle on the door at the same time both Piemur and J'hon had.

Dropping to his knees, Piemur tried to get his fingers into the gap between the door and its frame but his hands were too big, the join was too small, and he couldn't gain enough grip. J'hon held up his dagger and Piemur stood back. The bronze dragonrider quickly slid the tip of the knife into the narrow seam and dragged it up and down and all around the edges of the door. When he pushed the knife into the horizontal part of the frame at the top, they all heard the distinct sound of a click. They'd stumbled upon a hidden release catch.

Piemur swallowed a lump of fear.

J'hon twisted his knife between the frame and the joint and the door swung open a fraction. Leveraging his knife farther into the aperture, J'hon twisted it again and pushed the door fully open on its hinge.

The secret cellar was barely a meter square in size, with a slanting ceiling not high enough for even a small child to stand in. It was empty save for a dirty lump of fabric lying in a heap on the damp earth floor, and Piemur felt his heart skip a beat when he realized that this little hidey-hole, their last hope, held nothing but a pile of rags.

Then, suddenly and without a word, Menolly lunged forward and pushed Piemur's arm up, holding it so his glow shone directly on the rags. With dawning understanding, Piemur saw a brown curl poking out from the filthy material. He quickly put the glowbasket down, and then he, Menolly, and J'hon very gingerly tugged at the lump of material and managed to hoist it through the doorway and into the cellar room. The pile of rags moaned.

"Thank the first shard that fell from the First Egg," Piemur whispered as he gently lifted a piece of the rotting fabric away from the body lying underneath.

Menolly's sharp intake of breath was followed by a distraught cry, sounds that were almost a counterpoint to the guilt and empathy Piemur felt when he looked at the still form of the journeyman masterharper.

Sebell groaned, and his head rolled to one side, facing Piemur.

With wooden movements, Menolly unraveled the mess of rags that were tied around Sebell's head and mouth, and as the last rag came away, Piemur winced.

"It's not as bad as it looks," Sebell croaked through cracked lips, peering at them through one swollen eye. Carefully, Piemur and J'hon unbound Sebell's hands, while Menolly tackled the ropes on his legs. The journeyman masterharper was a fearful sight; his left shoulder sloped down at an alarming angle, and the arm to which it was attached lay limp and unmoving. His legs, visible through his torn trousers, were covered by dirt and caked blood, but not so much that his rescuers couldn't see that his flesh was lacerated and heavily bruised from knee to ankle.

When the rush of anger and shock abated, and Sebell's injuries had been silently assessed, they sat for several moments, uncertain how to proceed.

An odd noise, strangely familiar, came from farther along the passageway, and both Piemur and J'hon abruptly stood to attention in front of Sebell, ready to guard him in case Jerrol, Jentis, and Serra had returned. Menolly remained hunkered down next to Sebell.

"It's just Beauty with Kimi," she said. "I let them know where we are and that we've found Sebell."

Flapping wings sped toward them, seeming to drag all the air along, too, as they filled the confines of the passageway with their rapid beats. Kimi took a straight path to Sebell and then hovered for half a heartbeat before she landed on the ground next to him, cooing and chirruping, humming with joy and relief. She quickly furled her golden wings and, in two short hops, closed the distance between them to land on his uninjured shoulder, rubbing her head against his cheek repeatedly.

"Shh, shh," Sebell said gently, trying to calm her. "I'm here! So are you! We're both all right now. There's my golden girl."

She cooed at him again and he leaned his face toward her head. Kimi must have shared an image with Sebell, because he chuckled.

"I know, I know; it *was* frightening. Yes, Kimi," he said, "you stay right here and keep me in your sights. That's exactly what I need."

Then he looked up at his friends, reaching one hand out to grab Menolly's. "What next?" he asked, looking at them through his one good eye as Kimi clung to his neck. Piemur could see that Sebell was in a lot of pain, which nearly left him lost for words, but then something occurred to him: With those two simple words Sebell, who usually took control of any situation, had relinquished his welfare to Piemur and Menolly.

The realization had a cathartic effect on Piemur. "We need to get you to a healer, Sebell," he said.

"But we can't bring him back to Fort—or the Harper Hall," Menolly said, her voice breaking slightly. Tears ran down her face.

"You're right, Menolly," Piemur said, and he placed a reassuring hand on her shoulder. "Too many questions will be asked, and I'm not sure how we can answer them."

J'hon muttered an expletive through tight lips, and Piemur could see that the dragonrider was doing his utmost to control his anger.

"Wherever we bring Sebell, his condition will provoke too much interest. And if we rightly accuse Jerrol, Jentis, and Serra—or anyone—of beating a harper, we'd have to explain why Sebell and I were here. Then the threat to Jaxom—which we've been trying so hard to keep secret—would become common knowledge."

Sebell nodded as Piemur spoke.

"No, we can't tell anyone what happened here, though I sorely wish we could." Piemur spoke through clenched teeth. J'hon was staring at Piemur, a fierce expression on his usually benign features. Piemur returned his stare resolutely and then shook his head.

Menolly quickly wiped the tears from her face with both hands. "We need somewhere safe and where you aren't well known." They fell silent for a few moments, weighing the scant options they had.

"We could take him to one of the remote Weyrs. He'd be safe there," J'hon offered, but Sebell shook his head.

Again, Piemur spoke up. "There's no doubt he'd be taken care of in any Weyr on Pern, J'hon, but we can't travel far with him like this, and if his shoulder, or his arm, is as badly broken as it looks, he can't fly *between,* because the cold might destroy any chance of it healing properly. It's just too dangerous. And I think any dragonrider who sees Sebell would understandably want justice done on his behalf. No, we need somewhere remote, but not a Weyr, somewhere fairly isolated but not too far away . . ." And in that instant Piemur knew exactly what to do.

"I know where we can go. We'll fly Sebell directly to Crom, to my home!"

They wasted little time, and with Piemur and J'hon making a chair of their crisscrossed arms and Menolly acting as glow carrier and guide, they carried Sebell between them through the maze of passageways.

Once outside the Hold, Menolly went ahead of them with Beauty, and J'hon called Mirth, asking him to come as close as he could to the ramparts. As they made their way steadily through the throng of bustling holders and traders, several stopped and stared at the sight of J'hon and Piemur carrying a man in their linked arms, as if he were a person of great importance and not a battered, dirty jumble of grotty rags.

An elderly woman who bore a remarkable resemblance to Fronna frowned when she recognized Piemur's bruised face, and then gasped when she noticed Sebell's condition. As they passed by, her mouth fell open and she stood, silent, pointing one finger at them as she followed their progress away from the Hold.

They reached the clearing where Mirth and Menolly were waiting, the dragon already crouched low to the ground, Menolly astride him. When she saw them, she reached out as if to take Sebell in her arms, and Piemur saw that Menolly's face was wet again from fresh tears.

Moving Sebell as gently and carefully as possible, the three of them got him into place at the base of the bronze dragon's neck, Menolly just in front of him and Piemur behind, close enough to prop Sebell up and ensure the harper remained securely in place during the short flight. Finally, J'hon climbed onto his usual place between his dragon's neck ridges. At J'hon's signal Mirth took several steps forward, unfurling the sails of his wings and bunching the muscles in his massive haunches, and then pushed upward, making a deep gouge in the ground as he launched himself into the air.

His wings beat downward with huge force, propelling himself and his passengers steadily upward. The movement was turbulent and Piemur braced his arms more securely around Sebell's waist.

As Mirth beat his wings and rose higher and higher into the sky, several groups of people from the Hold looked up at the bronze dragon overhead, expressions ranging from curiosity to concern evident on their faces.

Piemur reached across Sebell and Menolly to tap J'hon on the shoulder, and the dragonrider turned his head to hear him.

"When you see Crom Hold, I can guide you from there to my family's smallholding," Piemur said, and J'hon nodded once before silently relaying their destination to Mirth.

They flew to the west of Crom Hold, gliding toward a broad, flat valley bounded on one side by a vast lake and on the other side by the butt end of the spiny range of mountains that extended from the Snowy Wastes in the far north, down through Fort, and all the way to the very tip of Southern Boll Hold. Piemur's family's small-holding was positioned on relatively sheltered high ground, over-looking the verdant meadows of the valley.

Once Piemur, J'hon, and Menolly had helped Sebell from Mirth's back and carried him to a long bench below a broadleaf tree, Piemur ran for help, though the arrival of a bronze dragon had brought many of the cotholders out of their dwellings to meet him halfway. When they saw who had arrived on the back of a bronze dragon there were cries of excitement. A group of Piemur's kin crowded around him, thumping him on the back or hugging him unreservedly, everyone asking him half a dozen different questions at the same time.

When Piemur returned a short while later, surrounded by a smiling crowd of family and friends, Sebell was lying motionless, his eyes closed. Kimi, shooed from his shoulder by Menolly, perched on a low branch right above him. J'hon was reassessing the extent of the harper's injuries, a grim expression on his face as he hissed under his breath. The dappled light that came through the leaves of the big tree did little to soften the signs of the horrific beating Sebell had suffered.

The cotholders, quietly nodding respectful greetings to J'hon and Menolly, eyed Sebell silently, their smiles and jovial expressions quickly suppressed as they took stock of his condition. One of the women held a cup of fellis juice to Sebell's lips and succeeded in getting him to take a long draft of the analgesic. It took effect quickly and Sebell was soon mercifully unconscious. Only then did the cotholders gently carry him to the smallest of the closely grouped cothold buildings.

As the sleeping Sebell was carefully laid out on a comfortable-looking bed, Piemur's family crowded into the little cottage.

"Dear gracious! How did this happen?" an older woman asked.

"Did he fall, Pie?" a tall man asked.

"Look at the state of him," another woman said in a hushed tone, beginning to pass her hands gently along Sebell's limbs to assess his injuries. "Who did this, Pie?"

"Can't say, Drina, and it'd be of no use to you if you knew," Piemur said uncomfortably.

"Don't look right to me," a ginger-haired man offered, and those standing next to him nodded in agreement.

"I sure as shards don't need all of you in here with me. Go away," Drina said gently, flapping one hand. "I'll look after Pie's friend now and let you all go about your day." And she nodded once, peering kindly but sternly at the curious spectators.

Menolly, J'hon, and Piemur made to leave the room with the rest of the crowd, but Drina reassured them that they were welcome to remain or leave, as they wished. Menolly released a held breath, moving to sit in a chair near the bed. But J'hon walked out of the cottage without a word, and Piemur figured either the dragonrider thought the little house was already sufficiently crowded or didn't want to witness in more detail the results of Sebell's torture. Piemur wondered if he should follow him.

But Drina stopped him. "You stay, too, Pie, and tell me what has befallen this poor man. You know it'll not go any further than me," she said as she lifted the torn material from Sebell's legs. She tsked under her breath when she saw the deep gashes and bruises.

"We were bashed about by some . . . some less-than-noble men,

Drina. They knocked me on the head, and while I was unconscious they took out their anger on Sebell. I think his left arm might be broken."

Drina pushed the sleeve of Sebell's tunic up and examined the arm from wrist to armpit.

"There's no break here, Pie. Help me roll him onto his other side."

Just then a burly man stomped into the cothold, filling the doorway and blocking out the light.

"Pergamol," Piemur said, and walked toward the older man, who engulfed him in a bearlike embrace.

"Ah, lad. It's good to see you, Pie! You've grown tall. This one, though"—he pointed a finger at Sebell—"looks a right mess. What happened?"

"I was telling Drina that we'd be grateful if what's happened to Sebell isn't mentioned outside the cothold, Pergamol. We were used as punching bags by some disgruntled, holdless men—I took a thump to the head and, I guess because I was knocked senseless, poor Sebell got the brunt of their abuse."

"'Nuff said, Pie, I'll tell the others." Pergamol looked at Drina. "What do ya need, Dri?"

"I need you to roll him over carefully so I can see the back a' his shoulder."

Pergamol easily rolled Sebell onto his right side, and Drina lifted his tunic. She sucked in her breath sharply and then tsked several times.

"I can't fix this one, Pie. You need a healer. It looks like someone yanked on his arm so hard the shoulder's been pulled straight out of its cup. I don't have the knack of getting it back in. Ama was good at that type a' thing, but she's not as strong as she used to be." Drina looked grave. "I can fix up most of his cuts and such, but a healer will have to tend to his shoulder. I think I can manage his eye. That'll need stitching." She pointed at the deep, messy gash over Sebell's swollen eye.

"Thanks, Drina," Piemur said, feeling a little queasy and glad for an errand. "I'll get a healer."

"Good lad," Drina replied. "Now leave me to get this man settled—and send Berry in to help, would you, Pergamol?"

Piemur left the tiny cottage, joining J'hon where he sat under the broadleaf tree. The dragonrider looked up at Piemur, who noticed the muscles in the handsome, usually calm face working and knew that the dragonrider was clenching and unclenching his teeth.

"Well?" J'hon asked in a dull voice.

"Drina says his arm isn't broken, but his shoulder has been pulled out of its socket. He'll need stitches over his eye."

"They should pay for this, harper. Blow for blow," J'hon said tensely, pounding a closed fist into an open palm to punctuate his point.

"I know how you feel, but right now we need to get a healer for Sebell. Someone discreet." Walking back to the cottage threshold, Piemur called for Menolly to join them.

"What healer should we use, Loll?"

"How about Brekke? She'd be discreet," Menolly suggested.

"She would be, but she's too prominent a figure in Benden Weyr. How could she explain her absence?" Piemur shook his head. "With everything that's gone on in that Weyr recently, I think we'd better look elsewhere for help."

"Does anyone know who Masterhealer Oldive has apprenticed under him?" J'hon asked. "He must have someone we can use."

"What about Toric's sister, Sharra? What's she up to these days?" Piemur asked.

"I don't think she has enough experience, Piemur." Menolly glanced toward the cothold, a worried expression on her face. "I should go back in there to him."

"Isn't Toric's new headwoman, Meria, healer-trained?" J'hon asked.

"Why didn't I think of Meria?" Piemur slapped his hand against his thigh. "She'd be perfect!"

They agreed that Piemur should go with J'hon to ask Meria for help. When Menolly fretted that someone should be watching out for Lord Jaxom until they could find out where Jerrol and his thugs were, J'hon reassured her that he'd already sent word to N'ton's dragon via Mirth. Menolly was relieved when the two men had no objections about her remaining with Sebell.

J'hon and Piemur returned with Meria within the hour, and then J'hon promptly departed again for Fort Weyr and his duties there, promising Piemur that he would return as soon as possible.

When Piemur ushered Meria into the cothold, he was relieved to find that Drina had not only done a good job stitching up Sebell's eye, but cleaned him up as well, dressing the gashes on his legs before she and Menolly changed him into a clean tunic. He made to leave, assured that the journeyman masterharper was in good hands, but Meria stopped him.

"You'd best stay, Piemur," she said. "I'll need all the help I can get to put Sebell's shoulder back in place."

With more than a little apprehension, Piemur took up his position next to her, while Menolly and Drina, under Meria's instructions, stood near Sebell's head, bracing his body.

"I'll hold on above his elbow, Piemur, and you clasp his hand. On my command I want you to pull hard and steady, and don't stop until I tell you to."

When Menolly and Drina were satisfied that they had a secure grasp on the other side of Sebell's body, so he wouldn't be pulled off the bed, Meria nodded.

Piemur braced his knees against the bed, and when Meria gave the order, he pulled for all he was worth. It seemed to take forever, and he didn't think it was possible to pull a person's arm that hard without it coming off in his hands, but when he felt a subtle *clunk* as the head of the arm bone slotted back into the socket, Piemur knew that they'd succeeded in relocating the shoulder. Sebell heaved upward, dragged out of his fellis-induced stupor by the pain of the relocation, his eyes shooting open.

"It's all over, Sebell. Just rest now," Meria said calmly. "Take another drink of fellis while we put some more numbweed on your shoulder."

Sebell closed his eyes again and muttered something unintelligible, but he duly drank from the proffered cup and then slumped back against the bed, sighing heavily as Drina put numbweed all across his shoulder. Piemur glanced at Menolly and saw that all the color had drained out of her face.

"I've a tincture-balm I like to use when the lads get thrown about by the young stock. It helps with bruising," Drina explained. "I'll just put it along his shins, betwixt the cuts. He'll be good as new right quick." She showed Meria a little jar of salve she had tucked away in a pocket of her tunic, and Meria nodded at her, smiling.

Menolly fussed over Sebell, settling a coverlet over him after she'd placed a plump cushion between his knees to keep the weight of the blanket off his bruised legs. Very soon they heard Sebell's breathing resolve into a steady rhythm and knew he was resting peacefully. Drina left Piemur, Menolly, and Meria to return to the demands of her family.

"I'll stay here for the night, Piemur," Meria told him. "To make sure he's suffered no ill effects from what we just put him through."

"Thanks, Meria. There was no one else we could ask to help." He gave her a lopsided grin, then furrowed his brow slightly. "If you don't mind, Meria, it would be best if this matter weren't bandied about."

"You have my silence, Piemur. Now, why don't you let me look at that cut on your head? I can clean it up and then take a look at the other lump, too. Were you trying for a matching pair?"

They left Menolly sitting next to Sebell and went outside. Piemur sat on the stone bench under the tree while Meria assessed the cut over his ear and the lumps on his head. She cleaned the dried blood from his hair and put some numbweed on the lumps, laughing softly when he confessed that the second lump had been self-inflicted.

Just as Meria was putting the last dab of numbweed on Piemur's head, a young girl, about twelve Turns old, came skipping toward them from the direction of the main group of cotholds.

"Hello, I'm Ais. Uncle Pergamol said to bring you some *klah*. I have it here." She held up a basket in one hand; in the other, she held two fresh glowbaskets tied together with twine. "Uncle said you should come up to his cothold for the evening meal. It'll be ready just after the light starts to fade. And he says you should stay for the afters, too." She deposited the basket and the twined glows on the stone bench and then loped away.

Piemur and Meria sat in comfortable silence for a while, but when Piemur's eyes began to droop, Meria wordlessly retrieved a blanket from the cothold.

"You've obviously been through a rough time, Piemur, so why don't you try and rest. I'll check on Sebell regularly, and relieve Menolly if she wants a break, so you needn't worry about him."

With a heartfelt smile, Piemur gladly pulled the blanket around his shoulders and curled up under the tree.

Dusk had descended on the pretty valley when Piemur at last woke up. Farli was in her usual place around the top of his head. He absently ran a hand along the length of the little queen's body, and she cooed gently in response.

"Renegade," he muttered fondly. He stretched deeply and then sat up. He could hear voices coming from the cothold, so he left Farli on the blanket and went to investigate.

Sebell was sitting up on the edge of the bed, talking with Menolly and Meria. A sling held his left arm across his chest. Piemur stood on the threshold, smiling at the obvious improvement in his mentor's appearance.

"You're looking much better," he said.

"And I feel much better, now my shoulder's where it should be. My legs are pleasantly numb, too, so I think I'll join you for the evening meal—Meria says it should be ready by now. I might hobble a little, but I could do with something to eat."

With Piemur on one side, Menolly on the other, and Meria leading the way with a lit glowbasket in either hand, they maneuvered Sebell out of the cottage and shepherded him toward Pergamol's home. The house was already filled with chattering people. Pergamol greeted the newcomers boisterously, then introduced Sebell, Menolly, and Meria to his extended family.

"Where's my Pie?" someone called from a seat next to the cooking fire.

Piemur hurriedly made his way past his kinfolk, quickly greeting each one as he passed by, finally stooping to hug a diminutive old woman who wore her gray hair in a long plait down her back and was smiling so much it dimpled her face.

"Ama," Piemur said reverently, "ah, it's so good to see you again."

"Look how tall you are, lad!" Ama reached up a hand, trying to measure his height but falling short of reaching the top of his head. "How are you, my Pie?" she asked, and she pulled him down for another hug, her eyes bright.

"I'm fine, Ama." He saw Menolly and Meria ushering Sebell toward him. "Ah, here, I want you to meet my friends.

"This is Ama. She fostered me when I was just a tot," he explained. "Ama, this is Meria. She lives in the new Southern Hold, and Menolly here is a journeyman harper like me. Sebell is a journeyman *master*harper. I'm training with Sebell now."

"Ah, that's my Pie. I knew you'd go far. You know: You never stopped warbling or crooning from the time you could first talk. You'll sing for us tonight, Pie." Ama's words were spoken as a statement rather than a question. "It's been a long time since we've heard any decent singing." And the old woman looked up at her foster son, her face bright and full of expectation. Piemur was momentarily unsure of how to reply, but he knew one thing for certain: He couldn't possibly try to sing in front of his family tonight.

"I stopped singing, Ama. When my voice broke," Piemur blurted. Although he was standing close to Ama, and he hadn't spoken very loudly, everyone heard what he had said, and the room plunged into a hushed silence.

A young toddler, hitched up on the hip of an older child, suddenly started crying. Someone shushed the toddler gently, and someone else made a tsking sound.

"Now, that's a true shame, my Pie," Ama said after an interminable silence. "I would've liked to hear you sing again." Then she patted him on the shoulder. "No matter, Pie, you'll find your way. I know you will. Just remember to listen to your instincts."

Piemur ducked his head, embarrassed by the attention his comment had aroused, but then, as if on cue, his kin carried on with their chatter, restoring the sound in the cramped space to a bustling, comfortable buzz. Piemur tried his best to look anywhere but into the eyes of his relatives until Ama gently pushed him into a seat and placed a plate of steaming-hot food into his hands.

When everyone had eaten heartily, they set their plates aside and fell into easy conversation. Piemur recounted some of the adventures he'd been on, and awed his family when he described Mikay's Impression of Nimath. After the plates had been cleared away and the family moved outside to sit around an open fire, Sebell asked Menolly and Meria to help him back to the little cothold. Piemur decided he'd had enough, too, and Drina made a big fuss over the bumps he'd taken to his head as she accompanied them back to the little house, holding a glowbasket high overhead to light the way.

While Meria and Menolly reapplied more numbweed to Sebell's shoulder, Drina bustled around in the cothold with two enormous young lads, whom she proudly claimed were the youngest of her brood, supervising them as they set up extra woven-reed beds with clean padding and blankets for Piemur, Menolly, and Meria to sleep on. When they were finished, they said their good nights and were about to return to Pergamol's cot, where the entertainment was still in full throat, when Drina turned to Piemur.

"Will you come back up with us, Piemur?" she asked.

"I might come up in a while, Drina. Thanks for asking," he replied.

The three harpers and Meria, not quite ready to turn in for the night, sat for a while under the big tree. Farli and Kimi had taken up positions on a low branch, Menolly's Beauty sitting on a higher one above them.

"Thanks for getting my shoulder back in place, Meria. I'm not sure if I said that already," Sebell said, smiling at the diminutive woman. "I guess you're wondering how we got in such a mess."

"Hm," Meria replied, smiling in return, "it is a little puzzling, Sebell. The dislocation of your shoulder isn't that uncommon an injury, but the bruising and lacerations on your legs make me more than a little curious, particularly since you asked for *my* help. Why didn't you get someone from your own Crafthall?"

"I know we have your discretion, Meria," Sebell said, searching her face for any hesitation on her part. When she nodded, Sebell sighed, puffing out his cheeks as he made a spur-of-the-moment decision. "We were trying to get more information about some men from Nabol who, we believe, are planning to act against Hold code." At the look of alarm on Meria's face, he stopped speaking. She pursed her lips and then gestured for him to continue, but her response piqued Piemur's curiosity, too. Why should Meria be concerned about the men from Nabol?

Sebell briefly explained what he and Piemur had been doing in Nabol, reassuring her, when she asked, that no harm had befallen Jaxom.

"And these men from Nabol, what will happen to them, now?" she asked, her eyes darting from Sebell's face to Piemur's. "What will you do, Sebell?"

This is odd, Piemur mused. Why would Meria have such an interest in Jerrol and his thugs? He could understand her concern for Jaxom's safety, but why was she asking questions about the Nabolese men?

"I'd honestly prefer to leave them to their Lord Holder," Sebell replied. "He is, after all, their kinsman, whether *they* like it or not. But I don't think punishing them would serve any purpose, not in their situation."

"But look what they did to you, Sebell!" Piemur cried, outrage propelling him to his feet. He stood with his fists at his side and his body thrust forward, his face suffused with anger as he stared at his mentor. Sebell merely held out one hand, gesturing to Piemur to calm down.

"Yes, Sebell, why don't they deserve to be punished?" Menolly asked, her brows furrowing deeply.

"They're hard men, and hardhearted, from what I witnessed," Sebell continued. "I know they were poorly treated by Lord Meron when he was alive, so it explains a great deal. What they need is for Lord Deckter to take them in hand instead of leaving them alone."

"You're amazing, after the treatment you received from them," Menolly replied, a deep scowl darkening her face.

Sebell shrugged his good shoulder and cast his gaze downward.

Self-deprecating as always, Piemur thought. Sebell always seemed to look to the broader picture. Piemur sat down again, trying to calm the anger that had risen in him so quickly. He glanced at Sebell, who caught his gaze and locked eyes with him, nodding once. Then Sebell looked at Meria, searching her face—for what, Piemur couldn't tell.

"You looked worried when I mentioned that the men who attacked us were from Nabol, Meria. Why?" Sebell asked.

Meria looked from Piemur to Sebell and Menolly, rubbing her hand along the base of her neck as she scrutinized the three harpers. She must have come to some decision, because she drew in a deep breath and then sighed.

"This is going to take a while. You'd best make yourselves comfortable."

"Drina said there was a small skin of wine in the cothold. Let me get it," Menolly offered. Holding up a finger for Meria to wait, she left them; when she returned, she was carrying the wineskin and cups, which she distributed before filling. Sebell took a cup, but Piemur turned the offer down with a shake of his head. After his experience in Nabol, he didn't think he'd ever again be able to stomach anything stronger than a cup of *klah*!

Meria sat down on the stone bench next to Sebell, while Menolly sat on his other side; Piemur sat on the ground in front of them.

"I'm an Oldtimer . . . from Nabol," Meria began, and quickly raised a hand when Piemur's brows flew up and he opened his mouth, poised to bombard her with a barrage of questions.

"I was born hundreds of Turns ago, when my uncle was the Lord Holder of Nabol. When I was a young woman, a dragonrider from Fort found me on Search and thought I had the right qualities to Impress a queen, so he brought me to Fort Weyr. Needless to say, another Candidate Impressed the queen, but I stayed on in Fort Weyr. I was enthralled with their way of life—and with a dragonrider, too. His name was S'han. We fell in love, and the Weyr became my way of life.

"When Lessa and Ramoth traveled all those hundreds of Turns *between* time and asked the five Weyrs to help fight Thread in this Pass I, like all the other weyrfolk, didn't hesitate to make the journey with her. I couldn't travel forward with my S'han, because he and his dragon were hauling supplies, so I came forward on B'naj's Seventh.

"Somehow S'han and Medith didn't make the jumps forward successfully, and they were lost *between*. I was devastated. S'han was the love of my life." Meria looked down at her hands. Her voice had taken on a tender quality that couldn't belie how keenly she still felt her loss. When she lifted her head again, what Piemur saw on her face was grief allayed with guilt and her deep sense of loss—a loss that spanned centuries.

"I didn't know what to do without my S'han, and yet I couldn't return four hundred Turns in the past. It was too much to ask of a dragonrider to make that journey, even if I *had* wanted to go back to my own time. And if one of the dragonriders had agreed to take me back, there wasn't anything in Fort for me to return to—all the Weyrs were empty, except for Benden. I was a grown woman by then and didn't want to return to Nabol. I would've felt like a stranger among my own kin."

Of course, Piemur mused, what Meria was saying about the empty Weyrs was absolutely true. Everyone on Pern had learned the words of the Question Song. It was one of the most important teaching ballads, though until Lessa's incredible time-traveling mission, no one had understood exactly what the ballad meant.

Meria continued, "The dragonriders and weyrfolk, *my* folk, were always so honorable, and they'd taken me in as one of their own, so I knew they were happy for me to stay with them even without my S'han. They were so kind to me.

"The Weyr Healer, G'reff, took me under his wing and taught me all he knew. But G'reff was an old man when we came forward, and he found it difficult adjusting to this newer world. G'reff's health began to fail, and gradually I assumed his duties as healer in Fort.

"Like so many of the others, I didn't approve of the way the more inflexible Oldtimers living in this Pass were behaving. Even so, when matters worsened and they were sent to Southern, I went with them, to stay with my friends, like B'naj, and to honor my Weyr."

Piemur sat up straighter when Meria mentioned B'naj's name. He was the Oldtimer T'reb had been speaking to in Southern, Piemur recollected. B'naj had tried to calm T'reb down before the volatile dragonrider dashed off to meet with the two men—what were their names? Tooban and Cramb? He dragged his attention back to Meria, not wanting to miss a word of her story.

"Life grew very difficult in Southern Weyr and the riders seemed to lose their sense of purpose, and so did their dragons. Eventually I felt I couldn't remain there any longer, but I had nowhere else to go—being holdless is not a thing people from my time can adapt to.

"Toric had been trading supplies with Southern Weyr, and when I asked him for help he offered me a place in his Hold. T'kul was furious at my decision and made his feelings known throughout the Weyr. It's with the deepest sense of regret that I've realized, all too late, that I did a selfish thing when I left the weyrfolk in Southern, because I was the only person among them who had an in-depth healer's knowledge." She paused, gathering her thoughts.

"I know you've heard often enough how stubborn us Oldtimers are," Meria went on, and a rueful smile briefly played across her lips, "and how the Weyrs of my time hold on to their autonomy like a crutch, unable to ask for, or accept, help from any quarter outside the Weyr. So when our firestone stocks were completely depleted, the riders and dragons grew desperate, because they had nothing with which to flame Thread. Their riders tried mining firestone themselves, but it was a disaster.

"I had left the Weyr by that point, and B'naj told me that almost the entire complement of dragons was at the mine to transport the stone back to the Weyr when the shafts gave way and caved in. He said the plume of dust that rose up from the mine must've been mixed with more than firestone dust, because it had a peculiar effect on everyone, although they didn't know it at the time. Those who had been at the mine started to grow irritable, and a persistent cough plagued a lot of the dragons and some of the riders, too. Then they developed chronic aches and grew more lethargic as their health continued to decline.

"Of course, they no longer had a healer, and were too proud to ask anyone from outside the Weyr for help. The sad thing is that I *know* I could have helped them. We used to use a root that grows in the north to help counter all sorts of woes. G'reff called it thujang, but I haven't heard it mentioned in this Pass. Perhaps it's vanished. I've been trying to find another root in the south that has the same healing properties."

Piemur suddenly thought back to that miserable, wet day in Nabol when old Laida had given him and Sebell the brew made from jango to help ward off chills after they'd gotten soaked in the rain. It probably wasn't the same thing, he reckoned, yanking his attention back to the present.

"Do you think *that's* the reason why they took Ramoth's egg? Because they were ill?" Menolly asked.

"Not entirely, but it played a part. You see, the Weyr has no weyrlings—no new blood—nor any queens young enough to fly to mate, and that only served to compound the sense of despondency many of the dragons and their riders were feeling. That's when a few members of the Weyr grew truly desperate."

"So they stole Ramoth's egg!" Piemur said in a hushed whisper as he stared at Meria.

"Yes, they did. But only a *few* members of the Weyr decided to do that, Piemur," Meria said, her tone earnest. "B'naj told me about the plan. He knew *when* they were going to take the egg to, and where. They had a drawing of the place where they planned to hide the egg—he even got a copy of it for me."

"I spied on the man who made that drawing!" Piemur blurted out. "And I saw T'reb, too, when he came to fetch it. Cramb—that was the artist's name—he kept one of the drawings, though. That must be the one he gave to B'naj!"

Meria nodded, a rueful smile on her lips. "Maybe you can see now that not everyone from Nabol is rotten, Piemur. Cramb is from

Nabol, too—he's a distant relative of mine. And for whatever it may be worth, B'naj and I planned to return the egg, but it was snatched up by someone else before we could get it."

"Do you know who returned the egg?" Sebell asked quietly. Piemur noticed that Menolly had grown very still. She wanted to know who'd returned the egg just as much as Sebell—as much as they all did.

"No, I didn't see who it was, and the riders guarding the egg were asleep when the egg was taken back. B'naj and I were too late." Meria looked down at her hands where they lay idle in her lap. She would have given anything to be the one to return Ramoth's egg, Piemur guessed as he watched the diminutive, likable Oldtimer. If she had pulled it off, it might have improved her standing in the Weyr and the precarious situation the Oldtimers now found themselves in. He glanced at Sebell quickly before Meria looked up from her hands, and the older harper gave him a piercing look.

"I guess it doesn't matter who took the egg back, though it was most likely an Oldtimer from the south," Piemur said, looking first at Meria and then Sebell and Menolly. Meria quickly lifted her head, a look of hope in her eyes. "All that matters, really, is that the egg was returned and the new queen has safely Impressed."

"I couldn't have said that any better, my friend," Sebell said, and smiled, his warm brown eyes crinkling up at the corners.

"I wonder what they'll do now?" Piemur said.

"I wish they'd listen to me," Meria said wistfully. "I'm certain the poor health they're suffering is due to the dust and fumes they inhaled at that firestone mine. I'm sure I could make them well again if they'd let me help."

"I feel sorry for them," Piemur said, crossing his arms in front of his chest.

Meria tilted her chin toward him, her expression one of curiosity. "Why is that?" she asked.

"They don't fit in anymore. They've left their Weyr and fled their lives. And they're sick, too. They haven't lived in their old Weyrs up north for more than six Turns, and they don't really seem to be living anywhere in this Pass. Shells, they're *nowhere*! How bloody awful they must feel."

Later that night Piemur tossed and twitched on his makeshift bed, trying, without luck, to fall to sleep. He finally got up and sat on the threshold of the little dwelling. The brief exchange he and J'hon had experienced with the head-in-the-wall kept playing over and over in Piemur's mind, and he clearly recalled the head's casual comment that Lord Deckter planned to brick up the network of old cellars. It made Piemur shudder when he thought of it. What if the head hadn't seen Piemur and J'hon struggling to get into the exterior door of the Hold, or told them how to find the door from within? Or what if Piemur hadn't kicked at the dirt floor in frustration so that J'hon saw the motes moved by the current of air? Ifs, ifs, ifs. There were too many of them!

When Piemur thought of what could have happened had the ifs not all worked out as they did, he was overwhelmed by a range of emotions. He found it difficult to fathom how those men could treat Sebell with such brutality and unwarranted disregard, such callous contempt. How could anyone do that to another person? he wondered.

The worst twist was that he *knew* they had to remain silent about their expedition to Nabol. He knew that the beating Sebell received would go unpunished—never mentioned. And Piemur knew *why* they could never disclose what had happened. But it didn't make it any easier to bear.

"What is it, Piemur?"

Piemur had thought Sebell was asleep. "Ah, it's nothing, Sebell. I'm just restless," he replied softly. "I didn't mean to wake you."

"You didn't wake me. Why don't we sit outside? Tell me what's on your mind and maybe I can help," Sebell said, his rich voice reassuring. The two harpers rose, and Piemur helped Sebell to the bench under the broadleaf tree. The skies above were partly cloudy, but here and there the stars peeked through.

"It's just—it's just that it's not right, that's all," Piemur said, plucking at a loose thread on his tunic.

"What's not right?"

"They shouldn't have done that to you, Sebell. Jerrol and his lot shouldn't have beaten you half to death and then stuffed you like a useless old bundle of rags in a dark hole. They should *pay* for what they've done!"

"You're absolutely right, my friend. What Jerrol and his lot did was unspeakable. And they should be punished for it. But you and I both know that the details of our little jaunt to Nabol must remain untold. That's how it has to be," Sebell said. "I know, Pie, that if we went to these men to mete out the punishment we think they deserve, we will have achieved only one thing."

"What?" Piemur asked.

"Retribution. Revenge. Retaliation, call it what you wish, but it would do absolutely no good. We have to find a solution to their problem so they'll never want to behave like that again. If we don't, we'll simply be showing them the same treatment they've always known and they'll never, *ever* have reason to want to change, or become more compassionate men."

Piemur sighed.

"Piemur, someone made those men into the people they are. They didn't start their lives with such adverse and damaged viewpoints. They were pushed to the breaking point after Turns of manipulation at the hand of someone else." Sebell leaned forward as he spoke, closing the distance between him and Piemur, eager to make sure his point was understood.

"But they beat you! They bound you and then left you for dead, Sebell! That part of the cellars was going to be bricked up! What were they thinking?"

"They weren't thinking, Piemur. They were reacting to Turns of mental torture that they shouldn't have had to endure. They'll never be able to change unless the chance to do so is given to them. I've been mulling this over, and I believe it's the only course we can consider—otherwise we're just *fighting* them. Perhaps turning *into* them."

"That can't be all that is done after what you suffered, Sebell," Piemur said. He knew he sounded belligerent—and probably looked it, too—but he didn't care.

"Don't you see, my friend? Dragons were prevented from fighting one another in the name of revenge! If everything that happened in Nabol came to light, the only outcome it would achieve would be to pit Craft against Hold. And we *can't* let that happen—it would be like permitting dragon to fight dragon," Sebell declared. "The only way this sickening behavior can be dealt with is at its root. If any of us were pitted against another it would cut to the very heart of our way of life. We all fit together in a unique way, and if we allow our guardians—the dragonriders—or our protectors and custodians—the holders and crafters—to come to blows, then we'll have undermined everyone's safety. And Thread would win."

Sebell turned his head to watch Piemur closely as the younger man battled with his emotions. "Do you see what I mean? We *have* to be prevented from fighting one another," he added, and then he leaned back.

"But it's not the same thing!" Piemur cried, and all his anger was expressed in those six words.

Sebell sighed. "The Oldtimers felt they were in a desperate situation, Piemur, and so they carried out a desperate act. In a way, I think that was their way of asking for help. Jerrol and his kin's actions, though different, were born from the same feelings of hopelessness. Holdlessness," Sebell said. It was Piemur's turn to sigh.

"Shards, those three men were probably treated so badly all their lives they no longer know what's right or wrong!" Sebell went on heatedly. "I remember when I was in Nabol for the Master, when Meron was alive. The way he baited his kin—it was nothing short of torture. He'd promise one nephew a patch of land, and the next day he'd renege on his offer and promise it to another kinsman. He used to laugh at their confusion and the anguish he put them through. It got so that none of them could trust the other. Meron made them all hate one another. Their very own flesh and blood, too! And all because they feared they wouldn't get what they should've been entitled to. It was appalling!"

"But what about the bricks, Sebell?" Piemur hissed; he couldn't stop thinking about what would've happened if Sebell hadn't been discovered.

"Don't think about that, Piemur. You found me, and I'm going to be fine."

Piemur stared at Sebell, the conflicting emotions welling up in him until he didn't know what to think. He wondered if he'd ever be like Sebell or Master Robinton, wise enough to see what was right and wrong, and strong enough to see past his own emotions, to discern the best choices to make for the good of everyone.

ELEVEN

JUST AFTER THE SUN ROSE THE FOLLOWING MORNING, B'NAJ FLEW into the valley to bring Meria back to Southern Weyr. She was content that Sebell hadn't suffered anything untoward as a result of his shoulder relocation, and that his other wounds and bruises were on the mend. She'd given the harpers instructions on how to care for him until he recovered, and left healing tinctures and balms to be administered. Rest was a key element to Sebell's recovery, she told them, followed by gentle use of his arm and shoulder over the ensuing week. Now that Sebell was on the mend, Menolly had to attend to her duties, too, and reluctantly sent a message to N'ton requesting a dragon to take her back to the Harper Hall.

Piemur walked with Meria to where B'naj waited with Seventh. The dragonrider stood proudly, one hand touching his brown's hide, and Piemur locked eyes with him. B'naj regarded Piemur with a composed and open demeanor, not a glimmer of arrogance evident. Unexpectedly Piemur recognized something in the older man's face that, up to this point in his life, he had never fully comprehended: What compelled B'naj and all dragonriders was an unconditional commitment to their dragons and to the code they lived by, a code that was so deeply embedded in all dragonmen and -women that it had become a part of their very essence: to protect, and to sustain the safety of everyone.

Piemur bowed to B'naj, trying in that one slight gesture to convey the deep respect the older man deserved.

"Dragonrider," he said, completing his bow.

Somewhat taken aback, B'naj dropped his hand from Seventh's side, while the brown dragon turned his head to look at Piemur, green eyes flecked with blue.

If only there were some way the Oldtimers could get back to where they belonged, Piemur mused, among the other dragonriders of Pern; somewhere not isolated, not *out of sight, or out of mind.*

As B'naj mounted Seventh and reached down a hand to help Meria, Piemur thought he saw a look of resignation settle on her face just before she turned to climb onto the dragon's back. Suddenly he felt compelled to stop her. He couldn't let her leave, let this moment pass without saying something.

"Wait a moment, Meria," he called.

"What is it, Piemur?" she asked, turning back as Piemur closed the distance between them.

Piemur spoke, loud enough so both Oldtimers would hear him.

"I thought . . . I just thought you should know—" He faltered and paused, searching Meria's face in the hope that his words would not be disregarded. The two Oldtimers patiently waited to hear what he had to say. He wanted to offer his help to them but knew they were too proud to accept it.

"I want you both to know something." He looked at Meria and then up to where B'naj sat on Seventh's back. "Even though it's very likely that you will never be credited with attempting to return Ramoth's egg, I admire what you tried to do. It was a noble, decent act." He smiled then.

He wished he could say much more, articulate more clearly all his hopes and good wishes for them, but this would have to do. It was not lost on Piemur that both B'naj and Meria probably had very bitter tastes in their mouths as they listened to him. Indeed, he realized, they must have fervently wished their situations were different from the reality they faced. They were living less than the fullest of lives; B'naj as a dragonrider banished with his Weyr, disgraced by the senseless act of a few desperate people; and Meria, banished from her adopted people yet desperate to help them.

"Safe skies, B'naj," Piemur said, looking up at the brown drag-onrider.

"To you, too, harper," B'naj replied.

As the two Oldtimers were lifted into the air on Seventh's wings, Piemur wondered how they would fare among their own. Would B'naj be maligned for acting with Meria, their outcast healer? And would Meria be forced, yet again, to remain outside the Weyr and live the rest of her life away from those she cared for the most? It seemed unfair to Piemur that they should not be rewarded for what they had tried to achieve.

Piemur spent the remainder of that morning with Sebell, noting that even though Sebell slept a lot, he seemed to be improving with every passing hour. Kimi, having been so dramatically separated from him before, never left Sebell's side.

Late in the afternoon the following day, Sebell went swim-ming. Meria had suggested that swimming would be beneficial for his shoulder, so N'ton flew Menolly into the valley on Lioth—enchanting the cotholders with yet another sighting of a beloved dragon—so that she could help Piemur with the pleasant task of getting Sebell into the water. One of Pergamol's kin had cleverly dug out a wading pool, separated from the main body of water by a high bank of earth and clay, so the younger children would have a safe and secure area in which to play. Piemur knew the water there would be warmed from the sun, and it was there that he and Me-nolly helped the injured harper into the shallow pool. With a soft sigh, Sebell sank down and allowed the water to lap over his legs.

Being sensitive to Sebell's condition, none of the group were in-clined to mention Nabol or any of the particulars relating to their time there. Menolly and N'ton relayed the latest news from the Harper Hall, the other Crafthalls, and the Weyrs, and then hap-pily talked about other minor matters. Eventually, though, Piemur thought he might explode and asked, "I'm sorry, but I have to know: Have there been any more developments with Jerrol and his plan to oust Jaxom?"

"The Masterharper received a message from Nabol today, just before we came here," Menolly replied, trying unsuccessfully to hide the smug look that spread across her face. "Jerrol and his kin have had their comeuppance."

"Yes!" N'ton said under his breath, punching a fist into the palm of his other hand.

"Lord Deckter and his primary holders found out what those three did to Sebell, and what they planned to do to Jaxom," Menolly told them.

"How?" Sebell asked, taking the words out of Piemur's mouth.

"It's the oddest thing, but some old biddy named Fronna recognized Piemur when he and J'hon were bringing you out of the cellars, Sebell. Seems she nearly had a fit when she saw the condition you were in, so she marched straight into Lord Deckter's rooms, fit to be tied, and demanded to know why two men leaving his Hold looked as if they'd had the stuffing kicked out of them. When Lord Deckter was unable to give her an answer she told him exactly what she thought of him. Candler heard her, as did everyone in the Great Hall! Her choice of words was great!" Menolly placed one hand on her hip and changed her voice to sound like that of a busybody old woman. " 'Lord Deckter, you cannot harbor the *despeakable* activities that's been going on in your own Hold. No, no, it's time for you to take better charge of your men!'

"When Lord Deckter quizzed her further, she told him how odd she thought it that a single dragon took off from the side rampart to the Hold, not where dragons usually arrive and depart when visiting Nabol. And she harangued another holder, who'd also seen Piemur and Sebell, and made him step forward to back her up. So Lord Deckter had no choice but to find out exactly what'd happened in his Hold, under his very nose. One thing led to another, and when Jerrol and his kin were found frantically searching every room in the deserted part of the cellars, the whole sordid mess was revealed."

"Did they plan to use Sebell to blackmail the Harper Hall?" N'ton asked.

Sebell cleared his throat. "I think they were using me to get the attention of their Lord Holder, *through* the Harper Hall," he explained. "Piemur, do you remember when we went to Marek's house? Before Laida let us in, there was a young boy knocking around outside. She shooed him away. Do you remember?" When Piemur nodded, Sebell continued.

"Well, it turns out he was a lookout for Jerrol and reported back to him as soon as Laida let us into her home. Jerrol took no small amount of pleasure informing me of that," Sebell said with a rueful grin. "The boy must've heard Laida call me by name, or perhaps she called me 'harper.' No matter. Our cover story was blown long before we entered Skal's brewhouse.

"After you got away, Piemur, I took a gamble and told Jerrol that there wasn't a chance he'd succeed in taking Ruathan lands. But I guess I must've been a little too convincing because—"

Sebell stopped short and shook his head ruefully as he eased his shoulder deeper into the water.

"When I explained that they'd never get what they wanted by holding my safety over the Masterharper's head, they really vented their anger." Sebell rubbed the base of his neck. "I'd hoped they were reasonable men, but my words just tipped them over the edge."

"I wonder what Lord Deckter will do with them now," Piemur said, absently rubbing a hand over one of the lumps on his head.

"Not half of what should be done to them," N'ton muttered under his breath.

"I hope Lord Deckter can see how frustrated they are," Sebell said, looking at Piemur. "They were wrong, but if he punishes them too severely, they'll always see life through bitter eyes, and they'll never have a chance. To change, I mean."

Some of what Sebell had been trying to foster in him over the last few days began to coalesce in Piemur's mind, and he thought he was beginning to understand Sebell's viewpoint.

Sebell closed his eyes and let his left arm move slowly back and forth across the surface of the water, easing the taut muscles in his injured shoulder.

"At least we don't need to worry about Jaxom's safety any longer," Menolly offered. "I don't believe he ever suspected how much danger he was in." She chuckled. "Shells, he saw more of me in the last sevenday than he has in all of the last Turn! He must be sick of me by now."

"I think Jaxom's been too preoccupied to notice," N'ton answered, and when Sebell raised one questioning brow, the dragonrider continued, "With a very fetching young woman, from what I hear."

"I thought he'd been acting fierce twitchy of late," Menolly replied. She had finally succumbed to the temptation of the lake and removed her boots; her feet were now immersed in the cool water. "Ever since we lost track of him at Nimath's Impression, Jaxom's been behaving strangely. Anytime I asked him what he thought about the egg being stolen and then returned, he always batted my questions away with questions of his own. He was very odd. Have you noticed that, N'ton?"

"He seems fine to me, Menolly, though I only see him when he's training with the weyrlings, so there really aren't any grounds for comparison."

"There was something very strange going on between Jaxom's dragon and all the fire-lizards, too—right up to about the time Nimath hatched," Menolly said, tugging distractedly at a hank of hair hanging across her shoulder. "They wouldn't leave poor Ruth alone for a moment. I can't understand why they pestered him so much. It's been driving me to distraction."

"Brand tells me Jaxom divides his time between duties in his Hold and his persistent interest in the sister of a smallholder in Plateau," N'ton explained. "It appears he's beaten such a path to her door that Ruth must know the place like I know the back of my hand." His brilliant-blue eyes shone mischievously.

"Well," said Sebell, glancing quickly at Menolly, "it's good that Jaxom has found a pleasant diversion." He raised one brow. "It should go a long way toward proving to the Lord Holders that he's more than ready to be confirmed as Lord of Ruatha. What does the Masterharper think, Menolly?"

"He'd agree with you if he was asked. He's been pushing hard for the other Lords to confirm Jaxom, but right now he's preoccupied with the Oldtimers in the north. They're not a problem like the ones in Southern, but since D'ram stepped down as Weyrleader of Ista, they're all worried about the stability of that Weyr."

"Master Robinton spoke about this with me and F'lar," N'ton explained. "Their Weyrwoman, Fanna, is too ill, and F'lar doesn't think D'ram has the heart to carry on without her. There's a real fear that D'ram might suicide once she dies and her queen goes *between*. He was deeply affected by the theft of Ramoth's egg—I think he felt that more keenly than any of the Oldtimers."

"D'ram's a fine, noble man, and still enjoying good health. It would be a huge loss if he decided not to carry on," Sebell said. The group fell silent at this comment.

"Does anyone know what's going to happen to the Oldtimers from Southern Weyr?" Piemur asked quietly, looking first at N'ton, then Sebell and Menolly.

"Huh!" N'ton slapped a hand against his thigh to show his distaste. "They made their choice when they took the egg from Benden. They'll have to live with the consequences now."

"But they weren't all involved, N'ton—it was just a few of them. We can't reject the entire Weyr because of a few desperate people," Piemur said, a note of subtle entreaty in his voice.

"They were given every chance to maintain their Weyr at full strength, Piemur, but refused all offers," N'ton snapped. "No, they were too stubborn to let go of their rigid old ways, clinging to their autonomy as if it were a lifeline. They can live with their choices now, the hidebound fools!"

Piemur had never seen N'ton so angry. He stared at him in dismay.

"Don't you see, Piemur?' N'ton went on. "Dragons expect us to know better—to do what is proper and for the benefit of everyone. They were designed to selflessly pit themselves against a dangerous enemy for the sake of the whole world. And they trust us to do our part in Pern's defense, too, not squabble and steal like dishonorable curs. The Oldtimers, even if it was just a few of them, violated a code that runs so deep among weyrfolk they may have corrupted the trust of our dragons."

Maybe now wasn't the time to remind N'ton of the part Meria and B'naj had played in trying to return the queen egg, Piemur reckoned. The Fort Weyrleader would know full well about their failed attempt from J'hon. Nonetheless, he felt compelled to try to show the Fort Weyrleader another point of view.

"I realize that, N'ton, far more clearly than I ever did before. But when it comes down to it, we all have impulses we can't ignore—or even control—sometimes. When we feel rejected, or under a burden, and can see no solution to our problems, then we're bound to behave badly. That's why we have to support and protect one another. What the men from Nabol and those few Southern Oldtimers did was dishonorable, unspeakable—" Piemur faltered for a moment, searching for the words to explain the idea he was trying to voice. "But it's as Sebell just said: They have to be given the chance to change, or they never will. To my mind, punishment followed by isolation is not the answer."

"Oh!" Menolly exhaled the exclamation on a single breath. "All that time you've spent on your own hasn't been wasted, my friend. I do believe you've become our very own deep thinker, Pie."

Sebell nodded, agreeing with Menolly, and leaned forward, his hand extended. Piemur clasped it tightly. N'ton's expression was still grim, but as Piemur watched him, he saw a glimmer of hesitation, and a softening in the dragonrider's brows. He hoped N'ton was beginning to see a different point of view.

Later, when the evening meal was being prepared, Pergamol strolled over to the little cothold and invited Menolly and N'ton to join them, claiming that he had an exceptionally large haunch of meat on the fire, which would only go to waste if there weren't enough mouths to eat it. Lioth was content to remain by the lakeshore, so Piemur, N'ton, Menolly, and Sebell made their way to the main cothold when the call to eat rang out over the valley.

Pergamol's extended family often pitched in at mealtimes, sharing the tasks of preparation and cooking, and on that evening they were roasting a side of meat in the open fireplace of a cothold that was in the final stages of being built. Piemur, Sebell, Menolly, and N'ton joined Pergamol in the little house, as another holder basted the meat from a pan of juices placed on the floor of the hearth. A gang of young children ran in and out of the unframed doorway, playing a game of tag. Across the main courtyard area, other holders were gathered in another house, preparing the tubers and vegetables that would accompany the roasted meat. A comfortable exchange of banter was passing from one building to the other, punctuated from time to time by laughter, or the sound of raucous guffaws when someone told a joke.

"Be sure Jamie covers the whole of the carcass with the juices, Pergamol," Ama called pleasantly from the doorway of the other building. "None of us want to eat a dry hank of meat."

"As if I'd let him miss a bit, Ma!" Pergamol called back, and they could hear Ama chuckling as she returned to her own preparations for the meal.

"Ama always says that," Jamie explained to the harpers and the dragonrider, nodding, "and I always get the meat cooked just fine." He winked.

"Who's this cothold for, Pergamol?" Piemur asked.

"Jamie's son, Jalla, and his woman, Nula," Pergamol replied, looking out the window aperture at the gang of children playing in the courtyard, while he slowly turned the spit. "They've already filled up the cothold next door with young 'uns. It's got so crowded for them now that we have to build another hold for the older children to live in."

Head bent to the task of basting the roasting meat, Jamie barely looked up from his task as he commented, "Shells, the man hardly has to take his trews off and she's got another bun in the oven!" His observation was greeted with hearty laughter from the visitors and he blushed, adding, "Never saw such a woman to breed before in all my life," before he reapplied himself to his task, scrutinizing a section of the roasting meat and then bathing it repeatedly with several ladlefuls of juices.

When the meat was sufficiently roasted and given time to rest, and the other victuals were cooked, everything was piled onto platters and placed on tables in the covered courtyard of the cothold, where Ama and some of the other holders had arranged enough chairs to accommodate everyone. Some of the smaller children opted to sit on a parent's or sibling's lap as they all tucked into the last meal of the day.

Piemur, like Menolly and N'ton, had taken the first free seat he'd been able to find, and as he ate his meal he listened with a growing appreciation to both the deep conversations and the light chatter the small community exchanged. There was a mixture of all ages around the table, with young seated next to old and adolescents mixed up in between. The man across from Piemur held a toddler on his lap; beside him, a heavily pregnant woman was gently remonstrating with a willful-looking young boy seated on her other side. *This must be Jalla,* Piemur speculated with amusement, as the man patiently held up a full spoon for the toddler. The small child batted the food away and then promptly anointed his father's chest with a small handful of mashed tuber, laughing gleefully as his father stared at him wide-eyed.

The atmosphere as they all dined was relaxed and easy, and Piemur noticed that Ama had taken a shine to the handsome Fort Weyrleader, insisting that he sit next to her. He watched as N'ton bent his head low, leaning in close to Ama, smiling as she recounted some family anecdote.

As he watched his family and friends, Piemur marveled at how the little community of people, who obviously lived much of their lives cheek by jowl, managed to maintain their equanimity so easily. Then, without warning, a chair was thrust back, scraping loudly on the stone paving, and everyone looked up. Jalla and Nula's young son said something to his mother in a fierce whisper and then pulled his arm out of her grasp sharply, storming from the table in a huff.

"Leave him," Nula said to no one in particular, her eyes fixed on her plate of food as the assembled diners briefly looked up at the commotion.

"Numie's a hothead and we all have to learn to let him cool

off," Ama said to no one in particular. "He'll come to his senses again given time, he always does. He knows we're always here for him—when he's ready to come back." And she chuckled at her own words, patting N'ton on the hand absently.

The diners resumed their meals, not at all deterred by the little scene, and when everyone had finished eating, the tables were cleared and returned to their respective cotholds, though most of the chairs were left in place.

Pergamol, who'd claimed Sebell as his dining partner, produced a small set of wooden pipes and also some hand drums and two fiddles, which he laid on one of the tables, gesturing for Menolly and Piemur to take their pick. Menolly opted for the pipes, while Piemur picked up a small pair of hand drums. There were still enough instruments left over for whoever else might want to play.

They passed a pleasant evening listening to music, or anecdotes, until some of the younger members of the large family took to the floor to dance while the onlookers clapped to help keep the rhythm. Ais and another girl were reeling each other around and around until they grew so dizzy they lost their grip and fell down, laughing. The youngest of the children who were not yet too tired played in a quieter corner of the courtyard outside, skipping ropes or jumping over ladders that had been scratched into the dirt; two young girls were practicing an intricate hand-clapping game together. The smallest members of the family, too sleepy to stay awake after their bellies had been filled, curled up in the laps of other family members, oblivious to everything but their own dreams.

Piemur watched Pergamol as he beat on a hand drum, keeping time while Jamie played a reel on one of the fiddles and Menolly sang a song.

"I see Numie has come to his senses," Ama said to Piemur as she sat down next to him. "He's forgotten all about his earlier upset. He can't stop his feet from dancing now." She chuckled as they watched the young boy clicking and tapping his feet on the solid floor, his eyes gleaming with delight.

Piemur smiled at his foster mother and they fell into a companionable silence as they watched their kin enjoying the evening together. Watching others enjoy themselves was a deeply satisfying way to spend the evening, Piemur reflected, and without realizing it, he sighed heavily.

"Don't you fret, my Pie," Ama said, taking his sigh as a sign of regret. "You shouldn't worry about what your voice sounds like since it broke. I bet it's still worth hearing. Just let it rip, my Pie, let your voice be heard." She leaned in close, putting a hand on either side of Piemur's face and pulling him toward her as she beamed into his eyes.

"Aw, Ama, I've tried. I sound like I'm croaking and get a squishy feeling in my throat. I have no control over it," Piemur said very quietly, and he leaned in closer to Ama so only she could hear him. "It's *hard* to be around music now. I can't join in as I used to."

"But you are good at other harper skills. You can't expect only your singing voice to fill you with self-respect and pleasure, my Pie." Ama looked at him sharply, though her words were spoken with kindness.

"But I was *good* at singing, Ama. It was the *one* thing I could do well without even having to try." And he shook his head, looking at her with a weak grin. A sudden rush of regret hit him, and he felt the loss of his voice as keenly as when it had just broken. Piemur had to look away from Ama quickly, afraid he'd lose his composure in front of her; he stared down at his hands instead, as they lay idle in his lap.

"I don't think, my Pie, that any of us could be happy in life by doing just *one* thing. Through all these long Turns I've lived, I've grown to see some parts of my life very clearly. It was the unlikely choices I made—where the sights I set my aim at were hardest to reach—that became the most highly valued feats of my life. Maybe it's because the goals were hard-won. I could not say for certain." She patted his hand. "You'll be fine, my Pie. Just be yourself, and always listen to your instincts"—she pointed a finger at his chest— "and you'll be fine."

She looked in his eyes again and smiled, then rose from her chair and reached out her arms toward Piemur. He stood, too, and amid all the dancing, chatter, laughter, and noise, they held each other in a long embrace.

When the entertainment was winding down and the younger family members were tucked into their beds, Piemur, Sebell, Menolly, and N'ton strolled back to the little cothold. Someone had lit a fire for them, which was blazing when they arrived. Four stools had been left around it, making a welcome seating area for the friends who were not yet ready to end their evening together.

"Your family are wonderful, Piemur," Menolly said. "It's delightful to visit a united cothold like this one."

"Thanks, Menolly," Piemur replied. "We have our moments, though, just like everyone does. I've been seeing my kinfolk in a new light. I guess when I was living here, and my family members were right under my nose, it was hard to appreciate them properly."

They sat companionably around the fire, exchanging gentle banter and enjoying each other's company.

"Do any of you ever have a notion you just can't get out of your head?" Menolly asked.

"All the time," Sebell replied. N'ton nodded, too.

"It seems like all I *ever* think about are the same boring thoughts," Piemur chimed in, his expression rueful. "Why do you ask, Menolly?"

"I guess I've been spending too much time in Jaxom's company. I couldn't help but notice some things. Odd things," she said.

"Like what?" N'ton asked.

"Do you remember when Mikay Impressed Nimath and we rushed to Ruatha afterward because Jaxom wasn't at the Hatching?"

"Yes," N'ton said. "Go on."

"Jaxom said the strangest thing at the time, and when I was about to ask him to explain, I saw the Masterharper glowering at me so I had to drop it."

"What did Jaxom say?" Sebell asked.

"You might remember, N'ton. It was after Jaxom said that Ruth always knew what *when* he was in." Menolly chuckled and scrunched up her face as if Jaxom had gotten his words mixed up. "You gave him a dressing-down, N'ton, and the Masterharper joined in, too, reminding Jaxom how tense everything was at Benden Weyr. I felt sorry for poor Jax, because it was obvious from his expression he knew full well the seriousness of it all." And Menolly paused, drawing in a long breath.

"Then he said, 'Dragons can't fight dragons—that's why the egg was returned.' There was a strangeness in his tone when he said that, and the way he phrased his words seemed so odd to me."

"What did he mean, N'ton, about his dragon always knowing what *when* he was in?" Piemur asked.

"He says Ruth always knows *when* he is if he *times* it, though it's not something I'd hasten to have him prove. It takes an awful toll on both rider and dragon to fly between times," the dragonrider said.

"Did you see how sheepish he looked when I asked what he was doing during Nimath's Impression?" Menolly said.

"That threadscore he got was nothing to be sheepish about," N'ton said to no one in particular, a puzzled expression momentarily washing across his face. "He's been so eager to prove Ruth's worth—I guess he'd give anything to show that his dragon's just as good as all the others. He had to *time* it to flame Thread with Ruth. But going back in time two days to the last Fall wouldn't explain why he looked so drained when we saw him with Lytol in Ruatha."

Menolly sat up straighter and pointed a finger at N'ton. "When we were at Benden, Jaxom collapsed right after the egg was returned. I know because I was standing right next to him. Wasn't that odd, N'ton? Or could he have been timing it much more than you think?"

N'ton shrugged. "Was anyone else affected in the same way as Jaxom?"

"No," Menolly replied, shaking her head.

"You did say that he'd been seeing a girl in Plateau a lot. All that to-ing and fro-ing could've knocked the stuffing out of him," Piemur said with a grin.

"We never bothered to follow him when he went up there because it's such a remote holding," N'ton said. "And his visits there were always last-minute. He snatched his opportunities whenever he could."

Suddenly Menolly grabbed N'ton's arm, and her eyes opened wider than Piemur had ever seen them before. Piemur could feel the atmosphere around the little campfire abruptly shift, and the air seemed to crackle with energy. The silence was so profound that Piemur thought his ears would pop as they all seemed to come to the same conclusion at the same instant. Before she could even utter the words, Piemur knew exactly what was going to come out of Menolly's mouth.

"Jaxom must have returned the egg!" Menolly cried.

"Of course!" N'ton said, a look of amazement on his face

"It makes the most sense!" Sebell chorused N'ton's exclamation.

"We only saw the bronzes as they were *leaving* Benden with the egg. There was complete bedlam after that, so anyone could've brought it back safely without being seen," N'ton explained.

"That's really been gnawing at me," Piemur said, frowning, then added: "Who could've been clever enough to return the egg without being seen?"

"You have a dragonrider's perspective, N'ton," Sebell said, the excitement in his voice contagious. "Would it be difficult for Ruth to maneuver in Benden's Hatching Grounds?"

"Not at all!" N'ton sounded excited, too. "Ruth is amazingly agile, more so than blues or greens, and he's smaller than all of them."

"Meria and B'naj said the dragon who took the egg from the southern hiding place was small and dark. That made me think it had to be a small green dragon—a blue would be too large," Piemur said. "But a green is too light in color," he added and frowned, realizing that his guesswork wasn't adding up.

"What if Jaxom did something to conceal Ruth's hide? Like covering it with something dark? Something that would hide his identity." Menolly was warming to this new theory; she was just as excited by this revelation as the other three.

"But what I don't understand," Piemur said, looking around at the others, "is why hasn't Jaxom *told* anyone? He could've owned up when you went to find him after Nimath's Impression."

"Maybe he just didn't want the attention," Sebell replied.

"I think I know why he hasn't said anything," N'ton offered. "Ever since Jaxom Impressed Ruth he's been under scrutiny from Benden, and Lytol—and all the Lord Holders, for that matter. His dragon is unique and after Ruth hatched we were all concerned he wouldn't survive his first Turn. Everyone's been hovering over that pair like a flock of nervous wherries, so poor Jaxom must've felt like he was slowly being smothered. I bet he's kept quiet because he doesn't want any more attention."

"That makes sense," Menolly agreed.

"And since Jaxom's been *timing* it against all good sense, and teaching Ruth to chew firestone without permission," N'ton added, "and basically bucking all the constraints that his well-meaning guardians have leveled on him, I think he's keeping his mouth shut because he's afraid the few freedoms he *does* enjoy will be curtailed."

Piemur listened as his friends continued to exchange thoughts and expand their insights into the theory they'd arrived at, and as he watched them he began to see Jaxom's intervention in the Weyrs' business as a picture in a larger frame.

"Do you think he knows what he's done?" Piemur spoke quietly. "What he's stopped from happening?" The other three fell silent, waiting for him to continue.

Piemur nodded slowly. "Dragons fighting dragons."

TWELVE

OVER THE COURSE OF THE NEXT SEVENDAY PIEMUR AND SEBELL fell into an easy routine at Pergamol's little cothold. With the continued care and rest Sebell was receiving, the strength in his shoulder increased just as rapidly as the bruises on his legs faded. Piemur taught the hold children several lessons, but he also helped Ama prepare food for preserving and assisted Pergamol with the runnerbeast herd.

After three long days of strenuous work with the runnerbeasts, Piemur was only too happy to eat his evening meal and quietly retire for the night while Sebell remained behind, entertaining the cotholders with some of the lesser-known harper tales.

Piemur was in a deep sleep, dreaming of dragon eggs and dragons lost *between,* when a voice called his name insistently and a hand roughly shook his shoulder.

"Wake up! Wake up!"

Piemur rolled away from the bothersome voice.

"You have to wake up, Piemur," Sebell said again, this time with more urgency.

Rolling onto his elbows and rubbing one eye, Piemur stared at the slender harper and muttered through dry lips, "What? What is it?"

"It's Ama, something's wrong. Drina says she's sick."

Piemur was fully awake in an instant, swinging his legs over the edge of the cot to haul on his leggings and then grabbing at his tunic to yank it over his head while his feet poked around the floor, searching for discarded boots.

"What happened?"

"She took a bad turn, that's all I know. Drina was with her. Go!"

Piemur stuffed his feet into his boots and was out the door of the little cothold in a flash, running as fast as he could to Ama's house. He didn't understand what might have happened to Ama: She'd seemed fine to him when he saw her that evening. As he ran Piemur grew fearful of what he would find when he reached her house. He arrived a few moments later, pushed open her front door—and was unable to take a single step farther. Pergamol filled the room with his large frame, though he was not alone; Drina and two young women were seated around the bed.

Pergamol grabbed Piemur in a quick bear hug, whispering in his ear: "She won't wake up!" Tears were streaming down his weather-beaten face. "Drina said she seemed confused. Then she just slumped over and hasn't woken since. D'you see how her face has changed? We've seen that before in other kinfolk. It's not good, Pie."

Wishing he were dreaming instead of looking at the still figure of his beloved Ama, Piemur sat down on one of the bedside stools, his movements wooden.

"Ah, Ama," Piemur whispered, a lump choking up his throat as he took one of her hands into both of his own and touched it to his cheek. "It shouldn't be like this."

Tears overflowed and ran down his cheeks. "Ama, wake up," Piemur implored, his voice low. "I should've told you at least a hundred times more how much you mean to me. How I'll always love you. No one will ever fill the place you hold in my heart." He laid a gentle hand on her brow and rested it there for a moment, silently surprised that it felt so cool to his touch.

With Pergamol and the other members of the family, Piemur sat by Ama's side through the rest of the night and on into the morning. He continued to hold her hand, silently hoping she would wake up, but his entreaties went unanswered.

Well past midday, Pergamol shook Piemur awake and made

him leave Ama's side to get some fresh air. A few other members of Ama's extended family took Piemur's place, and yet more family, fosterlings, friends, and neighbors sat outside the little cothold, quietly talking as they kept their vigil.

"Of all the dozens of fosterlings she's had, I think Ama held you closest to her heart," Pergamol said, a little smile tugging at his lips. "It could've been that sweet voice of yours that beguiled her, but I think it was all the antics you got up to—after she got over being vexed with you, of course. She always laughed at your windups, Pie. Didn't she?"

Wordlessly, Piemur nodded and then turned, grief-stricken, toward Pergamol, tears flowing down his face. "I knew this day would come sometime, Pergamol. Honest, I truly did. But my heart hoped she'd live forever. Aren't mothers supposed to live forever?"

"Aye, they are."

"I think a part of me is going with her. This hurts so much, Pergamol."

"I know. Our Ama will take a piece of *all* of us with her when she goes. But we'll keep the best bits of *her* right here, lad," Pergamol said, his voice faltering as he tapped a finger over his heart.

Chairs and stools had been placed all around Ama's bed so her loved ones could be close, and the hours passed by while the watchers silently listened to each breath she took. People from all over Crom came to offer support to those keeping vigil, consoling the grief-stricken with soft words or gentle silence. Piemur saw Sebell once, but it was only briefly and in passing, as the journeyman masterharper clasped Piemur's arms, offering his support.

As the sun started to fall and the new-season air began to cool, Ama ended their long vigil on one single inward breath. When the last lungful of air was expelled from her body they all sat, momentarily bewildered. When they knew that Ama had taken her last breath they all stood up and gently placed their hands on her head, or her face, on her hands or feet; on any part of her they could reach. They didn't want to part company with their Ama without one final caress.

Drina was the first to break the tableau as, sobbing gently, she turned from the bed. Pergamol pushed the door open wide and

everyone slowly left the room. Later, when Ama had been washed
and wrapped in a cloth, Piemur helped carry her slight body to the
woven-willow stretcher he'd helped make. It hadn't taken long to
weave the stretcher with so many hands to help.

With great tenderness they laid Ama's body on the rush padding
that topped the stretcher and then, one by one, each person placed
a small memento beside her body. Some of the younger girls, the
children of Ama's grown fosterlings, placed daisy chains or bunches
of fragrant wildflowers around the padding, and one little boy put a
small berry pie next to Ama's hand. Older folk secreted notes written on scraps of cloth under the rushes, and Pergamol placed a skin
of fortified wine near her hand because, he said, "She liked a nip or
two from time to time." Piemur laid a small stone near her head,
carefully turning it to expose where the shape of a heart had been
weather-worn onto its surface. When all the tokens had been safely
tucked around Ama, everyone helped hoist the stretcher up onto the
shoulders of those who would carry her onward.

Their task was not a burden. The cortege only had to bear the
stretcher past the cotholds and neighboring pastures, then over a
knoll to the lake. Each mourner lit a candle, secured in tapered
wooden cups, and then placed the candle cups on the woven stretcher
before it was taken into the water. They gathered in a tight group
around Ama's body, and on a single command from Pergamol, "Let
her go," they gently pushed her away from the shore.

As Ama's body floated into the center of the lake, one of the
women started to hum and looked to Piemur to begin the song. It
was a melody they had all learned as young children. Piemur's face
was awash with tears, and grief shook his shoulders. He felt bereft
that even for Ama he could not seem to find his voice, and when
he lifted his tearstained face toward Pergamol, he was grateful the
older man recognized his anguish.

Pergamol took the lead, calling out the song of lament:

On again, go again
Take your last step

Free your worn body
And send it to rest.

The dirge was a flowing, slow-paced piece and Piemur listened as Pergamol sang softly, his deep voice rich, even though it was untrained. Everyone grew silent, straining to hear the big herdsman, but then, as he sang the last three words of the verse, Pergamol faltered and then stopped as he, too, was overcome by grief. Silence hung in the air. Drina was standing next to Pergamol, and Piemur saw her reach up to lay a comforting hand on his shoulder.

The pause in the singing grew so long that Piemur began to wonder if Ama's farewell song would go unsung, and he closed his eyes. Ama deserved to be properly sent off. *Someone* had to sing the farewell song for her! Piemur closed his eyes, afraid to continue the dirge for Pergamol in case his voice might fail him. Fail Ama. But someone had to finish the song!

Even with his eyes shut tight Piemur could suddenly see Ama's face so clearly it was as if she were right in front of him.

Listen to your gut instinct! he heard her saying. *Just let it rip, my Pie.* And then, without a thought, Piemur listened to his instincts, lifted his head, opened his mouth, and filled the air with the sound of his voice.

Go again, show again
We'll see it right
Marching ye onward
Toward peace in the night.

His singing was soft and hesitant at first, but as each word rang out, Piemur let his breath get stronger. He stood tall, his chin lifted high, and though his cheeks were wet with tears, as he sang out the well-known words, his phrasing was as clear and perfectly timed as it had ever been. Growing increasingly assured as he sang each successive note, Piemur continued, his voice finally ringing out across the lake like a bell.

Go again, know again
You were loved true
Take heart in the honor
Shown b'those whom you knew.

Lifting his arms up from his sides, Piemur gestured for the mourners to help him finish the dirge, as was the custom, and as the group rose to the occasion, each man, woman, and child drawing breath in unison, Piemur believed he'd never felt prouder of his kin and community than he did at that moment, when their voices rang out together.

On again, go again
We'll think of you ere
Now rest our belov-ed
Turn to dust, turn to air.

After the funeral ceremony, Piemur spent a sevenday with his kin in Crom, promising Sebell, who had returned to the Harper Hall two days after Ama died, that he'd send word when he was ready to leave. He found it a comfort to be with his extended family as they all grieved; he slipped into the routine of the little community with ease, and every night he fell onto his sleeping mat exhausted from his day of self-imposed, strenuous travails and was lost, almost immediately, to a heavy, dreamless sleep. But he always woke, two or three short hours later, and spent the remainder of his nights in a turmoil of thoughts, worrying about a plethora of inconsequential things and falling into, and out of, a fitful pattern of sleep. Often, he wondered where his life would take him, and whether he'd ever fit into the part he was supposed to play.

During the endless, sleepless nights his thoughts always circled around to Ama and he was incapable of preventing his grief from flooding over him, pushing against his rib cage until he felt as if his heart were being compressed by a heavy weight. And when the aching grief slowly eased, as it always did, he felt as if he had been riding on a long, rolling wave.

Finally, early one morning, when he least expected it, he realized he was ready to move on. He had been drowsing, willing his body to rest even though he could not find sleep, while he waited for the sun to rise. It was at the hour when the day birds were beginning to rustle about in their nests with solitary cheeps and murmurs, calling to one another that they had made it safely through the night. It was then that Piemur experienced what seemed like a waking dream. Ama's radiant face was smiling at him, and although the vision appeared for only a moment he knew Ama was telling him that she was happy, and he would be, too.

"Ama," he whispered under his breath, and smiled. He knew that he could carry on as life demanded, and although the grief he felt was still sharp and raw, Piemur wrote a message and sent Farli to Fort Weyr to deliver it.

He was surprised, later that afternoon, when Ais sought him out as he was stacking fresh-cut wood, to say a dragon had flown in and a tall dragonrider was waiting for him near the lake. He hadn't thought his message would be answered so quickly. Striding behind Ais, Piemur could see N'ton seated on Lioth's forelegs, waiting patiently.

"N'ton!" Piemur called. "My thanks! I wasn't expecting such a quick response to my message." It was good to see his friend again.

"It's my pleasure, Piemur," N'ton said. "I'd gone too long without sampling your particular blend of humor. Lioth missed you, too." He smiled, his light-blue eyes full of warmth as he clasped Piemur's hand in greeting.

After Piemur went back to the little cothold to gather up his few belongings, he felt a pang of grief as he bade farewell to his family. He knew he was leaving behind him something much more than just family and friends; several large pieces of his heart would always remain in this little cothold in Crom.

He had said his goodbyes and was walking toward the lake to

join N'ton when Pergamol waved for him to stop. "Piemur! Piemur, wait!" He turned back and closed the gap to the burly herdsman, suddenly feeling that his heart might burst again with emotion.

"I know we've already said goodbye, Pie," Pergamol said slowly, "but remember something for me.

"Even though your young voice left you, there's naught to be ashamed about the one that came in its place. I know that was a hard thing for you to do, Piemur, to sing when you were so unsure of your voice, but I'm glad you did it. For Ama." Pergamol's chin quivered slightly as he looked down at Piemur. "Ama would've been very proud of you. You stepped up to the mark when you were needed, and I want you to know that *I'm* proud of you, too, Pie."

Then the burly, affable herder opened his arms wide, saying softly, "Don't stay away too long this time, auld son."

Unable to trust his voice, Piemur could only mumble the words "Thank you" before he stepped into the older man's bearlike embrace.

After Lioth had lifted off the ground and was wheeling above Pergamol's cothold one last time before flying *between,* Piemur looked down at his kinsmen and kinswomen as they stood waving goodbye. He felt that he was very different now from the Piemur who had arrived in the cothold such a short time ago, seeking help for Sebell. As Ama's influence on his life had been cleaved from him with her death, Piemur felt that something else had left him, too. And with a sudden jolt of recognition, he no longer felt that old sense of regret about losing his young singing voice; he could live without that voice, and he could make use of the one he had grown into. He smiled then, thinking back to how his voice had sounded when he sang for Ama. To his practiced ear, it wasn't half bad at all!

When Piemur returned to the Harper Hall, the Masterharper seemed his usual amiable self as they greeted each other, but Piemur thought that beyond the façade, Robinton looked distracted and, perhaps, a little sad. Sebell joined them, looking well recovered from his injuries and none the worse for his ordeal.

"I was so sorry to learn that your foster mother died, Piemur," Robinton said. "It is one of the most difficult things of all to bear—the loss of one's mother. They become such a constant part of who we are." The Masterharper drew in a deep breath and sighed.

"Much has happened since you left the Hall. At Ista, poor Fanna's condition has grown worse. It won't be long now before she dies and her queen flies *between*. Since D'ram stepped down as Weyrleader with Fanna so ill, Ista will soon have to find a new Weyrleader *and* a Weyrwoman. I'm always ill at ease when a Weyr is without its leaders, no matter how temporary, or how able-bodied the wingseconds are at filling the gap in leadership." Robinton rubbed a hand distractedly across the back of his neck.

"Ista has more than one queen, though. Do we know if any of them are ready to make a mating flight?" Sebell asked.

"I'm told Caylith will most likely be the first queen to take flight."

"Does Benden think her a good choice for the Weyr?" Piemur asked.

"I couldn't say," the Master replied, his tone abrupt, almost flat. That told Piemur there was still some discord between the Harper Hall and Benden Weyr, and he knew from Sebell's expression that he was right. It was a huge pity, Piemur reflected, looking down at his hands; allies such as Benden Weyr and the Harper Hall had to remain in accord. Lessa hadn't appreciated Robinton's insistence that revenge was the wrong road to take. It could only be hoped that Lessa would relent and see reason, once the rest of Ramoth's clutch hatched and Impressed, and life in the Weyr got back to normal.

"So, my Piemur," Robinton said.

A jolt of emotion ran through Piemur when he heard Ama's possessive name for him issue from his Master's mouth. Robinton carried on, unaware of how his particular choice of words had affected Piemur.

"I'd hazard a guess that your dislike of Nabol is more firmly fixed in place now than ever before. Such a pity: That province does have its merits, though they're often hard to perceive." The Masterharper looked fixedly at Piemur, but then his eyes softened and he smiled.

"Tell me, Piemur, are you quite recovered from your ordeal in Nabol?" The Master's tone was gentle as he searched Piemur's face, and Piemur nodded, grateful for such sensitivity. "You should take time for your own pursuits. Don't feel the need to rush off anywhere on harper business. You're always welcome here at the Hall, you know."

"Thank you, Master, your offer is more than generous, but I want to go back to the Southern Continent," he replied, squaring his shoulders. He hoped the Masterharper wouldn't push the invitation to stay on at the Hall; it wasn't that he was still uncomfortable around so much musicality but more an inexplicable urge to find what *else* he could do besides singing—what might inspire a new feeling of passion in him.

Piemur felt he'd turned some invisible corner in his life, and everything he'd been and done before was far behind him. From the moment he'd returned to Fort, he'd had an urge to be out in the open, wanting nothing more than to fly south, where he knew he would feel at ease. It was as if something inexplicable was pulling him back to the Southern Continent, and he could not ignore the subtle tugging.

"Ah, very well, Piemur," Robinton said, looking a little confused at Piemur's decision. "There's plenty more land to map in the south, of course, probably far more than we can imagine. Map as you go, lad, and send your sketches back here as often as you can."

"Thank you, Master Robinton," Piemur said, his tone solemn, as he inclined his upper body in deference to the older man. It had been ages since he'd observed such gestures, and Piemur realized that his relationship with Robinton had also undergone a change of which he had only now become aware. As he straightened his body and looked his Master in the eye, he saw that Robinton acknowledged their new footing, too.

"Go on, then, young man, and bring back something of interest," Robinton said lightly, his voice rising to stress the last word.

. . .

Piemur only stayed at the Harper Hall for that day, arranging with N'ton to return to the Southern Continent as soon as the dragon-rider could spare the time to take him.

It was late at night in the Southern Hold compound when Lioth touched down on the sun-warmed ground and Piemur heard N'ton exhale a long sigh.

"As much as I love being Weyrleader in Fort, I *do* like coming here to Southern," N'ton said. He turned to look at Piemur as they both unclipped their tethers from the flying harness.

"I used to think I didn't like it here, N'ton, but it feels more like home than anywhere else," Piemur replied, then he chuckled. "I know I wouldn't have felt this way a Turn ago. I guess I've grown accustomed to life here." He looked up at the huge southern sky above his head, saw the two moons glowing full and bright, and all the stars that sparkled, seemingly in competition with one another, as they lit up the night.

"Do you remember all that time you and I spent mapping the stars for Fandarel? You thought we'd never see the end of it." N'ton had pulled his flying helmet off his head, opened the clasps on his jacket, and thrown both legs over Lioth's neck, sitting sideways on the huge dragon so his back wasn't to his friend. He didn't seem in any rush to get back to the Northern Continent.

"When Fandarel first asked us to map the skies I thought he was deranged! Of course, when he explained *how* he planned for us to do the mapping, then I felt like a right dim-glow."

"You certainly were entertaining, Piemur. Remember that night you got so flustered because you thought the sky was all wrong, as you put it? Then the vellum fell out of your hand and when you picked it up again you saw that you'd been holding it upside down all along. That was a gem of a gaffe," N'ton said, laughing.

Piemur smiled, too, no longer embarrassed at the memory. He climbed down off Lioth's back and stripped out of his flying gear.

"What are you going to do next, harper?" N'ton asked.

"I'm not sure. I know I won't have to map this continent forever because at some point I *will* run out of land." Piemur shrugged, looking up at N'ton.

"I've spent so much time during the last three Turns thinking about my old voice and wishing so hard that it would come back, or that my mature voice would finally resolve and be just as good as the old one. But now it doesn't seem to matter anymore. You know, N'ton? I sang at Ama's ceremony."

The Fort Weyrleader looked surprised and quickly made one of his acrobatic dismounts off Lioth's back to stand next to Piemur.

"I didn't know that, Pie. How did it go?" N'ton asked tentatively.

"It was fine. Absolutely fine. And my mature voice isn't bad at all. But it's strange, N'ton, I was so positive that when my voice finally settled I'd want to use it all the time. Singing was what made me feel like I belonged at the Harper Hall, like I fit in there. Now I don't feel that way anymore."

Piemur looked at N'ton, who had been quiet throughout Piemur's revelation. The Weyrleader's lips quirked and his arched brows shot up and down in unison before he replied.

"You should do what you want, Pie, what feels true to you."

"Whatever it is, it's got to be something more important to me—more than singing. Or mapping, or scouting, or teaching. I want it to be worthwhile."

As N'ton placed a reassuring hand on Piemur's shoulder he could hear a gentle rumble rising up from Lioth's throat.

"My dragon says you will find what you want," N'ton said, and then paused for a moment as Lioth said something more to his rider. Then the handsome Weyrleader chuckled, adding, "Or, he says, it will find you."

Later Piemur said farewell to N'ton, and bowed politely to Lioth, whose eyes sparkled blue-green in the bright, moon-filled sky. Piemur watched the pair fly up into the night and then disappear *between,* but long after they had gone he stood alone, scanning the nightscape above, lost in deep thoughts.

·   ·   ·

When he rose from bed late the next morning, Piemur donned the lightweight, short leggings and sleeveless shirt he always wore in Southern. He wondered where Farli had disappeared to; she'd flitted off on her own the moment Lioth burst into the warm southern night from the flight out of Fort.

He pushed his thoughts outward, trying to locate Farli, pressing her to answer his call. She replied lazily, broadcasting an image of her lounging in the sunshine on Stupid's rump as the runnerbeast stood, one hip cocked, lips loose and droopy, dozing in a nearby paddock.

"Isn't it well for some," Piemur muttered to himself, pleased that his little queen could fit so easily back into life in the south.

When Piemur entered the runnerbeast compound, Stupid greeted him enthusiastically, repeatedly pushing his muzzle into the crook of Piemur's elbow to be scratched. When Piemur had given the runnerbeast an adequate amount of attention, and Farli had picked and poked at Stupid's hide sufficiently so that he was preened to her satisfaction, Piemur slipped a bridle over the beast's head and slung a saddle pad on his back.

Feeling aimless, and with no particular destination in mind, he struck out in the general direction of the sea, Farli flying in languid circles around Piemur and Stupid as they clopped along. At first Stupid moved in a lazy walk, doing as he pleased, but when a refreshing breeze blew in from the shore and roused him from his stupor, he increased his speed to a trot, his legs swinging forward at a steady pace.

The rhythm of Stupid's hooves on the soft sand reminded Piemur of the song he had been teaching the children at Pergamol's cothold before Ama died. The ancient verse known as the Question Song had been handed down from Pass to Pass, generation to generation, for over four hundred Turns, and was known by every person on Pern:

Gone away, gone ahead,
Echoes away, die unanswered.
Empty, open, dusty, dead,
Why have all the weyrfolk fled?

Now, why had he thought of the Question Song? Piemur wondered as Farli ducked and dove around his head, chirruping with excitement. He shook his head, and as Stupid's pace continued to increase, some of his critters' energy and excitement began to infect Piemur, too. Gathering up the reins, he squeezed his knees more firmly against the saddle pad and let his weight sink into his heels as he inclined his upper body forward, lifting his backside off the pad.

"Go on, then, Stupid," he said, pressing his heels into the runnerbeast's sides. "Let it rip!"

Without a moment of hesitation Stupid lengthened his pace, surging forward from the power generated by his hindquarters until soon they were eating up ground at a breakneck pace. Piemur leaned in close to Stupid's neck and stuck to the saddle tight as glue, his body moving easily to the rhythm of his mount. Encouraged by Stupid's eagerness, Piemur egged him on to a flat-out gallop, and the runner obliged. Piemur could hear the wind whizzing past his ears, obliterating all other sound. Farli flew beside them, making use of the offshore wind to help her maintain her speed. Riding a-dragonback was the only other thing Piemur knew of where the sheer speed and thrill of movement were so utterly exhilarating.

He galloped on, allowing Stupid to race across the ground as the wind whipped past them. In the near distance, Piemur could see an outcropping of large boulders that spilled out across the beach and formed a bluff that met up with the sea. He was nearly certain they'd be able to ride around the bluff, but since the water looked as if it might be deep where it met the boulders, Piemur was reluctant to race Stupid through it when he couldn't see his footing. Runnerbeasts were sure and fleet of foot, but they could turn over in less than a quarter of a meter of water, easily getting into difficulties if they thought their footing was undermined.

Piemur eased the pressure through his knees and squeezed on the reins so his runnerbeast would slow down. He straightened up from his forward position and gently sat back in the saddle pad as Stupid's pace steadily slowed to an easy lope.

"Whoa, there, Stupid," Piemur said, pulling on the reins again. Stupid slowed from a canter to a trot and finally to a walk with a dragonlength to spare before they reached the headland. They walked onward to where the sea washed into the shore, halting just short of where the boulders jutted out, and Farli landed on Stupid's rump while Piemur assessed the footing and the run of the water around the boulders. The long gallop had opened up Stupid's wind-pipes and he blew loudly through his nostrils, stretching his head low and sliding the reins from Piemur's hands so he could look at the water as it lapped around his hooves.

As they walked on at an easy pace, Piemur allowed his thoughts to come and go, enjoying his free time. He remembered the talk he'd had with Sebell, long into the night, just after Ama died. Sebell had been explaining the subtle role of a harper, a role Piemur was filling more often than he realized.

"There's a fine balance we have to keep, Piemur," Sebell had said, and he spoke slowly, his tone thoughtful and solemn.

"The stability of our way of life is everyone's responsibility, but as harpers, as curators of our accumulated knowledge and our heritage, it is ours to oversee in particular. You know that the Weyr-leaders at Benden were not pleased when the Masterharper coun-seled them to remain calm after Ramoth's egg was stolen. He had to press his point even when Lessa wanted revenge, regardless of whether her feelings were justifiable or not. What purpose, do you think, would retaliation have served other than to ease the sense of violation the Benden Weyrfolk had suffered?" There was a note of entreaty in Sebell's rich voice, and Piemur saw how hopeful his men-tor was that Piemur would grasp his point.

"The egg was returned," Sebell continued, "and though the in-sult remained, the wrong was righted. Remember, my friend: All the other Weyrs look to Benden for direction and guidance, just as the smallholders rely on their Lords Holders to provide protection and stability. We harpers are the men and women who keep the balance among all the groups—all those people who make up the weights and balances on the scales of our way of life."

Piemur shook his head, looking at his hands as they lay idle in his lap, a small frown on his brows.

"If you saw someone in trouble, perhaps without safe haven

from Thread, would you wait for someone else to help them?" Sebell asked, leaning forward to further engage Piemur's attention.

"Of course not, I'd help them straightaway! I couldn't be certain that they'd be safe before anyone else offered them aid," Piemur had replied.

"I know you would, my friend. And I think, too, that if you saw someone in less obvious mortal peril, but with a more complex problem, you'd offer them whatever help you could. Am I correct?"

"You are, of course. We all have a duty to help one another," Piemur replied.

"And that is my point, Piemur. We have a duty to one another, and that overrides everything else."

"I'm sorry, Sebell," Piemur had replied. "Sometimes it's hard to understand what *my* role is. I don't see how I can help anyone. I never imagined when I was in the Harper Hall that I'd do anything other than sing. And now that I've finally found my mature voice, and I'm comfortable with it, singing seems so unimportant to me. It's strange, Sebell, I thought finding my voice again would solve all my problems, but it hasn't. It all feels meaningless to me now."

"That's because you're so much more than just a singing voice, Piemur," Sebell said, his voice resonating with warmth. "You've a great many skills! You may take them for granted, but they're truly useful and important. You just have to trust yourself."

Piemur recalled that when Sebell had paid him that compliment, his cheeks had grown hot and he'd fidgeted with humility. It was odd to be on the receiving end of a compliment for something other than singing. Singing! He had thought about nothing else after his voice broke, and it suddenly dawned on him that for a very long time all he'd been able to do was to look back, toward what had been, not forward, toward what could be. He'd let his singing voice blind him to everything else. The oddest thing was that when he sang for Ama, and his voice rang true, he felt no different. No jolt of relief or rush of delight because he could sing again. He shook his head, musing that he had behaved just like the Oldtimers and had gotten stuck, longing for his past.

In a flash, as if he were being propelled from the darkness of *between* into the brightness of a southern sunrise, he felt his head might spin off his shoulders until, in a wonderful burst of clarity, all his musings and ideas fell into place. He knew exactly what he was going to do, what he *had* to do! Most important, he started to feel as if he knew his place, his niche, as a harper.

He squeezed Stupid's sides to urge him forward, but the runner-beast was playfully pawing at the soft sand underfoot and ignored him.

"C'mon, Stupid!" Piemur yelled, thumping his heels hard into the beast's sides as he gathered up the reins, wheeling the animal's head around and urging him homeward, fast. Stupid stumbled slightly but then, as the reins were gathered up and he was egged on by Piemur's frantic urgings, he collected himself and was soon charging homeward at full pelt. Farli flew next to Piemur's head, chirruping at him in confusion because the tranquility of their morning ride had been broken.

"We're going to show them, Farli! That's what we're going to do. We're going to show them how to look forward."

Piemur rode hard toward the Hold, and when he was within earshot, he bellowed out Meria's name until the diminutive Oldtimer rushed outside, staring at him in surprise.

"Meria, I think I know the name of the root!"

The Oldtimer looked at Piemur as if he'd lost his mind.

"When I was in Nabol with Sebell, we got soaked to the skin in the rain," he explained, all in a rush. "An old woman gave us a brew from a root she called jango. She said it would set us right. Do you think it could be the same as the root you used to know—the one G'reff told you about?"

"Thujang?" Meria asked, incredulous.

"Yes, that's it!" Piemur cried, unable to hide the excitement in his voice. "What if the real name of the root has been altered over the last few generations? And what if it could help the dragons in Southern?"

Within moments they put Piemur's plan into action. Farli was dispatched with a message to Sebell, and Meria hurried to fulfill her part in the plan. When she'd rushed off, leaving Piemur alone, he jumped off his runnerbeast, his legs shaking with spent energy and his head buzzing with what he had just set in motion.

It would have made more sense, Piemur thought afterward with a little regret, if he had grabbed his flying gear before climbing on Seventh's back. The journey back *between,* to when the Oldtimers had decamped, was far longer than any jump Piemur had ever made before. He decided not to count out the heartbeats in his head but trusted B'naj, who knew *when* he was taking them to, and who'd made the jump safely numerous times.

Piemur closed his eyes tightly as he sat behind B'naj, knowing that there would be nothing to see anyway, even if he did leave them open. *Between* had never felt so cold before! And when the words *cold, colder, coldest, blacker than all things* had wormed around his head, and he began to feel a tight knot of fear crawl around his chest into his heart, Seventh suddenly burst into the air above Southern's western Weyr. A warm blast of air washed across Piemur's face and he sighed.

Dragons were everywhere below them, probably twelvescore from what he could see. Makeshift, unlit campfires were dotted here and there around the clearing, and though rudimentary shelters had been erected to offer shade to the weyrfolk, it was a sorry-looking mess, Piemur thought, not in any way an ordered or fitting place for noble dragons and their riders. *Where is the proper settlement?* he wondered. The site was completely devoid of any of the facilities or structures that should have been there to accommodate a Weyr.

Piemur put a hand on B'naj's shoulder. "*When* is this, B'naj?"

"We came back twenty-five Turns, harper. When we knew there'd be no Thread to fight. The dragons would not have been easy here otherwise."

Ah, thought Piemur, *the Oldtimer dragons have run true to their instincts, unable to ignore the code ingrained in them, which runs to their very core.*

"I know it's an odd request, B'naj, but could you set down in the middle of the camp, please? And ask Seventh if he'd land among his fellows and allow me to stand on his back? I want all the dragon-riders to see me—and their dragons, too," he added as an after-thought.

B'naj nodded and Seventh quickly backwinged into the middle of the compound, blowing up grit and sand all around him. Several dragons nearby hissed or bugled in loud protest at the brown's un-seemly behavior. Piemur quickly stood up on the brown dragon's back, and B'naj slid to the ground, standing by his dragon's head.

"Dragonmen!" Piemur called, immediately attracting attention with the resonant timbre of his voice and the respectful tone he em-ployed. Roars and bugling rose up from several of the dragons in the settlement, and Piemur saw a few of the older dragonriders glower-ing at him. One or two men called out guttural cries, some coughing intermittently, and the air around Piemur grew tense. This might have been a very bad idea, he thought.

He raised his arms to shoulder height, palms open wide, calling out again in a deeper, stronger voice that could be heard throughout the compound.

"Noble dragons! Noble dragonriders! I beseech you to listen, please. Listen to what I have to say." Slowly he lowered his open hands, as if slowing the rising tension in the air. *It's now or never,* he thought. *I'd better speak my mind quickly, or they might sear me to char before I draw another breath.*

"My name is Piemur. I come from Crom and I am a journeyman harper. I was a singer once, but time changed that. Time changes all things." Piemur's tone was grave, and some of the calls from the angriest weyrfolk stopped midbreath. He grew hopeful, thinking he might have hit a chord.

"I want to offer my assistance to you."

From the corner of his eye, where he stood on Seventh's back, Piemur could see two queen dragons at the edge of the compound, and a small group of bronzes and browns perched in wallows nearby. Their light-amber eyes whirled steadily as they regarded him.

Shouts and a few curses rang through the air and Piemur could see small groups of dragonmen slowly walking toward him, anger plainly stamped on their faces. He had to change the atmosphere quickly or his plan would fail.

"I know that you have been blamed for things not all of you had a hand in!" he shouted. He tried to infuse his voice with a note of command.

"I know that you feel wronged. Cast out by the people of my time. You've been slighted when your noble acts should be lauded. But please listen to what I have to say!" The shouts and cursing calls stopped, and Piemur took a deep breath.

An older man, standing slightly stooped, walked out of the crowd to stand in front of them, an inscrutable expression on his face. At first Piemur didn't recognize him, but then he realized that it was T'ron, the Weyrleader.

"This is not where you belong! You should not be living here, in this time!" Piemur cried. A large number of dragons bugled in agreement and were quickly joined by their weyrmates. The noise was deafening.

"Your dragons know you should not be here!"

A low muttering started up among the dragonriders, and Piemur sensed that their old tenet of autonomy might be raising its ancient head.

"Noble dragonmen of Pern, set aside the rules of your time. Don't let your strict adherence to independence keep you isolated from the others of this Pass. I ask that you take my help and let me speak and act for you." As he spoke, he looked directly into the eyes of the men and women standing in front of him, projecting his words so they could be clearly heard, and keeping his expression and voice open and relaxed.

"None of us can survive alone, dragonriders, not without one another. And we can't exist as a whole when some of our parts are missing. Crafts, Holds, and Weyrs—we *need* one another. We are under constant threat from Thread and we have to defend against it together or perish. The Holds need the Weyrs just as much as the Weyrs need the Holds. And the Crafthalls enhance our lives. Together all serve to teach us that we must band together. Come back with me! Come back to where you belong in the Present Pass. You cannot face your future here. No one should have to face such difficulties alone."

A dragon coughed near Piemur, and then a voice from the back of the compound growled loudly.

"Bah! You are just one person! How can you help all of us? Go back to your own time, harper!"

A chorus of rumbles rose from the crowd and Piemur looked around him, trying his hardest to quell a mounting feeling of failure.

"Something has made many of you unwell," he shouted, looking around at the dragonriders and their dragons. "You've been fouled by something, made sick somehow when you were once robust and strong. And your illness has affected all other aspects of your lives. I know someone who can help you shake off your illness. When you're well again, we can work together to reunite this Weyr with the rest of Pern."

"They've cast us aside! We are of no use to them anymore!" someone shouted, and another rumble rose up from the dragonriders. Piemur held up his hands, waiting with patience for the Oldtimers to heed him again.

"Yes, I know how you feel! But you are crucial linchpins in the assembly of our social structure, and only *you* can take those first steps forward to come back to us." Piemur said, stressing the last few words. He lowered his head, wondering how he could make them see that he wanted to be their advocate, not their adversary.

"Noble dragonkind, I do not want to make judgment on whether your banishment was right or wrong. Or to mete out or seek justice," he said, knowing his choice of words would send a ripple through the crowd, making clear that he was referring both to the theft of the egg as well as to their own exile.

"We *could* fight with one another, seeking revenge and retribution until we're all but spent. But such actions are self-serving. They're not for the *good* of us all," he cried, and obeying an impulse he jumped down from Seventh's back and slowly walked into the crowd.

"You all came forward to help fight Thread and keep the people of this Pass safe for the future. I would like to help you find your rightful purpose again. In this Pass! I know you can teach us, teach your descendants, many things. Just as you taught our dragons and riders to fight against Thread. But would you let us teach you how we can live together in this Pass?" As Piemur spoke, he walked among the dragonriders, looking from one to the next in appeal. "I would be honored to act as your advocate, dragonmen." He came to a stop, his progress impeded by the stooped figure of T'ron, who had stepped forward, barring Piemur from progressing any farther.

"If you would allow me, I would be your voice—to speak on your behalf so your wishes will be heard." Piemur's words carried across the compound. He stood in front of T'ron, aware that all the Oldtimers were regarding him keenly. He crossed one arm in front of his waist and slowly dipped his upper body in a deep bow.

When he straightened up, T'ron had stepped closer. He glared at Piemur.

"We've listened to you, harper, and heard your words. Go, and leave us now!" T'ron's voice, loud enough for everyone to hear, was flat and brooked no argument. Piemur stared at the Oldtimer Weyrleader, his face contorted in anguish at the rebuff. T'ron reached out a hand and placed it on Piemur's shoulder, squeezing it for the barest moment before he openly pushed him away. Was he mistaken, Piemur wondered, or when T'ron touched his shoulder was he sending him another, subtler message? He couldn't be sure, and he could do nothing more about it now in this tension-filled atmosphere.

So this is it, Piemur brooded. *My great plan to be mediator for the Oldtimers has come to nothing. They don't want help.* He looked around at the dragonmen, aware that they regarded him with steady gazes as he searched among their faces to find B'naj.

With Seventh following close behind, B'naj walked with Piemur out of the Oldtimer compound where they could lift into the air with ease. Wordlessly Piemur climbed onto Seventh's back and strapped himself in behind B'naj. Moments later they were airborne and Piemur looked down one last time, true remorse washing over him as he watched the men and women who'd helped change

the fate of every person alive on Pern but who would not now allow
that debt to be repaid.

The journey home was long and cold, but Piemur felt so utterly
dispirited that he was barely aware even of the bone-freezing passage *between* as Seventh flew them forward through the Turns to his
own time. As soon as the brown dragon set down a short distance
from Southern Hold's compound, Piemur touched B'naj's shoulder
in farewell, threw his leg across Seventh's back, and began to climb
down. Suddenly Seventh trumpeted loudly. Piemur almost lost his
grip, but B'naj grabbed his arm. Piemur looked up in gratitude, but
the Oldtimer just gripped his arm tighter.

"You can let go now, B'naj, my feet are almost on the ground,"
Piemur said, trying to break free of the dragonrider's strong grasp.

"Seventh—and I, as well—we want you to know something."
The Oldtimer loosened his grip so that Piemur could continue to
dismount. When his feet finally touched ground, Piemur looked up
at B'naj. The Oldtimer had an earnest expression on his lined face.

"No harper has ever offered their support to us in the way you
did today. We are grateful that you tried to help. I'm sorry that your
offer was refused."

Piemur didn't know what to say in reply so he merely shrugged.
But then a thought occurred to him. "I hope that your Weyr will take
Meria's remedy. She's certain the jango will make them well again."

"It's my fervent wish, too, harper." B'naj dipped his head toward
Piemur, who returned the courtesy, bowing toward Seventh and his
rider. Without another word Piemur moved out of Seventh's way
so the Oldtimer dragon could return his rider to their Weyr. Just
before he climbed higher into the air, Seventh circled around to face
Piemur, his eyes whirling a startling shade of emerald green as he
bugled loudly. Then his voice was swallowed up *between*.

Piemur fell into an irregular schedule of work in Southern Hold,
never really finding an easy rhythm to his daily tasks. He felt like

he was stumbling and stuttering through each day. He helped teach the children; he helped grade and store a bumper crop of tubers; he pitched in to prepare a batch of numbweed that would see the Hold through to the following Turn, at the very least. But regardless of all the activity that kept him busy, Piemur's days felt empty; what he achieved had no meaning for him, and he realized after a sevenday that he felt very deflated and more than a little glum.

He couldn't shake the feeling of absolute disappointment that the Oldtimers had dismissed his offer of assistance so quickly and emphatically. Were they really that hidebound that they couldn't—no, *wouldn't*—take his help? Or did they think his words were empty, or that he didn't have the requisite ability? It was hard to shake his sense of defeat, and as the first sevenday passed into the next, even though his days were full of activity and worthwhile work, and he was surrounded by the friendly company of the holders, Piemur could not shake himself out of his doldrums.

Late one afternoon, a group of the hold children rushed back to the compound full of excitement because they'd found a clutch of abandoned fire-lizard eggs. Meria asked Piemur to help her and the children retrieve the eggs and keep them safe until their future homes could be determined. Fire-lizard eggs were hard to come by in the north, and would be used as a bartering tool for goods or future favors.

"You've been keeping busy, haven't you, Piemur?" Meria asked when the eggs were positioned in a safe place in the main Hold, out of harm's way. "I've hardly seen you at all these last few days."

"Yeah, I've been busy around the Hold, but I guess I should probably get back to mapping again." Even to his own ears Piemur didn't sound very enthusiastic.

"You did your best, you know."

"What do you mean?" Piemur asked.

"There was nothing more you could have done or said to those riders to change their minds. B'naj told me what you said; he told me about the offer you made to them. I think there are a few of the older dragonriders who are just too bitter, and still too angry, to embrace the possibility of a hopeful future. I'm sorry that they didn't accept your offer, Piemur. I think you would've been an excellent advocate for them."

Piemur pursed his lips in a brief grimace, nodding twice.

"But you should know that the dragonriders *did* hear what you said about getting help from me. At first, a group of about fifty riders asked B'naj for the jango root I had sent down from Nabol. They've had complete success with it, too, clearing up that wretched coughing once and for all. And when the others saw how improved their fellows were from the jango, the rest of the riders asked for some, too. I think their dragons put them up to it. If you hadn't guessed that thujang is called jango now, it might've taken far longer to make the weyr fit and healthy again. So you see, some good did come from what you did. I hope that makes you feel a little better."

"I'm really pleased the dragons and their riders are better, Meria. That *is* good news," Piemur replied, but he couldn't keep the disappointment from his voice. Meria scanned Piemur's face, searching his eyes for a moment, then she nodded once and reached out both her hands to clasp Piemur's. He could see that the gentle Oldtimer was trying her best to console him, and he smiled weakly at her.

The following morning, Piemur set out with Stupid and Farli to continue mapping the Southern Continent. They had left the Hold early and were making good ground through the dense tropical vegetation when they heard a muffled cry from above and behind them. Piemur stopped Stupid and turned toward the sound. There it was again, a woman's voice. And was that the whoosh and sweep of a dragon's wings? Sure enough, the next moment he heard Meria's voice calling his name.

"Piemur! Piemur, where are you?"

Quickly, he hopped up and stood on Stupid's back, while Farli flitted up high above his head. He waved his arms overhead, not sure if he could be seen.

"I'm here!" he shouted and was answered by the short bugling sound of a dragon.

"There he is, B'naj! Let's set down," Piemur heard Meria say.

A snapping, cracking sound came from several dragonlengths

behind him and Piemur waited, curious to know why Meria and B'naj had come in search of him. He could feel the air whooshing around him and guessed that Seventh was backwinging as he made to touch down.

Meria gave another call and Piemur replied, guiding her to him as he climbed down from Stupid's back. A moment later, the diminutive Oldtimer came rushing toward Piemur, trailing a piece of vine that had snagged under her arm and a long frond of fern that was caught in her hair.

"There you are! At last! We've been looking for you all morning. Quickly, Piemur! Go to Seventh. B'naj will explain everything. I'll take Stupid for you. Go! Quickly!" And she smiled at him, pushing him toward the waiting dragon and his rider.

"What is it, B'naj?" Piemur yelled, as he ran toward the brown dragon. "What's the matter?"

"I can't tell you, Piemur. You have to *see* it for yourself," B'naj replied, a smile splitting his face as he offered a hand to help Piemur up on Seventh. The brown dragon was hopping from one foot to another, impatient to be off again.

"But what is it—why can't you tell me, B'naj?"

"Not yet, Piemur," B'naj said, hauling the younger man up onto his dragon's back with one hand.

Bewildered, Piemur grabbed onto B'naj's waist as Seventh pivoted and began to run back through the forest he had flattened while making his descent. Quickly the dragon leapt into the air and beat his wings in half a dozen powerful strokes before he went *between*.

It felt as if they'd only been in that dark, cold void for a single heartbeat and then they were back in the warm, tropical air of the Southern Continent. Seventh backwinged, landing in the middle of the deserted main compound of Southern Weyr.

Leaning forward, Piemur grabbed the dragonrider's shoulder, on the verge of asking why they had come here, when B'naj held up one gloved hand.

"Wait," B'naj said, resting his arms in front of him on Seventh's neck ridges.

Piemur felt confused. What in the name of the First Egg was

going on? Was this some cruel game B'naj and Meria were playing, taking him to this abandoned Weyr—a clear sign of his own recent failure? And then his confusion was replaced by a growing feeling of anger. He tried to calm himself by remembering how Meria and B'naj had never been anything but kind and friendly to him, but his ire—or was it his shame?—was battling with his reason.

Then, without warning, he felt a change in the air pressure above him, familiar but much stronger and heavier than usual. He glanced upward. One moment the sky above him, bright blue and cloudless, was empty, and then within the single blink of his eyes, hundreds of dragons and their riders steadily filled the air, hovering briefly before they began their descents.

Seventh remained where he was, standing stock-still and bugling a welcome as the trees and vegetation all around them were buffeted under the huge draft generated by so many gleaming, shimmering dragon wings—gold, bronze, brown, blue, and green.

"They wanted you to know, harper—the riders wanted you to see them here again!" B'naj shouted above the noise of all the dragons. Piemur looked at him, unsure what he was saying, or what it all meant.

"What you said swayed them! They changed their minds and decided to return. To this Pass, to this time!" B'naj cupped his hands around his mouth so Piemur could hear his next words. "It was the dragons who made their riders see sense. They told their riders to listen to you, Piemur!"

Piemur looked at B'naj, mouth open, incredulous. A dozen or more dragons trumpeted welcoming calls, vocalizing their pleasure while Piemur took in the full import of what the Oldtimer had just said.

Surprised, exulted, and overwhelmed, Piemur jumped up on Seventh's back and spread his arms out wide in welcome, overcome with relief. As yet another dragon bugled a call of triumph, Piemur threw back his head, a huge smile spilling across his face as he welcomed the dragonriders home.

ACKNOWLEDGMENTS

This story could never have been written if not for my wonderful mother, Anne McCaffrey. She created Pern and its marvelous inhabitants over fifty years ago. Thank you, Mum, wherever you are, out there in the cosmos, for permitting me to play in your world.

A huge debt of gratitude is also owed to my brother, Todd McCaffrey, who generously stepped back and allowed his little sister to mess around in the treasured sandbox that he has been carefully guarding for so many years. To Shelly Shapiro, my editor, whose patience and indefatigable guidance encouraged me to keep writing even when I hadn't a clue where the story was taking me. Todd and Shelly, you two are true Champions of Pern.

To Diana Tyler, my agent at MBA Literary and Script Agents, for her gentle encouragement and endless patience; and to Jay A. Katz, most trusted Trustee, for thankfully never exerting an ounce of pressure on me throughout the writing process. Diana and Jay, treasured family friends for many decades, there could be no finer Guardians for Pern than you two.

To Richard Woods, O.P., for the most invaluable advice, guidance, and far too many admonitions to "Move it along!" For which I am most deeply grateful.

Hilary Taylor's musical guidance and expertise, especially with regard to singing; and Richard McDonnell's subtle insights into drumming, percussion, and the tensions required therein, have offered this novice a better understanding of that beautiful thing called music. Thank you both.

The music composed by Sheldon Mirowitz, for the original soundtrack to a film called *Troublesome Creek: A Midwestern* by Jeanne Jordan and Steven Ascher, was truly inspirational during the early stages of writing. Thank you, Sheldon, for your wonderful creation.

To John Greene, Maréchal de Logis, J'hon. Our memory of you carries on, my friend, and I know that you, too, are out there, somewhere in the cosmos.

For all the folk who grace the little haven that is the true heart of Ashford Village, the Chester Beatty Inn, and to her gracious patrons, Padraig and Mari Humby. Thanks to you all for the momentum you encouraged with your gentle nudges, asking "How's the book?"

To Micaiah Murray (Mickay), the Beautiful and Amazing First-Eyes Proofreader, my thanks.

Finally, to my husband, Geoffrey Robert Kennedy, and to our son, Owen Thomas Kennedy, for all your patience and encouragement. You are the finest men I know and all my heroes are based on you. You know you drive me crazy, but I love you both madly.

Mythago Wood, March 2018

ABOUT THE AUTHOR

GIGI MCCAFFREY collaborated with her late mother, Anne McCaffrey, on three short stories collected in the anthologies *Great Writers & Kids Write Spooky Stories, Mothers & Daughters,* and a German-language anthology titled *Das grofbe Lesebuch der FANTASY.* She also contributed an essay to *Dragonwriter: A Tribute to Anne McCaffrey and Pern,* edited by her brother Todd McCaffrey. She lives in the Devil's Glen, in the garden county of Ireland, with her husband, their son, and the infamous hound, Sidney.

ABOUT THE TYPE

This book was set in Sabon, a typeface designed by the well-known German typographer Jan Tschichold (1902–74). Sabon's design is based upon the original letter forms of sixteenth-century French type designer Claude Garamond and was created specifically to be used for three sources: foundry type for hand composition, Linotype, and Monotype. Tschichold named his typeface for the famous Frankfurt typefounder Jacques Sabon (c. 1520–80).